AMBIGUOUSLY PRODUCTIVE

Lavi J. Yves

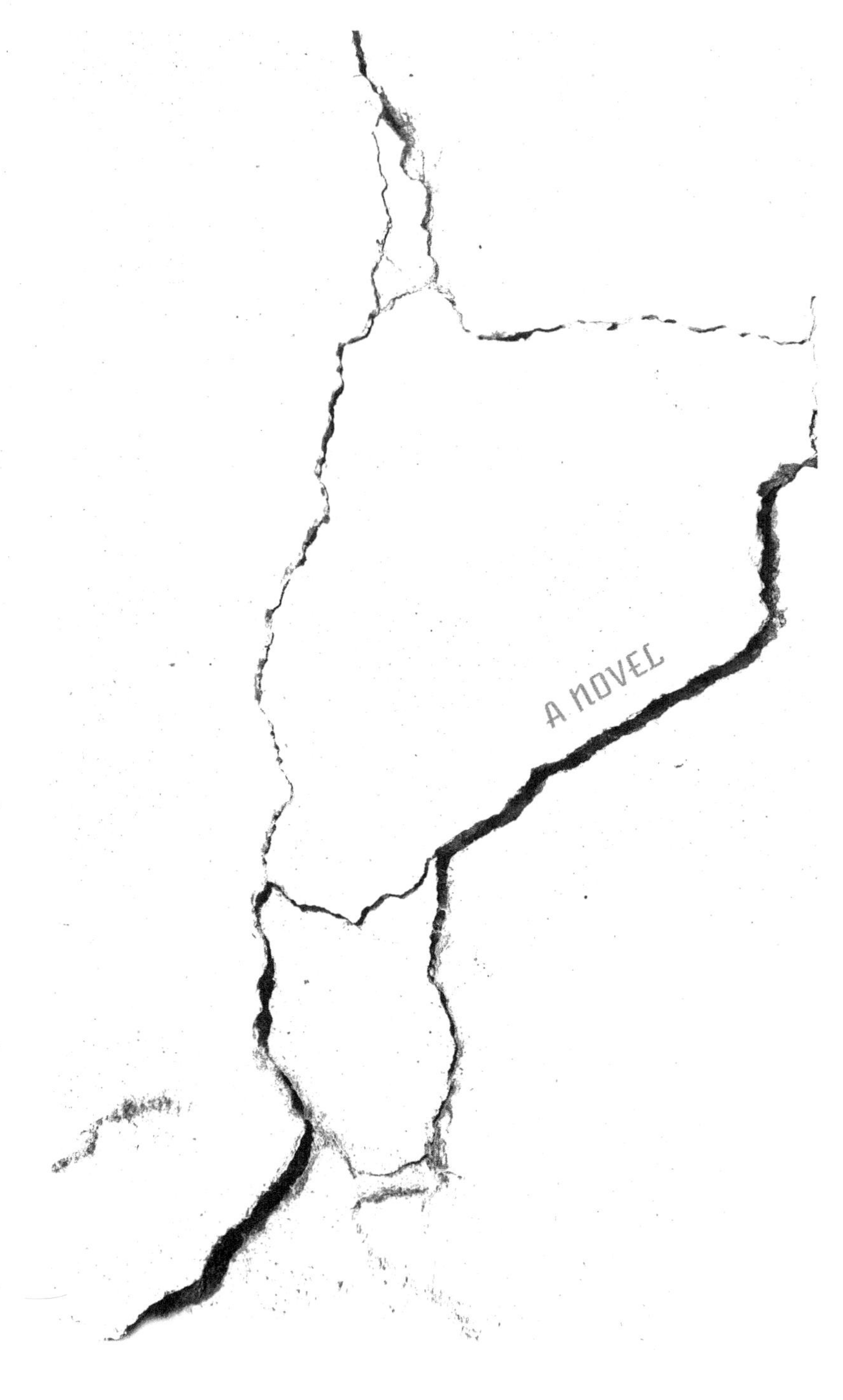
A NOVEL

ISBN: 978-1-0688812-2-0 (Paperback)
ISBN: 978-1-0688812-3-7 (eBook)

Editors: Stephanie Chou, Ophelia Mieux, Eliza Dee

Front cover image © Unsplash (Michael Discenze; Allison Saeng; Jr Korpa; Krakograff Textures; Drazen Nesic)
Cover design: Lavi J. Yves

www.lavijyves.com

You get on a bus, assuming it will take you to a stop on its route.

The engine halts halfway. You get off the bus to help.

Some of you tow from the front; some push from behind.

The bus runs everyone over and greases its wheels with your blood and flesh,

Until there's no one at the front, fleeing and screaming,

No one at the back, chasing and wailing.

It drives away, reaches the next stop, and swallows the next batch of passengers who think they know where they are headed.

1

NOLAN HAUT HAD two options.

One, he could grab the cardigan draped over the chair next to him and wipe Dan Barton's brains off his face. Two, pull the chair out of the way so Dan wouldn't break his neck from his fall. Given what had created option one, the chair situation seemed less problematic. The real issue was, Nolan had less than two seconds to make the choice, and he'd never been great with rapid-fire decisions under such time pressure, so he did neither.

A minute ago, things were fine.

Tim Kwan's family had booked the chapel for the entire day, and everyone was taking their time. The Level 13 Associates of Frenell & Co. lined up to pay their final tribute to the twenty-six-year-old. Each of them took a rose, stepped forward, shook hands with Tim's parents, left the rose with Tim, then moved on. When they ran out of roses, they made do with carnations.

When they ran out of room on Tim's chest, they planted the flowers alongside his body, the way you'd outline a crime scene silhouette.

The turnout was impressive. Most attendees didn't remember Tim Kwan as such a popular kid, and half of them had barely spoken to him. But Tim's parents had sent a heartbreaking invitation to his entire Year 5 cohort that would make even the most callous person say, "I'd stay for five minutes." Besides, they could record the time spent at the ceremony and the round trip between the firm and the funeral house as "Non-billable: Team Building," so the Associates hired a tour bus and arrived at the venue around 10:00 a.m., hung around for some light refreshments and lighter conversations, sat through an hour-long memorial service, then approached the bier where Tim slept. This was the last chance to say goodbye to a friend. Must not rush. Strictly one at a time.

When there were two persons left ahead of them, Dan turned around and told Nolan that Tim's casket was a "Lincoln poplar mahogany," which cost nearly six grand. Nolan did not ask Dan why he'd know something like that. He was more interested in the massive plastic sheet spread from Mr. Kwan's feet that looked like a transparent tarp for greenhouses.

Poplar mahogany—that was the color of Tim's father, a man tanned and weather beaten from a life spent under the unforgiving sun. He should be in his fifties but was worn beyond his years. The gardener lifestyle had carved deep lines around his mouth, and the sudden departure of an only child had dyed his hair gray.

With dignified calmness, Mr. Kwan asked each Associate a question as he shook their hand. As the line moved forward, Nolan heard what he was saying.

What's your name, son?

What's your name, young man?

Dan marched forward and grabbed Mr. Kwan's hand, offering the answer before the question.

"My name is Dan."

Mr. Kwan gripped Dan's hand and scanned his face. There was an eerie excitement under his veil of grief.

"Dan who, young man?"

"Dan Barton, Mr. Kwan."

"Oh, it's you," Tim's dad murmured. He shoved a hand inside his suit jacket and drew out a .45 Springfield–in, and out, smooth as shifting gears. Then he opened a window in Dan's forehead.

There was a hush between the gunshot and the screams. Nolan kept his mouth closed as the warm splash dripped down his face. *Just think of that time you cut an extra-juicy tomato,* he told himself and watched Dan collapse onto the tarp, still holding the carnation.

Mr. Kwan peeled the tarp from the floor and rolled it over Dan's body. He signaled Nolan to make some room with a backhand wave and pressed two fingers on Dan's neck before putting the gun back into its holster. In the meantime, striding across the chapel with a delightful smile, Mrs. Kwan announced to the fleeing Associates:

"It's okay, kids! We've found who we wanted. There's more sparkling in the back, anyone?"

"OKAY." HAYDEN HINS clapped twice after the last Associate had boarded the tour bus. "Everybody, remember to charge four point eight hours of 'Non-billable: Team Building' for 'Attend the farewell ceremony of T. Kwan and offer condolences to his grieving parents.' I'll circulate an email with the standard narrative so you can copy from that. Don't forget the period at the end, and use subcode 0041–that's the one including transportation. Most importantly, please refrain from speaking to the police or media until we have received Partner instructions on our position."

Ryuka Murong opened a fresh pack of alcohol wipes, pulled one out to clean her hands, then gave the rest to Nolan. She found a bottle of tomato juice in her bag, glanced at Nolan, then decided not to offer him this one. Nolan wiped his entire face over and over until he saw no more pink or yellow in the fiber; then he stared at the garbage piling up at his feet. In his reality, where time was valued in six-minute units, it took less than one billing unit to turn a person into that. He couldn't find the right emotion for this. Dan Barton wasn't everyone's favorite, but Nolan had rather neutral feelings about the guy. Dan could be a bully, a snob, a snitch . . . oh, maybe Nolan didn't like him either.

"I'm impressed with Tim's song choice—never pictured him as an ELO guy." Hayden dropped his butt in the center of the back row. "Gotta hand it to his folks—much better service than the one in March. That kid . . . shit, what was his face? The Year 3 who thought he was getting fired, but turned out Frenell was just fucking with him?"

Nolan was picking up the dirty wipes and Ryuka was swallowing her tomato juice, so Hayden turned to Sai for a response. Sai had moved one seat over as soon as Hayden had sat down and thrust her bag between them. Then she'd turned to the window with her earbuds in, pretending she hadn't heard anything from anyone. The "dodge, block, and ignore" was completed in such a smooth flow, as if she'd rehearsed for this scenario.

"Should you be talking to her?" Ryuka asked. Hayden ignored her.

By the time the Associates had returned to the office, Hayden had convinced himself that the name of the March kid was Ronan Shaw, which was only half right. He was thinking of Ronan Seymour, the Year 4 Associate who'd disappeared after he'd suddenly lost the ability to recognize human faces and everyone around him had become a talking animal. The Year 3 who'd flown off the rooftop two months before Tim had shot himself was Richard Shaw. To be fair to Hayden—those two kids did share a preference for Armani aftershave and Zara suits.

"TIM HAD BEEN a dedicated member of our team," Colleen Oakland, Frenell Partner and *Sauria Street Journal*'s "Top 10 Next Generation Stars to Watch 2027" finalist, delivered her speech from the podium in the freshly renovated Courage Room on Level 31. "I remember when we were on Project Gladiator, Tim would set an alarm for three a.m. every day to check his emails. Whenever any new instructions came in, he was always the first one to offer help. Never a tardy response. Never a complaint. Not even one passive-aggressive message that I remember. In the last few months, I'm sure a lot of you had seen him on the floor at midnight, faithfully holding his post in the front line. If you ask anyone on Project Rhapsody—"

She paused as the script reached the part where she was supposed to hand off to Dan Barton. After a quick scan of the rest of the page, she set the notes aside and improvised.

"Tim's departure is a tragedy, and a reminder for all of us—a reminder of how insidious mental illnesses can be, and how important emotional well-being is for this rewarding yet challenging profession."

Nolan closed his eyes and clenched his jaw. He'd known Colleen was going there, but he hadn't expected to hear it two minutes in. "Mental illness" was the default culprit in two scenarios: when a white man committed a domestic terrorist attack, and when anyone working in "professional services" killed themselves.

At Colleen's signal, the lights dimmed and the screen behind the podium started the well-being training video that Nolan had watched countless times. The video was about fifteen minutes long and looked at least fifteen years old. It had the cinematography, acting, and music perfect for in-flight safety instructions, and one simple message: Just ask, "Are you okay?"

Bump into a colleague in the pantry? See what they're drinking with their tea. Are they on medication, or just taking supplements?

Catch someone crying in a bathroom? Is it work related or personal? Gather details of their story and speak to their Handler about an intervention before they fall behind their peers.

When someone asks if you're okay, tell them. Mental health is a serious topic, and this is not the time to be shy. Help us help you. That's the only way to get out of a slump and be productive again.

As the upbeat outro music faded, someone from the Office of Inclusion, Diversity, Equity, Accessibility, Optimization, Productivity, Innovation, Operating Intelligence, and Data Science–OIDEAOPIOIDS, or, as the Associates preferred to call it, the Office of All Things Human, a.k.a. OATH–took the stage. She had a familiar face. Nolan might have seen her several times at firm drinks, but she wasn't the one stationed on Level 13.

"I won't tell you it's easy." The OATH manager spoke like a performing poet. "But you know that, don't you? Corporate life is never meant to be easy. It takes dedication. It takes commitment. It takes the will of a soldier charging onto a battlefield, knowing that he–or she!–might not return from the land mines or flying bullets. We know it–we know it too well, but we'd march straight into war anyway! Easy? We don't want it! Type A overachievers are destined for something bigger than themselves. If this intensely agonizing career is our cross to bear, so be it."

Nolan rolled down his sleeves and sank deeper into the chair. His skin was crawling with a sudden rush of goose bumps that wouldn't subside no matter how hard he pinched his biceps with his fingernails. The OATH manager had stepped off the podium and come to the edge of the stage.

"I won't tell you it's easy"–she choked up–"but I'm telling you it's worth it."

As the OATH manager fought back tears and regained her composure, the ocean of Associates stood up in synchrony, holding their right hands over their hearts as if to sing a national anthem. Nolan, Ryuka, and Sai exchanged a look, then followed the crowd as they saw the patrol robots cruising toward the back row.

"Who are we?" the OATH manager asked.

"We are the Frenells!" the Associates chanted.

"What do we believe in?"

"Hard work and purpose!"

"What is our bare minimum?"

"Above and beyond!"

"What is the best reward?"

"The smile of a happy client!"

"What is the worst atrocity?"

"Underutilization and presenteeism!"

"I thought the worst atrocity was 'absenteeism,'" Nolan whispered.

"That was last month," Ryuka said.

"What's 'presenteeism'?" asked Sai.

"Not enough enthusiasm," said Ryuka.

"Isn't that just 'underbilling'?"

"Same thing."

"Why so many different terms for the same thing?" asked Nolan.

"To accommodate people's vocabulary preferences for broader awareness reach." Ryuka sighed. "Like you can call Hitler a 'monster,' 'mass murderer,' 'the worst Austrian ever,' 'art school failure,' 'shit for a mustache,' or just the basic 'Nazi.'"

As the three compared notes and caught up on the terminology, a patrol robot glided over and stopped in front of them. It was the latest model. One hundred and eighty automotive-grade sensors, six 4K cameras, and twelve multifunctional mechanical arms, packed into this waist-high stainless steel tank. It tilted its touchscreen face upward and gave the three an accusatory stare.

"Oh hello, Edmund." Ryuka bent over and spoke in a baby voice. "Where's Edgar today?"

She patted the bald top of the robot as if it were a four-year-old. The staff manual specifically advised against that, but it hadn't been effective. These things were cute, like knockoff R2-D2s.

Edmund reciprocated with a mild electric shock, and Ryuka retracted her hand with a gasp. As she massaged her numb fingers, Edmund printed a statement on its screen:

You are displaying signs of presenteeism. Consider this your last warning.

Next to the flashing statement, a cartoon referee displayed a yellow card as a mechanical arm swam out of Edmund's body, holding an RFID card reader. Ryuka sighed and pressed her staff badge on the reader until the warning disappeared. She'd just lost ten minutes of Idle Time. Edmund folded its arm and hoovered away. These things also vacuumed the carpets.

"I don't like this one," Nolan said after Edmund was out of earshot.

"Total bitch," Sai agreed.

The motivational chanting continued.

"What if you don't record all your billable hours?"

"We are stealing food from the Partners' children!"

"What if you don't give your absolute one hundred percent?"

"We are committing white-collar thievery!"

Nolan wiped his clammy palms on the insides of his pockets. His skin crawl had turned into a shiver, rummaging through his organs and hooking a malicious craving out of the bottom of his stomach. A cold sweat broke out under his shirt, and he tasted a bitterness at the back of his throat—like he was getting carsick. Loosening his tie didn't help, so he sneaked out the back door. As he headed to the elevators, waves of chanting penetrated the premium wood panels and heavy padding.

We are the Frenells! We are the Frenells! We are the Frenells!

FRENELL & CO. USED to be Durham, Everett, Aldridge & Frenell International Limited. The firm was founded, allegedly, in 1875 by a certain Franklin Edison Durham Jr. as a legal practice that gained regional fame in maritime law, trusts and estates, personal injury, and aristocratic discordances. Over the next hundred years, it branched into oil, banking, real estate, insurance, aviation, and commercial litigation by acquiring the most talented minds the era had to offer. After "Frenell," they stopped adding names to the brand. Based on a piece of reliable research conducted by the top marketing and productivity institute at the time, most people could only remember the first four names anyway.

The firm had several good decades in the twentieth century; then the Durham family took a hit in its influence when Nixon went down. Shortly after, Clarence Aldridge ended up in jail for insider trading and perjury. In the nineties, Harold Everett III embezzled half the firm's trust money and fled to the Caribbean before they lost track of him—that was when the partnership realized maybe a rebranding was overdue. The elders of the firm wanted to maintain some degree of heritage, so they conducted a thorough investigation on the remaining name, Jefferson Frenell. To their pleasant surprise, the only questionable conduct of this man seemed to be a string of sexual misconduct allegations that had never moved beyond allegations. Maybe even the universe felt the firm could use a break—at the time of those alleged events, the attention of the entire public was seized by the Enron fallout, and MeToo wasn't a thing back then, so, nobody noticed. Even today, if you googled "Jefferson Frenell," you wouldn't hit anything outrageous in the first ten pages. With a great sense of pride and relief, the firm marched into the twenty-first century as Frenell & Co. with brand-new logos, letterheads, and website banners. The market embraced the decision with likes on the firm's LinkedIn announcement, and the Associates began to refer to themselves as "the Frenells."

By the mysterious force of the universe, the name change saved the firm. Over the twenty years that followed, through mergers, acquisitions, and local franchising, Frenell & Co. grew into today's global giant with more than eighty offices sprawling across six continents and forty-five countries, delivering unrivaled professional services in law, consulting, accounting, and forensic investigations—a one-stop shop for "Let us tell you what to do." Frenell & Co. became Frenell and only Frenell. Hardly anyone remembered Durham, Everett, or Aldridge.

The story of Mr. Jefferson Frenell was an inspirational one about perspective and hope: you can become a legend by being "relatively respectable."

Nolan strolled toward the front gate, which was flanked by people walking through metal detectors and picking up their belongings from the conveyor belts. The lines were short and seemed to be getting shorter each day. The lobby between the turnstiles and the elevators was decorated with pull-up banners. Nolan walked past one featuring a sad-looking Labradoodle and a rather indifferent British shorthair. The cursive words at the bottom said "You have left these to be here, so make every minute count." The next one said "Don't forget to kiss your kids good night over Teams," followed by an asterisked reminder: "Family events out of town or with no internet connection must be communicated to your team three months in advance." The building management had first put these up to welcome everyone back to the office after COVID. "Work from home" had died for a long time, but these banners had survived. *Who are these for?* Nolan thought. Some days he considered tearing one up on the spot just to see who'd come to the rescue, but the CCTV cameras in the lobby could complicate things.

He scanned his Frenell staff badge and pushed through a turnstile. Faceless, nameless, the badge revealed no identifiable information except the Frenell logo. It was linked to an arbitrarily assigned staff code in the Productive Assets Deployment and Utilization system, PADU. This scan would alert PADU that Year 5 Timekeeper NH23BRT9-C, who charged $800 an hour, had left the building, the purpose of which would need to be identified in his time sheet by the end of the day and classified as authorized work, potential revenue-generating activity, or unproductive Idle Time. That Year 5 being "twenty-seven-year-old Nolan Haut" was irrelevant in this context.

From the front gate of 113 Sauria Street where the name of Frenell & Co. was printed on top, the sixteen blocks up north to York Street, fourteen blocks down south to Clovis Avenue, nine blocks east to the Athena River, and six blocks west to Babylon Square made up the Central Business District of Grand Ivory City. Sauria Street was the artery of the CBD, where money was counted in millions and six figures was considered petty cash.

Nolan crossed the street at the first corner on the left, then swung a right onto Lynn Street, headed toward the Pollyanna Palace—headquarters of the Bank of Pollyanna. Behind him, the facade clock on the Frenell building struck three.

The bank faced the twin towers of the Grand Ivory monarchy—the Osireion Group. The three pinnacles were connected by a triangular skywalk thirty feet above the ground, sheltering a small courtyard underneath. To honor the general principle that an overpopulated city shall not have empty spaces, the courtyard nested a two-story social hub known as the Irrationality Prevention Center. The IPC strove to provide wholesome stress relief to its patrons—the place didn't even have a liquor license or a lottery booth. A café took up most of the first floor, leaving a small section in the back for a Rage Room where one could purchase six-minute sessions to smash plates against the walls. Upstairs was split into two halves. One for a compact gym with a single treadmill, a Smith machine, and absolutely nothing detachable or weaponizable. The other had a religion-neutral Peace Chamber with no altar but an abstract mural, which echoed the self-help nature of the place—it's your own responsibility to stare your enlightenment out of contemporary art.

Nolan checked in with his Frenell badge. His Idle Time allowance was running low, so he budgeted five minutes for his stay. Plenty of his peers were wary about the IPC, given that Sauria Street firms made up the majority of its sponsors, but this was the only place in the CBD where they could still find ten-dollar coffee and ham-and-cheese sandwiches under thirty. Nolan poured a paper cup of cooler water and walked toward his favorite booth, passing a suited young man who was rubbing some white residue off his nose as he strode for the door.

The corner booth already had someone in there. Someone with bright, innocent eyes that made him look like a college freshman, like the light inside him hadn't gone out yet.

"Oh, sorry." Nolan turned to leave.

"No, no, we can share." The young man gestured at the seat opposite him and held out his hand until Nolan sat down. "Calder?" he asked.

"Calder" meant Calder, Remington, Ainsworth & Farr LLP, a law firm in the Pollyanna Palace.

"Frenell," said Nolan.

The young man gave an impressed nod. Frenell was the only firm on Sauria Street with its own real estate.

"Miller?" Nolan asked, referring to Miller, Smit & Lange Global Limited. It occupied a couple of floors above Calder.

"Fischer," the guy replied, meaning Fischer & O'Brien Inc., a management consulting firm hidden in Sanford Lane. There had been some debate in the professional services world as to whether it belonged in the Sauria League, given that it was almost a whole block away.

Nolan responded with a closed-mouth smile, thinking that the only other group with pedigree-based greetings was dog owners. He took out a small tube of hand cream, squirted a blob into his palm, then worked it into his skin, even under his fingernails. He kept his hands busy so the tremor would be less obvious. What he really wanted was some sanitizer, but a dozen posts on Reddit had told him the smell could be triggering. The cream was bergamot scented, the only kind that helped with the headaches.

"Twenty-five?" the Fischer Associate asked. Nolan knew what he meant: "Is your billable target really twenty-five hundred hours a year?"

"Twenty-five fifty."

Now adopted across professional services, "billable hours" was the ninth wonder invented by lawyers to calculate their fees. Employees like Nolan, who were required to record their daily activities in time sheets, were called "fee earners," or "Timekeepers." Twenty-five hundred and fifty billable hours per year translated to 9.8 to 10.2 billables per day, assuming 250 to 260 working days. You could bring that number down to 7.0, if you worked every day including weekends. A Timekeeper was only allowed to bill the work that their firm was allowed to charge clients, such as reviewing a contract or drafting an advice. Time spent on their commutes, meals, coffee breaks, or any "unproductive activities," like crying in the bathroom, did not count as billables. Idle Time could become productive non-billables if, for example, the lunch or the coffee was for networking with a client or prospective clients. Non-billable targets were more manageable, and the industry standard in 2028 ranged between four and five hundred a year. Hardly anyone ever got fired for not meeting their non-billable target, unless the firm had been looking for a reason to boot them and had run out of patience.

So, clocking in at nine and checking out at five would not secure anyone eight billables. How long would a Timekeeper have to stay "at work" each day to meet a twenty-five fifty annual target? Twelve to fifteen hours, depending on how far away they lived and what kind of day they were having.

The Fischer Associate winced at Nolan's answer as if he'd smelled a carton of spoiled milk. He glanced around them, then stuffed a hand inside his suit jacket. His cuff links were color themed after the wig of a birthday clown. They weren't ugly, but they had violated an unspoken rule of corporate fashion—no more than three colors on you if you want to be taken seriously. He drew out a bottle that resembled a nasal spray, partially concealing it behind his lapel. Nolan had no idea what that was, and he didn't want to know, so he smiled and shook his head.

"This is good stuff—new formula," said Fischer.

"No, thanks, man. I'm just here to chill," Nolan said and picked up his water. The tremor had dissipated, but he still had an itch under his skin.

Fischer studied Nolan with a frown, then his lips formed a capital *O* as a light bulb moment hit him.

"If you want to 'chill'"—air quotes—"you need to go to Lodi Park or Edison Wharf. You on Facebook? I can add you to a group. The quality of chicks is a bit . . . meh, but still better than Tinder—"

"Dude—"

"—or Grindr, if you're on that team."

"No, seriously. I'm just here to . . . breathe."

A profound confusion crawled up Fischer's face and darkened his features. "M'kay, just trying to be nice," he mumbled. That made Nolan feel bad for a second, and worried—after all, relationships were the most valuable currency on Sauria Street.

"There's a Facebook group, you say?" Nolan logged on to Facebook with his dummy account. Fischer's eyes lit up. He grabbed Nolan's phone and requested to join Sauria Street Adventures on his behalf.

"I'm an admin—will approve you later." He grinned.

"Cool . . . thanks."

"Limit your messages to date, time, and location, and never use your selfie or your real name for your profile. Oh, and I'll send you a list of suspicious IDs. Don't respond to those 'cause we think they might be firm HRs, so they're a bit tricky. We haven't removed them 'cause we want them to think they have the upper hand."

"Thanks, dude, that's very—"

"But if you actually *need* an HR 'friend,' I can tell you the ones who are definitely not a sting."

"—thoughtful of you—"

"You play Fortnite? I got a PS7—preordered, first release. I'm usually home Tuesdays and Thursdays."

"Um—"

"Oh, oh, do you like ELO? The Electric Light Orchestra?"

Looking into those sparkly eyes, Nolan felt a nostalgic warmth—this guy actually wanted to be his friend. Before he could respond, his Frenell badge let out a string of beeps like a kitchen timer.

"Already?" Fischer frowned.

Nolan sighed and got up. "Twenty-five fifty." He finished his water.

Fischer lowered his head like a King Charles spaniel puppy that had been left behind when his human had gone to work. After a moment, he put his bored face back on and raised his half-empty coffee cup as if toasting to an invisible goddess.

"To twenty-five fifty."

"I STILL NEED two hundred and nineteen hours to hit a hundred and seventy percent." Ryuka stared at the result on her calculator.

"But why do you need one seventy?" Nolan asked. "One hundred percent is enough—that's what 'one hundred percent' means. It's a state of completeness. 'Complete' is more than 'enough,' am I crazy?"

"You're not wrong," Ryuka said. "But you'd only be right if the one hundred percent they told you were the *real* 'one hundred.' I've compared the metrics of the Star Billers in the last five years. The actual expectation is that you should bill *at least* thirty percent above your target, and that was the standard in 2023. Now, the new minimum is probably forty to fifty percent above, so one seventy is barely safe."

"You're gonna kill yourself." Sai shook her head.

"Do we even have that much work to go around?" Nolan asked.

"WPF is out there hunting whales," Sai said.

"Yeah, for like, four months." Nolan shrugged.

"WPF" was Wade Pendleton-Fitzpatrick, one of the Olympians on Level 28. Had he been born twenty years earlier with fewer letters in his surname, Frenell would've become Frenell & *Something* Co.

Nolan didn't know much about whale hunting, but he hadn't seen a piece of it. In the past few weeks, he'd been able to finish everything on his plate by 7:00 p.m., and those had mostly been non-billable assignments for BD–Business Development, which meant finding new clients and keeping existing ones, and KM–Knowledge Management, which involved making precedents and templates that your fellow Frenells could borrow. Nolan suspected his open-plan neighbors were in the same boat, based on how frequent their kitchen trips and bathroom breaks had become. Yet nobody would leave the office before eleven, and the Level 20 café was busy as it had always been at dinnertime. It was performance review season, so you'd better appear overbooked and stressed out.

The dinner line moved swiftly and silently. The Associates collected their plastic boxes of beef, chicken, or fish, then broke into predictable tables. The ones who dressed like they'd just come off the set of *Peaky Blinders* worked for the Partners who acted like that show was their backstory. The ones with flawless makeup and impeccable hair were under the Partners who had high expectations for female Associates' professional appearance. Then you got the extras for *House of Cards* and *Succession*–how could you not? There used to be a few brave ones who looked like the study group in *Community*. None of them were still here.

Sometimes, you'd see a lone ranger turn up with greasy hair and a five-o'clock shadow, often without shoes, jumping the line and rushing to the counter as if they'd escaped from a basement where they'd been imprisoned for six months, and Calais, the barista, would bring out a customized bento and hand it over with a free energy drink–those were the "cattle." Everyone needed a few "group dinner" entries in their PADU record, as the lack of such was a sign of "poor social skills." But the cattle were free to leave and eat their meals in peace, for they were the backbone of this place's balance sheet. Deep down, the others also wanted the cattle out of sight so they wouldn't answer their phones with a mouthful of food and annoy everyone by appearing more in demand.

"Project Rhapsody is gonna solve my problem," Ryuka said, still staring at her calculator. "Now that both Tim and Dan are . . . unavailable, they've gotta be looking for another pair of hands."

"You sure you can get on that case?" Sai asked. "WPF can be a bit . . ."

"Selective?"

"If that's how you put it."

"Please don't tell me you're playing that dumb game." Nolan shook his head.

Every May, the Frenells were expected to participate in Catch a Partner—an integral component of the firm's Culture, Coaching, and Development Program. This supposed morale boost allowed them to approach one Partner in person and deliver a one-minute elevator pitch on the value they'd created for the firm and how they proposed to better themselves in the future. The winner who made the strongest impression would be rewarded with every Frenell's dream—a dinner with their target Partner and a one-hour billable credit.

WPF had been one of the most popular targets, and one of the hardest to catch. Last year, Hayden had to pose as a mechanic and corner him in an auto repair shop.

"I have more class than that—I got intel." Ryuka grinned. "Angela's son turned thirteen last week. I got him that PS6 game he'd wanted for ages, so Angela showed me Wade's calendar. He has a window at three tomorrow, and I'm gonna recommend myself—I worked on Project Daffodil for TTC Pharmaceuticals and that monster advice for Osireion. He should be interested."

"You seem to have put a lot of thought into this." Nolan stared at Ryuka, then shut his eyes. "Jesus, Ryu, did you tell Tim's dad about Dan?"

"Keep your voice down!" Ryuka glared at him. "Poker face—poker face! And that's a hurtful question, dude. There are things I don't do."

Nolan raised an eyebrow.

"Fine, I cracked Tim's password," Ryuka said. "But that's all! Look, his dad begged me, all right? Have you ever seen an old man beg? And how would I know he'd blow Barton's brains out? You met Tim—everyone assumed he came from a long line of . . ."

"A long line of what?" asked Nolan.

"Of pushovers," she whispered.

"What else could he do anyway?" Sai said. "Just watch Barton walk?"

"Nobody's letting him walk." Nolan sighed. "There's an investigation. There are laws."

"Sure." Sai chuckled.

"We don't know for sure that Dan would've gotten away with it, Sai."

"Oh, he would. Ask Gina Roe."

"And Amy Wong," Ryuka added.

"Sandy Winslow." Sai nodded.

"Priyanka Sharma."

"And of course, Richard Shaw."

"Sai . . ." Ryuka peeked at Nolan when Sai mentioned Richard.

"You know I'm right." Sai shrugged.

"Well, you're not wrong—"

"In a way," Sai said, "the balance of the universe has been restored."

She could use some of that balance.

As Sai brought a lip balm to her mouth, she glanced across the café and met the stares and eye rolls from the other tables. So she put the cap back on and dropped it into her pocket. Nolan moved his chair squarely in front of Sai so all she could see was him.

"Have you called Kevin?" he asked.

"Been trying"—Sai sighed—"but I haven't heard anything since he got my CV."

"It's only been nine weeks," Nolan said. "Hang in there."

"I don't know if I should wish you good luck." Ryuka threw her plastic fork into the dinner box.

"We'll be around." Nolan did the same.

"Nobody leaves Sauria Street." Sai scooped up her trash and wiped the table with a napkin.

The facade clock struck 8:00 p.m. Two rows of patrol robots cruised through the café to time-stamp the Associates' staff badges and escort them back to their floors. Today's closing announcement flew out of the speakers as the panorama screen walls looped a firm promo video featuring flawless smiles and pristine dental work.

Dear Frenells,

We are pleased to inform you that Frenell & Co. has been nominated for the Inclusive Innovator Award, the Wellness Warrior Award, and the Employees' Choice of Best Workplace for 2028. We encourage you to participate in the voting, which will open on the 15th of May, next Monday.

We celebrate our Star Billers of April: Hayden Hins, Level 21; Jules Richardson, Level 24; Emma Abilene, Level 13; Wushan Yang, Level 9; and Scott Sherman, Level 10.

Your annual performance review must be completed before the end of May. Please schedule the discussion with your Handler at your earliest convenience.

As a gentle reminder: taxi fares will only be reimbursed if the receipt clearly shows the trip commencing after 11:00 p.m. If you have difficulty completing your assignments before the end of public transportation services, we encourage you to speak with your Handler and your team for possible adjustments in workload.

Your well-being is our utmost priority, and the firm appreciates your contribution.

2

MELODIE SIENA STOOD in the center of the open plan like an ancient Greek statue, without a single thread covering her body, yet all Nolan could see was her face. He wondered what the girl was taking—she seemed genuinely happy.

An hour ago, Melodie wasn't on Level 13, and Nolan thought his career was ending on Level 26.

"WE ARE PROMOTING you to Special Associate in June. It won't be announced until the end of the financial year, but I thought you'd appreciate a heads-up. As the Acting Talent and Resources Partner and the Principal Timekeeper Contact for OATH, I'd like to congratulate you on this remarkable achievement."

Colleen's office was on the west side of Level 26, the side facing the jungle of office buildings, not the side with the greens and the water. The afternoon sun penetrated her windows and forced her to roll down her blinds, dimming her glass castle to a cave.

"Thank you for letting me know." Nolan kept his back straight and his butt in the chair. It was too soon to excuse himself from the conversation.

"You've made it." Colleen spread her arms like a proud mother. "You've made it to the A-Team Floors, and you'll have your own office on Level 21."

"Special Associate." Nolan repeated that in his mind and felt indifferent. Before Frenell had adopted the title "Associate" for all Timekeepers from Year 2 and above regardless of their capacities, it used to differentiate them with descriptive names like "Lawyer," "Consultant," "Business Analyst," "Forensic Investigator," or "Researcher." But OATH had combed through all the national, industry, academic, and independent productivity reports of the past decade and concluded that a unified denomination would effectively reduce workplace conflicts caused by employees feeling they were better than one another.

Nolan didn't mind being a plain and simple "Associate"–he naturally sounded like an appendix, like a party tagalong who was allowed to mind their own business.

"It's an honor." He made brief eye contact, then looked away.

"Don't be so stiff." Colleen grinned. "Maybe we haven't properly caught up since March, but we did some great work together, didn't we?"

Nolan's eyes narrowed in a flash of rage, but he quickly returned to his usual inscrutable countenance. Colleen watched him, amused.

"We think you're on the right track to greater things–"

She thumbed her smart ring and projected Nolan's Timekeeper Profile onto the wall. His value as a fee earner for this establishment–quantified, dissected, and disseminated like a butcher chart over a deli freezer. Nolan felt a taste of sourness rise to his tongue.

"A hundred and five percent billables. Thirty percent non-billables." Colleen pointed at his "Productivity Summary" section.

"That's a good balance–you don't want to come off as desperate or slacking off. Your collection is only sixty but, well, you can't control when clients pay. None of us can, really. Good degree. Good grades. No job hops. Type A, ENTP, Capricorn. Good, all good . . . one area you could improve is your relationships. You're now at the stage where you need to build up a 'presence' within the firm, so you need to choose your connections wisely–"

She opened his Relationship Map. Nolan's headshot floated to the center of the diagram, encircled by satellites bearing photos of several other Frenell Associates. The sizes and distances of the satellites varied, reflecting the sentimental value of each relationship, calculated by the non-billable time invested and recorded in PADU.

"These are your friends?" She pointed at two larger nodes displaying Ryuka's and Sai's faces.

"They're my friends," Nolan said.

"Good friends?"

"Very good friends."

Colleen stretched the corners of her mouth as her gaze lingered on Sai's headshot. "Be sensible–these are not the old days."

"I should probably get back to–"

"Wade will like you–you're his type. Keep good notes on what you see, what you hear, who he meets, and what they do. Who knows, you might be able to catch him with his pants down in three months. Charge Professional Development, like the last time. You can use the same subcode . . ."

She paused to enjoy Nolan's silent dismay.

"A lot of people would kill to have Wade as their Handler." She winked. "How about a little smile?"

"I'm not doing it again." Nolan ground his teeth.

"This is not a request, sweetheart." Colleen pushed out of her chair and paced to Nolan's side of the desk. "As the Acting Partner for Culture, Ethics, Sensitivity, and Influence, I have the responsibility to monitor and investigate potential misconduct in this workplace. No one is above the Frenell values, not even the mighty WPF. Wade is trickier than Aaron Patucchi, but I think you're ready. Pop up to Level 28 and say hi when you get a chance. I'd suggest you go early in the morning–he's probably still jet lagged."

Before Nolan realized it, a scoff burst out of him. This "catch-up" with Colleen had accentuated the dull pain of chronic inflammation he'd acquired from this place. If monkeys understood English, this would be exactly how these people talked to them.

"I'm sure you can find another person for the job." He stood up to leave.

"If you're counting on that offer from Chalet & Gravelines, you can forget about it."

Nolan froze. He'd had a pleasant meeting with Alex Chalet and Jane Santos from that boutique firm two weeks ago, and Alex had made him a provisional offer on the spot. He'd told Nolan to keep an eye on his inbox and given him a pat on the shoulder as he walked him out the door. They just had to "tidy up some paperwork."

"I had a lovely weekend with Alex and his family in the Silver Mountains," said Colleen. "He spoke rather highly of you, but his wife owed me a favor, so he kindly agreed not to steal you. Although, it feels a bit silly now–why waste a favor when I could've played them this?"

She pressed a button on her smart ring, and a piece of recording flew out of her Bluetooth speakers. The processed clip had distorted the voices, so it took a few seconds for Nolan's heart to sink.

"*Rich . . . Richard? What's wrong with your voicemail? Gimme a call, man, everyone's saying you're dead, what the fuck–*"

"*You have reached the Frenell Well-Being Helpdesk. This is Sharon speaking. How may I help you today?*"

"*Put Richard on, please, I need to . . . fuck, did I vomit blood? My sink's red.*"

"*Sir, I have to ask you to refrain from using that language.*"

"*Oh, it's just wine . . . never mind.*"

"Sir, you have reached the Frenell Well-Being Helpdesk. Please describe your emergency and the assistance—"

"Can you bring pizza? No salami, ugh—"

"—you seek. Please note that services provided over the phone do not form medical relationships—"

"Actually, no, ugh . . . God, maybe I really should stop drinking—"

"—and are not a substitute for professional diagnosis or treatment. This call may be recorded for training purposes."

"—but some days are just impossible to get through without it . . . I should've listened to you . . . I wish I'd told you . . ."

"We offer emotional support and counseling in moments of crisis. Please describe your emergency—"

"You still got my address? No salami."

"Sir, you sound under the influence. Would you say you have a healthy relationship with substances such as alcohol, prescription drugs, or nonmedical drugs?"

"I can't find my remote control . . . sorry, who's this? Where's Richard?"

Colleen paused the recording and slipped into the gap between Nolan and her desk, pressing him back into the chair with her hands on his shoulders. He gave no reaction, and that pleased her.

Nolan remembered Friday, March 3, 2028, or at least part of it. He'd woken up on the floor of his bathroom before midnight and decided he should make a phone call. He thought he was calling a friend, or a pizza place, but the Frenell Well-Being Helpdesk was set as a speed dial on firm devices, and that was where the call went. He couldn't stitch the night together until Sunday afternoon, and even then he still had gaping holes in his memory. He had no idea how the call had ended, or how he'd woken up in the morning on his bedroom floor in clean pajamas. But he'd known he'd be finished if that call ever saw the light of the day. That was the day he went cold turkey. It'd been two months. He'd thought he was in the clear.

"As the Mental Health Champion of the firm," Colleen said, "it broke my heart when I first heard this. I'd like you to know that you can always talk to me."

"Those calls were supposed to be confidential."

Nolan felt stupid as soon as those words came out of his mouth. At Frenell, plenty of things didn't work the way they were "supposed" to.

"They are, technically." Colleen smiled. "You heard that, nobody could tell that was you—not without the right context. I'm a big fan of context. See, if we cross-reference the speech patterns and word preferences in the recording against your Timekeeper Profile, compare the time of the call with the activity level of your account, and run some targeted searches with details like the name mentioned across staff Relationship Maps—that *really* narrows things down."

Nolan turned to his profile on the wall. Next to Ryuka and Sai, a satellite of similar size framed Richard Shaw's shy smile and cropped out part of the messy hair he'd always worn like he'd never had a picture day in his life. The photo was in black and white, indicating the account was no longer active.

Colleen set her hip on the edge of her desk as she lifted one foot and squeezed it in between Nolan's legs. Her red stiletto looked like a blood-drenched dagger.

"You've always been my favorite, Nolan. You have this stoic look like, *I don't even want this.* That's cute, in a way, but I much prefer a good mix of disbelief, anger, and a little bit of fear on a pretty face—just like this, hmm . . . just like this."

She grabbed his tie and pulled him closer as she ground her high heel into his inner thigh. Nolan clenched his jaw and locked his gaze on Richard. His fingernails cut into the backs of his interlocked hands. He smelled the tobacco perfume between Colleen's collarbones as she pressed her face against his and loosened his tie with her forefinger.

"Did you think you could get away from me?" she whispered and nibbled his ear. "I like how your voice broke on that call.

Let's see if you sound as adorable when you cry in real life–maybe add thirty percent more quivering?"

He saw a paperweight near the edge of Colleen's desk. A brass tortoise the size of a wallet, bending its stretched neck backward to bite at the python coiling atop its shell.

That will fit right inside our hand, he heard the voice he'd been trying to ignore say. *Come on, the bitch deserves it.*

As he met Colleen's eyes and pictured her pulpified face, the fire alarm screamed on his behalf.

MELODIE SIENA WAS number 4 on the unofficial "Frenell 2023 Cohort Sinners" list. Two spots below Sai. Whoever had made that list noted she was "easy to impress," "needs people to like her," and was "highly agreeable, therefore boring," but good if "you want something with low MeToo risk."

The girl was a moving target, Sai thought. Striking enough to attract attention, imperfect enough to attract doubt. Open enough to turn up in the wrong place at the wrong time, withdrawn enough to keep the unspeakable to herself. Sai watched Melodie paddle her arms and read that as relief–maybe the girl believed that, this time, they'd finally leave her alone.

An hour ago, Melodie wasn't on Level 13, and Sai thought she was going to turn the Freedom Room into a crime scene.

"LET'S TAKE A step back–how did he know where you live?"

"When we first started at Frenell as Summer Cadets." Sai sighed. "I told you this before–he helped me pick up some costumes and tools for our final show . . . that's not the point, he wasn't invited that night–"

"We'll get to that," Christie Plains said as she scrolled through her notes. "So, you and Hayden had known each other for quite some time before the incident, is that right?"

"Why are we going through these old questions again?"

"We think context is important, like the nature of your relationship, your interactions leading up to that night, the dynamic–"

"We were not dating!"

"Okay, okay. Calm down. Not dating, just friends."

"He turned up at my door at eleven p.m. on Friday, March the third, drunk as a clown, and asked to come in. I said no; he wouldn't leave. He pounded on my door for fifteen minutes and woke my neighbor up–who's still mad at me to this day, by the way. Eventually he left, but he bombarded me with suggestive texts until two in the morning. I've repeated this more than enough times, and you're not getting a different story–"

"We're trying to help you, Sarah."

Katherine Waycross, the Chief Culture Officer from OATH, interjected without looking up from her tablet. Christie stopped typing and reached for the manila folder lying next to her laptop.

Sai's real name was Saidah. It wasn't complicated on its own, but with a surname like Sulaimaniyah, she'd made the sensible choice to apply for the job with the name Sarah to nudge her identity back to the "comfortably foreign" range. She'd asked to change it back after she'd passed probation, but it'd involve too many moving parts across OATH, Office Facilities, IT, and Marketing, so it'd never happened. Nolan and Ryuka called her Sai–"Sah-ee."

"We take these allegations seriously," Katherine continued. "And they carry grave consequences, so we must get the facts right–especially in today's climate. Things can get out of control pretty quickly. As Christie mentioned"–she snapped her fingers, and Christie passed on a stack of printouts; Katherine didn't take them, so Christie laid them out on the table, page by page–"you and Hayden had been friends. We have reviewed the texts you submitted. There, before the message 'wtf' at eleven forty-two p.m., there seems to be more to the chat history. What were you talking about before then?"

"That was–"

"Never mind. It was on your work phone, so IT has extracted the messages."

Christie spread out more pages in front of Sai.

"Take a minute to read them if you need to jog your memory," Katherine said. "It seems to us you were discussing weekend plans."

Sai grabbed the nearest page. The 11:42 "wtf" was followed by two rows of question marks, random words like *hello* and *horny* in all caps, then scrambled and autocorrected gibberish. Before it, there was a brief conversation about new releases on Netflix.

"A lot of emojis," Katherine added. "And you were talking about how you should hang out more, weren't you?"

"He said he wanted–"

"Fine, *he* proposed that you should, quote, 'hang out more,' to which you responded, quote, 'Sure,' smiley face."

"I work with this guy. Am I supposed to tell him–"

"He said 'we should hang out.' Then you said 'sure.' Yes or no?"

"That's not how I–"

"Did he touch you, yes or no?"

"Well, yes."

"Yes how?"

"He wouldn't let go of my door and he scratched my hand–"

"So you opened the door for him."

"With the lock chained."

"You opened the door, yes or no?"

"He kept pounding–"

"Did he touch any other part of your body other than your hand?"

"What, you mean he had to grab me–"

"That's a no. What does 'wtf' mean?"

"What?"

"Why do you think he said 'wtf'?"

"What the hell is this?"

"Exactly. 'What the hell is this?' It's a statement of confusion and frustration."

Katherine folded her arms and reclined in her chair. Christie began to put things back inside her laptop bag.

"Look, Sarah." Katherine sighed. "We know people are more sensitive about this kind of thing now because of all the social media madness. But as professionals, we shouldn't be so easily influenced like average people, and we must think critically to avoid turning this into a witch hunt. Not to say your feelings don't matter, and kudos for coming forward—we can see why you interpreted what'd happened the way you did, but this is just some unfortunate misunderstanding. What the evidence shows is that Hayden thought you guys were supposed to 'hang out' that night, so he came over—not in his best state, but it *was* a Friday. Then you seemed offended and turned him away, so he was confused."

Her voice turned gentle and proud, as if she were talking about her own son.

"You know how incredibly hard Hayden has been working. He just made Special Associate, and he has a lot to prove—he's the first of your cohort to hit that milestone, isn't he? Let me tell you, the first year on Level 21 is the hardest because he needs to build up his presence within the firm, so he has enough stress already. You're his friend. He needs your support."

"So you're telling me," Sai scoffed, "that because he's a Frenell darling, I have to suck this up."

"I already acknowledged your feelings."

"His behavior was not acceptable—"

"Oh, toughen up, princess." Katherine frowned. "You got some stupid drunk texts and a picture of a banana."

Except that if the banana was sticking out of a man's fly, was it still a banana?

"The point is, what happened was obviously just Hayden being Hayden. You need to learn to manage him, and manage this type of challenge in general. This is a relationship-based business. You will be ruining your own career if everyone has to tiptoe around you."

Sai's memory took her back to that night and replayed the part where Hayden tried to barge in like Jack Nicholson in *The Shining*. She zoomed in on his face and measured his intoxicated confusion, wondering if, by any chance, she had overreacted.

"I've talked to Hayden," Katherine continued. "He now understands your concerns, and he's promised to be more prudent going forward. He's also kindly agreed to attend a reconciliation meeting with you, which we'll leave with you two, but we do need written confirmation from both parties that the reconciliation has taken place and the subject matter has been resolved to your mutual satisfaction. I've briefed him on the process. He knows what to do."

"You gotta be kidding me–"

"If we don't receive the reconciliation slip by the end of this week, we will have to leave a write-up in your RAP that your sexual harassment complaint has been dismissed for insufficient grounds. Once an OATH ticket like this is opened, it must have a clear record of resolution, one way or another."

Sai went quiet at the mention of "RAP"–Record of Admonitions and Probation. A comprehensive work history that any employee of "productive age" was required to carry until retirement like their credit score and medical record. It was linked to their Social Security number, and any stain was just as permanent. Katherine seized the silence and took Sai's hand like a caring foster mother.

"I like you, Sarah, that's why I'm giving you the honesty you deserve. Some people will egg you on when you pick fights and burn bridges because they want to use you for virtue signaling and they don't give a damn about the repercussions *you* will have to face. Sure, you might feel powerful for one day, but then you'll *never* have a future at Frenell or anywhere near Sauria Street. Is it worth it? Be practical and think long term. Men like Hayden are a bunch of silly boys–they're pretty simple, and ninety-nine point nine percent of the time, they're just talking shit. You're smarter than them. Play dumb, laugh things off, let them know they can relax. They think you're cool and fun, then they send more good work your way and put in some good references for you–win-win. You don't have to give them anything real. That takes some practice, but it's an important part of people management. Learn to roll in the mud and avoid putting yourself in a vulnerable position at the same time, then everybody's life is easier."

Sai held her tongue. Katherine pulled away and nodded at Christie.

"I'll circulate today's meeting minutes," Christie said. "Please record zero point eight hours of 'Non-billable: People Management' for 'Attend meeting with relevant OATH representatives for interpersonal skills coaching.' I'll include the subcode and the standard narrative in my email."

"That's a lot to unpack." Katherine picked a loose hair off her blazer and dropped it on the carpet. "Take your time and reflect on it. Oh, we need the reconciliation slip by Friday."

Before the OATH hit squad stepped out the door, Christie turned around and whispered to Sai, as if to give her a precious cheat code for the game of life.

"Remember–dodge, block, ignore."

WHEN SAI RETURNED to her workstation on Level 13, her desk had been cleaned out. Well, not entirely. Her mug and family photo were still there, but the dozen binders for Project Eel barricading her spot had disappeared. Neither Ryuka nor Nolan was around, so she turned to the other Year 5 sitting two seats down the bench.

"James, did someone take my files?"

James Taree glanced out of the corner of his eye and saw who was talking. He slipped one hand off the desk and pressed a button under the wooden panel like a bank teller at gunpoint. Three black canvas screens sprouted out of the desk and constructed a

U-shaped cubicle around him. The flap behind his monitor rose twice as high, then folded over him, adding a lid on top of this private space. Inside these Productivity Shields, James resumed typing. In the meantime, Emma Abilene, another Year 5 and April Star Biller No. 3, marched over with a familiar binder in her arm and a frown between her eyes.

"Do you have the NDA mentioned at clause 22.1.3(a)?" Emma thrust the open binder under Sai's nose and tapped the paper with her pen. "And what's the billing protocol for this one?"

"They've put you on this case?"

"What do you think?" Emma let out an exasperated sigh.

"I'll send you the billing protocol with the narrative checklist–"

"I was supposed to go to a birthday party tonight, just so you know."

"I can help you. That NDA–"

"How?" Emma rolled her eyes before she strode away. "You can't work with Hayden anymore, can you?"

The other Associates in the open plan either had headphones on or their Productivity Shields up, and no one seemed to have noticed the exchange between Sai and Emma. Sai sat in the atmosphere for a second, then unlocked her screen. No new emails except a couple of firm-wide announcements about printer outages, after-hours air-conditioning, and acceptable use of the Meditation Chambers. The ramifications of "picking fights" had begun to manifest.

As Sai calculated how long her surplus billables could carry her before PADU flagged her as unproductive, a message from Christie landed in her inbox. The summary of her meeting with OATH was indeed a "summary." Other than the date, duration, and names of attendees, it contained two sentences:

After reviewing and clarifying certain details relating to the communications in question, the Claimant has agreed to attend reconciliation. Matter closed.

Her personal phone lit up and sent her heart racing–a call from Kevin Reese, Principal Scout of NoFuss Talent Warehouse.

The blaring fire alarm buried her yelp, so she didn't attract too much attention.

As the rest of Level 13 strolled toward the evacuation staircases, Sai ran the opposite way and hit the green button on her screen. The latch on the Meditation Chamber said "Occupied," so she pounded twice, then covered her eyes—special etiquette during performance review season. She felt two people rush past her, and no one else was coming out, so she hopped in, kicked the condom and tissues to a corner, and locked the door.

"I'm here, Kevin! Yes, hi! Sorry, fire in my building. No no no no no no stay with me! I can hear you! I can hear you!"

MELODIE SIENA HELD one hand to her heart and bowed her head, thanking an audience only she could see. She'd had the same pose after her rendition of "On My Own" from *Les Misérables* at the annual dinner two years ago. The girl had had a bright smile when she'd started at Frenell as a Summer Cadet, and her profile said her childhood dream was to be a professional musician. Ryuka wondered if that was still what she wanted.

Half an hour ago, Melodie wasn't on Level 13, and Ryuka was trying to set Mount Olympus on fire.

WRAPPED IN HER lucky suit, Ryuka listened to her footsteps echo down the hall. The echoes were pleasantly crisp from Level 26 and above. They used high-grade granite for these floors.

The thirty-one floors inside Frenell's Grand Ivory headquarters followed a simple numbering system: Levels 31 to 29 were the Perception Floors, with rooms named "Freedom," "Courage," "Vision," "Diligence," and the like. These were reserved for client conferences, board meetings, important firm events such as staff motivation assemblies, and, occasionally, political fundraisers. Levels 28 to 26 were the Partner Floors, home to twelve Equity

Partners, who were the true owners of this business, and twenty-one Salary Partners, who wished to become true owners one day. Levels 25 to 21 were the A-Team Floors, which belonged to anyone with "Special" in their title. Level 20 hosted Frenell's two intelligence services—the firm café and OATH. It also served as a border between "the Real Frenells" and "the Non-Specials" who sat between Level 13 and Level 9, from Year 5 Associates all the way down to Year 1 Graduates.

Level 8 and below were dedicated parking spaces and supporting services such as Office Facilities, the mail room, Accounts and Payroll, and of course, IT. Below the "ground" floor, a galleria elevated the building to five stories above the real ground for feng shui reasons and created a psychological comfort that anyone stepping inside this establishment had won at the starting line.

The buttons in the elevators stopped at Level 13, then jumped to Level 20. No one seemed to know why or what was in between. Ryuka thought it might be some really particular superstition, although they didn't seem to have a problem with thirteen.

Level 28 had an alternative name—"Mount Olympus." The Frenells preferred this one, as it highlighted the utmost importance of the small group of twelve that represented 1 percent of the Timekeeper force. The firm had a written policy that Equity Partners were not allowed to travel in the same aircraft or stay in the same hotel on business trips or retreats. If you saw someone step out of an elevator full of Frenell Partners without bowing to the pack inside, that one might be the designated survivor.

This alternative name also reflected another defining attribute of the gods on this mountain—the Olympians would not make direct contact with the mortals, unless they wanted to fuck them.

WPF's office was in one of the four corners on Level 28, overlooking Lodi Park with a glimpse of the Athena River. Ryuka clutched the binder containing her CV and work samples from her previous projects, rehearsing her pitch as she approached her target. Through the gaps between the blinds, she saw Wade in his reclining chair, facing the windows with his feet up on the coffee table, pondering, or maybe napping.

As she was about to knock, Angela grabbed her and pulled her aside.

"He's not in today."

"Then who's that?" Ryuka pointed at the office.

"He's on the phone."

"Wait, is he not in or is he on the phone?"

"He's busy."

"I'll wait, then–how's it going?"

"You should go. He's back-to-back this afternoon."

"But you said he has a window at three."

"Not anymore."

Angela took a plastic case from her drawer and shoved it in Ryuka's arms.

"Whoa, hold on. We don't have to do this." Ryuka put the PS6 game back on Angela's desk and covered it with a stack of invoices. "What's the matter? Damien doesn't like it?"

"Oh, he *loves* it." Angela rolled her eyes. "What's the matter with you? Getting him something like this–there are women twice his age taking their clothes off."

Ryuka bit her lip. One of the side quests was in the red-light district, and you'd have to socialize with the prostitutes for intel. So Damien had unlocked that one within a week. That was kind of impressive.

"What do you mean?" She played dumb. "It's marked thirteen plus and I double-checked with the retailer. They assured me there's no inappropriate content."

Angela ignored her. Ryuka pressed her face against Wade's glass wall and saw him lying in his chair with both hands laced behind the back of his head. Was there anything to stop her from knocking on the door and asking for *one* minute of his time? No, she could get it down to thirty seconds.

"If you barge in without an appointment," Angela said, "you'll *never* get a second of his time in the future."

Why? Ryuka thought. *Is this guy some kind of genie? If you rub the lamp the wrong way, he's gonna vanish into thin air forever?*

But she didn't say any of that, and she let go of the handle.

"Angela . . . I know you're the best—"

"I can't help you." Angela handed the game back to Ryuka and returned to her keyboard. At the press of a button, her Productivity Shields rose up and hid her face.

"Don't do this to me, Angela . . . seriously? Well . . . at least tell me if they've replaced Tim yet?"

The lid of Angela's Productivity Shields flipped down, sheltering her from distractions. Ryuka picked up the hundred-dollar game and suppressed the urge to slap it on the black canvas, then she stuffed it in her portfolio binder and shuffled away.

❦

"DON'T TELL ME anything I didn't ask."

Calais gestured a "stop" when he saw Ryuka had swallowed her water and was about to speak. Level 29 had no client meeting today, so it was hard to tell the status of the evacuation, but the fading fire alarm sounded like it'd descended below Level 26. Right now, the fire warden on each floor would be herding the occupants to the nearest emergency exits, which would lead them to the assembly points outside the building.

During the slow hours at the café, Calais worked in the main kitchen on Level 29. When the alarm went off, he'd been in the middle of preparing the staff dinner for tonight. As he stepped out to find the fire staircase, Ryuka dashed in and hid behind the doors, poking her head out to monitor the hallway.

"Was that you?" Calais pointed at the imaginary fire outside.

"I'll be quick," Ryuka said.

So Calais returned to the prep table and picked up the apple he'd been peeling earlier. One of the special bentos tonight had fruit salad.

Given the low traffic on Level 29, the fire warden of Level 28 was responsible for both floors. Ryuka saw Angela appear at the end of the hall, stroll a few steps toward the kitchen, then stop halfway.

"Anybody?" she yelled, then headed back the way she'd come after one second.

"Thanks, owe you one." Ryuka handed the empty glass back to Calais. His fingertips were cold from the washing and rinsing.

"Choose a different floor the next time. You're gonna get busted." Calais tossed a Granny Smith at Ryuka. She nodded as she caught the apple. It was solid advice—whole-building evacuation was too flashy even for her own taste. Her other option had been flooding the toilets, but there wasn't enough material to work with after they'd replaced paper towels with hand dryers.

Angela's screen was dark but unlocked. As the holder of "Most Forgotten Passwords" for three years in a row, she'd given up. Ryuka brought her Outlook calendars back up and saw that Wade's 3:00 p.m. to 3:30 p.m. was indeed open—the only opening of the week, as a matter of fact. She scanned for keywords "Project Rhapsody" and found a team briefing at 9:00 a.m. the day after tomorrow. Her heart sank—that indicated the team had moved on from Tim and Dan, and the ship was headed back into the water. Sticking an ear out for sounds of people returning, Ryuka combed through Wade's calendar before the scheduled briefing for anything that resembled an opportunity. This Olympian's days were diced into chunks of client con-calls, firm meetings, and Partner drinks. Nowhere for a lowly Associate like herself to appear for any natural reason. Eventually, her gaze landed on a five-hour "Busy" block from 3:00 p.m. tomorrow stretching into the night, marked "Private Appointment." Even Angela couldn't see its contents.

For someone who could affect millions' worth of business with the flip of a hand, Wade's desk was rather minimalistic. His computer was locked, which suited Ryuka well—she'd faint if she got access to the inbox of the mighty WPF. Under the forty-three-inch curved monitor lay a pack of pills, an empty coffee mug, a crumpled tissue, and the key of his Ferrari Purosangue. A stack of signed documents was left in a tray and pushed to the corner of the desk, waiting for Angela to collect. From underneath his mouse pad, a light-gray triangle poked out. Ryuka slipped it free and examined what looked like a loyalty card.

Dandelion had adopted a sophisticated design for its brand: asymmetrical blocks of gray and black painted a borderless background, with the cursive name of the business spelled out in the center in muted gold. *A jazz bar, maybe*, Ryuka thought. The back of the card displayed two rows of stamps with an empty slot for one last visit. The dates showed a pattern. Wade had been going to this place every Wednesday. Tomorrow would be Wednesday.

Before she fled the scene, Ryuka glanced at the tray of signed documents. The subject line of the memo on top read "2028–2029 New Special Associates." She saw a list of names that continued to the next page. She hesitated and did not pick it up.

On her way down the fire staircase, she tracked the meeting invite to her Handler for her performance review. No acceptance. No rejection. No response.

WHEN MELODIE SIENA appeared on Level 13, naked and disoriented, there were no gasps, only indifferent glances. The Frenells had seen some strange things in life, and they were still distracted by the fire alarm earlier, so most of them simply assumed Melodie had been showering when the alarm had gone off and she'd locked herself out, and now she needed to borrow a badge to get her stuff back.

Then she started singing "Sempre Libera" from *La Traviata*, which convinced the Year 5 Associates this was a practical joke or another random virtue testing. Some activated their Productivity Shields. As Melodie hit those top notes, her sonorous head voice morphed into squawks, then shrieks. She dragged her fingernails down her cheeks, leaving eight streaks of red and pink. That was when Nolan took off his suit jacket and rushed to cover the girl. Ryuka found Emma near her bench, watching this with a stern face.

"You got the first aid kit? Emma?"

"What . . . why?"

"Aren't you the first responder?"

"Yeah, but what is *this* supposed to be?"

Nolan had covered the torso of Melodie, yet he couldn't stop the scream. No one was offering a second cover. The girl had peed herself.

"Can't you just give her that sedative spray?" Ryuka reached out a hand for the key of the first aid kit. "C'mon, Em. It's Mel."

"Hold on . . . we don't even know what her condition is." Emma pulled away with a frown. "What if she has a bad reaction, who's responsible? You?"

"If the bots get here—"

Right then, Edmund the patrol robot entered the open plan and stopped in front of Nolan and Melodie. The sudden intruder caught Melodie's attention and hushed her for a moment. The top of Edmund's head cracked open and sent a rectangular screen to Melodie's eye level. Peaceful meditation music flew out of its speakers as its mechanical arm held out an atomizer to diffuse essential oil fragrance into the air. On the screen, a cartoon monster was dancing.

"We at Frenell encourage our staff to take care of themselves and manage their work-life balance." A confident female voice rose above the meditation tune. "Take a short break, look out the window for thirty seconds, and relax your eyes. Is your chair comfortable? Did you know that you might be eligible for a brand-new ergonomic office chair? Call Office Facilities at extension 9901 today for more information. Your well-being is our utmost priority, and the firm appreciates your contribution."

Glaring at the screen in terror, Melodie started shrieking again.

"Have you tried—" said the voice. Its follow-up advice was lost in Melodie's hysteria, and the screen froze for a second. The next moment, another mechanical arm extended from Edmund's body and sprayed some "de-escalator" over Melodie's face. Nolan caught her as she collapsed and laid her on the carpet.

As Edmund turned to spray Nolan, Sai pounced from behind and covered the bot with a fire blanket, sending it into defense mode. Edmund bolted and bounced between benches as its siren slit the stifling air open, calling for backup. It bumped its way to Emma's bench and charged toward her shins. Emma screeched and smashed Edmund on the side with a chair, knocking it over. Then she scrambled to its rolling body and pulled the blanket back in place before it slipped down, so the robot's cameras wouldn't catch her.

Half a dozen patrol robots arrived on the floor and surrounded the center of conflict. Two of them separated Nolan from Melodie and escorted him to the side, while the other four picked up the unconscious girl and dropped her on a large transparent spread. They flipped her over and scooped her off the floor as they rolled the spread up, the way Tim's dad had wrapped Dan Barton's body with that tarp. Melodie's necklace—a customized twenty-first-birthday present with her initials—snapped and fell off. Edmund, who had freed itself from the fire blanket and gotten back on its wheels, cruised over and swallowed it as if it were a piece of trash. The total of seven bots lined up and carried the Mel-wrap like the Seven Dwarfs carrying Snow White to her funeral. They slithered across the floor and disappeared from the view of the Associates.

The incident was contained in less than two minutes. They did not forget to return Nolan's jacket to him.

3

"WHY ARE YOU here?" Nolan whispered.

"Why would a strip club need loyalty cards?" Ryuka asked, then threw herself sideways and stood upside down on one hand.

"Nolan, can you hold her waist and give her some support?" Zoe said. "Keep your knees straight, Ryuka—like that, yes."

The three of them were attempting a pole dancing move called "cartwheel." So you'd graduated from a real college with a real degree, survived a two-hundred-to-one job-application process, overworked yourself till your soul left your body, and put everything else in life on hold. Who would've thought that waiting at the end of that road was a dancing pole?

Ryuka gave it another go and completed the move without external help. She bounded across the stage and wrapped Zoe in an exuberant embrace.

Nolan burned this scene into his memory, so that years later, when asked by his therapist and his AA support system exactly what, in those booze-fueled mornings when he could barely find his face, had gotten him out of bed and stopped him from jumping out of the window, he'd respond with all sincerity: it was the little things, mostly.

He glanced at the suited man over on the couch and couldn't tell if he was bored or drunk. Although WPF was someone who could make people do anything at any given time, Nolan doubted this was what he'd had in mind when he'd given him that invitation to Dandelion.

THE FIRST WORDS Nolan's new Handler said to him were "Don't move."

In the Level 28 men's room the size of three Special Associate offices, Nolan washed his hands till he felt his skin was peeling off. An itch that running water couldn't take away skipped all over the place, pinching the spots he'd missed, like inside his cuticles or the gaps between his fingers, and forcing him to glove his hands with more foam just to feel less exposed. In the middle of the last wash, he sensed another person behind him by the pronounced aromatic scent. Strong tonka base with amberwood and ginger, and a hint of geranium—a perfume that likely came in a dark-blue bottle. Loud and spicy. The smell of a pre-2008 investment banker knee deep in his second midlife crisis.

As Nolan lifted his head to check out the reflection in the mirror, the spicy man told him "Don't move" and started pacing. Nolan kept his head still, as if bowing to the water tap, and traced the figure in the mirror with his eyes. All he saw was the midsection of a double-breasted charcoal-gray suit that looked like a period piece costume. He cut the water, and silence fell over the sinks. The pacing behind him stopped. The spicy scent drifted closer.

"You're an alien who just arrived on Earth," the man said. "How would you convince me you're human?"

"I beg your pardon?"

"Five seconds."

"Wait–"

"Five, four–"

"Okay! Okay . . . why do I have to convince you in the first place? So what if you know I'm an alien?"

"Aha, challenge the premise–good! But I'll tell everyone you're not human, and you'll be in trouble."

"How would you convince anyone I'm not human?"

"Shift the burden of proof–that's right! If I film you and your alien ship with my phone?"

"I'll dispute the authenticity and integrity of your evidence, claim that's the alien who landed on a different farm, and contest your character and motive."

"Deny, deflect, and destroy–you know your Frenell bible. And if I call a hit squad to capture you and take you to a lab, cut you open and study you inside and out, learn your language, then work undercover among your species so I can raid your planet and uproot your entire civilization?"

"Is that really necessary?"

"Every step."

"Um, I . . . I will–"

"Don't think!"

"I will . . . ugh, I'll identify your weak links and crack them individually, bluff about the invincibility of my civilization and the consequences of defiance, plant doubts and pit your people against each other, lynch your rebels and chain your ordinary. What you have, I'll take it away; what you want, you'll never reach! You can scream, lament, and resent, but you will never speak, unite, or rise!"

A drop of water hit the porcelain, and Nolan felt his burning face cool down to a mask of ice. *Did you hear yourself?* The voice inside him chuckled. *It's almost like I'd never left, isn't it?*

You're not who I am, Nolan thought. *Fuck all the way off to Mars.*

The man strolled over to the mirror, and his face entered Nolan's view. Everyone at Frenell would recognize *the* Wade Pendleton-Fitzpatrick from all the marketing materials, yet as a person in the flesh, what struck Nolan about WPF was how "standard" he looked—his features arranged themselves in a way devoid of surprise. If this guy were twenty years younger, he'd have the perfect face for those generic IDs with names like "John A. Sample" or "Michael M. Motorist." Maybe Wade was self-conscious about that, which would explain the white bow tie and the triangular silk handkerchief sticking out of his breast pocket on an ordinary Wednesday.

Wade slid a light-gray card inside Nolan's suit, then pushed his spine back to an upright position with a hand on his chest. He was slightly shorter than Nolan, and much paler. "Three o'clock," he said and left Nolan with a gentle pat on the shoulder. The bathroom smelled like him for a long time after he was gone.

THE CLOSEST NOLAN had ever gotten to somewhere like Dandelion was at the age of nine when his uncle had taken him to a Hooters while on babysitting duty, and he hadn't quite understood the excitement surrounding him back then. Now, as the Prada-wearing receptionist punched the first stamp on his loyalty card, Nolan wondered if this was what his uncle had meant by "becoming a man" and he should indeed be proud of it—he'd peeked behind the curtain and seen the real endgame of the "professional" life. Once you'd proven you were a worthy asset to the firm, you could graduate from the Boys' Club and enter the Gentlemen's Club.

He found Wade and Hayden in a private room on the ground floor. Themed as a recording studio, the square room had a decorative grand piano in the corner and a U-shaped couch lining the walls. The mini stage in the center had a gleaming pole from which a tall blonde spun and dangled as if in a gravity-free zone. Wade lounged in the middle part of the couch. It was hard to tell if he was watching the dance or staring into space. A few seats to his left, Hayden froze for a second when Nolan walked in. His gaze shifted from Nolan to Wade; then he finished his drink without a word.

Wade had had a few drinks before Nolan arrived, and his eyes were honest about it. He spread his arms wide and signaled Nolan to settle down by his side, then stuffed his half-empty glass in Nolan's palm. Hayden caught this and pressed a button on the wall for room service without being asked. The potent aroma of neat whisky rushed into Nolan's nostrils and made his eyes teary. He squeezed out a smile at Wade and pinched his own thigh with his free hand. Thankfully, the dim lighting masked both his unease and the secret between the dancer's legs.

"Macallan eighteen." Wade pointed at the glass and nudged Nolan for a try. "Hayden's been obsessed with it. I think it's fruit punch."

"Thank you, Mr. Pen . . . Mr. Wade, but I don't drink."

Wade's smile froze. He retracted his arm from Nolan's shoulder as his bloodshot eyes inspected his expression.

"I have a slide deck that needs to go out tonight," Nolan explained. "I need to get back to the office—"

"That's a Macallan old enough to fuck," Wade said, his stare choking Nolan like a pair of hands. "Try it and tell me what you think."

Nolan averted his eyes and raised the glass, as slowly as he felt allowed to. Over Wade's shoulder, Hayden studied them with an expression that could be gloating or disgust.

Just have one, the voice said. *It won't hurt to just have one.*

There was only one gulp in the glass. Yet the pronounced smoky notes filled the empty space and hinted at the distinctive murky creaminess of an alluring Scotch that was eager to tell you how smooth it'd be on your tongue. This was good stuff, Nolan realized, maybe he was being rude to Wade.

The light on top of the door turned red–someone was waiting outside. Hayden pressed another button on the wall and let them in. A waitress in a white blouse and black suit pants approached with a tray. On top stood a single Glencairn glass, filled up to its tulip belly with two shots of amber liquid.

"Your Lagavulin twenty-five," she said, "Mr. Pendleton-Fitzpatrick."

Wade's eyes lingered on Nolan for another moment before he turned to his Lagavulin. Nolan peeked at the waitress, and his brain went blank. She stared at him, thinking exactly what he thought.

"It's, um, a new bottle that was flown in from London last week." Ryuka pulled her gaze back and crouched in front of Wade, holding the tray next to her face. "The one you kept here has run out."

Wade picked up the glass and stuck it under his nose.

"I liked Lagavulin three months ago," he said. "I might not like it today."

"If you want something new"–Ryuka smiled–"I have an Ardbeg nineteen that I can bring to the office tomorrow. I also have some experience in pharmaceutical regulation and commercial litigation that might be handy for Project Rhapsody."

"Get a number from Angela and do a phone screen if you want to play Catch a Partner." Wade swirled the whisky and nosed it again.

"I'm not playing that game, and I don't need you to hear my life story. I'm just offering my help–"

"How did you get in?"

"They're hiring dancers, so I proposed a one-day free trial."

"You don't seem like the right fit for the job." Wade glanced at her out of the corner of his eye.

"Dandelion is a nurturing and empowering believer in talent growth. If I successfully complete the six-month waitress internship, I'll be a contracted trainee for two years and rotate through bartender, DJ, booker, and host roles, and eventually progress to dancer with a balanced skill set. No one is choreography director from day one, wouldn't you agree?"

Hayden left his seat and wobbled toward Ryuka with a stern face as if to pull her away from Wade like a Hollywood bodyguard. Nolan debated whether he should intervene, but Wade stopped Hayden before he did. Hayden sat down on the other side of Wade, and they had a quick chat just between themselves. Then Wade sent Hayden back to his seat with a flick of the wrist and slouched deeper into the couch, finally taking a sip of his thousand-dollar whisky.

"I just need one chance, Mr. P.," Ryuka said.

"Chance is the most expensive commodity, young lady." Wade narrowed his eyes. "They're hiring dancers, you said."

"That's right."

"Well, why don't you go up there and let Zoe teach you a few moves?"

Hayden made a squealing whistle with two fingers in his mouth. Zoe was in the middle of a move called "birdcage" where she suspended herself horizontally above the ground simply by hooking the pole behind one knee. She climbed down and stood by the pole, waiting to hear what the men had to say.

"Let's see if we should take a chance on you." Wade gestured at the stage.

Nolan felt the urge to grab Ryuka and storm out, but Ryuka had already introduced herself to Zoe as she rolled her sleeves up.

"Please go easy on me." She gave an awkward smile. "I have, like, two muscles working at the moment."

Zoe shot a glance at the three men on the couch; then her gaze landed on Ryuka's slippery suit pants.

"You don't want to take your pants off, do you?" she asked.

"No—if that's possible—thank you."

She nodded and nudged Ryuka away from the pole, then she showed her the cartwheel—one of the easier variations, with one hand grabbing the pole and the other on the ground for support. Basically a regular cartwheel with a pole and more leg-spreading.

She landed on one side of the pole, light as a cat, then flipped back to the other side as a second demonstration before she stepped away and signaled Ryuka: all yours.

Ryuka hadn't been doing much gymnastics or exercise in general, and it showed. Nolan had seen her dance once. Her limbs and torso had moved like a couple on the verge of divorce. He watched Ryuka tumble onstage and struggle to draw a perfect circle with straight legs like Zoe had. Wade leaned in and took the glass from Nolan's hand while breathing down his neck.

"You." He shoved him forward. "Why don't you give her a little help?"

IN DANDELION'S CLOYING bathroom, Nolan scrubbed his hands like a pair of dirty sneakers, splashing his sleeves and shirt to a mess. He kept the water on the coldest setting so when he was about to spiral down the bottomless self-loathing, the sting would pull him back and whisper, *Forget, and move on.*

He slammed the lever shut. Not because he felt clean, but because he could no longer feel his fingers, and the lavender-scented hand wash made him nauseous. He snatched a rolled-up towel from the wicker tray, dried his hands with two careless wipes, then hurled it at the mirror. It left a smear on the glass and heaped up at the bottom of the tap.

His tube of hand cream was almost empty, so he gave it a violent shake, then squeezed hard. A generous blob burped out. He got most of it on the back of his hand, and a tiny bit on the tip of his nose. He tossed the empty tube into the trash and closed his eyes. After several deep breaths, the knot in his throat slid down and settled in his stomach. He slathered the cream over his hands until there were no more milky streaks on his skin, then he cleaned off the residue on his nose with one hand as he picked up the used towel and wiped the water he'd splashed outside the sink.

As far as Nolan was concerned, he had done nothing unusual. From the view of Wade, who had just barged in, all he saw was Nolan rubbing something into his nose while cleaning up the countertop. His face froze for a second, then lit up with the same spark of epiphany Nolan had seen on that Fischer Associate the other day. Just like that, the stone-cold Wade thawed and the drunk-warm Wade returned.

"I thought you young people would be into something trendier, but, well, you pick your vice, and there's nothing wrong with sticking with the classics." He strode to the urinals opposite the sinks and kept the conversation with his back to Nolan. "Is coke better these days, or do you kids cut it with something?"

It took Nolan a moment to catch on, so he missed the window to respond, but Wade didn't mind. He zipped his pants and bounded over to the sinks, stuck his hands under the tap for two seconds, then picked a towel from the tray. Something about the first towel displeased him, so he flung it to the side, grabbed another, and dabbed his hands dry.

"Is coke the cheapest option these days?" Wade asked.

"Weed is cheaper . . . I suppose?"

"Weed!" Wade cackled. "I bet coffee is even cheaper."

He stopped laughing and gave Nolan's reflection a long, silent stare before he drew out another card and left it on the countertop. It looked like a standard Frenell business card, with some drawing on the back.

"Consider this your second chance–and the last." Wade squeezed Nolan's shoulder before he left him alone. "We're in the relationship business. You can't walk around with a stick up your ass."

When Nolan stepped out of the men's room, Wade was dropping Ryuka a few words as he walked past her. Ryuka said something in response with a smile. Wade and Hayden marched away without waiting for her to finish.

"I'm in!" Ryuka hopped over. "Team briefing at nine."

The excitement on her face pinched Nolan's heart. He grabbed her wrist and led her to the exit in silence, ignoring her complaints until they were back in the open air and covered in sunshine.

"Why do you let people treat you like this?" he burst out.

"Like what?"

"Seriously?"

"I need Rhapsody, you know that."

"How is *that* worth it?"

"I can take care of myself." Ryuka pulled out of his grip. "And it's not like they saw *anything*—speaking of, did you see Zoe's abs? Holy. Shit. Maybe I should take a course with her—"

He turned to leave, as he felt he might yell. Before he walked out of earshot, Ryuka's voice traveled from behind.

"Nolan, are you going to Level 21?"

He stopped and lowered his head out of an inexplicable guilt. Right now, he was at the end of his fifth year with Frenell—the crossroads that'd determine if an Associate would rise above the land of the mortals, or plunge into "the Sisyphus Hell." The unwritten rule was that anyone who couldn't make the leap at the end of Year 5 was not "Frenell material" and they could forget about anywhere above the café.

Ryuka was the only Year 8 left on Level 13. She'd first applied for the promotion in 2025, two years after she'd moved from another firm on Sauria Street. They'd said she hadn't spent enough time here to prove her capabilities. The next year, they'd wanted her to work on her "leadership skills" until she was "ready." She'd applied again last April; they'd said she needed to establish a stronger case about her contribution to the sustainable growth of the firm.

"Congratulations." Ryuka caught up with Nolan and gave him a hug. She knew the answer as soon as she saw him with Wade and Hayden. That, plus the silence, those were all the hints she needed.

"It's nothing." He hugged her back.

"It is! And you should be proud of your achievement. I'm just a bit surprised–I thought you were leaving."

"Yeah . . . something happened."

"Have you told Sai? We should celebrate!"

"It really isn't a big deal."

"Stop saying that." Ryuka frowned. "Just be happy, dude. You're trashing something I actually want and have to–"

She stopped there, but Nolan knew what she was going to say: something she had to work so hard for–so much harder than he had to.

"I didn't mean to be insensitive, Ryu"–Nolan tousled his hair, trying to find the best words–"but I don't understand why you care so much about the Special Associate title. We both know it's not the answer. You can still get squeezed out anytime. Even the money isn't that much better–honestly, after tax and everything. It's a plastic trophy that provides no practical benefit but doubles the assholes you have to deal with."

"I agree with all that, and it's still important."

"But why?" He ran his palm over his face. "I mean . . . this job is like swimming in a river of shit. Who cares if you're fast?"

She chuckled and went quiet for a moment.

"Have you been to twenty-one already?" she asked. "I mean, *really* look around. You know the insurance company across the road? Did you know they had a roof garden with a myrtle? We can't see it on thirteen, and the Perception Floors are too high, so it's only visible on twenty-one."

"That's why you want to go up? To . . . see a tree?"

"I'm saying there are things you can only access from up there."

Something up there is important to me, she emphasized.

Years later, when invited by his therapist and his AA support system to talk about his old friends, Nolan would remember Ryuka. And what had he liked the most about her? Her refreshingly foolish optimism.

RYUKA WAS ONE of the expendables. Nolan knew it. Sai knew it. So did anyone with the correct amount of brains. She was three years behind schedule, her Handler was Morse Sachet, and she'd spent most of her time at Frenell on projects that'd been consistently voted "Meat Grinder of the Year" by the Associates. They might as well stick a Post-it on her back that said "Let's see how long this one lasts," yet Ryuka still thought she had a chance.

Morse Sachet was a Special Counsel who had been with Frenell for over two decades. He was half a century old, and he'd never left Sauria Street.

The first thing you'd notice about Morse was that, despite holding a senior position merely one step away from partnership, he sat on Level 13 in an office repurposed from a copy room, which added a sense of mystery to his status—the corporate equivalent of "lower upper-middle class."

The second thing you'd notice about Morse was that he had a mood like the weather of London.

September to December were usually his worst months—the season when Frenell would evaluate billing and BD performance of senior staff for the past financial year to decide whether they deserved to be elevated. For Morse, a season aptly named "fall."

January wasn't particularly pleasant for him, either, because that was when Frenell would introduce its new Salary Partners to the world, and when a lot of his old-time schoolmates chose to report their career progress and, strangely, family updates on LinkedIn.

Then there was also the awkward period from March to June, when Frenell would assess the Associates, reminding him of all the young wolves who might catch up with him sooner than he cared for.

So, Morse got up on the wrong side of his bed most months of the year.

This morning, after slamming a binder on Ryuka's desk, Morse marched away without a word. As Ryuka got up from her seat and scanned the contents of the binder, he clapped like a frustrated football coach and yelled in a volume that made the Year 5 next to him flinch.

"Come to my office! Should I send a taxi for you? And bring that with you! Why did you think I left it there in the first place?!"

Ryuka dashed to catch up with him and the door swung shut in her face, so she knocked. Through the glass wall, she saw Morse sit down behind his desk and start typing. She knocked again, yet he went on with his business. After a moment, someone else opened the door–Emma made a discreet "quiet" gesture as she let Ryuka in. Ryuka gave a look of confusion, and Emma responded with a subtle shrug.

"Leave it open," Morse said when Emma was about to close the door. So she let go of the handle and retreated to the corner with Ryuka. They stood against the wall like two waitresses attending to an indecisive patron.

"Morse . . . how can I help you?" Ryuka asked after a while.

Morse ignored her and punched his keyboard harder. So Ryuka and Emma kept their mouths shut and waited some more. There once was another Year 5 who'd had the idea for an invention called the Morse Meter, which would collect environmental data, such as the length of his mumbling, the frequency of curse words, and the amount of fidgeting noise and sounds of things hitting the walls, then predict and thermostat-graph a looming blowup so the Associates could seek shelter. But the production of such a device would've involved the high cost of bugging Morse's office and even his body, so it'd never materialized. It was a shame, as Sauria Street alone would generate enough revenue to sustain that business.

After Morse felt the gravity of his indignation had sunk in, he turned around and snatched the binder from Ryuka, rifled through the pages using his saliva, then tossed the whole thing on his desk, knocking a red pen onto the floor.

"Those figures don't make sense."

"I've checked with Accounts," Ryuka said. "They've confirmed these are the right Total Billed and WIP."

"No."

"No?"

"Check again."

"But Accounts–"

"Just do it."

"Okay–"

"How much did you bill for the Slaughterhouse case last month?"

"Um, I don't have the figure off the top of my head–"

"I do. Why did you need fifty-four hours? It was only a contract review."

"It was a master agreement for their distribution network, and they had dedicated equipment and software to deliver and track their inventory. The licensing and recycling of those needed to be factored in, and we had some difficulty getting instructions from the right people–"

"The team average for contract review is between twenty-five and thirty hours." Morse frowned. "I had to write off a lot of your time. You need to work more efficiently."

"Okay, but this one–"

"Where are the exhibits for Project Wire?"

"I've made two copies and brought them up to twenty-one–Rudy has them."

"So if I pick up my phone right now and call Rudy, he'll confirm what you just told me." He put a finger on the Speaker button of his phone and sneered.

"If you must." Ryuka sighed.

"Lose your attitude." Morse retrieved his hand and turned to Emma. "Is any of that true?"

Emma glanced at Ryuka–none of those were her assignments. Ryuka blinked once, meaning "affirmative," so Emma nodded.

Morse scanned Ryuka from head to toe for several rounds; then he swiveled back to his computer and stared at a draft email on the screen. After a while, he finally said "Close the door behind you" without turning around.

As Ryuka stepped out, something flew over and struck the glass wall next to her face. It was the binder containing figures that "made no sense" to Morse.

Emma picked it up from the floor and gave Ryuka a pat on the back. As soon as she closed the door behind both of them, she shoved the binder into Ryuka's arms.

"You need to learn to manage him. I don't have time for this."

She checked her watch and sprinted off, leaving Ryuka with her beaten-up binder. One of the rings had come loose, and several pages containing Morse's DNA had fallen out. Ryuka scooped them up from the carpet and peeked inside Morse's office through the blinds. This man had made a habit of throwing his tie over his shoulder when hunched over his keyboard. Today was one of those days when Ryuka pictured that tie as a noose.

As Ryuka returned to her desk and typed *Dandelion* into Google, a new message popped up in her inbox—an email from Morse to the Frenell Associates group address, which contained over six hundred recipients.

All,

At 11:03 a.m. yesterday, I circulated a request for assistance with a research task. Only 14 people offered to help or apologized for their lack of capacity.

I request that the rest of you reply to this email within the next 30 minutes and explain why you ignored the call for assistance yesterday.

He copied Emma on this email so she could collect the replies and tabulate them for his review later.

The third thing you'd notice about Morse Sachet, Special Counsel of Frenell & Co. and Handler of Ryuka Murong, was that he had the face and soul of a mouth breather.

"FRED GEORGIA, '03 Ivory University—ew, does he know Morse? Expert in data privatization, biometrics licensing, and artificial intelligence. Made Partner in 2022 on the Vietnam server farm project. Protégé of Senior Partner Harold Stun. Likes Wagner and pinot noir from Côte de Nuits. Brother is a Counsel at Calder. Wife is Cecilia. Two kids, seven and five. Two dogs, Lenny and Lucas. Don't mention shellfish 'cause he had a bad allergy six months ago—"

Sai went over her research notes one more time as the elevator took her to Level 42 of the Pollyanna Palace. Kevin had given her a list of two confirmed interviewers and a string of backups, accompanied by a dossier consisting of everything available on the first page of a Google name search. She'd spent the last twenty-four hours combing through their firm pages, news coverage, insight articles, roundtable keynotes, then social media. What books were they reading? Recent movies they went to? Political affiliations? Strong opinions on the Kardashians or the British royal family? Were they proud of their kids or at least pretended to be? Where did their kids stand on the Kardashians or the British royals? Gotta watch their dance videos on TikTok as well—how else would you know if they understood twerking was no longer a thing now, or if they were still in the age of dabbing?

She wasn't a natural-born stalker, but this had become an essential survival skill. She had a limited window to build rapport. She must make them like her within their attention spans. She had only one shot.

Lateral hires in the industry had plummeted since the third GFC. With the endless supply of fresh college blood, Sauria Street firms now much preferred breeding their own chickens—starting with a campus sweep every August, which allowed them to gather first-class eggs into their incubators and put them through an eight-week trial run as Summer Cadets, or interns by alternative names. Eggs that survived this first line of screening would debut as Graduates the next fall, making their first footprint on the cratered corporate road. This initial selection was crucial since only premium eggs could produce premium chicks that grew into premium chickens. Firm-branded and house-trained. Stay in their pasture, lay eggs during the day, and sleep in barns at night without dreaming about the greener grass on another farm. Taking in somebody else's chickens was a slippery slope–you'd never know what those second-grade farms fed their birds with, and what those filthy fugitives had caught and could pass on to your flock. It was also unnecessary. Twenty years ago, a chicken was considered a prodigy if it could deliver a TED Talk at the age of twenty-five without a full-blown nervous breakdown. Today, chicks came out of their shells with three to five years of working experience, two *Nature*-level academic publications, four Olympic gold medals, a lifetime Mensa membership, unicorn startup ideas and resources, and conveniently low self-esteem cultivated by the confusing times they lived in. If a rooster got its beak hacked off in some unfortunate event, the hatchlings could pick up the slack in a heartbeat, and there were always more eggs in the making.

According to Kevin, this opening at Miller, Smit & Lange Global Limited was a stroke of true serendipity. Months ago, one of their Associates had been found dead by the patrol robots in the morning. The good news: there were no signs of struggle or foul play, so it was either a brain thing or a heart thing that the girl had been carrying with her all along. The bad news: some slide decks that were supposed to go out first thing in the morning were delayed by more than four hours, resulting in a groveling apology from the project Partner to the client explaining that one of their PPT generators had, quite literally, died on everyone. It was a heart-wrenching disaster that shook the team, and nobody wanted to be reminded of all the crisis-management coaching, scary legal briefings, and workplace safety training they had to endure in the following week.

"That will teach them to keep a backup charger." Kevin let out a hearty laugh after the backstory; then he proceeded to explain that Miller's annual billing target was twenty-two hundred hours, subject to an annual increase of five percent by industry standard, and Sai's rank–if she landed the job–would be discounted by two years to Year 3 Associate, which reflected the commonly accepted price to pay for being a farm-switching crossbred chicken.

"Don't blow this, eh?" Kevin said before he hung up on her. "You're literally stepping over someone's dead body."

"WHY DO YOU want to join the Millers?"

Fred opened with a lot of interviewers' favorite pickup line–the corporate equivalent of "Tell me about your divorce."

No matter how honest it was, "Because I hate my current firm and you're hiring" was not an acceptable answer. In this economy, a job was only open because the person who had it could no longer perform their duties, physically or mentally, and a person was only looking for a new role because they couldn't keep on doing the current one for much longer. Yet multiple interviews remained indispensable because there were "right" and "wrong" ways to lie.

Because you want to do what we do? Market changes and tide turns. What we do today might not be what we do tomorrow.

Because you want to work on Project So-and-So? It's not up to you. You're not jumping ship because you have a helm to spin elsewhere. We're hiring because we need to plug a hole in our boat.

Because you want more money? That's a very short-sighted way of thinking and a huge red flag that you're incapable of long-term commitment.

Because you admire the team and the firm's culture? Hmm, let's hear some in-depth thoughts about the "people" and "culture" of a place you've never worked in.

Because you want a better work-life balance? Sunshine, you work long hours anywhere, and did you just admit you don't want to work hard?

"I've always dreamed of being a Miller." Sai pumped some enthusiasm into her voice. "Unfortunately, I didn't have the privilege to join this formidable team as a Summer Cadet, so I've been keeping an eye on the market. As soon as a position opened, I handed in my application, and it's a great honor to be here, Mr. Georgia and Ms. Milford—I deeply admire your work on the tech sector restructuring."

Fred nodded as he scanned Sai's résumé. He flashed the piece of paper to his co-interviewer and mouthed "Frenell." She shrugged and pulled her attention back to her tablet. Jen Milford was not on Kevin's list, but Sai had tracked down the entire department on the internet and remembered she liked Caravaggio, snowboarding, and her Thoroughbred, Crimson Wrath.

"We prefer to find the right talent early on and build them up as they grow with the firm," Fred said. "We have a very robust evaluation system and, frankly, you are either Miller material or you are not. What's the point of putting anyone through all the excruciating challenges if they have no chance of success anyway? So, tell us a little bit about your experience at . . . Frenell, if you don't mind."

Sai gave them a one-minute rundown of all the projects that had devoured five years of her life. Jen chuckled in the middle, but not at Sai or anything she'd said. She pushed her tablet toward Fred and showed him whatever she found amusing so he could have a good laugh too. There were a few seconds of dead silence before they realized Sai had finished.

"Tell us about a time when you successfully applied your interpersonal skills to resolve a conflict at work." Fred slumped into his chair while scrolling the touchscreen of his laptop.

If they progressed to the behavioral questions quickly, Sai remembered Kevin had said, it could be a good sign, meaning they were interested in you as a person. It could also be a bad sign, meaning they wanted to wrap up as soon as possible. It might also mean nothing and they were simply following a standard sequence of questions, which in itself could be a bad sign because your unique personality did not shine through. But that in turn could be a good sign because it meant you'd fit in well—hard to say. Human interactions are complex.

"When I was on this platform integration project," Sai said, giving her rehearsed answer, "we encountered—"

"Say you come in," Fred interjected without looking away from his screen, "somebody gives you shit, what do you do?"

"Would you . . . be able to clarify that question, please?"

"How would you manage someone senior and difficult?"

"'Difficult' as in—"

"Like they don't know what they want, or they know but they can't tell you. You need to follow instructions to a T, but be really comfortable with ambiguity. Work autonomously, but take responsibility when things don't go well. Oh, they're also not great with stress, so they might yell and throw things."

"Does that happen a lot?"

Jen Milford looked at Sai for the first time, giving her a glance that was barely enough to visualize her face.

"It's *really* just because they run a tight ship," Fred said.

"I will . . . do everything you just said—"

"Oh, by the way, have you ever worked with Colleen Oakland?"

"Yes, she's my Handler—"

"She has this bird fountain in the backyard of her summer house in Silver Mountains. Funny story: when we bought our place next to hers—"

Fred went on to tell Sai about his neighborly dispute with Colleen three years ago and how they'd made up, with Colleen sharing her secret barbeque sauce and Fred promising not to shoot her crows that shit on his grass. He still believed he was right and had been the bigger person for letting this one go. When he finished, Jen had stopped typing and flipped her tablet face down on the desk. She stacked the notepad she'd never opened on top, then stepped aside to appreciate the water view outside the floor-to-ceiling windows. Fred took out a pen recorder and spoke into it.

"Fred E. Georgia time entry: May the tenth, 2028, colon, zero point three hours, semicolon, interview Sarah Su . . . interview candidate for Year 3 Associate, end of entry. Thank you for coming."

He shook Sai's hand for half a second, then collected his stuff and strode to the door with a content smile, pleased to have crossed another item off his to-do. Sai extended her hand to Jen. She walked straight out without looking at her.

SAI COULD HEAR Kevin lose his interest by the second as it became painfully obvious that she wouldn't be the winning horse for his commission. After she described the unusual questions she'd gotten from Fred and how the conversation had unfolded, Kevin blew a heavy sigh into his phone that hurt Sai's eardrum.

"How could you not know how to handle that?" he grumbled. "Didn't you prepare? Don't you know the STAR method? You—fine, fine. It is what it is. I'll let you know."

Sai wanted to ask if he had any other openings as she suspected Miller had given her a "mirage interview" for a "ghost job," meaning they weren't seriously hiring or had already found the right person, and Sai was only there to contribute to their recruitment metrics. But the line dropped dead before she could open her mouth again.

The traffic light turned green. Pedestrians rushed past her in all directions, tutting and mumbling, scolding her for playing dead in the busiest area of the city during the busiest hour of the day. She zigzagged across the road, dodging impetuous cars that couldn't wait for the light to turn.

When she returned to her desk, she peeled off the Post-it note excusing her absence as a medical appointment, took out an ultrasound envelope containing an old scan from another time, and displayed it on the desk to complete the act. Still no real work in her inbox. She wasn't imagining it–they were drying her out.

As much as she hated to admit it, her mind turned to the reconciliation OATH wanted by Friday. She'd been ignoring Hayden's messages about it, but today's interview forced her to reevaluate. Miller wasn't interested, she knew that. But sometimes firms and recruiters ran checks on candidates they had no intention of hiring simply because they could. If she had a write-up in her RAP, she might never bounce back from the "Do not consider" pile. Gossip spread faster than STDs on Sauria Street. There'd be no warning letter or formal termination, and the career assassination would be done in seconds–clean, ominous, and quiet, like her inbox.

A Teams message arrived on her work phone. She picked it up and caught James staring.

"What?" she asked.

"I'm gonna keep that once you're gone." He pointed at the succulent next to her monitor.

"What are you talking about?"

He shrugged and put his headphones back on.

"Fucking weirdo," Sai mumbled; then she realized James wasn't the only one staring. One glance at the new message, she understood why.

It was a screenshot from Hayden, and a single line:

LOL, are we not paying you enough?

4

"SEE THAT?" RYUKA paused the video. "There. The bridge of your nose just shrank, and your eyes were creepy purple for a second. And here—"

She fast-forwarded to one minute later and hit play.

"When she rolls her head back, her face dissolves. See? Her eyes and nose are blurry and floating above the skull. Let me show you again—"

She rewound the video for five seconds, then replayed at half-speed. On the screen, a woman with Sai's face was riding a naked guy twice her age. Sai turned her head away. "Occupied!" Nolan shouted at the person banging on the door of the Meditation Chamber and signaled Ryuka to kill the video.

"This is most likely just some old porn with a deepfake face swap," Ryuka said. "It's gonna be okay, Sai. Remember last summer? That whole drama about Jo?"

"Jo had tattoos on her boobs." Sai sighed. "Everybody knew that wasn't her."

"I know, I know." Ryuka stroked her hair. "The point is, people know you can fake this kind of garbage these days–easy. This one is pretty sloppy. They can tell it's not you."

"I doubt it." Sai gave a ghostly smile. "Even if they could, they'd play dumb."

In an age when the paramount mission of humanity was colonizing Mars, the most intuitive and economical way to destroy a person was still to strip them. For a man, you'd have to go the extra mile to make him a pedophile, throw in an animal or a dead body, or, depending where they lived, another man. For a woman, she just needed to be sufficiently naked.

"Occupied!" Nolan yelled again.

"I really gotta go." Ryuka shoveled her stuff into a one-armed hug. "I've downloaded the video and screenshotted the page with the user name, upload time, view count, and comments. I'll send them to you later. You should call the police and ask the website to take it down–police first. The user ID says they're in Grand Ivory, but that's not reliable. Without direct communication, I can't see their IP, and they can always use a VPN. I'm afraid this is all I know for now."

"I've also saved what's posted in the Facebook group," Nolan said. "I think I'm friends with one of the admins, so I'll ask him to help. It's gonna be okay."

Ryuka unlocked the Meditation Chamber and bolted out, almost colliding with the couple waiting outside. "I saw nothing!" she shouted without looking back. Nolan switched sides with Sai, shielding her from the open plan and the people in it. Sai kept her head low and her eyes on the carpet. As they walked away, she heard a faint comment of confusion from behind:

"Really? Threesome at nine a.m.?"

≈

WHEN RYUKA ARRIVED at the Diligence Room on Level 29, Hayden was already there, snuggling up to Emma and keeping her updated on the latest Frenell gossip. Ryuka recognized the background music—it was the part where fake Sai was sucking on a peeled banana with a comically suggestive look. "Morning," she announced as she sat down on the other side of the table, which did not provoke any reaction out of the two. Emma kept her expression neutral and her gaze aloof while Hayden continued to encroach on her personal space with his giggling face. Once the video had finished, Hayden put his phone away and started interrogating Emma about her weekend plans. Neither Ryuka nor Emma had expected to see each other here, so they acted like they didn't.

Wade wobbled in when Hayden had run out of small talk and Tinder daily swipes. Without greeting the room, Wade let his hollow stare fall on Ryuka. A shiver of sheer terror ran up Ryuka's spine as she wondered if WPF had forgotten his approval for her to be here. Fortunately, he didn't ask her to justify her presence and let out a loud yawn as he dropped his butt in the head seat.

"So we have everyone." Hayden projected his desktop onto the wall. "Today is a quick catch-up—"

"Did they change their oat milk on Level 20?" Wade asked.

"I'm . . . not sure," Hayden said. "But we can definitely check—"

"Somebody be a doll and get me a triple espresso." Wade yawned again.

"Oh, I'll have a flat white, then," Hayden said, then turned to Emma.

"A latte for me," said Emma.

The room fell silent, and Hayden stared at Ryuka.

"I'm okay, I had one this morning," Ryuka said. "Before we start, Hayden, could you please approve my confidentiality clearance for this matter? It's still pending in the system—"

She stopped as she realized Hayden had continued to stare at her. Emma cleared her throat and devoted all her attention to her laptop. Wade was scrolling on his phone without looking at anyone.

"Um, I'll call the catering staff in." Ryuka popped up and headed toward the admin panel next to the door.

"Actually, it'd make everybody's life so much easier if you could kindly take the orders down to Level 20 in person." Hayden smiled. "It's just . . . sometimes the staff get things wrong even when they have the best intentions. Please ask the barista to put precisely one dash of his premium oat milk in the triple espresso—tell him it's Mr. Wade's order, he'll get it."

Ryuka read the room and realized she didn't have a choice. She closed the door and texted Calais the coffee orders in the corridor. *Precisely one dash of premium oat milk*, all caps. Calais responded with a thumbs-up emoji two seconds later, and Ryuka counted to a hundred before she stepped back inside. The team had moved on without her.

"We've received some updated data points from Team Osireion. Oh my God." Hayden shook his head and chuckled. "These guys are hopeless. Their Excel skills are embarrassing."

"You should see their graphs," Emma said.

"Anyway, we still have to incorporate those changes into the slides. Emma, if you could kindly help with that, you'd be an absolute champion. We need more academic references in the exhibits, specifically on the definitions of 'craving' and 'drug-seeking behavior.' I'll put a minion army together for that. The chapters on Serotane's therapeutic effects need to be redone—Dan Barton was useless, may he rest in peace. I heard there's a kid on Level 9 . . . what's his face? Anyway, basically Tim 2.0, always eager to help, never talks back, does everything Dan could do at half the cost, so I'll loop him in and it's all under control. Speaking of cost, we are over the sixty percent mark of the Stage 2 budget . . ."

He paused there and glanced at Wade, who seemed to have fallen asleep with his eyes open. Hayden called out his name, and Wade snapped out of what looked like a silent seizure. "Where the hell is my goddamn coffee?" he grumbled, clawing the back of one hand with another, scratching his skin ashy pink.

"The coffee's coming," Ryuka said. "Speaking of the budget, I'm more than happy to help with a memo to clients on fee updates. If you could please clear me in the system—"

"We'd appreciate your help with a very specific moving piece," Hayden said as he thumbed his smart ring and brought up a profile on the wall. "This is one of our independent experts. We've received his draft report, and there are certain things we'd like him to reevaluate. He's been . . . difficult."

Ryuka studied the face of Laurent Cheong, the man who'd dared to be "difficult" to Hayden Hins. Assistant professor at Université de Saint-Cloud in Paris. Relocated to California three years ago and currently a lecturer at Eldridge University. Kempt, austere, a face that reminded her of her own father.

"He still got a problem?" Wade asked. "Unbelievable."

"Said he wasn't 'convinced.'" Hayden made a single air quote.

"Preposterous," Wade scoffed. "I have no idea how to deal with these people. Typical—they know how to take exams, I'd give them that, but that's not how real life works."

"What Wade meant," Hayden explained, suddenly turning to Ryuka, "was that Mr. Cheong is more of an academic, and we'd like you to bring some practical perspective to our dialogue with him—"

"They have their own ways, fine, but now they want to tell *us* what to do?"

"As in, Mr. Cheong's perception might not fit in the legal context." Hayden kept his eyes on Ryuka and smiled wider. "And we need to make our own judgment in our job—"

"They gotta lose that attitude if they want to get along with everybody. Look at him." Wade glared at Laurent's headshot. "Probably jerking off to anime chicks at night."

"Um—"

"No wonder they eat bats," Wade finished with a mammoth yawn and some disapproving headshaking.

Hayden's smile froze as his brain searched for the best translation of Wade's remarks. Thankfully, the door of the meeting room popped open, and Calais's new intern brought in the coffees. Wade watched this Vietnamese girl put his espresso in front of him. His stare was intense, his breathing was loud, he'd scratched the back of his left hand to a rash, and he seemed to have noticed none of that.

"*Ni hao*," he blurted out as she turned to leave. The girl returned a confused yet polite smile. Wade said something else that he believed was Mandarin and received no response. He repeated the sentence to Ryuka, who couldn't give a better reaction but did give the girl a chance to run away. "See?" Wade tutted. "You folks don't appreciate it when people make an effort."

Back in the days when Frenell had thought it should hop on the Chinese gravy train, it'd formed an Emerging Market Strategy and Cultural Enrichment Task Force that had delivered a twenty-four-month immersive training program, including a four-week crash course in Mandarin for senior staff. Ryuka was moved that Wade still remembered what he'd learned, but she wondered if she'd misheard him because what he'd said sounded very much like *Ten dollars is a rip-off, how about eight?*

"Emma will send you the draft report from Mr. Cheong after this. Won't you, Emma?" Hayden pulled Ryuka's attention back to the real conversation.

Emma lifted her face from her palms and nodded with half a smile.

"Have a read," said Hayden. "We'll set up a call for you two."

He stopped at that and stared at Ryuka. The room fell into the same silence as before the coffee run.

"Well, we won't take more of your time," Hayden said.

"Um, maybe I can finish the briefing so I have the big picture?" Ryuka asked.

"Oh, it won't be necessary." Hayden chuckled. "Emma will send you all you need to know, and Osireion has been pretty cost sensitive lately, so we try to keep the team lean."

He stopped again for Ryuka to take the cue. Ryuka remembered when she was a Year 3, Hayden had joined Frenell as a Graduate and had been assigned to her as her Buddy—the spring chicken you were supposed to take under your wing and help them survive the farm. He'd been a very different kid back then, or he'd appeared to be, and Ryuka had been a new lateral hire, so they'd had some good times figuring things out together. It hadn't lasted, as Frenell had soon noticed Hayden's value and paired him up with a "better fit."

She got up and stacked her stuff into the pile she'd come in with, grabbed her blazer off the back of her chair, and folded it to cover the dry-cleaning tag she'd just noticed. She paused for a second, then headed to the door. Behind her, Wade slammed his coffee on the table.

"They've changed the oat milk."

WHEN CALAIS WAS inspecting his last stock of "premium oat milk" with his nose to determine if it had expired and who he should feed it to, Nolan was at the bar, trying to decipher the second riddle from WPF. The drawing on the back of the business card was deceptively simple. It seemed to be an eye, judging from the almond shape and the five strokes on top that indicated lashes. Except that the sclera was crimson and the central dot was milky gray, like the lens of a cataract patient. He hadn't seen this symbol in recent TV shows, memes or video games, and his Google search on *crazy eye* plus *cult* had returned nothing spot-on. The badge reader in front of him made the "five minutes left" beep as he foraged for hints page after page, getting nowhere.

"You're on *that* now?" Calais asked as he handed the coffee tray to his intern.

"Huh?" Nolan looked up from his phone.

"That." Calais pointed at the drawing.

"What's this?"

"If you don't know, don't worry about it."

"Is it some sort of club?"

Calais sealed his lips and wiped the steam wand clean.

"Help me out, man," said Nolan. "I need to know what this is, or I'll lose my job. Calais? C'mon."

"Who's asking?" Calais said. "You, or someone else?"

"Someone else."

"Someone you care about?"

"Not really."

"Then I know a guy."

That was how a lot of successful businesses started–a guy knew another guy.

After he'd returned from Dandelion yesterday, Nolan had turned in the loyalty card to Colleen and given her a TL;DR on what had happened. He'd explained that he hadn't gotten the chance to photograph or film any part of the event, but chances would come since WPF and Hayden were clearly regulars.

"I'll get him in the same frame with a stripper," Nolan said. "I might even be able to catch him doing drugs."

He examined Colleen's expression closely, searching for a window to slip in his request for the destruction of the recording.

"Hmm, they've finally changed their design. Much better paper." Colleen thumbed the loyalty card, then flicked it across the desk. It landed in front of Nolan before sliding off the edge.

"Oh, nothing." Colleen snorted as she met Nolan's confused eyes. "That place was pure trash before it got a new marketing director. They rebranded a couple of years ago and did a huge campaign. Some of the boys upstairs signed up together for a group discount–one of those 'Refer a friend' things."

She wandered to this side of the desk and pressed on Nolan's shoulders from behind, as if he were a skittish bunny that might run away.

"My bad–I should've made my instructions clearer. Silly stuff like a strip club membership might be enough for small fish like Aaron Patucchi, but you can't fry a whale with a toaster. Here are some rules of thumb for you, okay? Wade doing drugs: nobody cares. Wade dealing drugs: depends–who are his clients?

Will they diminish the Frenell brand by association? Wade paying a stripper: nobody cares. Wade killing a stripper: did he do that on company property? Sex video: useless and gross. Rape video: now we're talking. Saying crazy shit on Twitter: depends on how much his target matters. Saying crazy shit offline: unless caught on film, it never happened. Focus on the Big Three: 'money, honey, body.' Embezzlement, cheating with another Partner's wife, actual murder—those are the high-value findings. Don't let the peanuts sidetrack you."

Nolan listened to this real-life wisdom that the world had been hiding from him and wondered if he should sue his college for negligence.

"I have fifteen minutes before the next call, so this is what happens next." She slipped one hand into his open collar and turned his face toward her with another. "You'll get under this desk and kiss where I ask you to kiss, leave when I say you're allowed to leave, then you'll go out there and find me a nuclear weapon."

"YOU WANT ME to do what?" Sai thought she'd misheard something horribly wrong.

"Melodie is down, so they could use some new resources. We'll modify your employment relationship, so you need to resign first, then get a new contract with our staffing agency. Oh, and an NDA, obviously."

Before Sai could comprehend the concept of her "new assignment," Katherine had moved on to the specifics. They were in a much more humble room today—a meeting cube with one square desk and no windows or customized name declaring what it stood for. From this close, Sai could see the face-down bullhorn Katherine's laugh lines drew around her nose and smell her cologne.

"You get to keep fifty percent of your salary, and you can still sit on Level 13 three days a week and participate in Frenell projects, subject to approval. No one other than the Partners and OATH needs to know the technicalities. As far as your peers are concerned, you've gone part time and that's all. If I were you, I'd grab this offer with both hands."

"Would you like a thank-you note with compliments?"

"I don't care either way, Sarah, but can you afford this attitude right now?"

"It wasn't me in that video. You know it."

"I don't, actually." Katherine smiled. "Neither do most people, and that's the problem. It's a trigger for termination without notice if you, quote, 'adversely affect the firm's image or reputation.' Now, the Partners are willing to issue a supportive statement to give you the benefit of the doubt while the matter is being investigated. You have the right to provide technical evidence. They're even willing to help you with some of the reasonable costs. I've been with Frenell for over twenty years. They are not always this generous–must've heard the story about Farid."

The mention of Farid sent Sai off her seat. She reached for whatever she could hurl at Katherine, then she remembered Christie had collected all her belongings and taken them away.

"You want an assault charge on top of everything? Sit down."

Katherine drew a bottle of mineral water from the ice bucket behind her and set it on the desk. "Sit down," she repeated. "Let's run the math together: you have two options."

She picked up a blue pen and laid it in front of Sai.

"One, take the offer and you have the firm behind you. I know it's an unorthodox line of work, but you can still do well on that team. Help your family, pay your debts. Your life will be normal, and stable. Your other option–"

She picked up a red pen and set it down next to the blue one.

"Play tough, and you have at least three problems–first, your indecent footage. That's your personal affair. Whatever actions you want to take, the firm has no obligation to get involved. Second, your complaint against Hayden, is that video helping you or what? Third, your RAP write-up and your career prospects in general. Let's say you also sue the firm for unfair dismissal—why not? All the investigations and legal proceedings, out of your own pocket, and they're gonna take you months, even years. Can you fight this fight without working at all? Fine, you look for a new job, who's gonna give you a reference? This is a tight community and, you know, they've probably seen everything by now. I can go on, but do you need me to?"

As Sai stared at the two pens in front of her, Katherine twisted off the cap of the mineral water and slipped the bottle into Sai's hands. Her fingers were slimy like the lick of a toad.

"Two months ago, in this very room, I had a chat with Tim Kwan."

That caught Sai's attention, and Katherine nodded.

"I also talked to Amy Wong and Richard Shaw before they had to wrap up their runs with Frenell. It's a shame, but you know how I feel when I think of all of them? I feel angry. They were all so young and talented, but so foolish and entitled. They picked a fight they had no chance of winning because they didn't understand the importance of biding time. They lost and got bitter, and what Tim's dad did? Barbaric!"

She raised a hand to swat the ghosts of bad memories.

"If you think I went too hard on you at the last meeting, please understand there are things I can't say with Christie around." She smiled, and the corners of her eyes wrinkled with tenderness. "You were making the same mistake and I was so frustrated. I'd hate to see you become just another statistic. You want to get even with Hayden, don't you?"

"I'm not sure 'get even' is the right—"

"C'mon, he was an absolute disgrace! I'd shoot him and stage self-defense if he pulled that bullshit on me. But you know what you did wrong?"

"What did I—"

"You weren't ready." She sighed. "I've seen this script a million times. It's always the same shit show—girl complains; people freak out; firm gets annoyed; competitors laugh in your face; it gets maybe one week of attention on social media; boy may or may not get sacked, then what? In your case, then this: Frenell keeps Hayden, and you go out no matter what. He has good experience and good network, and he generates good revenue. He's more valuable–ask *any* firm."

It was a blunt remark, but Sai couldn't deny it. The cohort had started at the same line, but it had soon become obvious that Hayden was going to be the next Frenell poster child. There had been rumors that he was already on the Partner track.

"And it's not like you have a bombshell–he didn't rape you; he never really touched you. You couldn't even win an argument with *me*, remember? Fine, say you successfully MeToo him and get him fired, he can get another job down the road or even join a client. Maybe he'll have to lay low for a bit, but eventually he'll land on his feet. But you? You get your name and face on a controversy like this, you're done. This is a relationship-based business, and you're too high a risk. So prepare to stay underemployed for the rest of your life and rebuild your mental peace at your own expense–doesn't sound so pleasant, does it? Then years later, when people see the jarring disparity between you two, you think they'll feel sorry for you? No, they'll try to get on Hayden's good side, and they'll remember you as someone that's okay to fuck over. And the worst part? If they ever revisit your claim against him, all they'll say is, that's it? That's all she was bitching about?"

Katherine leaned over and pressed her face against Sai's.

"You must thrive in the future to make what's happening today not okay."

"What do you mean–"

"Work harder! Rise above! Do better than him, then you can pin him under your thumb. Isn't that a much better revenge?"

"You're saying–"

"Work your ass off! Let the Partners see your contribution. Keep your mouth shut and get your work done, then tomorrow's

Sarah will thank today's Sarah, who in turn will thank tomorrow's Sarah for saving today."

"What?"

"If Future Sarah is nobody, Present Sarah will never be anybody. But if Future Sarah is somebody, what does that make Present Sarah?"

"Isn't Future Sarah dependent on Present Sarah?"

"Vice versa."

"Vice versa what?!"

"You're disappointing Present Sarah."

"Hang on, this is getting weird." Sai rubbed her temples. "So, if you fuck someone over, it's only problematic if that person is successful later–otherwise whatever you do to them *now* is fine because they *will be* a loser in the future?"

"It's counterintuitive, but think about it."

"But you'll never know if it's okay to fuck someone over *at the moment* you fuck them over."

"In a sense, yes."

"So it's like . . . Schrödinger's Assholeness or Quantum Bullying."

"Fine, if you have to make up some silly hashtags for TikTok! Call it 'Time Travel Justice' if you want. But you get it, don't you?"

"This can't be right."

"It's not about right or wrong. It's whether it's okay."

"This can't be okay either."

"Well, what brilliant ideas do *you* have about how the world works?"

"I don't know, how about not fuck anyone over in the first place?"

Katherine's face looked empty for a moment, then she slumped into her chair and folded her arms.

"You're not gonna tell me something like 'The world is not supposed to be like this,' are you? Actually, you know what? Say it, I dare you–say that to my face and tell me I just wasted all this time on you. Say it. Say it!"

"Katherine—"

"Say it!"

"We don't have to—"

"What? You don't have the guts to say what you think?"

"The world is not—"

"I can't hear you!"

"The world is not supposed to be like this! Jesus!"

"Well, guess what, honey? You're not changing the world and the world is not gonna change for you! We don't live in a perfect vacuum, Saidah: *somebody's* gonna get fucked. Better be them, not you. That's right, I remember your name all along, but I don't care. And why can't you make me care? Because you're weak. 'Sulaimaniyah' is not harder than 'Pendleton-Fitzpatrick,' but you're not WPF. Playing the victim won't get you anywhere. If you can't roll with the punches and get back on your feet, you have no right to cry over the pain. If you can't transcend above prejudice and give people *absolutely* no excuse to discriminate against you, it's your own problem and no one gives a shit!"

She took the water out of Sai's hands and held it at the tip of her nose, like dangling a carrot in front of a horse.

"Do you want people to call you by your real name? Why don't you earn it?"

SAI DIDN'T REMEMBER what had been discussed after that, or how she'd gotten out of that meeting. She vaguely recalled signing something and getting her phone back. She remembered the nausea she felt when Katherine patted her back as if to congratulate her, and the mind fog that smothered her with a thought she couldn't put her finger on—a thought that finally took shape hours later, when she was home alone and her brain replayed the meeting while she sorted her mail in an unlit room:

How the fuck had she lost that one?

After getting rid of all the ads, coupons, election campaign flyers, and shady recruitment cards for "adventurous girls between eighteen and twenty-nine," all she got was a notice from her landlord that, from next month, the rent for her 175-square-foot studio would increase by 5 percent to reflect market rates. She salvaged the coupons from the trash can and stuffed the notice in it instead.

She punched her monthly take-home into the calculator and subtracted her student loan, the mortgage on her family house on the other side of the city, the emergency medical fund for Farid, the living expenses for her siblings, her minimum credit card repayment, then her own groceries and utilities. She could save about fourteen hundred dollars a month, and her current bank balance could last her ninety days.

The laptop at her feet had finished loading, and the browser took her to a new page. After devouring her résumé and additional "equal opportunity information" including her age, gender, ethnicity, country of origin, citizenship status, sexuality, and disability, the smart job application platform returned with "No matching jobs found." She hadn't heard anything from Miller or Kevin, and she knew she wouldn't. The last time she'd called Kevin, the line had cut dead without reaching his voicemail—he'd blocked her.

She opened a new browser tab but couldn't find the courage to start another job search, so she typed in "clinics near me."

Her new assignment needed some blood tests.

FIVE MINUTES AWAY from Sai's apartment, Nolan was shaking a homeless person's piss off his shoes and reassessing his life choices.

The "homeless-free zone" ended two blocks from Sauria Street, and the sky was no longer dissected by high-rises after another eight. In the past few years, the housing crisis had claimed pockets across the city. These camps would typically disappear after a crackdown, then reemerge in different spots like mushrooms post-rain. After several failed cleansing attempts, the government had to concede that this problem was "unfixable," so instead of eliminating the camps, it consolidated them into one major tent city by the Athena River and urged sensible taxpaying citizens to steer clear. As a result, on the west bank of the river, you had this time capsule from the 1930s. Meanwhile over the water, the artificial island Oleander had become the richest zip code in Grand Ivory, with its median household income surpassing half a million earlier this year. Fortunately, the river was wide enough for both communities to forget the other existed. For people caught between the two realities, the west bank became "the wrong side of the Athena River."

Nolan watched the tent city residents line up along the bank and collect their free meals from a charity called Uphill. He called out to Calais, who was enjoying a hand-rolled cigarette by the water, and asked how much longer they'd have to wait. Calais took a drag and pointed at something over Nolan's head, and Nolan heard a cough. A drunk guy who wanted to empty his bedpan but decided the water was too far was slinging its contents off the edge of the bank. Nolan sprang away in time, but he still caught some on his feet. Now he too smelled like bad ideas pickled in misfortune.

"Ah, twenty-five fifty!"

The Fischer Associate waved at Nolan as he skidded down the embankment.

"You're late," Calais said.

"No, I was early," said Fischer. "I bumped into an old colleague and we just had so much to catch up on. You guys want me to introduce you? His tent is bigger than everyone else's."

"Maybe another day," Nolan said.

"You got the stuff?" Calais asked.

Fischer took something out of his suit jacket and handed it over—the same nasal spray he'd offered Nolan the first time they'd met at the IPC. Nolan saw that the labelless clear bottle was only half-full.

"May I . . . get a new one?"

"Not from me–I only bought a little for myself."

"So why get rid of it?"

"It makes me weird."

"How does it work? You get high through your nose like cocaine?"

"Orifices," Calais said. "You can also drink it, but it takes longer to kick in."

"Squeeze it in your butthole if you want a more steady release," Fischer said. "I wouldn't recommend it, though."

Nolan stared at the bottle in silence.

"Nah, this one is fine." Fischer read Nolan's thoughts and gave him a nod of confidence. Offended by Nolan's hesitation, he grabbed the bottle and stuck the tip in his nose.

"The guy who sold me this said it'd turn people into animals." Fischer sniffed. "It's almost like a superpower, like, you can see their souls and that's pretty awesome. Everybody should know if they're a turtle or a mongoose . . . by the way, have I told you you're a lovely gecko?"

"You have now," said Nolan.

"I like geckos!" Fischer laughed. "They're calm, resilient . . . they make great company, and they're cute! I've seen a lot of wishy-washy blobs, like melting slugs . . . like, their souls have no shape, know what I mean? Am I bleeding or just crying? No? Good. I don't–"

He bent over to retch. Nothing came out. After a few deep breaths, he pulled himself upright and gazed into Nolan's eyes. His lips parted to say something, but he lost track of his thoughts and blanked out for a moment. As Nolan waved a hand in front of his face, Fischer broke into a radiant smile as if he'd just spotted an old friend in an engulfing crowd rushing him toward an unknown destination.

"Oh hey! Twenty-five fifty!"

"I'm just gonna assume he's always been like this." Nolan turned to Calais.

"He does seem to have more fun than average people." Calais took the nasal spray from Fischer's hand and gave it to Nolan as he stroked Fischer's back, which made him giggle.

"You're a good man, Vince," Fischer said and hugged Calais.

"Vince?" Nolan asked, to which Calais responded: "Don't worry about it."

"What have we got here?"

A female voice turned their heads. In the twilight, a slim figure hopped down the bank. The honey-toned glow over her taut contours and the untamed raven curls dancing around her glimmering eyes captured Nolan faster than anything else, so it took him a second to notice the piece of metal in her hand, which looked a lot like a .22 automatic with a silencer. He put his hands up and glanced at Calais, who didn't seem worried about anything other than stamping out his cigarette. Then he saw the plastic dinner box in the girl's other hand and the Uphill logo on her shirt.

"I thought you'd stop doing this after you got a job," Calais said.

"I count this as my non-billable pro bono," said the girl.

"What?" Nolan stared at the two.

"Is he okay?" The girl tilted her chin at Fischer, who was holding his face up high, counting invisible stars.

"He's in his happy place," said Calais, so the girl pouted a little and put the gun away.

The pistol-shaped dispenser contained shots of a hybrid antidote called Revilox, which bound to the neurotransmitter receptors affected by the most common drugs on the market. It had a higher affinity than the drugs and no agonist effects, so it would sweep over the receptors and displace the intoxicating substances rapidly and, as a result, reverse an overdose, like how a carbon dioxide fire extinguisher would cut out oxygen and cool the burning materials. It'd become essential for anyone volunteering in drug-related charities.

"Have you met your Buddy yet?" asked Calais.

"They'll let us know the pairings before the Debut tomorrow." The girl kept her eyes on Fischer. "Are we sure he's okay?"

"You just want to shoot him, don't you?" Calais said.

"No . . . ?" She looked away and finally noticed Nolan, who was still holding his hands up in surrender. As Nolan debated which question to ask first, Fischer turned to the girl and stared at her for a long moment.

"Ah, a gray wolf," he murmured and flashed a childlike grin. "I like you."

5

ALTHOUGH CALLED DEBUT, the event was to celebrate the Graduates who'd survived their six-month probation and earned their initiation into the Frenell clan. Ten years ago, these kids would get their welcome drinks and meet their Buddies when they first got on board. As the dropout rate crept higher each year, Sauria Street had moved the rituals to a more sensible milestone. No point hyping up the cast of a show when any one of them could get canceled before release.

"We're pleased to see so many young bright minds joining the Frenell family and embracing the Frenell values. I am especially proud to see the demographic shift in our talent reserve. Back in my days, our gene pool was like a bowl of macaroni and cheese. Today, we have sushi and butter chicken."

Lindsay Mason Frenell paused to reap the handful of dry laughs and coughs from his audience as the OATH assistant cut to the slide with multiple charts in pie, bar, and line shapes demonstrating the firm's achievements in Diversity, Equity, and Inclusion. The charts broke the makeup of Frenell down to every data point that was legal to collect and matched each one to its representation rate in the general population. The results showed that Frenell had traced the American societal fabric to fiber level, like a comforting wrapping tutorial that covered every corner with laser precision.

Despite his last name, Lindsay Frenell had very little interest in the firm's business. But he didn't have a better option for a "career" and he was a Frenell, so he stayed on as the only Founding Principal of the firm. His responsibilities had been refined to socializing with his old friends, attending golf tournaments and cocktail parties, giving speeches at summits and conventions, and appearing at marketing events as a mascot. To avoid confusing the firm with the human, the Associates called human Frenell "Mickey Mouse," or "Lord M," meaning an asset that was hardly producing anything new but was retained for IP purposes.

"We're also pleased to see a steady increase in our annual intake. 2027 was a strong run, and we expect to sustain the same growth in this financial year—"

"I guess the trip to Geneva paid off." Colleen swirled her pinot as she watched Lindsay from the back of the Level 20 café. "Should we get a team ready for incoming instructions?"

"We gotta start putting caps on LSAT and GMAT," Wade grumbled as he stared at the balcony, where a dozen Indian and Chinese kids congregated.

"That reminds me," said Colleen, "how's Abbi doing?"

"Poor thing needs Valium to sleep 'cause some little rats with no life drove up the scores and ruined the game for everyone." Wade squeezed his glass as if to crack it with his bare hand. "These days you can just come over on a boat, open a filthy deli, and breed like rabbits, then your kids will set you up for retirement—what kind of parents exploit their own kids like that?"

"Careful." Colleen coughed and glanced at the crowd in front of them. "Not everybody here is deaf."

"So you think now that you're a Partner, you can tell everybody what to do? What happened to the lovely Collie?"

"Times have changed, Wade. They can send you into training for saying things wrong."

"When you're billing as much as I do, I'm all ears."

"I probably am." Colleen smirked. "Wouldn't it be nice to see some blubber from that whale?"

Wade scowled at Colleen, his lips pressed razor thin.

"Everything you have, Collie, I gave it to you and I can take it back. You talk like a big girl now because I pulled you away from the kids' table. Whether you're really cut out for this, I think we all saw your spectacular performance earlier this year. Enjoy your lucky streak while it lasts, but if you're gonna fuck up again, give us a heads-up so our insurers can get another twenty-eight million ready to go."

Colleen clenched her jaw, and Wade walked away from behind her. As their bodies overlapped, he squeezed her ass and whispered:

"Like it? You worked twenty years for this."

AFTER LINDSAY WISHED for a prosperous 2028, the speech segued into the introduction of the April Star Billers. Hayden had the floor and gave the new Grads a sermon on the Frenell Ten Commandments:

Clients are always right.

Follow instructions religiously. You know nothing.

Meet deadlines, or you'll know why they're called "deadlines."

Do not be the first to leave or the last to arrive. You'll have no friends.

Do not barge into a Meditation Chamber. You'll regret it.

Record and close your time every day. Even if you're having a heart attack, you do that in the ambulance.

Round only upward. Twelve minutes is 0.2 hours; so is seven.

Put all your time in, even if you think you've spent too long on a task. Do not self-censor. Do not self-censor. Do not self-censor!

The last one was so important it counted as three.

The panorama screen walls highlighted Hayden's top ten assignments, nine of which were Frenell's spotlight projects of the year. His utilization had reached 210 percent, which translated to fifteen billables a day. No weekends. No holidays.

There had been rumors that Hayden was one of the Stars who'd figured out "time padding." An older version of PADU had a bug that allowed a user to alter historical time entries that had already been exported onto invoices and archived in the system. So if anyone having a lull wanted to tinker with their past billables and give themselves some anxiety relief, they had the means to do so.

The developers had released a patch twelve months ago, but not all users had installed the update. Around that time, Frenell restructured its IT and decentralized the system administration duties, including software updating, to endpoint employees because it was believed to be more "empowering." After the Timekeepers were empowered, the IT department of the Grand Ivory headquarters was streamlined to three specialists with an eight-hour shift each, plus an overseas call center.

This issue hadn't caught much executive attention because the tampering was rather easy to detect—if OATH decided to audit a Timekeeper and dug out their original productivity reports. So anyone who padded their metrics would be playing with fire. There had also been a tinfoil hat theory that a handful of Partners were aware of the practice and a handful of Associates had the "don't ask, don't tell" pass for it. Morals aside, it was a handy trick to build someone up as the next rising star and plant your golden kids in the major league. Most importantly, they were adding time in, not writing time off. Who'd care if a salaried Year 5 pumped his billing by 30 percent? They were not the ones getting paid by the hour.

"Wow, two hundred and ten. Does this guy sleep in the office?"

Nolan responded with a shrug. Other than the suit and the Chelsea boots, the Uphill girl looked the same as he remembered, except that now he knew her name was Keahi Ka'uhane and she was one of his spring chickens.

"Wushan is pulling one eighty, and he camps here," Keahi said, referring to Wushan Yang, the new Grad on Level 9, April Star Biller No. 4.

"Jealous?" Nolan asked.

"Of Wushan? Why?"

"He's got a leg up and a shout-out."

"If he's happy, then good for him."

"Ah, you're one of those."

"One of what?"

"The 'you should do what makes you happy' people."

"Right, those 'meaning and purpose' bitches."

"Your words." Nolan turned to Luc Edward, his other Buddy. "Did you know Keahi is an angel from the tent city?"

Luc shrugged as he scanned the floor, looking for a "cool kids" circle to join. As his ambivalent gaze found a focal point, his spine straightened up and made him half a head taller.

A hand landed on Nolan's back.

"May I steal your mama hen for a moment?" Wade grinned.

Keahi gave a polite smile and pivoted one step aside. Luc leaned in for a self-introduction, but Wade had left with Nolan before he could open his mouth.

WADE LET OUT a loud moan and pinched his nose hard. He stumbled backward and grabbed hold of the stall partition, batting his watery eyes as he swallowed a half-charged sneeze. He held up his forefinger as if to say something but decided not to ruin the moment with words. A few seconds later, the rush subsided, and he followed with a chaser hit. One for each nostril.

Men in Wade's age group and shape would normally get advice against strong stimulation, like too much cocaine, too-kinky sex, or any amount of squash. Nolan felt an offbeat sense of amazement. It was like seeing a mall Santa do a flip.

"I see, yep." Wade nodded. "Yep, yep, yep."

He took a money clip out of his Armani jacket and peeled a twenty from the fold, then splayed it in front of Nolan's eyes like the first step of a magic trick.

"Um, it's two fifty . . . Mr. Wade."

A bottle cost five hundred dollars, but Fischer had charged him half for half.

"What do you see?" asked Wade.

"Twenty . . . dollars?"

"No, you see it as payment. I see it as capital. That's why I'm where I am and you're where you are."

"Capital for–"

"An empire! The future! The–" Wade's arm froze in midair. His bulging eyes gleamed with the same empty exhilaration Nolan had seen on Fischer last night. It hit Nolan that this guy could be having a heart attack and, instead of "alcoholism," he'd have "supplying drugs and causing Partner death" on his RAP, or both.

Um, run? the voice said. *You don't have the skill set for prison.*

As Nolan attempted to extricate the bottle from Wade's hand, Wade inhaled sharply and grinned at whatever he was seeing Nolan as:

"Here's your whale, motherfuckers."

NOLAN COUNTED TEN alligators after Wade had left the men's room fresh as a daisy. As he stepped out, Colleen pulled him into the handicapped restroom and caged him against the door with her arms.

"Spill it," Colleen said.

"What?"

"I saw you with Wade."

"We both had to use the bathroom, what's the big deal?"

"You both had to take a twenty-minute dump?"

"Drugs." Nolan shook his head and palmed his face. "Just drugs. He does drugs, he likes them, and they're probably gonna kill him one day, okay?"

"What else?"

"You just gave me this assignment on Tuesday."

"So?"

"So there isn't enough time for 'what else' yet. Why the rush?"

Is there another negligence claim coming? Nolan thought, but he didn't say it. Colleen had gotten some heat earlier this year for missing a critical risk in a merger which should've slashed the price by at least a quarter, then Aaron Patucchi had been conveniently outed as a regular at a local gay brothel and had taken some attention off her back.

"What drugs?" She narrowed her eyes.

In a flurry, Nolan chose not to tell her the whole truth, so he tapped his nose and said nothing.

Colleen examined his face, then pulled away. As she paced and pondered in the middle of the bathroom, Nolan grabbed the door handle.

"We're not done yet." She stopped him.

He turned around and saw her sit on the toilet, back against the tank and legs wide open, one foot stepping on the seat.

"No," said Nolan.

"No?"

"You want dirt on Wade, I'll get you that, but I'm done with this–"

"You don't get to cherry-pick your work." Colleen rolled her panties off her legs and dangled them from her ankle. "'No' is a privilege. You have to earn it."

"You know what? I don't think that stupid recording proves anything." Nolan clenched his fists. "And I haven't had a drink since March. It's fucking killing me, but I don't have a drop of alcohol in my blood right now. That's a fact."

"Good for you, but you don't understand." She folded her panties and stuffed them inside her bra. "If that recording gets out, it won't stop at 'you got shitfaced and dialed the wrong number.' It won't even stop at 'you had a problem back then, you might still have a problem now.' What people will be really curious about is what led to that. Are you sure you're ready to answer *everything* you'll get asked?"

She locked her eyes on him and ran her pinkie along her lips. "You can avoid one shit sandwich, then get hit by a truckload more. Or, we can get this over with."

Nolan's mind rebounded to his last night of blackout drinking, and there was a bolted door in his memory stopping him from going further. His feet moved on their own, carrying him toward her while his paralyzed brain watched. In a moment of desperation, he called for that voice that wouldn't shut up when he wanted it to. Something to tell him what to do. Anything.

But this time, it left him alone. The next thing he knew, he was kneeling in front of her.

"Why me? You know I can't do this." Nolan groaned, close to begging.

She grabbed his brown curls and yanked his head back so she could have a good look at his face. Soft skin with no scars or bruises. Teeth that had once been in braces. His eyes–they weren't sharp, unlike those of a predator. What they had was a glimmer of sadness. Life had given him a few reality checks here and there but hadn't shown him all it had in store. He looked like he could be the son of any of those pigs out there.

She tightened her grip, tugged him closer, and smiled.

"That's exactly the point, sweetheart."

Once they were done, Colleen dusted her clothes off with a damp paper towel and reapplied her oxblood lipstick. Nolan sat against the wall and watched her slip back into her stilettos.

"Will you let me go?" he asked. "Ever?"

"Don't be so cold, I can still feel you. The next time I catch you, you'd better have something more interesting."

She sauntered out and closed the door behind her.

He sat on the floor like that for a while. Then he took out the twenty from Wade and shared a moment with an indifferent-looking Andrew Jackson.

"AH, YOU'RE STILL alive." Keahi paused her conversation with Calais when Nolan approached the bar. Nolan forced a smile.

"Yeah . . . had to get something done."

"Yuck, work?"

"Sort of."

Luc sneaked up from behind and inserted himself between Keahi and Nolan.

"Do you work for Mr. Wade?" His eyes sparkled. "What's he like?"

Nolan stared at him for a second, then said: "Challenging."

Luc then described how he'd attended a Frenell scholarship competition as a sophomore and Wade had given him such heartfelt praise–and his customized business card–which had led to him pursuing a career in this profession. He went on and on, and Nolan could no longer tell if Luc was talking to him or polishing his material with a live crowd. He raised a hand to catch Calais's attention. Calais handed a bourbon and Coke to someone waiting, then put a tall glass in front of Nolan and reached for a large bottle of mineral water.

"I'll have a vodka tonic, please," said Nolan.

Calais paused and read Nolan's face, then he retrieved the tall glass and mixed the drink ordered. He covered the drink with his hand for a second when he set it down in front of Nolan and tried to catch his eyes one more time. Then he let go and walked to the other end of the bar.

Nolan kept his head low. Neither the glass nor the seemingly innocuous liquid reflected his face.

Well, well. Look who's crawling back.

While his mind searched for a dignified excuse, his clammy hand grabbed the glass and sent it to his lips. The thirst that had been brewing inside him finally saw the light and crawled up the dry well.

It's okay. Let me drive. The voice chuckled. *We both know I'm better at dealing with stress. Don't beat yourself up–you've had a good run.*

The first sip went down like a burn, and his throat almost shut off. He put the glass down and snapped his face to the less populated side. His body tensed up to suppress the spasms as he coughed with his mouth closed. The sickly familiar spicy taste buzzed through his nerves and heated up his pulse like an erotic punishment. Jaw clenched, he drew a deep breath and straightened his back, then he emptied the glass in two gulps and wiped his lower lip with a thumb.

From his throat to his stomach, it hurt, like his digestive tract wanted to invert itself to get rid of the toxin. The revulsion fired up a blinding migraine. He forced himself to sit still, so he could feel the pain he deserved.

Calais replaced the empty glass with some water, then stepped away. He hadn't forgotten to drop a wedge of lime in it. That gesture of care hooked a dry laugh out of Nolan and nudged him to face people again.

Luc was explaining to the small group that had gathered at the bar how he'd finished two degrees in half the time that "normal" people would've because he just seemed to have difficulty forgetting things. Nolan smiled and nodded, quietly picturing the kid's eyeballs in a jar.

WHEN HAYDEN FINISHED his sermon, they kept the snapshot of his accomplishments on the screen until the applause subsided. Ryuka calculated the reported revenue of those spotlight projects in her head, ballparking the profit Hayden had generated for this place and what that figure would let him get away with.

"They said I needed more local experience," So-yeon said, peeking at Ryuka. She was answering the question of why she was "only a Grad" despite having worked overseas for years. Based on what OATH had told her during the recruitment process, she'd been under the impression that they were bringing her on board as an Associate. But "impressions" were not enforceable.

Ryuka nodded as she scanned the café for the sight of Morse. Earlier today, the Teams group chat named Mortification had published a table listing the Associates who'd have to speak to Morse at the Debut, the time they expected to need, and whether their stuff was bad news so they'd better follow one of Morse's favorites. A few years back, some Associates had noticed that they'd have a better chance of holding a peaceful conversation with Morse when he was dizzy, so they'd started saving up less-urgent matters and cornering him at firm events to deliver those in one briefing. They only had a thirty-minute window for that—while the Partners were still around and Morse couldn't yell at anyone—so coordination was key.

Before the lateral market collapsed and before he settled down with Frenell, Morse had spent some time with three other firms. The Associates had stalked him on LinkedIn, trying to work out which place had made him the way he was. But Sauria Street firms were a collective force with a cumulative effect, like tobacco companies. It was hard to ascertain which one of them put the cancer in there.

Ryuka had a five-minute slot tonight to remind Morse of her performance review. It was fairly late for her as most people had already gotten it done and dusted—especially if they were Year 5 and looking for a Special Associate nomination from their Handler. Theoretically, she still had two weeks to get her review in.

Theoretically.

She spotted Morse talking to Emma on the balcony. Morse was leaning against the railing and sipping his wine, even chuckling a little, so it seemed Emma was making good use of her ten minutes. She got a larger chunk of time because the guy following her had to tell Morse that the expert witness on his case had gone into chemo and wouldn't be able to deliver his report on time. Gnawing at her fingernails, Ryuka watched the chemo Associate join the chat and carve a deep frown on Morse's forehead.

"What's the team like?" asked So-yeon. "I've heard–"

"Excuse me," Ryuka muttered and dashed to the balcony as soon as Morse dismissed the bad-news bearer with a flick of the wrist. Morse saw her approach and began to leave. Ryuka called out his name and stopped him.

"Have you . . . seen my invite?" she asked, catching her breath.

"I need to work out my commitments first. Will let you know when I'm free."

"Thanks, I was thinking–"

"I don't believe we've met." Morse extended a hand to So-yeon, who'd caught up with Ryuka. So-yeon glanced at Ryuka, then gave Morse a quick handshake and answered his follow-up questions with simple words and a smile.

"Look what you've achieved!" Morse raised his glass after hearing about So-yeon's previous experience and recent relocation. "I might need your help with some translation work in the future."

Ryuka tried to steer the conversation back on track, but Morse had turned his back on her and given So-yeon his full attention. The Year 4 following Ryuka on the schedule had come over, standing next to Morse and tapping on his watch as he shook his head. He seized the moment when Morse took a sip of his wine and delivered the update that the client of his case had fucked up version control, so they'd have to trace two drafts back and there'd be some cleanup first thing in the morning. Annoying, but manageable.

Morse rolled his eyes but nodded, then went on to ask about the Year 4's weekend plans. Ryuka walked away in silence and returned to the inside. The night suddenly felt colder.

Why does she have to follow me around? Ryuka frowned when she noticed So-yeon by her side. *Can't she go hang out with her kind?*

The real reason Ryuka wasn't so buddy-buddy with So-yeon was that she didn't like her.

When Lindsay Frenell was describing the culinary benefits of mixing sushi and butter chicken, the presentation slide claimed that people who identified as "Asian" made up 6 percent of Timekeepers below Special Associate level—rounded up from 5.7 and matching the representation in the general population.

Six percent. That was not the statistic of the Asian population in this state. Not the statistics of Asian matriculants in the "default" law schools or business schools expected on the CV of a Frenell. But it was *a* statistic, and it was the one that had become the allowance.

"Morse seems nice," So-yeon said.

Ryuka halted. So-yeon kept on walking a few steps forward, then turned around, perplexed. Ryuka examined the woman in front of her: She wasn't Chinese or Japanese. She wasn't tanned or athletic. She spoke with a faint accent and had a makeup style that hadn't been Americanized. She wore designer clothes—tonight was a Chanel tweed over a Ralph Lauren dress, and they fit like skin. Ryuka couldn't picture her in an oversize suit or any loose pile of fabric that could bury her petite figure. She was eight years behind, but she thought carefully before she spoke, which made her appear more mature and alert. She had so much hope about this place, and she thought Morse Sachet was fucking "nice."

They were nothing alike, yet she was the reflection Ryuka saw in a mirror.

They were nothing alike, yet they had to race in the same lane and fight for that 6 percent of nectar trickling down Mount Olympus, because as ingredients for the Frenell stew, they sat on the same shelf for "Oriental spices." A pinch could exoticize a Michelin fusion dish, but too much would turn it into a food court bento.

So-yeon Bae was her certified "peer" and her designated competition because although everyone was born free and equal, they're free and equal in their unique ways. Some have the freedom to ration the world for others. The others have the freedom to take it or leave it.

"Did I do something wrong?" So-yeon asked. Her frown could mean hurt or annoyance. Either way, Ryuka realized her own expression must be hideous.

"No . . . no, I was just . . . distracted . . . come on, let me introduce you to some friends."

They came to the bar, where Luc was talking about his involuntary memory retention. Ryuka let So-yeon pick the stool next to Keahi, then she sat down at the far end of the row. She saw Nolan across the bar, and they shared a light nod when their eyes met. Nolan was muddling the wedge of lime with the straw to infuse the water, the way he liked it. She mouthed, "Where's Sai?" He shrugged.

Over a bottle of San Pellegrino, Ryuka saw a little smile emerge on So-yeon as she eased into the chat with her Grad gang. That made her feel slightly less guilty about being an asshole earlier. She waited a few moments, then slipped away and pulled an Irish goodbye.

She sat in the evacuation stairwell for a bit, replaying the interaction with Morse earlier, wondering if there were alternative ways to interpret that. Months ago, she'd asked about moving under a different supervisor. OATH had responded that firm policies prohibited changing Handlers at will, as it wouldn't be fair to the others.

"We expect our Associates to demonstrate good relationship skills and their ability to adapt to different communication styles as required for the job," Christie had told her. "It's up to you to make it work, Ryuka."

She opened Perspective on her work phone. It was a guided wellness app designed to, as the name suggested, put things into perspective. The AI assistant looked cute, but God it was dumb—Frenell had definitely cheaped out on the learning model—yet Ryuka talked to it at times. It was like talking to a turtle munching on its lettuce. There was a certain therapeutic peacefulness to it. Some days, that was the only peace she could get. Besides, it'd count toward her "Non-billable: Personal Development."

I don't think my Handler likes me, she typed.

We should be cautious when assuming negative intentions, said the assistant. *Not everybody is out to get you. Some people might be under a lot of stress at work, or going through a difficult time in life. Give them the benefit of the doubt and see their good side.*

The good side of Morse? Ryuka thought hard and managed to find some. Morse had a horrible temper and he picked favorites. He had a lot of petty power plays and liked them. But he wasn't *evil*. He'd kept his hands to himself, he wouldn't blackmail to get what he wanted, and he hadn't killed anyone—not that she was aware of.

I just wish I could be less invisible, she typed. *I don't even get to be a cattle.*

Merriam-Webster defines "cattle" as "domesticated quadrupeds held as property or raised for use," said the assistant. *It's a fine summer's day for grazing, and I stomp my happy hooves in the pasture. MOOOOOOOO—*

She let out a soft laugh and closed the app. Then she turned around and climbed up the stairs, away from the jubilation that didn't involve her.

At first glance, Level 21 fit an outsider's stereotypical imagination of a firm like Frenell. Offices delineated by frosted glass panels and solid wooden doors. Plush carpeting in emotionless steel gray. An open kitchen at one end and a Meditation Chamber at the other. The centerpiece was the artistic statement that really brought the quarter-million-dollar renovation to life—a Zen garden with an enclosed watercourse, circulating a rainbow cascade between the summit of a crystal mountain and the gravel base. A unique feature on Level 21 to celebrate the new Special Associates who had evolved from bulk material to named individuals.

Hayden's office sat directly above Ryuka's workstation. She stood outside his glass walls and peered at the insurance company across the road. The rooftop myrtle wasn't particularly glamorous even during daytime; it was reduced to a shapeless cluster under the night sky. But she hadn't even known the myrtle existed. She knew now, and that was something.

The whirring of a patrol robot startled her, and she almost fled the scene, then she recognized that constant off-course veering and the bumpy motion that resembled a limp. They still hadn't fixed the wheels on this one.

"How have you been, Edgar?" She stroked the head of the bot. "Made any new friends?"

Edgar tilted its screen upward and printed a smiley face, accompanied by a string of upbeat jingles. Then it flashed the time and circled behind Ryuka, gently nudging her hamstrings, meaning, "It's late, you should leave."

She sent the bot on its way and watched it snake down the hall. As she turned to the exit, a fleeting thought hit her.

When she had left the Partner Floors through the fire staircase on Tuesday, there had been a suspicious pause between Level 20 and Level 13. She vaguely remembered that she'd had to hop down several flights of stairs in a doorless spiral before she'd seen the number "13" painted on the wall, but her mind had been occupied by her meeting with Morse and the name list of new Special Associates on Wade's desk, so she'd let it slide.

She entered Hayden's office and came to the window. The insurance company employee facing her workstation might be a German immigrant, as he'd hung a national flag over his territory. She couldn't see that flag from here even if she pressed her face against the glass.

There were far more than two stories between Level 13 and where she stood, so that number jump in the elevators wasn't just a superstition. Maybe Frenell had sublet those floors for some extra cash, although there were no signs or directories of other businesses in the lobby.

Or, maybe that's where they hide the skeletons. She chuckled to herself.

&

THE SECURITY GUARD took Sai's electronic devices at the entrance on Level 15 and wielded a metal detector around her torso for suspicious beeps. It was the common model that Sai had seen at airports—the one that looked like a shrunken paddle with the brand label printed across the scan surface in lemon yellow. He waved her in after two seconds of work as he let out a huge yawn—probably still recovering from his other job, or jobs, she wouldn't know. She did know the guy wasn't paid enough for this.

She turned to leave, but Katherine cleared her throat loudly, so the guard picked up his wand again and bent over to scan Sai's lower half. Slow and reluctant, with a pained grunt. Could be osteoarthritis.

Across the hall, a suited man had finished his check-in at the guest section, which offered basic cloaking services. Eyes glued to his screen, he almost crashed into Sai, but he sensed the presence of another body and changed course in time, successfully making his way through the entrance while typing furiously on his phone.

Sai left Katherine, who was still lecturing the guard about the value of diligence, and followed the man down the doorless hallway, which was about the width of a hotel corridor and illuminated by two neon trails along the ceiling. After a few turns, she picked up the muffled thump of a bass line. Rounding a corner, the guest pushed through a swing door, and the music detonated. Synthesized melodies and euphoric beats washed over her, then pulled her deeper into the space like a rip current.

She found herself entering a sumptuous lobby spanning two conjoined floors vertically. On her right, the bar swam forward till it hit the end wall. Behind the counter was a familiar face. Sai recalled she was Calais's new intern at the café. On her left, against the night sky and the floor-to-ceiling windows, plush chesterfield sofas and wingback chairs wove enclaves that could harbor a cozy conversation or a quick break between dances. In the boardroom-sized open space before her, a boy was guzzling down a box of red, fraternity-hazing style, while a circle of suited men cheered him on and someone in a catering uniform drifted past with her canapés. Sai had never met the boy, but she knew he was a host because of the Frenell badge attached to his belt. He might have sat on Level 9 or Level 10, given he seemed young enough for anyone to call him a "boy" without being offensive.

The boy finished the last drop from the box right before the facade clock struck nine, and that sent the crowd into a round of hollers. Two men heaved him up and bounced him on their shoulders in a parade. The kid sealed his mouth with both hands and clamped his cheeks between palms. His Adam's apple jerked up and down, yet it didn't stop red streams from dripping through his laced fingers.

I misread the job description, Sai thought. *I've joined a cult.*

"I see you've found your way in," Katherine whispered from behind.

"I guess I've been sleepwalking for five years straight," Sai said.

She was being hard on herself. The conversion had been done way before her time.

To the extent allowed by the load-bearing structure, Frenell had removed the concrete between Level 15 and Level 16 to amplify the visual gratification from a high ceiling and top-to-bottom glass enclosure. Walls enhanced by damping compounds and multiple dry layers encapsulated the space and prevented sound transmission. Outside the dual-glazed glass panels, the needles of the facade clock glided across the view as time went by, casting elegant geometric patterns on the floor. Beneath her feet, Level 14 had been reconstructed into a buffer with mass-loaded vinyl flooring and noise-absorbing insulation. Over her head, Level 17 to Level 19 offered business lounges, accommodations, and amenities including a spa and a massage parlor.

There they were, the "missing" in-between floors with their separate entrance, separate elevator system, and separate rules. For the hosts, a hidden Red Sea that could either drown them or lead them to the promised land. For the guests, a bustling hub connecting and directing the flow of power and money like an airport terminal. Exclusive. Private. Safe. No cameras. No record. No evidence. What happened in the Red Sea slept with the whales.

Brokers come and go. The marketplace will outlive them all.

Sai followed Katherine upstairs as she received her induction tour. They passed a business lounge and stopped for an oversweetened rendition of "Everybody Loves Somebody" by Dean Martin.

"Hmm." Katherine closed her eyes and nodded. "It does have its charm, if you're into this kind of breathy voice."

Sai peeked inside and realized it was a live performance. On the mini stage at the front of the lounge, Pace Tivoli, Year 2 Associate, was singing in a 1920s flapper dress.

Instead of her skills or her personality, Pace was most well known for having the wrong kind of mentorship with a Partner from Level 27, Gerald Dover or Denver—one of the two. Sai could never remember because the Associates just called him "the Whore."

Although Sai had never worked with Gerald, she'd always known he was a bit off. Back in the days when she'd still had so many naive assumptions about Frenell, she hadn't expected a Partner's first greeting to a twentysomething employee in the public firm café to be "Where have you been my entire life?" Thanks to being in different practice groups with little professional overlap, she'd managed to dodge him so far.

Meanwhile, Pace was exactly the kind of girl that Gerald would get his hands on. If you were a thoroughbred with a regal family tree, and the biggest challenge you'd had in life was surviving a spiritual trip to a third-world country with limited sanitary facilities, this guy would be pretty harmless. Most

Associates thought it was because those women were too high maintenance and high risk, but Sai's theory was that Gerald had tried enough of them. He had bagged a Cornell-then-Yale-trained wife from old money and produced two pre-law, pre-med kids with one more on the way. He had stroked enough shoulders wrapped in grade A cashmere and heard enough cocktail chatter about ski holidays and equestrian training. An affair with essentially a preview of his own daughter would bore his eyeballs out of their sockets, just like a hog that had been hunting truffles its entire life wouldn't bother with some saffron under its snout. But those girls in flimsy polyester suits and glossy PU heels, girls with unsettled glances that darted from side to side as if someone might jump on them at any second, girls who needed to calculate whether it was appropriate to laugh or speak at any given moment, girls that he could just call "girls" before sending them off on a coffee run–girls like Pace–those were an all-you-can-eat buffet of wild poppies.

Pace hadn't ended up in the Red Sea because she'd assumed she was Gerald's only poppy. She'd ended up there because she'd thought she'd be his last. Sai didn't know if Pace and Melodie knew about each other.

Sai glanced across the lounge, and her gaze landed on the largest table in the back. Five suited guys were sharing some stories with their expressive faces and their expressive hands. A clean-shaven man with slick hair listened, occasionally tossing out a few words in response, or giving a light nod of acknowledgment to someone who'd refilled his drink.

It'd been a while, and Andrej Bovec had changed a lot in his fashion taste and temperament, but the one difference that almost made Sai mistake him for another person was how calm yet commanding his presence had become. Sai had met Andrej when she was a Summer Cadet and he was a Year 5. Andrej used to talk like he was in the first five seconds of a YouTube ad before the Skip button showed up. He was obsessed with condensing his statement to no more than three bullet points, and he would rush through his reasons because he was too used to getting interrupted. The way he'd run out of breath midsentence till his eyes teared up reminded Sai of how prisoners consumed their food, and how squirrels stuffed their faces until they became overinflated balloons.

She'd heard people call him Andrej Try-Hard behind his back and taunt him for being a doormat to his face. It'd sucked particularly hard for someone like Andrej because he was actually good at his job. It seemed he'd finally realized that. There wasn't a single trace of the constant fear by which Sai remembered him. Right there, all she saw was a halo of formidability over his head. She reckoned getting promoted to Deputy General Counsel at Osireion would do that to a person, or maybe it was before that. It was leaving Frenell that made him realize he wasn't a piece of trash and he didn't have to let people treat him like one. Either way, she felt happy for him, and intensely jealous.

While Andrej's former superiors desperately tried to overwrite his memory about them with pleasant banter, the look on Andrej's face conveyed the typical standoffishness of someone who had recently completed their food chain climbing. There was something tawdry about that formulaic power shift and the people who legitimized it. Sai looked away.

Katherine had received a phone call and stepped to the side. Her face hardened as she listened on and wandered farther down the corridor. "Keep people away and get the Revilox." She kept her voice low, then stormed off in silence. Sai hurried up to follow Katherine. A cheerful voice stopped her from behind.

"Saidah? Saidah Sulaimaniyah?"

She snapped around and caught a young man with wheat-blond hair and half-rim glasses staring at her in beaming excitement. Her eyes widened, and she wished she had some magic dust to make her disappear in a puff. There'd been too many unexpected cameos for one night, and it'd begun to feel like a setup.

"I thought it might be you!" Henry exclaimed, then he scanned their surroundings. "You . . . work here?"

"I work at Frenell." Sai squared her shoulders, then looked around them, copying Henry's expression. "Do you come here . . . often?"

"Not really." Henry shrugged. "They kept asking, so I was like, I'll stay for one drink. This isn't my kind of show. You know me."

It was true. Henry Carrollton had never been a party boy even in his college days. During the semesters when she was tutoring him in Corporate Finance and Pricing Strategy, he'd missed only one session for a family reunion. Even after they'd started going out, she couldn't remember him ever showing up hungover. She'd liked Henry, just never as much as he'd wanted her to. They were both young, but he was the one who'd acted like a child. Then she'd graduated; he had two more years to go. Something changed in those two years, and before she noticed, they hadn't spoken for three months. She wasn't as upset as she should've been, and that upset her more than the ending of "the thing" between them.

"So . . . if I come here again, will I see you?" Henry asked, biting his lip. The same look of anticipation that he'd had every time he'd wanted them to spend some time together. Some things hadn't changed, and that warmed Sai up from the inside.

"I'm so glad you made it!" Katherine reentered the picture before Sai could respond and planted herself before Henry. The keenness in Henry's eyes faded, replaced by bare minimum diplomacy. He folded his arms, and the tips of his feet started turning as he addressed Katherine's questions with a single word or a silent smile. Sai did not miss that.

"Thank you for having me. I've gotta go." Henry shook Katherine's hand and pulled away before she could say anything further. He nodded at Sai, leaving her with a light touch on her arm and a lingering gaze. Katherine did not miss that.

❧

"YOU AND HENRY, good friends?" Katherine asked after Sai had reclaimed her stuff from the guard.

"Okay friends," said Sai. There was a new text from an unknown number in the notification bar of her personal phone. She turned off the screen, but Katherine had seen it.

"Are you really not worried at all that I might tell people everything I just saw?" Sai asked in the elevator to the ground. It made Katherine snort.

"Keep talking like that. They'd think you're pure."

As they stepped out the back door behind the building, Katherine left Sai with some wise parting words.

"There are presumptions about how the world should operate, then there are rules about how the world really operates. We want people who confuse the two to vocalize their misbeliefs. That's how we filter out the idiots."

Sai waited till Katherine had exited her vision before she opened the new message from a "stranger."

Just to see if you still use this number :)

She replayed the last part of her night and pictured Henry in a way that was completely different from how she used to see him in college: He wore a plain gray suit, a slightly wrinkled white shirt, and a brandless belt. Casual dress sneakers. A backpack for his laptop. No accessories except a Fitbit on his left wrist and a signet on his right pinkie. Subtle soapy, clean scent with no luxurious signature. Without any prior knowledge, you wouldn't assume Henry was from the family he was from. The most expensive thing on this guy had always been his attitude.

He could afford to say no to anyone in that place, and he'd saved her number for years after they'd stopped talking.

An idea lifted the corner of her mouth as she tapped on the message and selected "Create New Contact." If she played her cards right, the Red Sea could be her ticket to the outside.

6

IT WAS ALMOST six in the morning, and the Perception Floors were dead. In the Vision Room, Ryuka went through the documents in her binder one more time and finished her second triple espresso, getting ready for someone "difficult."

"Difficult" was good. If she could fix "difficult," she must be good.

At precisely six, Laurent Cheong's face appeared on the wall-mounted TV. He looked younger in live footage. Framed glasses, unstyled hair, visible stubble, no tie over white shirt. He'd be a perfect archetype of "cattle" if he worked at Frenell.

"Good evening, Dr. Cheong." Ryuka showed all her teeth. "Thank you for meeting with me today! How was the trip to Singapore?"

"Hello, Miss Murong. The flight was all right. I had a fifteen-hour layover in Hong Kong, so I went to see the area I lived in when I was a kid."

He had a classic French accent and ate his *h*'s. She did not dislike the way he pronounced "Murong."

"I love Hong Kong!" Ryuka exclaimed—maybe she could diaspora-bond with this guy after all. "I lived there until nine, so I speak Cantonese and Mandarin. If you want to continue the discussion in Chinese, that's totally fine."

"That's impressive, but my English is all right," said Laurent. "If my memory is correct, Tim also grew up in Hong Kong. So did Amy before him."

"That's right!"

"Does your team have any more Chinese Associates?"

"We . . . hmm, no, actually." Ryuka tilted her face and crossed the names off in her mind one by one. "Oh, wow, I'm the last one standing."

"Well, I guess you're the last one, then." Laurent let out a sigh of relief. "May I ask if Tim is still on this case?"

"Tim is not with us anymore." Ryuka cleared her throat. "But I've read his notes on your previous meetings, so we can pick it up from there."

"I've made my position abundantly clear to Frenell, multiple times. As far as I'm concerned, there's nothing left to 'pick up.'"

"There are a couple of things we'd like to discuss—not to change your mind, just to make sure we don't misunderstand or misrepresent your opinion." Ryuka turned to her file and read from the notes. She could tell she hadn't warmed Laurent up as much as she wanted, but touching the printout relaxed her a little. Work was always easier than people.

"The core dispute in this case is whether it'd be appropriate to regulate 'beta-9-tetramethylenedioxythetamines,' a.k.a. compound B9-3T, as a drug with 'a high potential for abuse' under the Controlled Narcotics and Chemicals Act. In light of that, we sought your input on the long-term effects of B9-3T."

"You did."

"And you have concluded that, I quote, 'B9-3T appears to induce compulsive post-treatment redosing, indicating an elevated risk of dependence.'"

"I have."

"Meaning it's addictive."

"So there's nothing left to discuss."

"Maybe I should clarify the question, Dr. Cheong." Ryuka looked up to catch Laurent's eyes. "Whether B9-3T seems 'addictive' to average people is different from whether it should be regulated. When interpreting a piece of law, not just the meaning of its words, its context and legislative purpose are also important. You see, things like heroin and cocaine are regulated because they pose a much higher risk of abuse, but there has been no conclusive evidence suggesting that B9-3T is comparable. If I could remind you of the review by Professor Daniels in 1997–"

"That review–sorry to interrupt–it only covered twenty-one clinical studies done within five years. They all had rather small sample sizes between fourteen and fifty subjects and lasted six to eight weeks. Their purpose was not to test the safety of the compound either, but to demonstrate its effects on short-term mood regulation based on self-reported data. You seem to have done your homework, Miss Murong, so I assume you also know that review was sponsored by Ithaca Pharmaceuticals, a member of the Osireion Group, your valuable client."

Yeah, she knew.

B9-3T was the active ingredient in one of Ithaca Pharma's best-selling drugs, Serotane. Ever since they'd gotten wind that the Department of Substance Administration was thinking about a ban, the big boys at Osireion had been gathering ammunition to shoot down the change. This wouldn't be the first time anyone had flaunted that study to portray Serotane as a godsend.

B9-3T had been around for almost half a century, and the noise warning about its risk had been growing especially in the last decade, but no real action had ever come through, until the

DSA got a new secretary. In her first public interview, Secretary Berlin emphasized that this long-neglected hidden crisis would be one of her top priorities to address, then she shared her personal experience of being prescribed Serotane, then losing two years of her life to battling the withdrawal–some people just couldn't comprehend that not everything was about them.

Against that backdrop, the DSA had completed its investigation at light speed, and a proposal of action had been published in the Federal Register. The Department had also released a study by Professor Lindau of Johns Hopkins University that provided enough scientific details and patient testimonies to make a textbook on addictions. It was said that Netflix had booked a documentary.

As the manufacturer of Serotane and the B9-3T distributor with the largest market share, Ithaca Pharma had requested a hearing with the DSA where it could submit evidence against the alleged "addictiveness" to hopefully convince Secretary Berlin to abort or at least moderate the ban. The hearing was in less than two weeks, and Frenell was supposed to have gotten a "silver bullet" from Laurent a month ago.

Ryuka still hadn't gained access to the matter folders in the system, but she'd found the backstory in Tim's bus memo. The "bus protocol" required all Timekeepers to file their emails and work products in order and prepare a memo, updated weekly, on the current state of their assignment, so anyone hit by a bus could be replaced within less than thirty minutes of downtime.

"I'm glad you mentioned the sponsorship." Ryuka smiled. "Osireion has always been the leader in psychopharmacology and it is committed to bringing effective and affordable solutions to people who are struggling, and helping them regain control over their lives, which is exactly why we're fighting this fight. Dr. Cheong, to prepare your report, you reviewed the medical charts of two hundred patients who were prescribed Serotane between 2008 and 2018, and those charts recorded their activities up to three years following their treatment, is that right?"

"That's right."

"First things first–on the writing style, we've noticed that certain language seems vague and leave a lot of room for misunderstanding. For example, section 4.8, last line: 'B9-3T may cause intoxication' all the way down to '*severe* psychological or physical dependence.' I'd suggest avoiding words like *severe* unless we can quantify it precisely."

"If someone is burning through two boxes a day, I think it's fair to call that 'severe,' wouldn't you agree?"

"I did see that, thank you for reminding me. There are seven cases that seem a bit . . . unthinkable. One of them was taking *sixty* pills a day."

"That's how much tolerance it can build up for some people."

"But the recommended dose in Serotane's prescription guideline is between point five milligrams and two milligrams. That's two pills. I'd suggest we remove those seven cases–it feels needlessly sensational. They're outliers anyway."

"I'm afraid I can't do that." Laurent shook his head. "Once the user has developed tolerance, they won't follow the recommended dose. Also, I believe the latest delivery method for B9-3T's recreational use is in its highly concentrated liquid form, then you get forty pills' dose in ten milliliters. We could see much higher doses pretty soon."

"But Serotane is sold in tablet form, Dr. Cheong."

"You can vape or smoke. Nicotine is nicotine."

"The point is"–Ryuka took a breath and acted like Laurent's pushback didn't annoy her–"if patients are getting creative with where they get and how they use the drug, that's not in our control. Serotane was never meant to be a pair of permanent crutches. It was meant to lift people up for six weeks, so they have the energy to sort their lives out. That reminds me–figure 2A shows that fifty-six percent of patients reported 'strong craving'–again, vague words–twelve weeks after treatment, and twenty-six percent obtained additional doses. Something obviously happened in those twelve weeks, but that's the patient's personal life. If we zoom in on the prescription period, only eight percent felt any kind of 'craving' and less than one percent requested additional doses within those six weeks."

"B9-3T has a longer half-life than its comparable drugs on the market," Laurent explained. "Which means it takes longer to metabolize. The dependence manifests more slowly because this compound has an insidious cumulative effect. The leftover will continue to circulate through the brain, which makes the withdrawal milder, so the patient might not feel the cravings until they drop below a threshold level."

"Are we comfortable with omitting the observations outside the prescription period? We could maybe extend that to eight weeks–that'd give us nineteen percent craving and five percent using. That's not too bad."

"No."

"We just don't want to distract the secretary with irrelevant information."

"It's not irrelevant."

"I'm gonna make a mental note 'cause we might need to come back to this."

"My answer will be the same no matter how many times we come back."

"Dr. Cheong, Serotane is currently the most effective and economical solution for chronic depression on the market. If it becomes a controlled drug, a lot of people will suffer. They need your help."

Laurent smiled. "You mean Osireion needs my help."

"Fine, Osireion needs you to help it keep this drug accessible."

"I'm engaged as an independent expert, Miss Murong–at least that's what my contract says. My job is not to write down what Osireion needs me to say."

That hit a nerve. *Self-righteous people die young, Doctor*, she thought. *Apparently the rest of us are all crooks because we choose to defend Big Pharma.*

Irritation aside, she was more concerned about another question: How had they gotten here in the first place? Normally, uncooperative experts would've been weeded out during the initial selection. If they went rogue halfway and refused to rectify their unfavorable opinions, their evidence would be abandoned. It was extremely rare for a firm like Frenell to be in a position where the hearing was around the corner and the expert evidence was the exact opposite of "helpful."

Most likely, all the other candidates were either conflicted out or wouldn't say anything different anyway.

That means what's said in the Lindau study is probably true, Ryuka realized. *That means B9-3T is, probably, addictive.*

But that's irrelevant.

"If there's nothing new to discuss," Laurent said, "I'd appreciate it if Frenell could accept my report as is, then we can all get on with our lives."

"There is," Ryuka blurted out. "I have some new theories to test with you."

She didn't, but she couldn't afford a solid no.

"I'm, um, waiting on some data points. You know, these pharma cases can get quite complex, especially with addiction—it's never only one culprit, am I right? I'm expecting some papers coming out of . . . not Stanford, somewhere else—"

Laurent stared at Ryuka. She put on a bright smile so he couldn't tell there was nothing behind that. As she began to wonder if his computer had frozen, Laurent opened his mouth.

"Do you need this case, Miss Murong? I mean, you, personally."

"Well . . . it's interesting. I'm definitely learning a lot—"

"That's not what I asked." He chuckled. "Your team has been working me for quite some time. They must've realized by now they're not getting what they want, but here we are having this last-minute conversation anyway. If it's important to *you*, I don't mind hearing what you have to say. But if you don't even need this case—"

"I need this."

She immediately regretted that. Now that he knew he had something she needed, he was gonna make her jump through hoops and bark for it.

Laurent nodded and looked down at something below his screen.

"I have to go now, but tomorrow looks good to me. We can do any time before nine in the morning and my night is open, so feel free to pick a time easier for you."

For a second, Ryuka felt lost. Was Laurent being . . . nice? This feeling was as foreign as the man in front of her, and it confused her to the extent of discomfort.

But "nice" was good. "Nice" would give her a way in.

RYUKA GOT A call on Teams in the elevator on her way down to Level 13. Her binders and documents slipped out of her hug and fell on the floor, but she saved the laptop and picked up her call before it rang out. Morse's face and his home study appeared on the screen.

"I need to know the extradition arrangements with Vanuatu," he said. "And the case law on the extraterritorial operation of the Computer Fraud and Abuse Act."

"Oh, okay, I can have a look. Sounds interesting." She crouched down and swept her stuff into a pile. "Do we have a matter number for this one?"

"Nobody pays for research."

"Um . . . maybe I should still record my time but you can write it off on your end? So it still counts as my billable–"

"Since when did you give *me* instructions?"

"When do you need this?" She pursed her lips.

"I have a call at eleven, so before that."

"Oh, sorry, Morse, I don't have the capacity today–"

"What do you mean you don't have capacity?"

"Sorry, I should've mentioned earlier. I'm doing this expert evidence that's already late and there's a lot of medical research to catch up on–"

"So you're not gonna do *my* work? Is that what you're saying?"

"Look, can we get a Grad to help with some preliminary research, maybe? We have some really smart ones–"

She paused, as Morse's frown had deepened into a scowl. Then a smirk crept onto his face as if a million-dollar idea just hit him.

"Since you've been chasing, let's do your performance review now."

"What?"

"I'm opening your Timekeeper Profile."

"Um, Morse, can we please wait till later this week and when you're in the office? I'd really appreciate it if we could do this one in person."

"Your billing is low. I thought you were busy."

The elevator had stopped on Level 13 for a while, waiting for its next ride. It was early, and traffic was light. Ryuka sighed and sat down in the middle of scattered papers, back against the glass wall.

"My overall utilization is a hundred and sixty-two percent," she said. "And my collection is over eighty."

"I'm talking about this month. If you're quiet, ask around. Don't just sit there and twiddle your thumbs."

Well, it's a slow month, so thumbs have been twiddled, Ryuka thought. There had been fifty-three new BD slide decks created in the system in the last two months, and a Year 4 had fist-fought a Grad over a proofreading task last Thursday, so, there was likely more twiddling down the road.

"Why do you think people don't want to use you?" Morse asked.

"I'm actually on Project Rhapsody. That's the expert evidence I was talking about–the one I have to work on today?"

Morse raised an eyebrow and took a few good seconds to let that sink in.

"Wade's Rhapsody?"

"Yeah."

"What do they need *you* for?"

"Like I said, the evidence–"

"So you're using Wade to push back on my work. Is that what you're doing?"

"No, that's not what I'm doing, Morse." Ryuka pressed her temples and felt a migraine coming. "The timing is unfortunate. It's a confidential matter, so I can't say too much, but Osireion is having a hearing in ten days, and they *really* need this done as soon as possible."

Morse narrowed his eyes and scanned Ryuka's face for any signs of lying. All of a sudden, he seemed to have lost interest in this conversation.

"Make yourself useful, then. Don't bite off more than you can chew or the others will have to clean up after you. Still, your billing has gone down, so do more work. Oh, hope you get something that's 'good enough' for you. You obviously don't want mine."

He lifted a hand to press the hang-up button on his screen. Ryuka panicked. Was that all? Her most important phone call of the year would just end like this?

"Morse!" She stopped him. "I feel there's more to discuss, so should we pick this up later? I'll update the invite–"

"What else to discuss?"

"Um, we talked about this before, but I'm wondering if . . . you could nominate me for the Special Associate promotion this year?"

For a moment, Morse looked deeply confused. Then he held his chin high and gazed down at Ryuka's face as if looking at a messy kitchen sink he didn't have the time to clean.

"You're not ready."

"Morse, I've waited three years–"

"It's not time based. It's merit based. You saw the top ten projects on Friday. Which one of them has your fingerprints on it? You think Rhapsody makes you a big shot now? That's not enough. If I let you through but the committee doesn't even know you exist, that's a waste of everybody's time."

"I've prepared a case for myself. If you just let me do the interview—"

"I have another call."

He cut the line right there. Teams pulled up a black screen with five empty stars in the center, asking her to rate the quality of the call while reflecting her glum face. She slammed the laptop shut and sat in the elevator for a second. The car was still parked on Level 13, which seemed to be the highest she'd ever reach in this building. She raked her fingers through her hair and picked up her laptop, returned to the notes for her meeting with Laurent, and stared at the bullet points for a moment. Then she logged in to the Frenell research portal, which had access to countless online libraries of statutes, precedents, and academic journals. In the next twenty-four hours, she'd find out everything about B9-3T. Laurent Cheong would reconsider what he had to say, and Serotane would not be addictive because Frenell would not allow it to be. Then Wade would remember who she was, and Morse could keep his wrong opinion to himself.

"WHY ARE WE meeting this guy again?" Nolan popped a mint into his mouth as he watched Zoe set down a Negroni in front of Fischer and a bottle of sparkling water for him. Their waitress intern had broken her hip in her transitional dancer training, so she was helping out. Nolan liked Negroni. Sometimes he'd use it as a chaser for the neat gin traversing through his system right now.

"Wholesale orders need approval from a regional manager or above," Fischer said. "That's what this guy is."

"Has buying drugs always been this complicated? Is this some sort of societal pact to reduce addiction with bureaucracy?"

"You never had a dealer?"

"I don't do drugs."

"What do you do, then?"

"Nothing . . . really—"

"Ah, right, you're in my hookup group. About that thing you asked me—"

Before Fischer could continue, a suited guy stepped in. One glance at him was enough to convince Nolan that drug dealing was the next discipline to be gentrified. The guy dressed like he worked on Sauria Street, and he was here for a meeting about "Opportunities and Challenges on the Horizon for 2029—Top 10 Jobs to Disappear and What Will Replace Them." The three of them could leave Dandelion, find a random end-of-financial-year party to crash, and blend right in. Not only his outfit, his face looked familiar too.

"Ed? Ed Chateau?"

Despite being his contemporary, Nolan didn't have any remarkable memory about Chateau's time at Frenell, but he remembered everything about his departure. The morning of April 2, 2026, Nolan had arrived on his working floor—being Level 11 at the time—to find that his entire workbench had been vacated and secured as a crime scene for vandalism while a group of patrol robots cruised around for forensic procedures. Several workstations were demolished. Monitors shattered, laptops squashed, Productivity Shields torn, and ergonomic chairs broken to pieces and tossed aside. An educated guess would be that someone had come in early, trashed the place, then left with no intention of returning. So Nolan had asked Ryuka the obvious question: Who'd won the lottery?

Chateau hadn't won the lottery per se, but he'd secured first-round financing for his start-up, which produced a gadget called the Smile Enhancer. A transparent elastic band that you'd wear under your chin and secure over your ears to position the facial muscles, fine-tune your smile, and optimize your friendliness in remote meetings. The Smile Enhancer targeted the broad corporate workforce over the age of eighteen, college educated and trained in industries with a paramount focus on "relationship skills." It attracted viral media attention, and the investors were optimistic about its growth potential. They were particularly pleased with the marketing slogan: *Got a hard sell? Start with a better smile!*

Oh, it might be worth mentioning that Chateau was the one who'd come up with the concept of the Morse Meter.

It didn't take long for other businesses to smell the opportunity and launch their competing products like the Hostile Frown Neutralizer, the Psycho Stare Softener, the Power Pose Corrector, and, of course, the unicorn of the year—the Resting Bitch Face Remover. The Smile Enhancer also faced challenges from counterfeits and substitutes sold for $19.99 instead of $129.99, a war it had no means to win or even make it worth the legal costs. When grilled by the investors on the lukewarm growth, the board reportedly stated that they regretted focusing too much on immediate profitability, while they should've scaled more aggressively before the competition and knockoffs inundated the market.

Nevertheless, the real event that sealed the fate of the Smile Enhancer was the regulatory ban introduced across the white-collar industries. Inventions like the Smile Enhancer were classified as "enthusiasm defeat devices," which were believed to have profound detrimental effects on company culture and workplace camaraderie. A spokesperson for the Secretary of National Productivity denounced products like the Smile Enhancer as "a cowardly attack on the fundamental values of this great nation—the will to work hard and thrive above misery," and called their creators "grifters preying on the tired and the poor with a false promise of effortless success." The secretary also recommended an investigation into these companies' ties to foreign political influences, since their business model sparked suspicions of a joint-force conspiracy to infantilize this country's most productive generations.

Stories like this often reminded Nolan of the significance of a seemingly ordinary job—or the lack of it. You took the stability for granted, you thought you were better than the mundane spreadsheets and PPT aesthetics, you quit the job, and now you were a national security concern.

Following the regulatory crackdown, Chateau and his investors announced changes in the company's mission and embraced their new chapter. Unfortunately, none of the subsequent products took off like the Smile Enhancer. They burned through the seed funding faster than expected, and the next time the start-up made any splash in the news was about its "leadership change." Chateau stepped down from his position as the CEO, and his LinkedIn profile disappeared two months later—the telltale sign of someone falling off the corporate wagon, which was always a tragedy in itself: another life reduced to the meaningless waste that would never experience the wonder a thousand-dollar suit could do to neutralize an invalidated childhood.

OATH had been following Chateau's trajectory since his epic exit. The week after the CEO change, it hosted a roundtable on "Temptations and Pitfalls in the Age of Opportunities." The panel had discussed one real-life case study without revealing any personal details, yet all the Frenells under the stage had known exactly whose heartbreak that was. As the Acting Champion of Frenell Alumni and event moderator, Colleen had offered her advice for the younger generation: "We strongly encourage our employees to pursue their ambitions, but we also firmly believe that self-awareness and humility are the most important capital for long-term success."

"How much capital do you have?" Chateau cut to the chase.

"We're thinking maybe fifty grand?" Nolan said slowly, gauging Chateau's reaction before proposing a staged financing plan. Maybe they could work out something on a pay-per-use basis, like cloud services.

"Wholesale minimum is a hundred vials." Chateau shook his head. "So it'll be ninety-five, at least."

"Wait, what? I thought it was five hundred a bottle." Nolan looked at Fischer, who nodded in support.

"It was. But Rhapsody is our star product and we sell at market price–this morning it opened at nine fifty."

Nolan and Fischer stared at each other.

"If you don't have the budget"–Chateau sighed–"you can always get in touch with our retail agents for small purchases."

"Would you . . . take a five percent deposit?" Fischer asked.

"No."

"So what can we do now?" Nolan asked.

"Don't do drugs, I guess." Chateau got up to leave. "Even a shitty coffee costs twenty dollars these days. Get a job or something."

"Wait!" Nolan stopped him. "We can work this out . . . um, are you hiring by any chance?"

"What?" Chateau frowned.

"See, what we had in mind was more of a . . . brand ambassador deal. I don't use the drug myself–nothing wrong with your product! Just not my thing. Do you have a partner program or any . . . associate support?"

Chateau took a good look at Nolan's face as if he'd finally seen him for the first time since he'd walked in.

"Did we work together?"

"We did, yes," Nolan said. "Frenell, Year 3? We sat at the same bench?"

That information only got an ambivalent nod out of Chateau but did bring him back to the couch.

"If you want to be a Rhapsody Advocate, there is an option, but let's clarify some important details about the business so everybody's on the same page–we're not your average cocaine shop."

Chateau took out a notepad and started diagramming.

"Rhapsody is relatively new, but it's already gaining traction because of the utmost pleasure that no competitors can deliver.

We welcome the market reception and the fast growth, but our mission is more than selling a product. We pride ourselves on building a community where our customers can enjoy an exclusive, luxurious experience, and our distributors can grow into visionary, resourceful entrepreneurs. I'll send you a form after this so you can make an application. I also need a credit check and three letters of reference. Once you've been accepted, you can call yourself a Rhapsody representative and start working on your downline. You still need to carry some inventory–samples, freebies, relationship gifts, that kind of stuff. If you don't have enough funds to buy your stock outright, a limited amount of credit can be considered, but it depends on your rank–you start as an A1 Advocate, and the maximum advance we offer for your level is ten vials. As you develop your client base, build up your line of credit, we can talk about increasing your capacity. We evaluate your sales and your rank every month. According to our holistic approach, we consider not only your hard number of sales but also the quality and potential of your recruits, which we believe are good indicators of your project management and leadership skills. If you want a hundred pieces solely on credit, you need to be A7 at least–that's Vice President. It can take you . . . two years? Five years? Depends on your performance. Questions?"

"Yeah . . . this is very helpful." Nolan nodded as his brain scrapped all the old data about Chateau and opened a new file for this guy. "How long have you been doing this?"

"About six months, but I'm already A4. Buy me a drink if you want tips."

"Right, right. Is this all you do now?"

"I'm working on some new inventions," Chateau said and drew a circle in the air with his finger. "Dandelion gets some strategic advice from me every quarter, and I also do some consulting on the side."

"Oh yeah? What kind of consulting?"

"Detection of enthusiasm defeat devices and assessment of lost productivity." Chateau grinned. "Strong demand from Sauria Street—a good place to start your distribution network, by the way. You'll be selling to people with at least one income source and a clear predisposition to substance dependence, and it's hard to feel sorry for those sons of bitches."

"What if we need a large stock before we could move up the ranks?" Fischer asked. "Any chance of fast-tracking?"

"I'm afraid that won't be possible," Chateau said. "We have a robust system to ensure we target the right demographic and generate high-value users organically, which is more sustainable for the business in the long run."

He took two nasal sprays from his suitcase, then leaned over and winked.

"Since you two are my new recruits, here are some welcome freebies on me. Congratulations on your first step to true freedom. This might seem daunting at first, but don't worry, a good product sells itself—Rhapsody is a beast, and people *will* miss our juice once they've tried it."

"DID WE JUST get a second job?" Fischer waved goodbye as Chateau disappeared around the street corner.

"Side hustle," said Nolan. "How many leads do you have?"

"You, for one," said Fischer, followed by a long pause.

"We have no real-life skills." Nolan shook his head.

"About your friend's video in the group." Fischer finished the thought he'd had before Chateau had joined the conversation. "I've checked the account. It'd been marked for caution 'cause we thought he might be an HR—remember Eric Farlan? He took some Summer Cadet applicants home after a firm social and did *not* let them into the interview rounds? Anyway, he's with a different firm now, and his account went dormant for a while. That video was the first thing he'd posted in two years. I'm not sure if it's still him, but thought you should know."

&

"THANKS FOR TELLING me." Sai switched the phone to her left hand as she closed the balcony door and muted the smooth jazz behind her. The name Eric Farlan didn't mean much to her, but she thanked her friend for trying to help and said she'd update the police. Deep down, she wasn't holding her breath.

"You okay?" Nolan asked.

"Yeah, good." She rested her back against the balcony railing and examined the living room in front of her. Larger than her entire apartment and well lit with a soft glow that spoke of home, the room resembled a frame from a witty dramedy about middle-class New Yorkers finding the meaning of life—something Woody Allen or Noah Baumbach would make. A sanctuary that would welcome any aspiring artist with a trust fund. Henry was behind the kitchen island, playing with half a dozen bottles and giggling to himself. "Good," she repeated.

A sobering night breeze brushed her face and her bare shoulders, cooling her cheeks as it traveled down her midi dress. It wasn't cold; nevertheless it felt like a slap and made her shiver. The moment she stepped onto the balcony reminded her of the dramatic transition in a clichéd perfume ad—the scene where an actress enters a sparkly realm and her modest outfit turns into a bewitching evening gown—but in reverse. She said good night to Nolan and threw herself back into the hug of those warm lights. She had entered her sparkly realm, one that smelled like chocolate brownies and made her hungry.

"Try this." Henry handed over a double-walled tumbler containing a gulp of amber liquid. Sai accepted the glass with both hands and smiled at him from under her lashes. She'd never cared for the forceful character of spirits, but she took a sip and widened her eyes to look pleasantly surprised. As she breathed out, the aromatics passed through her nose and tickled her heart.

"This might be my best work!" Henry laughed and swirled his drink under his nose. "That limited edition of Ravenmore

ACE-50 used first-fill sherry casks for the majority of the aging process, but they transferred the whisky into bourbon casks for the last two years to give it a subtle wood finish. That delicate balance between the sweet, fruity quality and the woody accent is really hard to get right since the stuff from liquor stores has such prominent toffee notes, it could easily overpower the signature charred oak, and then it'd just taste like straight bourbon. A common trap is to add peat to somehow bring back the scotch attributes, but that's a dead giveaway of a blended drink. But guess what? I've found some awesome cedar extract and just the right type of peppercorn, and voilà!"

He went on to explain the difference between American and Japanese distillation processes and why he'd pick pot still over column still any day of the week. She listened, smiled, and nodded. Then she watched him funnel and filter the amber liquid from his punch bowl into a bottle that resembled a miniature museum. He filled it up to two-thirds to make a cognac backdrop that highlighted the bold, golden "50" at the front.

"This is gonna be *so good.*" He cradled the finished product and gave her a mischievous wink.

The playlist cut to an old song, and Sai recalled halfway through the first verse that it was the one Pace had been singing last Friday night—"Everybody Loves Somebody" by Dean Martin. Henry took her hands for a slow dance. His grip was gentle yet firm. His hands were gracious as to where they went, leading her in a way free of transgression. He froze for a second when she rested her head on his shoulder, then he stood her against his fridge and leaned in for a kiss. She dodged and slipped away, leaving him with a grin and a peck on the cheek. Holding on to her hand and gazing into her eyes, he made an adorable, whiny groan from his throat, until she hopped back and hugged him. Together, they cleaned up his lab and put away the bundle of forty-dollar whiskeys, assorted spices, and caramel coloring that they'd picked off the shelves earlier tonight. Sai tossed two empty mini bottles into the trash. They gave a dull clink that made her want to fish them out and smash them against the wall to hear them shatter.

Later, he drove her home. She asked him to drop her off on the last stretch of the homeless-free zone. It was quite a bit of a walk to where she lived, but she'd walk all right. He pulled over under a streetlight and teased her for treating him like a serial killer. She kissed him good night on the forehead.

Her lock was more stubborn than usual tonight. No matter how she jiggled it, she couldn't stick her key in. For a moment, she considered leaving this apartment and everything inside, moving on from this city and everything she remembered it by. She sighed and took out a plastic library card and slipped it into the gap next to the doorknob–worked like magic with old latches. She wrestled the door open and secured the jammer in place. The only window in her studio, for whatever reason, was located on the side of the corridor instead of the building exterior. So most of the time, she'd kept it shut and the curtains drawn, unless she wanted to be observed by strangers like a classroom pet. It took a moment for the damp smell to enclose her, and the invisible weight she'd temporarily escaped from seized her and dragged her down. There were days when she felt that weight had planted her feet into the soil, and she might never leave the ground again. She was having more and more days like that.

She walked across her studio and counted her steps. Seventeen feet from her front door to the end where she put her bed, then ten feet from one side to the other. That'd give her half of Henry's kitchen.

WHEN SHE FINALLY got through the line to the police station, the officer greeted her with a loud yawn before stating her name.

"Hi." Sai cleared her throat. "I'm calling to follow up on the case I spoke to Officer Haley about last week–"

"If it's Haley's case, you need to call him tomorrow."

"I just want to give him a name—"

"He's not in. Call back tomorrow."

"Would you please take a message—"

"I can't help you. It's Haley's case. Do you understand me?"

Sai took a deep breath and steadied her voice.

"It's really just a name I want to give him because I think it's relevant and he should look into it. It's two words."

There was a brief silence, then a long sigh. "You think it's relevant," the officer muttered, but she took down the name after all. "Eric. Farlan. M'kay?" she grumbled as she wrote. The line went dead on her last syllable.

Sai's phone screen returned to her wallpaper, and the notification bar displayed a new message from Henry.

I had a great time tonight.

Then a smiley face—the one with the rosy cheeks.

She set a timer to reply in half an hour. She'd use this time to craft a dignified answer thanking him for his hospitality, telling him that she'd enjoyed his company, and complimenting his taste in music and drinks. Overall, a message that would make him propose the next meetup without her saying it—the typical post-date response from a "high-value lady." She'd also need to google some of the things he'd said tonight so she could add her own thoughts to them. The first thing she typed into the search bar was "Ravenmore ACE-50, limited edition," and the first thing she saw was a price tag of seventy-five thousand dollars.

After scrolling back to the top of their chat history, Sai went through each text word by word, analyzing the tone and examining if she'd missed any nuance or made any unwise move that she'd need to remediate. In her mind, she read out Henry's part in his voice, adding a personal touch of tenderness or playfulness as appropriate to the context. She played back their interactions, from the first night he'd found her in a hall of disgrace till minutes ago, when he'd said to her: *I had a great time tonight.*

Yeah, so had she.
So had she.

7

"EXACTLY WHAT'S THE pain point?"

Wade rested in his reclining chair with his feet up on his desk, staring at the ceiling as he digested Nolan's report.

"The . . . pain point," said Nolan, "is basically, we want the drugs, but we don't have the money."

"Have you considered staged financing?"

"They don't have much appetite for that, I'm afraid."

"So you just came back like this?" Wade glanced at Nolan. "I thought your profile said you have a 'can-do' attitude."

"We did explore an alternative—"

"Right, the pyramid option!" Wade exclaimed. "That's your brilliant idea, isn't it? Or have I misunderstood you?"

"It alleviates the capital pressure and helps us remain agile because of reduced physical transactions. Once we've found enough ambitious, autonomous downline recruits, this can turn into a passive, compounding money machine—"

"Except the coordination and collection would be a pain in the ass. We don't need more pain-in-the-ass nitpicking slow-paying clients. This is the kind of low-value work that'll tarnish the Frenell brand."

After the Grads' Debut, Nolan received a generic notification from Frenell's project management system that he was now the lead Associate on a new matter for "Happy Place Inc." The project involved "strategic advice on fast-moving consumer goods distribution and assistance with business presence establishment." Any revenue generated from the "side hustle" that Nolan set up with Wade's twenty-dollar angel investment would be billed to this matter and recharacterized as "professional services fees."

Wade's whale hunting hadn't gone as expected, so he'd captured an octopus and painted it blue.

"If we want a more streamlined B2B model"—Nolan took a deep breath—"there are the conventional wholesale or franchise options. But again, the initial capital—"

"We're running in circles." Wade threw his hands in the air. "If a client asked you, 'How do I build my drug dealership?' you'd just tell them, 'You need money'?"

"Well . . . money definitely helps."

"You think? If it's something that easy, why would clients come to us, then?"

"Mr. Wade, I'm not a magician."

"Turn into one if you want to stay here." Wade took his feet off the desk and leaned on his elbows. "If God wanted to send a second flood to Earth, he'd first ask Frenell how to do it."

Nolan sustained a polite smile and pondered how to end this conversation without resorting to violence. His insides were in knots, and he struggled to keep his thinking coherent since he hadn't had his "cure" this morning. As part of his drinking ethics, he maintained a strict sixteen-hour dry window between two benders. It kept the alcohol from seeping through his pores but made him slightly more murderous. To make things worse, Wade's leg shaking seemed to be getting noisier by the second.

Suddenly, Wade sprang out of his chair and paced in front of his floor-to-ceiling windows. The shower of sunlight did not mellow him, and he bounded to the guest side of the desk, towering over Nolan and pressing his face down from above like an angry deity. Nolan smelled a trace of ammonia on his breath.

"How much do you have on you right now?"

"Money? Or—"

"The stuff! Jesus!" Wade slammed both hands on the cherrywood. "What's wrong with you today? Go do a line in the bathroom so you can keep up!"

"Okay! Okay!" Nolan raised his hands in surrender, then took out the welcome gift he'd gotten from Chateau yesterday. Wade snatched it and shoved the tip inside his nose, pumped twice on each side, then groaned like a relieved asthma patient. He returned to pacing in the sun until his hands stopped trembling and his breathing steadied. Once he'd strolled back to his seat, he twisted off the nozzle and squeezed a thin stream into his leftover coffee. When he put the bottle down, it was half-empty.

Wade wiped the rim of his nose with his thumb, then rubbed the residue on his gums. "That's better." He smiled with his eyes wide open. "Where were we? Right, I don't want to hear money, money, money, money, money . . . so you will stop asking for it. Next time we speak, there will only be one item on the agenda: you show me everything is ready to go, and I'll start signing invoices."

"If you want drug money, Mr. Wade"—Nolan kept his voice low and calm—"why don't you invest in a proper drug business? Why would you want to divert that revenue to Frenell, which you'll have to share with the other Partners?"

"Because, son," said Wade, "I'm not a filthy drug dealer."

&

NOLAN'S SMART WATCH buzzed when he picked up his ristretto from the counter of the IPC café—the dry window had expired. He rushed to the Rage Room in the back, stood by the door, and listened. No weeping, yelling, or smashing sounds, so he went in. It was empty. After all, it was only nine in the morning. He put his coffee on top of the credenza storing the plates and drew a mini bottle of Jack Daniel's out of his jacket. He downed the drink and stuffed the empty back into his pocket for later disposal. Then he took a sip of the intense brew and pushed it around inside his mouth with his tongue, until it had covered every inch where alcohol had passed through. Once the coffee cup was also empty, he left the Rage Room and headed toward the gym.

He opened the locker labeled "out of order" with the code in the text he'd received. Lying inside was a canvas pouch. He took it out and counted its contents, frowning.

The advance is ten, and I paid for a whole dozen, he texted Chateau.

Tip No. 1 from A4 senpai: never put all eggs in 1 basket, suppose you get robbed? Chateau replied. *Unload these, then collect your next batch.*

Are you guys hoarding the supply? Nolan asked. Rhapsody had opened at eleven hundred this morning.

No response.

Nolan slammed the locker shut and strode toward the exit. As he passed the crowd surrounding the checkout counter, a familiar voice flew out of the ring of conflict.

"Call your manager out! This is unacceptable!"

Luc Edward was demanding his cold brew, which was already ten minutes late. His watery eyes bulged as colorful words spewed from his lips. His face flushed not with anger but with anxiety, which was understandable—he'd have to justify his Idle Time spending. If someone else could get their shitty coffee in ten minutes, why would you need twenty?

&

"I'M WRITING A fifty-page advice on synergistic optimization of value chains and frictionless multijurisdictional scalability," Luc said as he fidgeted with his coffee cup. "The key is to channel the momentum of technological revolution and leverage the hidden value of a company's data assets, while intersecting AI and conventional management to enhance the efficacy of resource command, therefore promoting holistic decision-making in a fragmented global landscape and achieving real-time agility and resiliency against black swan events. Forget about blockchain and metaverse—this is the real 'next big thing.'"

Under normal circumstances, Nolan wouldn't choose to hang out with Luc. The kid talked like he was a fictional character and his creator was really worried about hitting the word count. But if he was going to dope the kid up, the least he could do was let him charge "Team Building" for it.

"Interesting. Do you have a tech background?" Nolan asked.

"Nope, but I'll pick it up."

Five years ago, something that complex and gibberish-sounding would've been an Associate-level job. "Capacity stretching" had become an open secret on Sauria Street. Once the newbies had demonstrated what they were capable of and how desperate they were to prove their worth, the heavy lifting began to roll down the hierarchy until it buried the ones at the bottom like a landslide.

Timekeepers were salaried, and "professionals" were exempt from minimum wage and overtime laws—besides, their contracts explicitly stated they'd put in extra hours as required by the workload. So, a firm could swap one twelve-hundred-dollar Special Associate for two six-hundred-dollar Graduates, or stretch one day of someone expensive to two days of cheaper labor, and like that, the project suddenly had more hands on the deck or more actual working hours. It was the same budget and the same turnaround, but a different bucket of resources who were eager to please and ready to give up their nights and weekends for the "recognition."

The Partners were happy because it made cost control easier. The clients were happy since every budget crunch seemed to be accommodated, leaving room for the next slash. Even the Graduates were happy, as they were gaining hands-on experience with high-value work from day one.

It's not exploitation if it's voluntary.

But what was left for the Special and Not-So-Special Associates in the middle? Growth generation: watch the market and unlock those opportunities hidden under the debris of financial crises. People management: the hardest goddamn job in the entire goddamn world. And of course, relationship, relationship, relationship.

"I want to be a Star Biller this month, and all the months after," Luc said.

"How do you unwind?" Nolan stared at Luc's jittery hands. "How do you . . . take the edge off? Know what I mean?"

"I jog." Luc peeked at Nolan, then looked away.

"It's okay. Part of my Buddy responsibility is to give you a safe space to say things you can't tell a Partner. You know what? I'll go first—I do coke, every other day, and molly, but not recently 'cause there haven't been any deep house concerts since . . . forever. Oh, and there's a decent chance that I'm addicted to sex."

He took out his phone and showed Luc his feed from Sauria Street Adventures. Someone was in the mood for a quickie before lunch and waiting for offers.

Luc studied Nolan's face, then cleared his throat, his gaze hopping from corner to corner.

"My doctor gave me something to relax . . . real doctor. I don't even take it that often, just when there's a big meeting coming up and I have to be on top of my game, or when the work is a bit challenging, like . . ."

"Like a fifty-page advice on something you don't really understand?"

Luc fell quiet.

"So what happened back there? Missed your chill pill this morning?"

"Good days, bad days." The boy shrugged.

Nolan glanced around them, then pushed a bottle of Rhapsody across the table with two fingers.

"Try it. You'll never need another prescription for anything else. I can give you a Buddy discount."

"I'm not sure–"

"You want to work for Wade, don't you? That's a really tight ship. You can't have bad days. If he sees you lose control like you did with that barista, you're done. Imagine you feel overwhelmed and lash out at a client–"

Luc grabbed the bottle but kept it away from his face. He stared at it for one second too long. Nolan tutted and reached out a hand, palm up.

"It's your choice. You don't want it, I can take it to your peers–"

A ghostly grin emerged on Nolan's face when Luc bent down under the table and took a hit. When the kid bolted back up, his gaze landed on Nolan and sliced right through him.

"I see what's wrong with the structure now–the part about supply chain risks should come before platform integration. And we need an overview of the architecture or the whole thing will be on stilts."

He drew a deep breath and smiled at Nolan.

"I need to get back to work."

"This is a marathon, not a sprint." Nolan patted Luc on the back and helped him stow the spray in his pocket. "Don't mix your drugs."

"HELP ME UNDERSTAND why Serotane makes people feel so good, Doctor." Ryuka turned to her notes. "So, B9-3T is a synthetic cocktail that raises both the level of dopamine and the level of serotonin in a user's brain."

"That's right. B9-3T inhibits the reuptake of those neurotransmitters and therefore increases their concentration in the synapse, meaning there will be more dopamine and serotonin to bind to their receptors when B9-3T is present, compared to the normal situation without the drug."

It was 9:00 p.m. in Singapore, and Laurent Cheong had just returned from the gym. Without the glasses, the shadows under his eyes made him seem tired, but Ryuka preferred him this way—exhausted, off guard, plain as an open book.

"Let's be careful with words like 'normal,'" said Ryuka. "We don't want to inadvertently reinforce any unconscious bias. In your study, were you able to isolate the dopamine stream of B9-3T's action from the serotonin stream? I'm asking because section 1.6 of your report recorded different rates of increase."

"It's true that B9-3T elevates the two neurotransmitters differently." Laurent nodded. "But we weren't able to 'decompose' the compound so it only affected one of the two, if that's what you meant. You're right that the compound has dual properties, but it's not simply adding one on top of another."

"So it's not like cocaine and molly had a baby."

"If you have to put it that way." Laurent chuckled.

"I'm glad we've clarified that." Ryuka smiled. "You see, Dr. Cheong, this gives us some technical difficulties in regulation. I won't bore you with the legalese about the Controlled Narcotics and Chemicals Act, but it has five schedules that assign the regulated drugs to different groups, and these drugs have quite distinct mechanisms. For example, opioids affect endorphin transmission and they're in Schedule II. Benzodiazepines bind to GABA receptors and they sit in Schedule IV. We mentioned in the last meeting that context is important in legislation. If we can't ascertain how B9-3T works on each neurotransmitter and which one of its dual streams is more . . . significant, then we might have trouble scheduling it accurately. In light of that, maybe a more prudent conclusion is that we need further studies on B9-3T's working mechanism? Not to say that we'll never regulate it, but maybe for now it's premature?"

All the above was true except the "if" part. The law didn't group the drugs by the neurotransmitters they affected but by the level of their potential for abuse, their possibility of safe use, and the consequences of their abuse. On its own, the obscurity in B9-3T's mechanism of action wouldn't be enough to keep the drug off the hook, but it might be enough to get Laurent to say "there is limited scientific knowledge regarding the pharmacological effect of Serotane at present," which was one of the key factors that could possibly stop an immediate ban from the DSA.

Ryuka had had two hours of sleep last night and spent every waking minute looking for holes in Laurent's report and the Lindau study. It hadn't gotten her far and made her realize she was looking at a near-perfect specimen of an "open-and-shut case." Her best hope would be to nudge Laurent away from "addictive" and into the gray area of "inconclusive"–*Hey, we don't know enough yet, so hold your horses.*

Laurent gave her question some thought, then he grinned at Ryuka and responded in the tone of a college professor facing a first-year know-it-all:

"If we focus on the classification of B9-3T, Miss Murong, we'll miss the big picture. The telltale sign of addiction is the pattern of use, tolerance, and withdrawal. The case studies we reviewed demonstrated a clear and consistent cycle of craving, which started with intrusive thoughts, then progressed to compulsion, physical craving, and at last, drug-seeking behavior. It doesn't matter how you shuffle the drugs on paper, 'addictive' means addictive. Also, I might not be a legal expert, but I did some research on the Controlled Narcotics and Chemicals Act for the study. If my memory is correct, the classification of a drug in the schedules is based on its risk of abuse rather than the neurotransmitters it targets, am I right?"

"Let's look at this from a different angle." Ryuka cleared her throat. "According to *Merriam-Webster*, 'addiction' is 'a compulsive, chronic, physiological or psychological need for a habit-forming substance, behavior, or activity having *harmful* physical, psychological, or social effects'—I'm not gonna read the whole paragraph, but basically, Doctor, addiction is the state of 'needing something that's *bad* for you.'"

"Okay?"

"So the supposedly 'addictive' substance should cause *harm*."

"That can't possibly be where you're going—"

"I am going there, actually. The well-documented effects of Serotane include: instant boost of motivation and clarity, reduced feelings of despair, reduced anxiety, and improved concentration. About forty percent of users also reported better sleep and better social interactions."

"You're describing Serotane's treatment benefits. If you turn to section 2.4 of my report, you'll see a wide range of physical pain and discomfort, extreme mood swings, return of depression symptoms with prolonged episodes, hallucination, even delirium."

"Side effects are different from harm."

"Those are not 'side effects,' Miss Murong. They're symptoms of severe withdrawal. You don't get those when using the drug. You get them when you want to stop but can't."

"They *can't* stop, or they don't want to?"

"I'm sorry?"

"A lot of people drink to relax, to feel better, and to be less awkward at social events. Sure, sometimes they might get an itch, especially when they're fresh off a bender, but does that mean we should bring back Prohibition?"

"You can't be serious." The smile on Laurent's face disappeared. "Unless you've been living under a rock, you must've seen what this drug could do by now. Ten minutes on YouTube alone should be enough."

Ryuka knew what Laurent was referring to. Every now and then, she'd get clips in her social media feed about the horrifying state Grand Ivory had fallen into. They all seemed to have the same formula: set in a tent city, most likely the "headquarters" near the Athena River; featuring a selection of people who used to be people and were now just shadows of sadness, yelling at trees or drifting into eerie peace, with God knows what unfolding behind their smiles; then a doctor or a pharmacist would explain the danger of the substance, and anywhere in between you'd get a YouTube warning to disable your ad blocker. She might have opened the first one or two. The rest, she'd only scanned the titles. It was getting hard to keep up with every new "epidemic" or "crisis" that came out every six months.

"Addiction is a disease of the brain." Laurent spoke in a low, restrained voice with an edge he was trying to contain. "Nobody would *choose* to live like that."

He tousled his hair in frustration and stared outside the frame in silence. Ryuka recognized a familiar emotion that pinched her stomach. An emotion that she'd been exquisitely well trained to detect over the years: disappointment.

Why do you think people don't want to use you?

"Thank you for your insight, Doctor." She lowered her eyes and shut off the unwanted commentary. "But we don't make laws based on what's trending on YouTube. I also have to point out that none of the reports to date have concretely identified Serotane as the cause of the madness out there. We can't stop the public from speculating, but we can't regulate everything that has a conspiracy theory, or we'll turn this country into everyone's nanny. I hate to sound unsympathetic, but in this profession, we have to defend the undefendable by design of the system. The people you see in those videos . . . there's more than one thing going wrong in their lives, and they probably have more than one drug in their diet."

"Please don't say things like that—"

"That reminds me, is Serotane even B9-3T?"

"I beg your pardon?"

"I assume you're aware of the 2023 study by Professor Lieu-Fuller et al., which found that, when B9-3T was ingested, it was metabolized to the cytochrome enzyme CYP4B6 and a variety of inactive metabolites, including 3-hydroxythetamine—let's call it HT-3. A unique feature of Serotane is that it contains 4,6-trimethylbenzoic acid, which activates the typically inactive HT-3 and gives us another compound, TPT-6. A separate study in 2025 by St. Kingsman University found that TPT-6 appeared to have therapeutic effects that strongly resembled two other commonly used antidepressants on the market: sertraline and escitalopram. Dr. Cheong, would it be possible that what gives Serotane its power is not B9-3T but this new compound, TPT-6?"

She tossed out her last card. If all efforts to keep B9-3T off the Schedules failed, Osireion might consider rebranding as an alternative. They'd have to do something about their labeling and get additional advice on what "active ingredient" meant, but they'd be able to keep the drug on the market, which would be their second-best outcome, and hey, it could also mean more work for Frenell.

Laurent was taken aback by this proposition and stuttered for a second.

"But . . . the active ingredient of Serotane is B9-3T."

"Dr. Cheong, you'll see that the studies I just mentioned are fairly new. This could be a new development that we should take into account."

"If you take Serotane, you're taking B9-3T. That's how your client Osireion and Ithaca have been marketing this drug all these years."

"Let's forget about marketing for a second. The point is, there are two candidates for Serotane's effects, and we may have been giving credit to the wrong one."

"This is getting ridiculous—"

"Fine, maybe B9-3T is addictive, but Serotane is not B9-3T."

"For the purpose of my study—"

"You can't say for sure it's not TPT-6 that's working."

"Please let me finish—"

"You don't know, do you?"

"It doesn't matter!" Laurent raised his voice slightly and drew a deep breath. "My apologies, but what I've been trying to tell you is that in those cases, Serotane was administered as a whole instead of an isolated B9-3T compound. Whichever ingredient is more . . . 'active,' B9-3T or TPT-6, it doesn't matter because what we've found addictive is the pill itself."

Don't bite off more than you can chew, or the others will have to clean up after you.

For a moment, there was no sound on either end. Laurent had returned to the poised man he'd been when they first met. He looked at Ryuka with a faint smile as if he felt sorry for her.

"Miss Murong, you can argue that Serotane has a different formula for addiction, a different degree of addiction, or it's not even what we think it is at all, which I don't believe is true. They clearly mean different things to lawyers, I see that now, but they all mean the same thing to me. As a neuroscientist, I'm telling you: Serotane is addictive, and it's a dangerous drug."

You're not ready . . .

Ryuka sank into silence as she munched on Laurent's words. A fleeting spark flashed across her mind, and she snatched it.

"You're a neuroscientist, you say?"

"Well, yes."

"So you're not a chemist or a pharmacologist."

"No, I'm not."

She flipped to exhibit A of Laurent's draft report, which set out his CV. As she went through his education and qualifications, the vague "off" feeling she'd had when researching Laurent's previous assignments became clearer—both his PhD and master's were in neuroscience. No background in medicine, chemistry, biology, or pharmacology. And his bachelor's degree? Ha! Psychology—not even a real science!

She burst out laughing, which must have been an extraordinary laugh given how concerned Laurent suddenly looked. Ryuka Murong was not finished. She still had one more card to play. If you can't edit the things being said, edit the person who says it. If this guy wouldn't say what he had to say, he might as well forever hold his peace.

"WE SHOULD REPLACE the expert. I know it'll take extra time, but we'd be better off not using his evidence at all. I've found two new candidates, one in Hamburg and one in New Zealand. The DSA released a supplementary report from Lindau yesterday, so we might have some ground for an extension. Let's put someone on a plane to track down a substitute so we can show we're not dragging our feet—"

"Hold on, who gave you all these instructions?" Emma pulled her face out of her stack of binders and looked at Ryuka with a frown.

"Um, no one, I just thought them up."

"Just do what you were told, please." Emma let out a loud sigh. "So what's the verdict? Addictive or not?"

"Well, it's hard to make him budge—"

Emma pursed her lips and shook her head.

"You owe me two hundred dollars."

"Huh?"

"You just made me lose two hundred to Hayden." She flopped back into her chair and tapped her chin with her red pen. "We thought it might be worth it to let you have a go, but, well, it is what it is. I think it's time you tell your guy that if he wants to stay in this country, he'd better reevaluate his position. We need the report signed by tomorrow, and it shouldn't contain any inflammatory words like—"

"Wait, wait, wait . . ." Ryuka pulled back as if to examine an abstract painting she didn't understand. "What are you talking about?"

"The guy is on H-1B and Eldridge University is sponsoring his visa. Osireion has been a pretty generous donor for a bunch of universities, including Eldridge, so they could've asked someone from the faculty to have a little chat with Cheong to move things forward, but Andrej didn't want to go there unless absolutely necessary. That's where you came in. Remember, I'm the one who had faith in you, and it cost me two hundred bucks."

Ryuka felt a punch in her gut.

"Is this what you planned to do this whole time?"

Emma shrugged.

"This is . . . wrong." Ryuka took a few good moments to find the right word.

Emma gave her a funny look, then she opened a new tab in her browser and navigated to Laurent's Instagram. The latest post was a soft-smiling woman holding a child up against an illuminated aquarium tank so he could say hello to a turtle.

"Technically, he's an employee of Eldridge. He should do what's in the best interest of his employer, and you have to do your job—there's nothing personal. Look, he's an easy case—his wife and kids just moved here last year and his son is about to start school in August. Cute, huh? It's gonna be a shit show if he has to uproot their lives again and get everything back on track in three months, yeah?"

"No, we don't have to do this." Ryuka frowned. "Let's call the two substitutes first and see what they say—"

"Please don't create more work." Emma dropped her face into her palms and hunched over her mountain of binders. "I just . . . no more work, no."

THAT DAY, RYUKA finished early and arrived home around 9:00 p.m. She skipped dinner, went straight into the shower, then straight to bed. She slept until she fell out of sleep at three in the morning, and the lump she'd felt in her stomach was still there. The first thing she did was reach for her phone. Nothing new in the world called for her attention except for some force-fed ads she couldn't disable, plus a new message on her LinkedIn. Groggy and somnolent, yet she recognized Laurent's face in his profile. That kicked her out of her drowsiness.

Why was this guy messaging her? He would've been instructed early in the project to minimize written communications with Frenell–a common practice to avoid leaving discoverable records of lawyers' involvement in the expert evidence in case a legal professional privilege claim failed. That said, there was nothing stopping Laurent from sending a simple email if it was work, yet he'd taken the trouble to search her out and make contact outside the Frenell realm.

"Please don't be a dick. Please don't be a dick," she muttered as she opened the message.

It wasn't a picture of any body parts or a request for such. It was a YouTube video filmed on the wrong side of the Athena River. A reporter from a local network gave a simple opening before entering the land of the forgotten. Among the tattered tents and makeshift shelters, the residents had found some sort of order out of the chaos and carved out a thin path across the maze. It was daytime; the ones who hadn't gone into the city were tending to their living spaces, doing their laundry by the water, or resting under cover. They either flicked a disdainful glance at the camera when it got too close for their liking, or they were too engrossed in their own business to notice they were on display. Near the water, two people next to a bridge pier caught the crew's attention. A gray-haired Uphill volunteer was snapping her fingers in front of the eyes of a homeless man as she called out his name and checked his pupils. Facial hair had obscured his features yet had not removed all traces of youth. As the frame centered on the man's expression, the voiceover began to explain how he'd encountered the new Four Horsemen: unemployment, multiple criminal charges, homelessness, and addiction. Once those four had closed the loop, they would create a séance trap that was almost impossible to escape.

In the middle of the narration, the man's stuporous face thawed and broke into an exuberant smile.

It was then Ryuka recognized that sharp canine tooth on the left side of his mouth and the asymmetrical stretch of his upper lip. With great certainty, she knew underneath that beard there were dimples that were no longer visible. An estranged name emerged: Ronan Seymour, the former Frenell Year 4 Associate who had woken up one day and lost the ability to see human faces.

SAI ADJUSTED HER pendant and nestled it in the center of her wrap dress's neckline so the micro camera could get a clear view. She laced her fingers and cupped her hands over the pocket of the jacket draped over her shoulders. Touching the edges of the rectangular object soothed her. That, and knowing that her phone was capturing the circus show.

After her induction, she'd found the product specifications of the wand metal detector online. Its sensitivity configurations enabled it to pick up a medium-sized pistol from nine inches away, a large knife and box cutters from five, razor blades from three, a .22 long rifle bullet from two, and for items as small as foil-wrapped drugs or tiny jewelry, it had to get into the one-inch range. She recalled the way the guard had scanned her—like a half-hearted knighthood accolade performed by a drunk. There was a decent chance he wouldn't pick up anything. Even if they got a beep, he'd need a pair of hawk eyes and several good moments to realize this petite onyx charm was more than a decoration. It offered a 180-degree ultrawide field of view, and the battery could hold up to six hours. This thing had cost her five hundred dollars, so it'd better do what it said it would.

She had sawed off the rubber sole of her right platform boot and hollowed out a compartment just big enough to sleeve her phone. The bottom half had then been realigned to the underside of her boot and secured in place with four pairs of magnets. She'd walked in front of the mirror to test it out, and mimicked a security check to see how far she'd have to bend down to get to her ankles. There was also a decent chance that the guard would be having a really bad day with his osteoarthritis.

She'd felt optimistic about taking chances because she would have her lucky charm with her tonight.

As she "turned off" the dummy phone she'd bought online for fifty dollars and dropped it into the collection tray, the guard stared at the clingy fabric that highlighted the contours of her body and the absence of any irregular bulges that could be a weapon. He blew out a loud sigh but glided the detector across her torso anyway. No beeps. Then he gazed at her boots. That was when Henry hopped over like an eager usher. Sai gave the guard an apologetic smile and a little shrug as she hooked Henry's arm–guess they wouldn't have the time to take her shoes off. With a backhand wave, the guard dismissed her and scorned behind her back.

Once the coast was clear, she visited the bathroom, where she took out her phone, connected the camera, and flipped the hard plastic case backward to cover the touchscreen so the rubbing and bumping inside her pocket wouldn't accidentally turn off the filming. Then she found Henry and sat down on the edge of his booth without saying a word. Nobody paid attention to her, as they were captivated by Henry's anecdote about how he'd won this "Ravenmore ACE-5o" in a freestyle ski contest against a friend of his father's.

Flanking Henry and his center seat, Wade was on chardonnay tonight while Lindsay had a fancy cocktail in front of him. A gin martini with a floating hollow ice sphere through which a shot of dry vermouth seeped and gradually turned the martini into a tuxedo. Opposite Sai, Pace stared at her fingernails with a light pout. She had as much passion for whiskeys as she did cars and gardening. Andrej passed by and planned to move along after some pleasantries, but he sat down next to Pace when he heard the last name Carrollton. Wade signaled Pace to swap with Andrej, which drew his old-time Asset into his arm's reach and pushed Pace back to the edge.

"I heard someone made an NFT for this whisky," Lindsay said while Henry poured a round of his masterpiece.

"Someone has, indeed, but unfortunately I don't own it." Henry smiled.

"Is NFT still relevant? I thought crypto had crashed," Pace chimed in as she sniffed the drink. No response from the table except for a cackle from Lindsay.

"Crypto is crypto, honey. NFT is art."

Pace rolled her eyes discreetly and took a sip, then she performed the same "impressed peasant girl" act that Sai had put on when she'd first tasted the juice.

Andrej studied the liquor with mild curiosity before he brought it to his lips. The first sip went down easy but did not spark excitement commensurate with that backstory. Then he finished his one serving the same way anyone would finish any drink on a quiet night. He politely turned down Henry's offer for another one and ordered a sparkling water with lime, looking as bored as he had been before the drink. Next to him, Wade did not let the mysterious nectar access his sacred palate until he'd completed the full swirl-and-nose ritual. There was a subtle pause before he swallowed. With a flawless smile, he repeated the swirling and nosing and took another sip. Then he put down the glass and never touched it again for the rest of the night.

"Beautiful!" Lindsay exclaimed. "The complexity of it!"

"Please, do elaborate." Wade presented Lindsay to the group with a palm-up hand. "Lindsay is our expert on anything that has depth and history."

"I'm getting a really gorgeous butterscotch head note with a hint of a fruity taste, maybe peach." Lindsay closed his eyes and nodded. "It doesn't linger at the back of your tongue. They likely did that on purpose to give a philosophical sense of fleeting and imply something scarce and precious, like time. Oh, I'm getting the retronasal olfaction just now . . . quite a kick, this one."

"It's certainly a memorable taste," Wade concurred.

"Interesting," said Lindsay. "The maker is obviously bold for going against the mainstream and making their whisky not as smooth. But it's also intelligent in counterbalancing the strong opening with a sweet aftertaste. Hang on . . . is it honey?"

"What can I say? It *is* honey!" Henry gave a golf clap.

It was a two-dollar Wild Turkey mini. It had real honey in it.

"A mild burn with a thin finish—now, that's a statement. There also seems to be an accent grain. Could be rye or corn, which adds an extra layer and really enriches the character of the drink."

"Isn't 'single-malt' supposed to be just one type of barley?" Andrej asked.

"Well, it depends on the way you look at it." Lindsay stared into the distance as he pondered. "What does 'single' mean? If we mix multiple parts of the same grain, from the same distillery, but of different ages, are they still the same malt? Say, the five-year-old you, the present you, and the fifty-year-old you, are they all the same person? And if we take 'malt' as a verb for the process of malting, then even if the mash contains various grains, arguably the product can still be called 'single-malt' as a reference to one consolidated malting process."

Andrej raised an eyebrow but did not press further.

"And one thing I find particularly fascinating is this unexpected pop of a dry, spicy taste coming through the base note." Lindsay rubbed his chin as he inspected the liquid. "It's quite subtle, and it only bounces back up after it goes down. Confident, very confident, like an audacious declaration that says: I'm here, and I'm not going anywhere."

Sai was impressed. Lord M still had it—he'd detected the vodka.

That was the highlight of the night, and the rest was less eventful. After finishing his water, Andrej stretched an arm across the table to shake Henry's hand and wished him a good night, then extricated himself from the scene before Wade could grab hold of him. Lindsay had enjoyed Henry's special blend so much that he proposed they start an exclusive drinking club to share rare finds, and maybe he could give Henry some elder wisdom in exchange for Senator Carrollton's insights about the weather on the Hill. He'd feel less enthusiastic about the idea the next morning once the hangover kicked in, but he'd blame it on that overengineered cocktail he'd had earlier.

"God, I wish I could film that! I can't stand those pretentious buffoons!"

Henry skipped alongside Sai as he walked her to the subway and sobered up at his own pace. She watched him with a smile and let him bump into her without a complaint. This was the old Henry she remembered. Five years ago, she'd found his temperament silly. But now, his childlike exuberance peeled off the layers of pretense that had been clinging onto her like a crust and electrified the air around them. It brought out a comforting scent like the fresh linens in her own room, reminding her of somewhere she could be safely bare.

As they reached the Sauria Street Station, Henry stopped and scanned his surroundings with a stern face, as if watching the world shift back to its true shape.

"The thing is, I wish I enjoyed that stupid shenanigan," he said. "But I zoned out halfway 'cause when I looked at those talking heads, all I could think of was, is *this* what I'm turning into? God, those people bore me out of my mind. Everything is a dick-measuring contest and nothing is important except money and status, because those are all they know and those are all they have. Their fortune did not make them better. It only helped them mask what they really are. But I think people are catching on, Saidah. People are sick of forty-dollar liquor with a thousand-dollar price tag, and one day, they'll realize how much angrier they should've been this whole time. That scares the hell out of me, and I can't wait for it to happen."

He lifted his face and shouted into the night sky.

"The emperor is naked! That asshole has always been naked!"

Then he laughed. Even the city looked alive for a moment. Sai swung herself in front of him and hooked his neck with one hand. On tiptoes, she sent her lips to his. His eyes widened, then he closed them as he circled her waist and drew her to him, lifting her heels farther above the ground, then gently letting them land.

"I'm so glad I went to that Frenell party." He brushed her hair off her forehead to take a good look at what he'd found. "You're different, Saidah. You've always been. With you, I feel I can be completely honest."

He held the back of her head and leaned in to kiss her again. She stopped him with a hand on his chest.

"I need to tell you something . . . because that's also how I want to be with you–completely honest."

Henry tilted his head and gave her an intrigued stare. She cradled his face with one hand and thumbed his cheek. His blush had faded a little.

"You work for Secretary Berlin of the DSA, don't you?"

8

"THIS IS NICE." Ryuka sipped her double espresso. "When was the last time we had coffee together? In the sun?"

"Been a while," said Nolan. "Wish Sai were here, though."

"What's she doing these days?"

"No idea. We need a proper catch-up."

"Totally . . . so are you gonna tell me what *that* is about or are you waiting for me to ask?"

They were sitting at a square coffee table on the balcony of the Level 20 café, facing each other. On Ryuka's left, there was this random dude she had no memory of meeting. On her right, Luc's body slouched into a wheelchair, which she'd correctly identified as their priority. With the oversize sunglasses covering half of his tilted face, Luc looked like he'd dozed off in the warm sun.

That wasn't how Nolan had found him.

Earlier that morning, Nolan had descended to Level 9 to collect the second installment for his first sale. Yesterday was payday, and he'd like to get to Luc before his landlord and Whole Foods did.

The moment he entered the open plan, he thought he was back in the tent city. A dozen Grads had brought sleeping bags to the office, and some of them still had a body inside. The empty ones lay open across the floor, airing out the human residuals from the night before while their owners freshened up in the bathrooms or the communal showers on Level 4. Frenell might not be the perfect workplace, but it'd done its best to provide every life necessity, from sugary snacks to disposable grooming kits, so their staff would never have to return to their real homes. The ones who chose not to sleep in the office had stuck Post-it notes on their monitors that recorded the time they'd checked out last night and the time they'd expected to clock in to imply that they weren't losing more productivity than their peers simply because they preferred to brush their teeth and chew their cereal the old-fashioned way—in private.

There was a big eDiscovery and a tax audit document review in progress, which had made up 40 percent of the revenue in the last three months. Given the low complexity and the intense labor required, the work was retained below Year 2, which had brought two April Star Biller titles down to Level 9 and Level 10. Some senior Associates were bitter about it, especially the ones whose billables had been dwindling. *This rewards mindless labor and turns Frenell into a low-value sweatshop*, they said.

Nolan glanced at the floor that resembled a music festival camp and recalled Chateau's tips on starting his client base from Sauria Street. That advice sounded more appealing than the first time he'd heard it, maybe because he was seeing with his own eyes a solid market for something stronger than energy drinks, maybe because he was on his second vodka shot and he felt motivated.

He found Luc at his workstation, slumped over his desk with his face buried in his arms. Poor kid had probably gotten up before sunrise, then fallen back into one of those "recovery naps." Some Grads would do that so the sensors under their chairs could pick up the weight of their butts and mark an "early start" on their accounts. Brownie points add up.

"Hey, buddy." Nolan shook him by the shoulder. "Rise and shine–"

Like a wet dishrag, Luc slid off the chair and heaped onto the sleeping bag folded at his feet. Nolan crouched down and saw Luc's eyes were open. The whites of his eyes had turned crimson, and his lenses were cloudy as if cataractous. His fist clenched the bottle of Rhapsody, which had gone down a third. Inside Luc's jacket, Nolan found his orange prescription bottle. The lid wasn't shut properly, and pills had piled up at the bottom of his pocket. Nolan sighed. The kid had done the one thing he'd specifically told him not to.

He considered stuffing Luc back into his sleeping bag and letting the others discover him "naturally," but this abnormal face of death was bound to draw attention, and he'd like to keep Rhapsody off the radar for a bit longer. The next idea was to remove Luc from the building, but he didn't drive and there was very little he could do to make a body run on its own. So, while Luc's de facto roommates were in their morning routines, Nolan stole a foldable wheelchair from the emergency supplies on the floor and grabbed everything Luc had laid in plain sight–his phone, his Frenell badge, his Ray-Bans with his initials on the frames. Then he'd gathered the people who could get him out of this one.

"Help," Nolan whispered.

"With what? CPR?" Ryuka whispered back.

"It was an accident."

"Then why don't you call the police?"

"I kinda caused that accident."

"Did you? What are *you* doing these days? We really need to catch up."

"Totally. Where do we put him?"

"Who's 'we'?"

"It's just like that time we got rid of Dr. Marshall's tortoise together, remember?"

"Franklin wasn't dead!"

"Listen." Nolan leaned in and took Ryuka's hand. "Wade is my Handler now. You want to get to twenty-one, don't you? You help me; I help you."

She stared at him for a long moment, catching a trace of the cologne she hadn't smelled on him for a while.

"Are you drinking again?"

"Hi, I don't think we've met." Fischer reached out a hand across the table while Nolan tried to come up with a response other than silence. He then retracted it as if Ryuka's glare would burn his fingers off.

"You're my best friend, Ryu," said Nolan.

Ryuka pulled her hand out of Nolan's grip and sank into her chair. After staring at her own fingertips for a second, she assessed their surroundings.

They were between the two morning peaks of Level 20 traffic–the first at nine when the Frenells needed something to sustain their denial of a new day, and the second around eleven when they were desperate for a pick-me-up before lunch. So, there was no crowd except for the table of four near the cash register, which seemed to have some Non-billable Team Building going on, the kind that would usually turn into group therapy where the participants took turns to spill all the emotional garbage they could no longer contain. James Taree was there, next to a Year 3 whom Ryuka had briefly worked with but never spoken to again after the girl had realized Ryuka wasn't someone "going places." The other two, she only knew they weren't Year 5s. Judging from their exaggerated expressions and dancing hands, they were too invested in their own stories to notice anything. The few loners by the coffee machine were tethered to their phones. One by one, they snatched their orders without looking, then scurried away like ER doctors on call.

It wasn't an hour of idling, so if they wanted to contain this, they'd have to do it now.

"Step one: stop being the last person who saw him," Ryuka said to Nolan.

"A bit late for that, no?" asked Fischer.

"Are you just here for commentary?" Ryuka rolled her eyes. "Which floor are you from?"

"I don't work here, actually."

"You don't?"

"I'm here for—" Fischer stopped as Ryuka held up a forefinger.

"You know, you kinda look like a Luc." She studied Fischer's face, then asked Nolan: "What do you think?"

"Yeah, maybe not this Luc, but definitely *a* Luc." Nolan nodded.

Fischer's gaze bounced between the two as he caught on.

"Is it too late to mention I'm not white?" He stared at Luc in the wheelchair.

"He's a Grad! Nobody remembers what he looks like!" Ryuka turned to Nolan. "Let some people see you two together, but more importantly, make sure they see you part ways. Throw off the timeline and get an alibi."

"Good thinking," said Nolan. "What's step two?"

"We'll figure it out after step one."

So Nolan and Fischer stood up and pretended to appreciate the heavenly weather outside, shielding the table from the eyes on the floor until Ryuka unlocked Luc's phone with his biometrics. She took a Smile Enhancer out of her pocket and helped Luc wear it. Nolan didn't ask why she carried that around but thought it was a nice touch to soften the intimidating mirrored aviators.

Ryuka left Luc's badge and phone on the table, then wheeled the kid away. Before she stepped into the elevator, she glanced over her shoulder at Nolan. He didn't catch her looking.

Nolan and his new Luc shuffled toward the now-empty cash register, keeping a natural distance from the table of four.

"What can I get you, Luc?" Nolan asked, loud enough for the group to hear.

Calais stepped out from behind the coffee machine to take orders. He paused for a second when he saw them.

"Yes, Luc, that's my name." Fischer held Calais's gaze. "Um, a piccolo?"

"A piccolo," said Calais.

"Yes, please."

"Oat milk or almond?"

"Which is better?"

"Never mind. We're out of oat milk anyway." Calais turned to Nolan. "The usual ristretto for you, I suppose."

"Look–"

"Don't tell me anything I didn't ask."

As Calais handed the to-go cups over, Fischer scanned Luc's badge on the register reader, and it was simple as that–Luc Edward was officially resurrected at 9:45 a.m., May 17, 2028.

A wave of laughter swept the table near them, so the two seized the moment and joined the party. As the group passed a phone around, Nolan realized the source of their laugh was a LinkedIn post by an Alan Graeme who had been a Frenell Graduate as of yesterday. Under his headshot cradled by the humiliating "Open to Work" green ribbon, Alan expressed his gratitude toward Frenell for the invaluable opportunity to work alongside the brightest in the industry, then announced that he was now looking forward to a new chapter in life and he'd welcome all invitations to the next adventure. The notice from OATH said Alan had decided to explore "alternative career paths," and the firm wished him all the best for his future endeavors, but James confirmed that, right before his departure, the kid had volunteered some feedback about firm culture in Sensible Echoes–Sauria Street's favorite anonymous whistleblower app.

"That was obviously a trap!" James guffawed. "I can't believe people still fall for that."

"Every couple of years, you get one of those," said the Year 3. "Two days after Debut, is that the shortest Grad survival record at Frenell?"

"At least he'll be remembered as a legend," another Associate chimed in after finishing his mocha.

"And an idiot who made James lose five hundred bucks," the Year 3 added.

"The kid looked smarter, I swear." James shook his head, then pointed at the Year 3. "Don't laugh too soon, your horse is gonna be the next."

"You wish. I'm gonna keep that bitch a bit longer." The Year 3 turned to the mocha dude. "She's just been staffed on Project Moonwalk. Take care of her for me, would ya? Ben? Benjamin, look at me–bros before hoes. If she goes through *one* day without crying herself to sleep, I'm on your ass."

"Chill out, queen," said Ben. "What do you want? A full-blown meltdown?"

"She's stopped wearing that stupid Chanel, that's a good start."

"I know exactly who's gonna be the next." The last Associate at the table finally opened his mouth as he stretched his suspenders. "Lindsay's Grad is on annual leave today."

The entire table gasped, including Nolan.

"Maybe it's just normal leave," the Year 3 said, almost looking sympathetic for a second.

"Then why is Lindsay asking for 'urgent translation help' all of a sudden?"

"Jesus, did the kid kill Lindsay's dog or something?" asked Ben.

"Lindsay played Frenell Trivia with him, and the kid got his weight wrong."

The other Associates groaned in terror, then erupted into peals of laughter. Frenell Trivia was a game Lindsay had invented to test people on their knowledge about Frenell–not the firm, the human. It covered topics including his physical attributes, his tastes in arts and culture, his iconic moments and career highlights, and quotes from his previous speeches. It did not include his relationship history or political stances, thank fuck.

Nolan tasted a familiar disgust in his mouth. He knew exactly what would happen to that Grad when he returned tomorrow–he'd get a reprimand from OATH about his "no call, no show." He'd explain that he had applied for leave in the system, which remained pending, but Lindsay had verbally approved his time off, which Lindsay would deny. He'd lecture the kid on the importance of "diligence, loyalty, and availability" for this job, then send him into a performance improvement plan for his unforgivable misconduct of "abandoning his post and leaving the team stranded." By that time, the kid was as good as fired.

The last Associate Lindsay had pulled the same stunt on was Richard. His reason? Lindsay had asked Richard to pick him as his Catch a Partner target for this year, and Rich had said no.

Some Associates had this theory that Linsday "Lord M" Frenell might have an unknown ailment that had severed the neural connection between his brain and his dick, and this behavioral pattern was his attempt to reestablish that pathway. Every time the big head decided to leave a bad taste in someone's mouth, it'd send out a beacon across the boundless vanity that was this man's existence, hoping that one day, it'd catch a crackling response from the little head: *Houston, I'm coming home.*

"Why didn't you warn him?" Nolan asked, and it hushed the table.

"No intervention allowed," Suspenders said. "That's cheating."

"And we'd never get anything done around here if we had to give common sense training all day long," James added.

"You call that common sense?"

"Isn't it?" James frowned. "Don't believe it when people tell you they want your 'honest feedback.' Don't flirt with someone's ex-boyfriend if you need them to like you. Never pick fights. Never make your superiors look like fools. You shouldn't need anyone to tell you any of this if you're over twelve. They're basic social skills."

"When I was twelve, 'social skills' had a very different definition."

"They walk into a place like this, they know they're gonna suck some dicks. They chose this, Mr. Nice Guy, what are you giving *me* shit for?" James stretched his neck toward Fischer. "You knew you were getting fucked, didn't you?"

"Um–"

"For those delicate flowers who don't understand that"–James turned back to Nolan–"we don't need them on the team, pissing off clients and sinking the ship for everyone. They can sort themselves out elsewhere. Nobody here has the time to wait for them to grow up. Speaking of–" He pointed at Fischer. "What's the deal with that Moana chick in your cohort anyway?"

"Moana chick?" Fischer glanced at Nolan.

Nolan knew who James was referring to. There was only one.

"Her name is Keahi. She's Hawaiian."

"Potato, potahto," James said. "Is she loaded?"

"Why?"

"She certainly acts like she doesn't need a job."

"What do you mean–"

Before Nolan could finish his sentence, Luc's phone rang. The screeching ringtone startled Fischer, then he realized the others were giving him a suspicious look. He picked up on the fifth ring, and an angry man's squawk blasted out of the speaker, forcing him to hold it farther away.

"Yes, I am working today. . . . The value chain optimization advice . . . um, yes, it's coming, I'll send–sorry about that. . . . Well, something came up–I said sorry. M-Mister, there's no need to–actually, shut up. Shut the fuck up!"

Fischer drew a deep breath and scanned the dumbfounded faces at the table. He spoke slowly as his eyes landed on Nolan.

"The thing is, I hate this place and I'm gonna go. Never call me again. I'm dead to you."

Nolan heard more screaming from the other end of the phone before Fischer cut the line.

"Exhibit A." James sighed and pointed at Fischer. "Juniors are impossible to manage these days. Well, enjoy the unemployment gap on your RAP. Let's move before those things tag us for loitering."

He stood up and signaled his gang to follow. Nolan and Fischer looked over their shoulders and realized what "those things" meant. A squad of patrol robots appeared on the floor and headed toward the café. The screen of Luc's phone had turned black, with nothing but a banner in the center that said "Access Revoked." The other three Associates rose in unison and joined James, sharing a few whispers and giggles on their way out. As they stuffed themselves into an elevator, Ben shouted "Respect!" at the top of his lungs. It set off another wave of laughter, which was quickly muffled when the doors closed and the metal box took off.

Fischer scrubbed Luc's phone with his sleeves until he couldn't see any prints even on the screen. He handed it back to one of the bots and scanned Luc's badge on the reader of another before the third one confiscated it. At 9:58 a.m., May 17, 2028, Luc Edward was allowed to die.

The robots then formed two lines, waiting for Fischer to leave on his own. They could've wrapped him up like they had Melodie, but Fischer held his hands up to show them violence was unnecessary.

As Fischer stepped into the elevator, he pulled a guest pass out of his pocket and hung it over his neck, then he punched the button for Level 30 and headed to his ten o'clock interview. The opening was meant to replace Dan Barton. Frenell met half a dozen candidates and eventually made that role redundant, but that wasn't important.

"I have some pitch decks to finalize today and a BD meeting," he told Nolan before the doors closed. "Will text you before that meetup, yeah?"

"Seriously? You're going back to work after this?"

"Why not? I didn't quit my own job."

RYUKA TAPPED HER foot on the elevator floor as she watched the number jump up one at a time, taking an eternity to reach Level 29. She needed somewhere quiet to hide until she could come up with a real plan, and those Perception Floors were the quietest place in the entire building these days. Also, the days were getting warmer, so she'd better find appropriate storage for her cargo.

"Hey, you–"

A woman stopped Ryuka as she pushed Luc out of the elevator and toward the kitchen. For a split second, it crossed Ryuka's mind to leave Luc here, but those busy high heels had caught up to her before she could run. She turned around and saw an unfamiliar face that might be wearing a Smile Enhancer itself.

"Are you here for the diversity photo shoot?" The OATH manager looked at Ryuka, then at Luc in the wheelchair. "Perfect."

She bustled away, then stopped again when she noticed the two weren't following. She clapped her hands twice, which lit up a light bulb in Ryuka's head.

"I don't in fact work here." Ryuka put on a stiff accent. "Me, um, sushi chef. We interview at chicken–I mean, kitchen."

The smile disappeared from the OATH manager's face as she inspected Ryuka. It was a regular working day with nothing fancy in her schedule, so Ryuka was wearing a plain white shirt over black pants and sneakers. She looked like she could use an apron.

"So who's this?" The OATH manager pointed at Luc.

"My supervisor," said Ryuka. "He negotiates dinner menu."

She spun the wheelchair around and bent over as if whispering into Luc's ear. Her hand reached up and peeled off the Smile Enhancer. Luc's muscles had cramped up, so she squeezed his face like a handful of clay. When they swiveled back, Luc's smile was gone, and the sunglasses gave him the stern look of someone being inconvenienced.

"We're late." Ryuka pursed her lips.

"Kitchen's over there." The OATH manager tilted her chin at the far end of the floor. "And you should take the freight elevator when you're done."

Ryuka thanked her and wheeled Luc away, not long before she heard another call from behind.

"You! Stop—"

The busy high heels rushed forward and a hand tapped Ryuka's shoulder.

"You're here to discuss your catering services, you say?"

"Yes . . . ?"

"Once you finish your interview, why don't you bring some samples to Level 20, like some assorted platters? We can give you some feedback. You see, we have a very good relationship with Procurement, and we might be able to put in a good word for you."

"Sure, why not," Ryuka mumbled and hurried away.

The OATH manager watched the duo leave and nodded to herself: *Multiculturalism is indeed important. Look at our food.*

"I HOPE YOU'RE not thinking about my freezers."

Calais rested his back against the doorframe as Ryuka sat on the kitchen floor, staring at the body in front of her.

"I'm not thinking about anything at this point," Ryuka cradled her face and sighed. "I'll just sit here and stare at the problem until it goes away."

She had a few ideas, but all of them involved some form of mistreatment of the boy's body. Her memory of Luc since the Grads' Debut was already fading, but that didn't mean he deserved to be chopped up or tossed out with rotten lettuce.

"Can't swing a witness. Can't hide a body." She buried her face in her elbows. "Maybe I'm not cut out for this job."

"Why are you doing this?" Calais asked.

"If I didn't do it, nobody else would."

Calais looked at her for a moment, then stepped over and took hold of Luc's wheelchair. Without a word, he pushed the boy to the far end of the kitchen and made a turn into the side room where the pantry and the scullery were. Ryuka followed and found him standing in the corner, next to what appeared to be a back bar refrigerator with double sliding doors. She peeked over his shoulder and noticed that the empty fridge didn't have any shelves, then she saw the switch panel on the side of the frame with two buttons indicating up and down.

"Don't wander too far, you could get lost," Calais said as he crammed Luc inside and signaled Ryuka to make more room. "Leave him in the open area. They have a protocol for something like this."

"Who's 'they'?" Ryuka asked.

Calais shrugged and folded Luc's legs. Ryuka pressed her back against the wall and drew her knees up to make herself small. Luc's body tumbled forward and collapsed on top of her. His neck and chest had begun to stiffen, his bloody eyes wide open and inches away from her face. Ryuka wiggled farther into the corner and lodged Luc's chin on her shoulder without touching his cold cheeks. The space smelled of bacon and brine. She took a second to register where she was and what she was doing.

"Is this supposed to be normal?" she mumbled as she smashed the Down button and shut the door.

The dumbwaiter moved slower than an elevator. Two minutes in, they were still descending. Ryuka kept her breath shallow and started counting, keeping her mind off the smell of stale food, and the smell of Luc. Another minute had passed, and an intrusive thought that she'd been suppressing ballooned into a paralyzing terror–this thing could break and she could get stuck in a tunnel that she clearly shouldn't be caught in, with a dead kid that could put an end to the life she'd known.

Her chest tightened and the metal box seemed to be contracting with each beat of her heart. Just when the increasingly pungent odors gripped her neck, the dumbwaiter stopped and she crawled out, pushing Luc's body out of her way and letting him collapse onto the floor. She stayed on all fours to catch her breath and managed not to puke. Slowly, she got up from the rubber mats and realized she was under a bar counter. The place was well lit but quiet.

She poked her head out, and the palatial atrium eased her breathing. The bar and the shelves had been cleaned and tidied, yet the ghosts of a good time lingered. The hour hand of the facade clock slashed through the grandiose windows diagonally, splitting the light and framing the shadows. A loud chime shook her out of her stupefaction. It was ten o'clock.

Ryuka took Calais's advice and did not wander. She dragged Luc by the shoulders and heaved him into a booth bathed in sunlight. She positioned him semi-sideways to face the windows and draped his arm over the back of the couch for balance, then she set the sunglasses back on the bridge of his nose, leaving his eyes open. They were in a place that shouldn't exist, and she was doing something that felt like a hallucination, but the radiant sky out there was undoubtedly real, and the lively image of a prosperous city was mesmerizing. She suspected that when this kid had joined Frenell, he'd hoped to see a view like this, someday.

"MISS MURONG?"

Ryuka snapped back to reality and met Laurent's eyes.

"You seem distracted today." He smiled.

"My apologies . . . strange day."

"Is everything all right?"

"Yeah . . . yeah, everything's fine, I think."

The conversation dropped dead like a long-distance call with poor connection until Laurent picked it back up.

"You mentioned Professor Crowley?"

"Yes, right. Sorry." Ryuka pretended to search for something in her binder. Crowley was the dean of Laurent's faculty and Osireion's designated "nudge." "Doctor, you've been with Eldridge University for almost three years, is that right?"

"You have my CV." Laurent nodded.

"Do you like it there?"

"Yes, I like the work I do, and my colleagues are friendly, bright, and quirky in their own ways. I've thoroughly enjoyed my time at Eldridge."

Ryuka closed her eyes. She'd hoped Laurent wasn't so happy with where he was. She'd rather he resented what he had to do, or at least felt indifferent–like a normal person–and Eldridge was no more than a job that he'd stayed in because it looked good on paper or simply because he wasn't ready to leave. It would've made him less vulnerable. It would've hurt him less when the work he'd thought had meaning turned into asswiping for exactly what he despised about the world, when the people who asked for his respect and loyalty threw him under the bus without pulling the knife out of his back.

"My family joined me about a year ago," Laurent continued as Ryuka said nothing. "And there has been some serious discussion about settling down, but we are reevaluating that. Théo is about to start school. Claire and I think it might be better for him to lay the foundation at home–getting properly scolded by a French teacher is important for character building. If he wants to pursue higher education in the States later, he can choose that for himself. We will also be less worried about his safety."

Ryuka looked up and saw Laurent grinning.

"You can tell them Laurent Cheong isn't desperate to stay in this country, so there's nothing you can do."

"How do you–"

"I had lunch with Professor Crowley the other day, and he asked about this assignment since I was supposed to have finished it a while ago. I guess the conversation took off on its own, and he ended up telling me more than he'd planned. Well, he didn't spell everything out, but I can put two and two together. I see you've been staring at an empty page since we sat down, so let me make things easier for you."

Ryuka flipped her binder shut while her eyes locked on Laurent and her racing mind searched for clues on this man's face. She'd had enough confusion for one day, but what she felt right now was more perplexing than the secret tunnel she'd had to carry a body through, or the forbidden palace she wasn't ready to discover. This confusion screamed danger from its bottom, and it was morphing into anger.

Was this some kind of test Frenell pulled on her? To see how she'd respond under pressure or if she was corruptible? Was this one of those "damned if you do, damned if you don't" situations–if she did as she was told, she lacked judgment and integrity; if she refused to push Laurent, she was insubordinate and pompous?

And what was in it for Laurent? Was he one of those who wanted a "lawyer friend" in their back pocket? Did he want to sleep with her? Over Teams? How? Was this meeting recorded? Was this part of Eldridge's evaluation of him, and he was just playing a character?

He must've wanted *something* from her, but she had no idea what it was.

report about her discussions with Laurent from their first encounter, the arguments and evidence each of them had put forward, his final opinion about Serotane, and his reasons. She finished by saying they should respect Laurent's expertise and that it would be futile and inappropriate to push further. She addressed the email to Hayden and copied Wade and Emma. As she hit Send, for the first time since she'd started at Frenell, she felt she was part of something important.

The only response she received was from Hayden two minutes later, which included one simple line:

I appreciate the proactivity, but do not contact Wade directly unless I have okayed your message.

She read that one more time. Strangely, she felt nothing but insipid boredom. She tried to picture a kind of life where not every sentence uttered had to be manipulative or ferocious, not every interaction had to end up with one person's face stomped into the dirt, and it got her nowhere.

Her work phone buzzed once. The Perspective app reminded her to get up and walk around her bench for a minute, which had been proven to boost energy and improve productivity.

Am I a pair of rubber gloves? she typed into the chat. *Someone people use to handle things they don't want to touch? Is that why I keep getting cleaner jobs?*

The assistant took longer than usual to scoop an answer out of bubbles.

Certain work may appear less exciting, it replied. *But that doesn't make it less important. Someone has to get it done right. If not you, who? The firm appreciates your contribution and values all talents equally.*

She stepped over to the window and flattened herself on the floor, peering at the insurance company building across the street. She pressed her face as low as she could, trying to catch a glimpse of the roof.

Still couldn't see that myrtle from here.

9

"WHAT'S A . . . LEVEL II Assistant Deputy Vice President?" Nolan asked.

"That's the title for A5—at least that's what the guy said in the Facebook group," Fischer said as he texted the ADVP their location. "So he should have a higher credit and a decent downline."

"Why is he selling his account cheap, then?"

"Cash flow crunch. He got involved in NFT derivatives, so he has to liquidate some assets fast to keep his position 'cause they've margin called him. He's not that into drugs anyway."

When you don't have enough time to build a business from scratch, one option is to acquire an existing one. In the last forty-eight hours, Nolan and Fischer had made two sales combined, and one of them had become a write-off by dying.

"What if he gets close enough and sees it's not real?" Nolan watched Fischer pop the magazine out of the ".22" in his hand.

It was fully loaded with ten antidotes. The finale of the sunset illuminated the barrel, giving it a dangerous glimmer.

"That's exactly why I have this—so he won't get close enough."

The ADVP was selling his account at 60 percent of its book value, but it'd still cost $90,000. For a legal business that you don't have the money to buy, you identify enough high-risk concerns in the due diligence and push for a lower price. With illegal businesses, there's always the Scarface approach.

"Shit, not now . . ." Fischer murmured and fumbled in his pockets. He pumped the near-empty spray, then rubbed his nose with such vigor that it reminded Nolan of Wade.

"Dude, I thought you were quitting," said Nolan.

"I was. Not anymore."

"You can't?"

"Don't want to."

"Why not?"

Fischer sniffed and held out a hand to see if it was still trembling. Then he gave Nolan the empty look he'd had earlier today when he'd quit Luc's job for him.

"I figure you go up, or you go down. There's no standing still. Up, I know where the limit is—I get high, it gives me a rush, and I see some animal heads. The other way? I can't see the bottom, and I have no idea what's waiting down there. That's the thing about going down—you always have farther to fall."

Nolan stared at him for a moment and asked the question that he'd been withholding.

"How does it feel?"

"It feels . . . it feels like acceptance." Fischer wiped off a reflexive tear. "A comfortable paralysis. Your mind takes you to places you forgot existed or didn't want to look. It breaks your heart, but then your heart will never break again."

The ADVP showed up on time, alone, and suited. This seemed to be his first encounter with the wrong side of the Athena River. He kept peeking at the tents over the embankment, his gaze unsettled and timid. He refused to come near Nolan or Fischer and tossed them a spiral-bound pitch deck from twelve feet away. Nolan liked what he saw—he was no doubt dealing with an amateur.

On paper, the business looked promising. The guy moved forty to fifty bottles every week on average, with a steady upward trend. He had about two dozen regulars plus their referrals, and he'd developed a line of A2 to A4 recruits who would bring in additional commissions. The accounts receivable sat around $300,000, and they were looking at a comfortable six-figure profit in the coming month.

"And you're selling your book for ninety grand?" Nolan gave the guy a look that meant "Now show me the catch."

"Well, as I said in the group, I don't see myself as a dealer." The guy averted his eyes, then pointed at Nolan's backpack. "How about let's see some cash and get this over with?"

"How about let's see some inventory before we talk green?" said Nolan.

"Same time?" The guy raised his briefcase.

"Sure." Nolan took the backpack off his shoulder and swung it forward as they counted to three, then he feigned a throw and hauled it back by the strap while the guy's briefcase landed at Fischer's feet.

"Fuck!" the ADVP exclaimed and grabbed his own head.

Fischer snatched the briefcase and checked its contents. One glance, he tutted loudly and drew out the Revilox gun.

"It's just paper," Fischer said as he kicked the open briefcase to Nolan.

"Calm down, dude!" The seller raised both hands high up. "It's not normal paper! Look at them!"

Nolan picked up a piece and examined it. It was the size of a diploma and had a cotton fiber texture. The calligraphic name "High Hopes Inc." sat on top. Underneath, some legalese spread across the page with a bolded name, a number, and a date filling the blanks. The illustrated bloodshot eye in the center of the stamp triggered a flashback of Luc's face. Nolan had to blink it away.

"What are these?"

"They're holding certificates."

"What?"

"Look"–the seller took a breath–"we have some supply issues, okay? This thing is exploding and we can't keep up. The company still owes me half of my stock, so I've made these to track orders. It's a proof of ownership and the customers can use these to redeem their purchases later."

"So you're selling . . . drug shares?"

"Stimulant options. You've seen the price and it's not coming down. The users buy in early to hedge against future increases. It helps us lock in the market and scale before the competitors move in."

Nolan considered this. It seemed to add up–he still hadn't received the rest of his inventory, and Rhapsody had opened at twelve hundred fifty this morning.

"I'm not feeling good about this guy." Fischer held up the gun. "He's a chipmunk. Why are you unloading? Are the cops onto you?"

"No! No! I want out 'cause it's becoming like my job! I already got a job–"

The guy stopped talking as Fischer moved the gun to his own temple.

"I can't go to jail," Fischer mumbled. "I'm not good with confined spaces."

"Dude, put that down." Nolan raised a hand, but Fischer stepped out of his reach. *I can't go to jail*, he repeated.

"Hey, nobody is going to jail." Now the seller looked nervous.

"Why is this getting so complicated?" Fischer yelled. "Are you a banker?"

"No! I'm a consultant!"

"What consultant?!"

"Huh?"

"Tell him what kind of consultant you are! For fuck's sake!" Nolan yelled.

"ESG! ESG . . . um, corporate responsibility? A-and government strategies! It's true! I work at Fischer & O'Brien! My Handler is Michael Sanders!"

The mention of Sanders seemed to have won some credit in Fischer's book, but he wasn't fully convinced.

"How much does Fischer pay you?"

"Um, a hundred grand plus gym membership."

"Wait, you're a Grad?" Fischer stared at this guy, who seemed to have his college years way behind him.

"No! I'm a Year 4—oh . . ."

"Yeah . . ." Fischer lowered his gun. "Maybe talk to Michael about that in your next performance review? The bottom is one fifty, just so you know."

He snapped around to say something. When his eyes landed on Nolan, a fleeting moment of disappointment washed over his features.

"You look . . . different. I don't know if I like you this way."

Then his breathing became labored.

"Shit, I'm coming down . . . I don't want to come down."

He dropped the Revilox gun and whipped out the spray, finished all that was left, then paced in circles with his head held high to walk off the kick. Abruptly, he stopped and gaped at the sky. Then he turned to Nolan. A crimson mist had clouded his eyes.

Nolan gasped and scooped up the Revilox. He charged forward and caught Fischer as he collapsed to his knees, then he pressed the muzzle against Fischer's chest and pulled the trigger. The dispenser made a muffled pop. Fischer's body jerked, and his face slumped onto Nolan's shoulder.

The ADVP attempted a dash toward Nolan to recover his briefcase. But as far as he was concerned, this guy had just shot his partner, so he made the sensible choice of leaving everything behind.

Nolan propped Fischer up and held his head. His eyes weren't muddy, but they weren't reflecting anything either. For a second, Nolan panicked that he might never see the Fischer who'd call him "twenty-five fifty" again. After what felt like forever, the crimson faded, and Fischer uttered a soft groan.

"Fuck, that hurt . . ."

"Seriously?" a familiar voice complained.

Nolan looked up and saw Keahi holding another Revilox gun, aiming at Fischer's back. Once again, she put her unfired lifesaver away with a pout.

"SHOULD I CHARGE 'Team Building' or 'People Management' for this?" Keahi grinned as Nolan put a canned espresso in front of her. The firm café had closed, but the vending machines were working fine.

"Charge 'Meet and Greet' if you want." Nolan laughed. "I have a lot of respect for what you've done."

"And now you're gonna tell me to stop."

"I like you, Keahi. I kinda want to keep seeing you around. Those above Level 26, no matter how considerate or 'open-minded' they claim to be, not *one* of them is interested in your idea about what to change in this place. They won't fix whatever you complain about. They'll just replace you with someone who doesn't complain."

"What I did isn't really complaining, though."

Not complaining. Protesting, Nolan thought.

After her Debut, Keahi had added a little ritual to the end of her day. At ten o'clock every night, she'd shut down her computer, tidy up her workstation, and leave the office without logging back on from home. No time-stamped Post-it notes. No immediate response to midnight emails. No apologies for her unavailability. She'd simply walk out and let the others whisper behind her.

The news permeated the floors in no time, and the Associates started asking questions: *What does her family do? Is she related to a client? Who's her Handler? Are they "dating"?* Some even traced back to the recruitment process to find out who'd let this one in. People started from different angles, but all the questions converged to one: *Is this really the best way to make a point?* That was when they reached the consensus that Keahi Ka'uhane should improve her communication skills.

"I know all the Grads have been working really hard," Nolan said. "But unfortunately, that's just the nature of this profession. Look at the bright side for a second–as long as Frenell isn't underpaying you, even if you work fifteen hours a day, your hourly rate should still be pretty viable–"

"Thirty-five dollars," said Keahi.

"Sorry?"

"I've done the math–I make thirty-five dollars an hour."

"See? Not to say it's a fortune, but you still get paid okay money–better than a lot of people in this economy. This has been a demanding job since the beginning of time. It's the same shit show wherever you move on Sauria Street, and you're already in one of the best theaters."

"It's not just the hours," Keahi said. "Something is not right about this place. Every other day, I'd catch a different person crying in the bathroom. When we first started, some Grads had never done drugs in their lives–they do now. Something has gotta be wrong if, I don't know, you need metal detectors downstairs so nobody can shoot up the entire office, then themselves."

"To be fair, the metal detectors were only there *after* the Chateau incident."

"A friend of mine is a journalist and she's doing a piece on professional services. This one will focus on bullying and gaslighting 'cause the exploitation and harassment stuff is not even news anymore. We'll meet up next week, and some of the Grads have agreed to come forward–anonymously, of course–and we've lined up a football team."

The vague grin Nolan had been wearing disappeared. In the dark café solely illuminated by the lights from the vending machines, he looked like he was in pain.

"Don't do it."

"Why not?"

"Nobody does that."

"Nobody?"

"Nobody does that without losing a leg of their own." He sighed. "This kind of claim . . . it's really hard to prove. Even harder than sexual harassment. We're not talking about people who make you miserable by calling you dumb names or tripping you over as you walk past–straight shooters like that wouldn't even get anywhere near Frenell's door. It's always subtle, it's ambiguous, and it's teamwork. Your 'bullies,' so to speak, they have been here longer, and they're probably more popular than you. All they need to do is get one of their pets to say 'So-and-So has always been nice and supportive to *me*,' then immediately, you will become the suspect and this will become your interrogation. Why isn't the same person nice and supportive to *you*? Is it because you have poor social skills and you don't know how to build relationships? Are you incompetent and you frustrate them? Did you just mention you use drugs? Maybe we should address that first. And what did they actually do to you anyway? They're probably just stressed. Don't assume bad faith. Don't take anything personally. Why don't you take them out for coffee or buy them chocolate so they like you more? We're here to listen, but if you can't prove anything, I'm afraid our policy requires us to flag in your RAP that your bullying claim is dismissed–not to punish you, just to remind other managers what might happen when they work with you so they understand their staff better. Trust me, Keahi, you don't want to be in that witness box."

"Did you get burned before?" She chuckled.

"I don't have to. I have eyes. Just look around–only people who are used to getting away with things would be *that* comfortable being assholes."

"But they really shouldn't be."

For reasons Nolan couldn't articulate then, the word *shouldn't* irritated him. Today alone, he'd found a dead kid in the morning and gone to a drug deal an hour ago. His delayed hangover was fracking inside his skull, and this woman who was barely legal to drink wanted to tell him what to expect in life and how to feel about it. He gulped a mouthful of his coffee and let the bitterness suppress the anger.

"Look, every couple of years, you get one of those 'horror stories' about the 'toxic culture' of some big firm, and people gossip on Reddit for, like, forty-eight hours, then they move on until the next post complaining about pretty much the same practices. The cycle has been going on for decades, and what's changed? Nothing. Nothing! You see more stupid titles and you get more window-dressing training to justify those stupid titles–that's all. Firms like Frenell will never change because they will never run out of cannon fodder *pouncing* on these jobs. Because as horrible as it is, you can still live off this one salary and you work indoors, sitting down and not surrounded by dangerous machines. You don't have to pee into a bottle or wear motion trackers–"

"Is that the bar now? As long as you're not facing imminent risks of death or mutilation and you still have bathroom breaks, it's worth a college degree. Maybe *nobody* should have to hold down two full-time jobs to get by or pee into a bottle in the first place, because there's no guarantee that person would *never* be you. I've spent so much time on the wrong side of the Athena River, Nolan, one thing I've learned is that we're all much closer to that rock bottom than we'd like to believe."

"Are you lecturing me now?" Nolan frowned.

"No." Keahi averted her eyes. "I just thought you were someone who'd say something different."

That stung.

"Why are you still here, then?" he asked. "Why don't you leave? Sure, the market is shit, but there's gotta be something out there. Go bag groceries or stock some shelves."

"Why should I? I have the education for this job. I have the capabilities for this job. I worked hard to get to where I am today—"

"Exactly!" he scoffed. "You applied for the job, voluntarily. You jumped through all the hoops, voluntarily. You could've said no at every single step, but you're still here 'cause you want to be 'elite.' I'm sorry, but being 'elite' is hard. C'mon, we all have to deal with everything you complained about, and we all know that bullshit is just part of the package—"

"So we all asked for it?"

"Well . . . yeah! In a sense."

"I, for one, did not choose abuse."

"What *abuse*?! There's no law against being a shitty person! If you can't prove it's discrimination on a protected ground and it's not sexual, then it's just . . . people being people."

"People will be the kind of people they think they're allowed to be. If we keep racing to the bottom, eventually there will be no bottom at all. Someone has to be a 'whiny bitch' to stand up and say, 'Maybe it's not okay to treat others like that.'"

"Noble—very noble. I-I respect that, but you know you're not the first 'whiny bitch' who thought they had a chance, don't you? You think those people didn't make a difference because they didn't try hard enough?"

"One voice can only say so much, but a river of voices might resonate." She smiled. "It's also in the firm's interest to listen. Wouldn't it improve productivity if the working environment were a little bit more pleasant?"

"Have you heard *anything* I said at the beginning?" Nolan shut his eyes and palmed his face. After a moment, he looked her in the eye and pressed his hands together as if begging someone to step down from the roof of a building. "Please, like you said, you worked hard for this. Don't throw it away. Bide your time. Get a few years in, then maybe you have a little bit more authority to make people listen. Hell, you could be the first Partner who actually gives a shit! But not now, not like this . . ."

She stopped smiling and chose her words carefully.

"I'm not saying this to hurt you, Nolan, but you've only been here for five years, and look what you're telling me right now."

Nolan's throbbing headache had turned into a drilling pain between his eyebrows as if someone were pointing at his forehead and laughing about how much of a joke he'd been. All these years he'd spent between these walls, he'd felt he was tied to a chair, *Clockwork Orange*–style, and watching people march toward an avoidable demise he couldn't prevent. He bowed his head so he didn't have to look at her.

"Fine, it's your career." He slumped into his chair. "Don't come and cry to me when you no longer have one. Good luck changing the world."

"Sauria Street is not the world."

"It *will* be. This is where we're going, Keahi, this is what *every* job is going to become, so you'd better learn to deal with it unless you don't have to work at all. I'm sorry, are you loaded?"

"Not loaded, just dumb."

"What. Is wrong. With you?"

She twisted the can of coffee with one hand. Cold water dripped down and wet her fingertips.

"I guess I just don't want to live in a society where the ultimate standard for power and success becomes whether you can comfortably be an asshole without any accountability. Whether you can belittle and intimidate someone because they're not bending over backward to please you. Whether you can constantly gag people and tell them 'The world doesn't care about your feelings,' 'Toughen up,' 'Stop playing the victim,' 'You're overthinking,' 'Systemic injustice doesn't exist, you're just not good enough,' or the best one–'It is what it is.' You fuck up someone's mind so hard they question their own sanity just so you can brag to the others: 'See that? I made that one cry on

Monday.' You wake up every day, can't wait to puff your morning breath down everybody's face 'cause you have to take your own misery out on *someone*, or simply because you can, because your life goal is to spread PTSD and congratulations, you live in the best age for sociopaths, so knock yourself out. The world is not supposed to be like that. I did not choose *that*, Nolan. If I ever did, I wouldn't have priced myself at thirty-five dollars an hour."

She slipped a twenty under the can to repay him for her untouched coffee and left. Nolan said nothing to stop her. He didn't move at all. Not even following the girl with his eyes. He let her disappear from his vision, convinced of two things: he'd never see her again, and he'd drop dead if he didn't get a drink right now.

That night, Keahi repeated what she'd always done–she logged off at ten and left Level 9 with a clean desk behind. As the faint elevator chime traveled across the open plan, So-yeon at the next workbench shut down her computer, tidied up her desk, and walked out.

ANDREJ RETURNED TO the first page of the document and skimmed the key points again. He nodded slightly, then dropped it inside his bag.

"I trust Michelle will be pleased with this development." Wade stuck his face closer to read Andrej's expression.

"Ms. Joplin will consider the implications and the strategy going forward." Andrej stood up from the banquette. "If she has any further instructions, I will pass them on."

"Look at you!" Wade patted Andrej on the shoulder and pressed another hand on his chest, guiding him back into his seat. "One more thing–"

"If it's about the fees again, that topic is closed."

"No! No, we don't talk about money tonight."

Wade handed two envelopes to Andrej.

"We'd like to invite you and Michelle to our one-hundred-and-fiftieth anniversary party. It'd be nice to finally meet Michelle in person—I wanted to say hi in Geneva but didn't get the chance. We'll also organize some entertainment after—"

"Ms. Joplin has a tight schedule this month, and I shall also mention that she has very different tastes from Brendan."

Wade nodded as his smile gradually stiffened. Andrej opened one envelope and rubbed the invitation between two fingers, feeling the texture and weight of the cardstock. It was the same design as the RSVP email he'd deleted weeks ago, but the paper made a stronger case to avoid the bin.

"Relationships are delicate, aren't they?" He chuckled. "It takes one person to die to shove you back to square one. A hundred and fifty years, huh? Impressive."

"We owe it to our esteemed clients like Osireion, so this event is also an opportunity for us to express our appreciation. We trust our next hundred years of collaboration will be even more fruitful."

"Good to see Frenell has such confidence in its future." Andrej nodded. "I'm sure Arthur Andersen also assumed it'd be around forever."

Wade's face dropped.

"Andrej, you have done well, but as your former mentor, I must remind you to remain humble and grateful for the people who nurtured you and put you where you are today—"

"You can get a drink on me anytime, Wade. We have a tab at Dandelion."

"I think I deserve a little bit more respect than you're showing right now!"

"Everyone knows you Frenells are full of self-respect already. Any more from me would be excessive."

"What's this animosity about? The team missed you."

Andrej burst out a sharp laugh and met Wade's eyes.

"You miss how much of a pushover I was, but I don't need to be reminded of how spectacularly stupid I used to be."

Wade stared at Andrej for a moment, then he seemed to have recalled how he used to talk to this young man.

"Since I've got you here, as the Managing Partner for Project Rhapsody, I have the duty to remind you that our last four invoices remain outstanding, and Osireion has over two point seven million dollars overdue for the last quarter alone–I guess we have to talk about money after all."

"We wrote you a handsome check in January, so be very careful what you accuse us of. The rest was–and still is–rejected for the lack of clear description of services provided. I'm sure you got that email a long time ago."

"All of our bills have detailed narrative–"

"It doesn't prove value." Andrej sighed and took a tablet out of his bag. He opened an app and brought forward a dashboard. "Between February third and March first, our Vendor Management App detected a significant increase of repetition in billing narratives from multiple Frenell Timekeepers on Project Rhapsody, which indicated a group task, but the only job we gave you during that period was some advice on directors' liability, which shouldn't have generated a billing pattern that resembled a massive document review."

"We've checked the record," said Wade. "Those Associates were reviewing internal reporting materials to ascertain the level of knowledge of the Board–"

"Similarly, between March twenty-seventh and April fourteenth, you charged us four hundred grand for a fancy table copying and pasting academic papers. Those Timekeepers' hourly rates ranged between seven fifty and twelve hundred dollars. If my memory is correct, those are Year 4 and above. They shouldn't be doing grunt work like that. Our app has run its prediction model for tasks of comparable difficulty and concluded that the work could've been done within half the time at one third of the cost. This is clearly a waste of resources caused by mismanagement and gross inefficiency."

"That summary involved more than copying and pasting." Wade shifted in his seat. "They were highly technical and required people with knowledge about the core dispute to first determine their relevance–"

"I know how your firm works, Wade." Andrej stowed his tablet away and zipped up his bag. "Osireion is not paying for unproductive paper shuffling or gravy train rides. Drop it."

"Andrej, we did the work, and we expected to get paid." Wade's mouth pressed into a grim line. "The amount of outstanding fees has exceeded Osireion's credit limit. I have the Board and the other Partners to answer to. If we can't reach an amicable agreement, I'm afraid I will have to refer this matter to our Office of General Counsel for them to decide the next steps, including potential legal actions."

"You do that, Wade." Andrej leaned in and patted the back of Wade's hand. "And I'll wait for the pitch decks from twenty other firms on Sauria Street that will explain in great detail why they can do everything you do at a more sensible price. Actually, how about I go up there right now and tell everyone what you are about to do so they can prepare for what's coming their way? Yep, I'm gonna take this one for the team–"

He sprang off the banquette and strode to the mini stage at the front of the lounge, grabbed the mic standing in the center, and caught the attention across the floor with some mild feedback.

"Good evening, everyone, I'm Andrej Bovec from Osireion. Some of you, I've met. Now, I'd like to thank Frenell for its continuous hospitality, and I don't know if you have heard, but the firm is having its hundred-and-fiftieth anniversary this year! I know, right? Tonight, we have Frenell's Senior Partner, Mr. Wade Pendleton-Fitzpatrick, with us, and guess what? He just told me–"

He glanced at Wade and saw that he'd left his seat, gaping in this direction while what was, without a doubt, a glimpse of panic climbed up his face.

"–that he was so excited about this milestone he'd like to sing us a song as precelebration! Excuse me, Miss DJ? Do we have the national anthem on karaoke? We do? Perfect."

As the triumphant brass and percussion replaced the bossa nova, Andrej orchestrated a round of laughter and applause from the tipsy crowd, which formed an invisible hand nudging Wade forward. The Frenell Olympian seemed disoriented for a moment as he entered the spotlight. Andrej greeted him with a wide grin and guided him to the center of the stage.

Before he stepped away, Andrej covered the mic and whispered: "Cheer up. You worked thirty years for this."

HE GAVE IT to him, Sai texted in the dim corridor outside the lounge. *Hard to tell what Andrej thinks, though.*

This is gonna be soooooooooo good, Henry replied.

Sai added a smiley face to her response–the one with the rosy cheeks–then deleted it. It'd been less than twenty-four hours since she'd last seen him, but she'd been checking her phone more and more often for new messages. Something she certainly couldn't tell him. So she told Henry she'd keep him updated and moved to a spot that gave her a better view of Andrej's face. He was showing Wade something on his tablet as they spoke, and he seemed amused, but Sai wasn't sure if it was because of the document.

The other night, after she'd told Henry about her "assignment" and asked about Secretary Berlin, Henry was lost in his thoughts for a while. When he snapped out of it, he had this uncanny smile that she'd never seen on him. He grabbed her by the neck and kissed her till her lips were numb. "Brilliant," he murmured as he let her breathe. "Those clowns think I'm one of them. Let them remember this one."

They will remember this one. He chuckled.

A couple of hours later, when Sai got out of the shower, Henry handed her a large yellow envelope marked "Strictly

Confidential." She skimmed the contents of the five-page memo inside, then gave him a quiet grin. They sealed the envelope together, then she let him touch wherever he wanted to touch. When his fingers ran down her neck and brushed her chest, they ignited an aching desperation, making her want to offer herself up to the flame.

An incoming call put an end to her dream. Her heart dipped when she saw the name Inaya, but she hit the green button immediately and dashed down the corridor to find a quiet corner. Behind her, they started playing the national anthem. *Seriously?* she thought.

"Saidah? Saidah, can you hear me?"

"Yeah, yeah. What's wrong?"

"Nothing . . . how you doing?"

"Ina, what's wrong?"

There was a pause. Sai could hear her sister breathe.

"Mom saw that video," Ina finally said. "Look, I've shown her what you sent me, but she's still really upset."

"How did Mom see it?" Sai closed her eyes.

"It's Harun." Ina sighed. "He had a fight with Mom about something super petty, and his son saw that on Facebook or something . . . are you coming home this weekend?"

"I can't. Gotta work."

"We haven't seen you for ages. Farid is on some new treatment, and Mom is swamped. We could use some help around the house . . . I know you're busy. I'm helping too, but this month is killing me. I got two papers due—"

"Okay, okay. I'll see what I can do." Sai rubbed her forehead. "Tell Mom I've called the police, okay? But it takes time, this kind of thing."

"I will."

"You okay with money?"

"Huh? Yeah, um, don't worry about that, I got some gigs . . . I should probably go. See you this weekend?"

Sai confirmed and said goodbye. Before Ina hung up, Sai caught her and put on an upbeat tone.

"Ina, you've done a great job. Good luck with your papers."

She stood in the dark corner and stared at her empty screen for a moment. Her mind wasn't ready for the three-hour train ride back to her family's house in Clover Hill and the guaranteed chaos between those flimsy walls, so she strode back to the lounge and peeked inside. Andrej was chatting with some insurance executives in a different booth, and Wade had disappeared. Opposite the entrance, the casual catch-up between a venture capitalist and a start-up founder had grown into a serious pitch, judging from their brushing knees. In the back, some bankers were hitting the sweet spot of inebriation and getting handsy with the hosts. With a stiff smile on her face, Pace kept glancing at the door while dodging the grabs, as if to see if Gerald would miraculously march in and take her away.

Sai felt she was looking at a jigsaw puzzle and she wasn't a piece in it. She was just the glue smeared over the assemblage and smoothed into the gaps. Once all the pieces had locked into place, there would be no trace of her in the picture at all. She didn't want to go back in, and she didn't want to join the other group at the bar on Level 15 either. The rumors that someone had overdosed there earlier today made her sick to her stomach.

She opened WhatsApp and saw two blue checkmarks next to her last line. No new messages from Henry.

Turning away from the lounge, she headed to the ladies' room on the other side of the floor. She'd freshen up a bit, then clock out early and tell Katherine that she was feeling unwell, which she assumed wouldn't be a problem. After all, she'd just delivered a big job.

As she pushed the bathroom door open, someone grabbed her from the inside and threw her at the sinks. She hit the granite edge with the side of her body, and the pain brought her to her knees. That someone picked her up, pressed her against the countertop, and forced his mouth onto hers. She struggled one hand out of his grip and pushed his face away. That was when she recognized him.

Panting like a horse, Wade grabbed her wrist and twisted her arm behind her back. His pupils seemed dilated, and his tongue felt like a warm slug. Sai tried to knee him in the groin but only got him in the thigh. Wade made a small jerk and cocked his neck. He put a little distance between their bodies, then slapped her across the face. Instantly, she lost her hearing on one side and hit her head on the partition wall. He flipped her around and bent her over. As she tried to stay on her feet and steady her spinning vision, she realized he'd pushed her dress above her waist and pulled down her underwear. She swung a hand backward to push him away. He shoved her head down, and her left eye hit the arching faucet. She heard a disturbing squishy sound, then a sharp pain spread across her face and choked the faint "No" back down her throat. With the one eye left open, she saw red spots on the porcelain. As she grabbed the faucet to keep her balance, he squeezed himself inside her.

"What the fuck do you think you are . . . you piece of shit?" he mumbled over her head.

It finished in less than thirty seconds, and she felt like she had been hit by a train. From the crown of her head to her shaky ankles, everything throbbed with pain, and she couldn't feel the blood dripping down her thighs. She glanced in the mirror, and the sight of Wade zipping his pants made her retch. In a moment of dissociation, she remembered she hadn't had a single drop of alcohol tonight. That drew out an unbecoming sense of relief–at least they wouldn't be able to say she was drunk.

The bathroom door busted open, and Pace rushed in crying. She gasped and froze when she saw Sai collapse to the ground as Wade fastened his belt.

"What are you looking at?!" Wade shrieked.

Pace met Wade's bloodshot eyes and hiccuped uncontrollably. She stumbled out of the bathroom and shut the door behind her. Wade stormed out shortly after, leaving Sai on the floor, curling up as if to stop her body from falling apart. A silent vacuum enclosed her for a moment, then she pulled herself up and fixed her clothes. She kept her head low and emptied her stomach in the sink before she was able to face her reflection. Her left eye was still in its socket. The impact earlier had cut her brow ridge and left a blood spot in her sclera, but it hadn't blinded her, not completely. Her cheek felt swollen, and the corner of her mouth cracked. She found a bruise on one side of her forehead when she ran her fingers through her hair. More would appear all over her skin tomorrow.

Then she saw her necklace. The camera that had been dangling in front of her when what had happened, happened. The thought that she might have caught her own violation on film did not console but repulsed her. She pulled her blazer back over her shoulders and drew her phone out of the pocket, hesitant to unlock it. Then it dawned on her that the filming had stopped when she'd started texting. As the physical pain converged into prick points, her mind pendulumed between two realizations—there was no footage to use as evidence; there was also no footage to remind her it wasn't just a lucid nightmare.

She stood behind the closed door for a long time, rehearsing how she'd walk out and leave this place like nothing had happened. *Get out, and act normal*—she couldn't remember who'd taught her that, but that had always seemed to be the first to-do in this scenario. The bathroom door swung open, and someone in a catering uniform stepped in. The café intern didn't expect to bump into anyone, so she gave Sai a standard "Oops" smile, which faded as her gaze traveled down Sai's body, then back to her face. Sai thought she'd run away like Pace had done. She didn't.

"Excuse me," Sai mumbled as she walked past.

"If something happened," the girl said, "they have a protocol for that. If you don't want them to tell you what to do, you can't just walk out like this."

ᘓ

THE DUMBWAITER HAD a lingering smell of chocolate fondue and macarons. The girl held the drape up as Sai crawled out of the service trolley and transferred into the metal box.

"Use the freight elevator at the back of the kitchen," the girl said.

"Thank you," said Sai.

"I'm not here." The girl shut the door.

The freight elevator took Sai to the loading dock. From there, she got back on Sauria Street and found the line of taxis waiting outside the front gate of the Frenell building. These lines had been getting longer as the CBD became the last spot in the city with a decent level of late-night business. She approached the first one in line, and the doors were locked. The driver rolled down a window and asked her where she was going.

"I've been waiting for over an hour," he grumbled after he heard she was going to a hospital merely six blocks away. "Get a street cab, or just walk."

"Please, it's an emergency," said Sai.

The driver rolled his window back up and faced forward, staring at the revolving door of Frenell & Co., waiting for a "high-value" customer to emerge.

Sai repeated the exchange at the end of the line, then she opened Google Maps and headed toward the nearest emergency room on foot. A street cab picked her up after two blocks and dropped her in front of the hospital. When the driver asked for the fifty dollars shown on the meter, she realized her wallet was still in the check-in locker of the Red Sea. They tried to sort out the payment with an app on her phone, and that was when she discovered she'd maxed out her credit card. Sheepishly, she asked if the driver could wait for her and she'd pay him for the round trip when she got home.

"Call a fucking ambulance the next time!" the driver yelled as he decided it'd cost him less to take his loss and move on.

A homeless man hovering outside the ER heard that and applauded the passion in the driver's complaint.

The harsh fluorescent lights thrashed her as she stepped into the ambience of a place trying to save lives. Near the entrance, a woman lay on a stretcher, puking into a bag strapped to its frame. Two paramedics were checking the pupillary reflex of an old man who was clearly under the influence. The waiting area was full, and every patient seemed cocooned in their own consciousness, separated from the world around them. A nurse in blue scrubs dashed past and made Sai notice she was blocking the way. She spotted the triage station across the lobby and moved forward in heavy, small steps. Against someone's blood trail, her shiny PU heels looked like a corny punchline.

Should she just tell them she'd been attacked, then they'd know what to do? What kind of insurance would she need for this? She no longer had any after she'd become a "contractor" of Frenell's staffing agency. Ever since she was old enough to understand the subtext behind people's stares, this particular ER trip had always been lurking in the shadows of her mind, yet it'd failed to prepare her.

When she was steps away from triage, she snapped around and bounded back to the entrance for some fresh air, almost colliding with her reflection on the glass door. The image made her heart sink. She stood there like a misplaced mannequin.

"What are you looking at?!" the homeless man shouted outside.

She was wearing one of her wardrobe staples—a black knee-length pencil dress with shoulder straps and no sleeves. Cute, versatile, and some would say just a little bit too low, too short, and too tight to report an assault in. She'd wrapped her suit jacket around her body, but the slim cut helped very little. Times had changed, so she was told, yet she couldn't shake off the vivid image of people rolling their eyes when they heard "She can wear whatever she wants." Had her eyeliner and mascara been this heavy the whole night? Or was it because they were smudged?

She couldn't recall the precise reason why she'd chosen this wavy hairstyle—not to be intentionally alluring, she knew that, but was that obvious to everyone?

Then she thought about the "investigation" that would follow. They'd ask her what she was doing there in the first place, what kind of "relationship" she'd had with Wade, whether she'd had any "relationship" with anyone she worked with. They'd dig out her complaint against Hayden and the record of its dismissal. They'd ask her about that video.

They'd ask her about Henry. Worse, they might ask Henry about her.

She stared into the dark night and pictured Henry receiving a long line of unexpected questions. She pictured his expression changing from confusion to shock to unease, then eventually, annoyance. Then she pictured herself in a witness box, desperately trying to justify every thought and action leading to this night, while her distressed family watched from the public gallery, knowing that none of them could help her.

Outside the ER and next to the mirrored image of her petrified face, the homeless man kept on shouting.

"What are you looking at?!"

THE TAXI DRIVER who took her home did not scream at her, and he let her get out of the car without paying, but he kept her phone as collateral while she picked up her cash. Her keys were also in her wallet, so she borrowed a plastic IKEA card from the driver to bypass the latch. She reclaimed her phone after the driver got his money. No missed calls or new messages.

She secured her door with the jammer, then went straight into the shower, turned on the water, and let it run. Inside the plastic caddy was a new bottle of shampoo she'd bought yesterday. She couldn't get over the sophisticated mix of neroli and sandalwood from the one she'd tried at Henry's place. According to YouTube reviews, this was the closest dupe.

She squeezed out a palmful, foamed it with her hands, and covered herself in it. Her hair, her face, her neck, her breasts and thighs, every inch of her skin with a bad smell that she wanted to remove. Then she closed her eyes and crouched down, hugging herself in the steamy, synthetic scent of a fake garden, pretending she was elsewhere.

10

"WHAT'S WRONG WITH good old cash transactions?" Chateau flipped the holding certificate upside down, then back, in his hands.

"Nothing. We can certainly preserve them. But I present to you three reasons why this new model will facilitate swift scaling and drive sustainable growth."

Nolan peeked at Chateau as he stressed the word *scaling*. He'd mention that word a few more times because he knew how much it'd remind Chateau of the fatal mistake he'd made with the Smile Enhancer. The woman next to Chateau was listening, but so far she'd displayed as much emotion as the *Mona Lisa*. Chateau hadn't given a proper introduction when they'd turned up together, except that the matter on today's agenda required deliberation of two manager-level Advocates, and she was that second vote. She looked like she'd come straight from horseback-riding practice–snow-white show shirt with a ratcatcher collar, double-front charcoal jacket with a pleated back, chestnut hair in a braided bun, and slender fingers in a pair of black sueded-cotton gloves. Fischer was convinced that he'd met this woman somewhere before but couldn't recall where or when, and that was the one thing that'd distract him throughout the presentation. Wade's face lit up when she walked in, then he lost interest as soon as he realized she wasn't Zoe's new colleague.

"First, the holding certificate serves as a powerful tool to mitigate the disruptive supply shortage, which can compromise user experience," Nolan said. "As evidence of commitment, these certificates can guide supply coordination and ensure that available stock is triaged and allocated to high-value users according to their positions on the priority scale."

The stack of "stimulant options" that the ADVP had dropped last night certified ownership of over fifty thousand dollars' worth of purchases and tracked their incremental redemption and balance on the back. This rudimentary system didn't record user habits or length of the customer relationship, and that was the first thing Frenell could fix.

"The stimulant options can be so much more than a simple IOU, which brings us to our second point–we should acknowledge the holding certificates as a product in their own right. This helps us tap into the market of people who don't use drugs themselves. Someone who despises social media may nevertheless own Facebook stocks. People who know nothing about blockchain may still hold Bitcoin out of FOMO–the fear of missing out, the most potent sales driver of the decade. It also alleviates the legal pressure because they're not in possession of an illegal substance, only the idea of it. Unlocking the non-user market will let us access the whole iceberg instead of just the tip and, accordingly, scale to the next level. We're optimistic about market reception given the consistent and strong interest in Rhapsody. You can find at exhibit 1B a line chart visualizing its retail price increase over time."

Chateau and the woman flipped their glossy-covered booklets to the exhibit, where the page laid out an inspirational up-trending curve that was never stiff enough for the esteemed "investors." Wade let out an audible yawn that almost let Nolan see his fillings. His stare trailed off along the underutilized dancing table they sat around, and the look on his face could be described as "solemn." Nothing hits harder than an empty dancing pole in a stagnant economy.

"This sounds like a logistical nightmare." Chateau shook his head.

"Great point." Nolan nodded. "That's why we invite you to imagine a new way of drug dealing. Businesses must remain adaptive and agile in this era of uncertainty. I believe you have noticed that, these days, everything is a service, and every service has a platform. The next chapter of High Hopes Inc. will no doubt be the digitization of the transactions."

He spread his arms and started drawing invisible blocks and hierarchy charts in the air.

"Envisage an integrated platform where we have the users, the distributors, and the non-user proprietors. The users register their purchases and track their consumption through their accounts. This helps with their budget control since they can visualize their drug spending over a period of time. If they wish to apply techniques like dollar-cost averaging, they can certainly do so. The distributors have access to an informative dashboard that exhibits their customer preferences and sales trends. We can also connect them to a centralized order, delivery, and customer services network as part of our seller support. Then we have the non-user holders. They get real-time bid-and-ask prices for the product and a secondary market consolidating their potential trading parties in one place. We can charge a commission for each buy and sale for some extra income, but we think the best use of this group is to create an active market and sustain the hype about Rhapsody in order to attract more users organically. Let me pause here 'cause I think there might be questions?"

Nolan gave his audience an encouraging nod.

"Yeah . . . just . . . why would we do any of this?" Chateau asked.

"In our line of business"—the woman uttered her first words since she'd walked in—"we prefer to keep a low profile."

"Another great point!" Nolan exclaimed. "This brings us to our third and final stage of High Hopes' evolution. Once we have locked in all three groups and secured our market position, let's streamline our services by removing the tiered distribution and franchise. Instead of physical drugs, we sell managed-use solutions. Products can only be redeemed at our designated collection sites, so users don't risk getting worse stuff off the streets, nor do they have to pay any middlemen. They enroll in autonomous metered programs where they have full control over how much they use, how they want to taper, when they want to stop, if they want to come back. In the future, we can move to a subscription model—like those monthly groceries and meal plans, or mystery boxes for designer drugs, but let's not get ahead of ourselves. This model offers our users safe, predictable consumption and lets us give back to the community and play a meaningful role in combating the ongoing drug crisis."

"You want us to do what?" The woman turned to Chateau. "Are we still drug dealers, or have we restructured into something else?"

"Don't ask me." Chateau shrugged. "I didn't open the last three newsletters."

"This is the end goal we should aim for." Nolan leaned forward on his hands and kept his gaze sharp. "The war on drugs is unwinnable, and individual rehabilitation is highly inefficient. If we take more responsibility in this virtuous cause, we no longer have to be vampires. High Hopes will stand proudly under the sun, not as the creator or enabler of the crisis but as an essential stabilizing agent for an inevitable epidemic of human weakness. The users get better services. The investors profit from a product that will never be out of demand. Even the regulators will benefit from our success because of the resources we're able to devote to do their job. That's a four-way win-win."

Team High Hopes exchanged a look, then burst out laughing.

"There seems to be one group missing in your beautiful new world," said the woman. "Our distributors, so basically, every drug gang in town."

Nolan nodded and put on a compassionate tone.

"That's a fair point, and I hear you. But unfortunately, those distributors might not survive with or without us. With the abundant cheap materials and chemists available overseas and the growing need for cost control by automation, the challenge that small-scale gangs face is structural. It's time we accept that drug dealing and organized crimes are major league games. In the big picture, it'd be far more effective for those who have risen from the ashes to carry the torch and illuminate the path for the rest of humanity. For centuries, we've tried to 'do well by doing good.' Let's reclaim that motto and transcend it—this is the age for 'integrity by prosperity.'"

The woman held a ghost of a smile with her parted lips and stared at Nolan. Then she closed her eyes and chuckled.

"You are one magnificent piece of shit." She followed with an approving nod. "That's a compliment."

She laid a bespoke business card in front of Nolan with two gloved fingers. Clean layout on a piece of textured cardstock, with a matte finish that conveyed tasteful luxury. No watermark, that was a shame.

"Let me introduce myself—I'm the Vice President of High Hopes Inc. in charge of innovation, technology, and growth opportunities in the Great CBD Region. You've made an interesting proposal, and we're always on the lookout for talent—"

She paused as Wade reached across the table, snatched the card, and flashed it in front of his eyes.

"I think that's enough warm-up. How about let's get to the real business, Miss . . . Goldman."

"And you are?"

"He works for me." Wade tilted his head at Nolan. "And he's not looking for a job. We have a lot to do, so we'd better get on with it."

"Send a fee quote to my email." Goldman shrugged.

"I'll also attach the detailed project proposal–" said Nolan.

"What we had in mind was something different," said Wade. "This is a complex project, and no one understands it inside out and backward like Frenell. We believe High Hopes would get the most out of what we have to offer as a business partner, instead of as a client."

He then addressed the broader audience.

"First things first, research offshore manufacturing options. Start with Mexico, that's a no-brainer. Second, identify the steps in the process that can be streamlined. For example, to automate the delivery and collection of products, we can learn from the post offices and copy what they've been doing. Networking can be a bit particular in this business. We need some good precedents . . . what's that movie about cocaine with Michelle Pfeiffer and a bunch of Cubans?"

"*Scarface* . . . ?" Fischer said.

"That." Wade nodded. "We probably won't deal with Cubans, but gotta start somewhere. Okay, does everyone know what they should be doing?"

The group looked at each other in silence, sharing one collective thought: *Did this motherfucker just give us assignments?*

Nolan was speechless–Wade hadn't gotten to where he was by chance. He wished one day he'd have the guts to tell a drug dealer, "You know what you need? A boss." For the first time since he'd met Wade in the Level 28 bathroom, he experienced a profound sentiment toward this man that almost felt like respect.

"So"–Goldman clicked her tongue–"you want a piece of my business, you want to run your own show with my people, and now you want me to watch *Scarface*?"

Wade's eyes stayed on Goldman's chest for a second, then turned to Chateau. "We'd like to suggest a fifty-fifty global profit distribution. We trust we bring enough value to the table to make that a fair and reasonable deal."

Chateau said nothing and turned to Goldman.

"If you want to be a partner," said Goldman, "you go through the same system and start from A1 like everyone else. I don't see why we have to make an exception here."

"I've spent my entire life in the CBD, and I know these streets like the back of my hand." Wade pinned his eyes on Chateau.

Chateau looked down to check his phone as he raised a hand toward Goldman.

"A lot of our Advocates came from a similar background," said Goldman. "Myself included."

"Maybe this is something we should bring to a higher level for discussion?" Wade asked Chateau. "If you could kindly make an introduction to your senior management team, we'd greatly appreciate that."

Chateau gestured at Goldman for the third time.

"Wait . . . is she Jen Milford?" Fischer leaned in and whispered to Nolan as he navigated to the Partner profile of Jennifer Milford on Miller's website. The woman in a pinstripe three-piece suit looked squarely into the camera—an intense gaze you'd want to see on someone you considered hiring for a million-dollar project, as long as it was neutralized by a pair of appropriately curved lips that implied she was still "easy to work with." That subtly disdainful expression reminded Nolan of Colleen.

"Seriously, you don't see it?" Fischer raised his phone and aligned the screen with Goldman's face. Nolan pulled his hand down and responded, "It's probably just the vibe."

"It'd be far more productive if we could speak with the right person." Wade smirked. "It won't work if it's just you and us."

He then swiveled a full ninety in his chair and slouched against the table, pretending to read Nolan's pitch deck and giving Goldman his side.

Goldman smiled.

"You don't want to talk to me, how about I send you to Tony Montana?"

She hopped on top of her stool, leaped across the table, and landed in front of Wade. From the leather sheath strapped to her right ankle, she drew out a clip-point survival knife, hoisted it high above Wade's head, and drilled it straight into the crown of his head before he could react in shock.

Two competing thoughts jumped into Nolan's mind: Goldman was wearing moto boots, which was outrageous–it wasn't even smart casual season–and with that knife handle sticking out of his skull, Wade looked like a candy apple.

No one around the table made a sound, until Fischer conceded, "Okay, she's not Jen Milford."

"You have *one* rage kill per year, woman." Chateau put down the pitch deck he'd held in front of his face as a shield. "And you spent it on this guy?"

"He talked too much, and he had a really annoying voice." Goldman pulled the knife out of Wade and seemed annoyed by the mess she'd have to clean off the blade, so she stuck it back inside the eighth hole she'd opened in Wade's head.

"What if tomorrow you run into a sex trafficker or a child molester?" Chateau asked.

"You haven't used yours, have you?" She skipped off the table and brushed some dust off her pants. "Give me your credit, or I'll tell the board you've been using company resources for your side project."

"But I'm saving it–"

"Your credit, or your gadgets."

She picked up her card and slipped it into Nolan's palm, leaving a bloody smear on both sides.

"Think about it." She winked, then instructed Chateau, "Let's go collect the dues. Is Zoe working today?"

Chateau let out an exasperated sigh, then left Nolan and Fischer with a hearty piece of advice.

"I swear to God, some days this job really gets on my nerves . . . work for yourselves, guys. Lay off the Kool-Aid."

"YOU'VE GOTTA BE fucking kidding me."

"You did great with the last one!"

Ryuka looked at Wade's body crammed inside the trunk of his Ferrari Purosangue and thought this was exactly what was wrong with the corporate world: the only reward for good work is more work.

"The last one was nobody!" She glared at Nolan. "*I* can't even remember his face, and I was literally the last person who saw him! This is W-fucking-PF! People could be looking for him, like, right now! God, Nolan . . . you can't do this to me . . ."

She felt a wave of dizziness, and her breathing intensified. For a moment, the smell inside that dumbwaiter returned to haunt her, and it didn't blend well with underground parking.

"Um, if you need to chill out–" Fischer extended a nasal spray to Ryuka. Nolan clamped Fischer's wrist and pulled it away.

"Look, I'm really sorry!" He groaned. "I didn't mean to do this to you, but it happened too fast . . . we were just trying to sell some drug shares–"

"Stimulant options." Fischer corrected him.

"Whatever! Then . . . then this VP woman–right, she was with Ed Chateau! You remember Chateau? Anyway, Wade pissed her off–"

"Because he gave her a to-do list," said Fischer. "Never ask clients to do things. They don't even like reading emails–"

"The point is! The point is . . . something about *Scarface* rubbed her the wrong way and she just lost it and stabbed Wade straight down the skull. Jesus! Have you seen a *proper* Mafia kill?! God . . . how the fuck did I get here . . . I don't know, the first person I thought of was you, Ryu. You're the only person I trust in this place, in this whole world maybe . . ."

He stopped there to catch his breath and gave Ryuka an awkward grin.

"Okay . . . so I'm hearing . . . that you didn't kill him." Ryuka stared at Nolan as she extracted the keywords. "Did you kill him—actually, don't answer that, and there's a Mafia lady who might not be totally done with this."

Nolan and Fischer looked at each other for a second.

"I may have used the word *Mafia* loosely," said Nolan. "She seems more of a . . . an independent contractor."

"Yeah, that lady has a really strong mercenary vibe, damn," Fischer added.

"Please, Ryu . . . help me out," Nolan said. "I'll do *anything* for you. Anything."

Ryuka stared into Wade's half-open eyes and tried to sketch his final thoughts. Yesterday, she'd spent the night coping with the revelation that she'd never have a future at Frenell again, for she'd blown her chance of being approved by its god. Today, Frenell's god was curled up in a fetal position, with a dagger poking out of his head like an antenna and shadows in the crotch of his suit pants that seemed like stains of incontinence. Her chest tightened again, and the world in front of her retracted and distorted as if captured by a fish-eye lens. Silently, she counted and named the things in her vision to register where she was and what she was doing. Maybe she'd never left that dumbwaiter and she was still traveling through the tunnel. She pictured herself reaching the bottom. There wasn't a new dimension, only the stone-cold walls of a well. At the end of all that falling, all she could claim was a Post-it note that said, "Louis Vuitton seat covers won't make your brains any less sticky."

She chuckled a little.

The mighty WPF was dead.

She mustered all the life experience she'd acquired inside the grandiose glass cage above them and imagined the worst sin she could commit and how she'd get away with it. For example . . . what if she was cat-sitting and the fur baby ran out on her?

Get a new one and hope the owner won't tell the difference.

RYUKA MURONG LIVED in a warehouse.

Not the kind of luxurious Manhattan loft with an edgy touch from its exposed bricks and industrial ceiling. It had as much interior decoration as the one in *Reservoir Dogs*, and it had to be called a "warehouse" because it was too big for a "storage unit." Nolan ran his eyes along the steel-gray concrete and rusty pipes, wondering if Ryuka had been looking for someplace to put all the gadgets she'd hoarded, then she'd seen the kitchenette and the bathroom and decided she might as well move herself in, save some human-domicile rent, and maybe one day retire.

"How long have you been living here?" Nolan asked.

"Since I started at Frenell, so . . . about five years?"

"Wait, what was that cozy one-bedroom you took us to last Christmas?"

"Oh, that was an Airbnb decoy."

"What?"

"So we need a full scan of Wade's face and his fingerprints for biometrics. Bring him over." Ryuka led Nolan and Fischer to a small studio behind the partition screens next to her bed and turned on the softboxes around the chair. She let Nolan hold the handle of the dagger to keep Wade's head in place, then she dragged a handheld scanner across Wade's face as if checking his temperature from different angles.

"Okay, if we're gonna scan his retinas, don't ask me to hold his eyelids." Fischer took a step back. "I'm not good with intimacy."

"We don't have that level of security at Frenell," said Ryuka. "But this is a gaming scanner, so the raw images will need some touch-up. Find some pictures of Wade online, you know, with more lively expressions."

Fischer downloaded all the professional headshots and interview photos he could find of Wade from open sources, then dug into his social media. The guy was on every platform, exclusively for liking and reposting family updates from his wife. It took a decent amount of time to trawl through that gallery and collect the samples documenting Wade's appearance in the last three months. Ryuka fed Wade's face scan and the downloads into a 3D modeling software, and they watched the claylike base flourish into a fleshy mask, refined with the correct pink undertone, realistic imperfections, and precise wrinkle distribution. After one song's worth of time, the severed head of Wade opened his eyes and grinned.

For a copy of Wade's voiceprint, they extracted his prerecorded voicemail and cut hundreds of training samples from a dozen hour-long public seminars and BD recordings featuring him.

"Hi, my name is Wade Pendleton-Fitzpatrick. I have been to hell and back. Pleased to meet you too." The head practiced Wade's microexpressions and cadence on the screen without the involvement of a body.

"Reset his password, just in case," Ryuka said after they'd unlocked Wade's Frenell laptop with facial recognition. They tried to find a record of said password on a sticky note or a .txt file on Wade's desktop but then decided it'd be faster to call IT for help.

"When you speak into this mic"—Ryuka plugged Wade's phone into the laptop hosting his head—"this app washes your speech with the Wade clone track so it comes out as his voice. It also has text-to-speech conversion, which could be handy when you can't open your mouth. I've made a looping video with his face and locked his default camera to the feed of that footage. It's not foolproof, so only show it for the first few seconds of a meeting, then find an excuse to turn your camera off. Never say you got a cat or a dog wandering around, though. People will want to see it."

"Is Ryuka Murong your real name?" Nolan asked.

"At this point, what is 'real' anyway?"

"That shouldn't be the answer to that question."

Jake from IT picked up the call on the second ring. Ryuka nudged Nolan and signaled Fischer to stay quiet as a mouse.

"Hi . . . Jake, is it? How are you? This is Wade, um, WPF." Nolan steadied his voice. "I don't seem to be able to recall my log-in password—sorry, long day. I'm wondering if you might be able to reset it for me on your end, please."

"Mr. Pendleton-Fitzpatrick?" Jake asked.

"Yes, hello."

"You need a password reset, you say?"

"Yes, if that's not a problem. Actually, can we please do this on the call right now? I have a meeting in ten minutes and I'd really appreciate it if we could get this sorted immediately. Sorry about the short notice."

There was a long pause on the other end of the line. Nolan panicked and almost hung up as he was convinced they got busted and Frenell was tracing this call to track them down. Then Jake responded:

"I hope this doesn't land the wrong way, Mr. Pendleton-Fitzpatrick, but you seem uncharacteristically polite today. According to our security protocols, I have to ask you a few questions. Now, would you be able to tell me the name of your first pet, please?"

Nolan froze. Ryuka shoved him to the side and took over.

"You listen to me—whatever your name is—I've got eight minutes left before my next call, and you just wasted another thirty seconds. Do you know how much money that translates into? Whoops, there goes another fifty dollars. Should it come out of your next paycheck? Get this fixed *now* or you'd better get that old apron out 'cause you're about to go from help desk shifts back to coffee shifts."

There was another pause, followed by some rapid typing, then Jake said:

"Mr. Pendleton-Fitzpatrick, I have completed the reset and your screen should be prompting for a new password now.

Kindly note that the firm's policy requires a strong password to consist of–"

Ryuka cut the line while Jake was still talking and clenched her fists in silent victory.

"Why . . . do you . . . work at Frenell?" Nolan asked.

"It's my dream job." Ryuka shrugged.

They went through Wade's calendar to figure out where he needed to be in the next eight hours, then set his Teams status to "Busy." Nolan and Fischer moved his body back to his car and promised to take both somewhere they'd never disclose to Ryuka even at gunpoint.

"Ryu, I remember what you said the other day outside Dandelion," Nolan said. "I think Wade has the authority to approve new Special Associates. If you wish, we can make it happen."

Ryuka glanced at Wade in the trunk. They'd put a black garbage bag over his head and tied the collar around his neck. She recalled the last moment she'd spent with Luc–at least Luc had had the sunshine.

"Nah, I'm good." She slammed the lid down. "Actually, there's something better we can do."

They sent out an email from Wade's account before they parted ways. As Nolan started the engine, Ryuka knocked on his window and stuck her face in.

"Nolan, never dump shit like this on me again. I'm not your cleaner."

WHILE THE AD hoc gang of three was busy resuscitating Wade, the Grads of Frenell gathered in the Loyalty Room on Level 31 for an ad hoc assembly announced five minutes ago.

"I'm shaking right now." The OATH manager onstage put a hand over her chest. "I haven't had an hour of sound sleep since that video came out. We–the Partners and OATH–feel deeply hurt and disappointed that the person chose to communicate in such an immature and unhelpful way. It felt like someone had pulled the rug from under us."

Although she didn't say it out loud, the Grads knew what video she was referring to. Last night, Keahi hadn't been followed by just one Grad but a squad of ten who'd performed the same ritual, then walked out one by one. The group sentiment quickly transformed from "Wait, are we doing a thing?" to "Holy shit, this could be our *Do you hear the people sing* moment." Someone had filmed it and put it on TikTok with improvised hashtags like "the Spontaneous Walkout." In the next hour, it swept all social media in existence, even the one for knitting enthusiasts, because somebody's grandma wanted to show her grandkid at work.

"Our colleagues had to work overtime to address the misinformation in those posts," the OATH manager continued. "And some of the comments we saw . . . they were not only hostile and abusive, they were simply untrue. It's been a very traumatizing experience—"

She broke into tears, so Colleen took the podium and let her process her grief off the stage in her own time.

"We at Frenell always welcome constructive feedback from our employees," Colleen said. "But there's an appropriate manner for such communication. We believe those who engaged in this unprofessional outburst had the best intentions but operated on a temporary lapse of judgment. The Partners encourage them to come forward, and as the Acting Talent and Resources Partner, the Acting Partner for Culture, Ethics, Sensitivity and Influence, and the Mental Health Champion of the firm, I'm here to address any concerns you may have."

She paused to scan the crowd. No response or eye contact. She let the silence ferment and cloak the room, until the Grads realized they were gonna be here for a while.

"It can be daunting to speak up." Colleen smiled. "So I'm going to make an executive decision and pick a representative—"

The screen behind her put up a collage of still shots extracted from the video in question, and a collective gasp sucked all sounds out of the air. The author of the video had only started filming after the walkout had taken shape, so Keahi and So-yeon weren't caught on camera. But she'd captured more than enough. Three full-frontal shots, five profiles, and one accidental catch of someone who'd walked too close to the frame. Nine faces, not mosaiced with the slightest effort. Some Grads glanced around furtively for the author who'd presumably turned in the unedited film, but they couldn't find her anywhere.

Colleen relished their reactions. With abundant clues, including the shooting angle, the seating plan, and everything else posted on that TikTok account, it had taken less than ten minutes to identify the author. They could've matched the outfits and gaits of the protesters with lobby CCTV footage, of course, but going to the source was far more efficient.

"Adam," she called out. "Nice haircut."

Adam Sulley, the second Grad who'd followed Keahi out and the face on the top left corner, flinched at the sound of his name. The next moment, his staff badge, and eight more across the floor, made a humming noise that repelled the bystanders surrounding them and opened nine pockets in the crowd, each containing a rebel inside. The wooden doors flanking the stage popped open, and two rows of patrol robots marched in. They broke into pairs—two bots for one rascal.

"Let's hear from the heroes," Colleen said.

One of the robots next to Adam extended a microphone to him. Not getting an audible response, it thrust the mic forward as if pushing a dick into his mouth. Adam whimpered and turned his face, breathing heavily like he was having an asthma attack. The rest of the Grads lowered their heads and stared at their feet. The room sat in mournful silence for a whole minute until Colleen spoke again.

"If you don't have a case to make, I regret to inform you that it is a trigger for termination without notice if you obstruct the conduct of business, fail to perform your duties, or adversely affect the firm's image or reputation. However, we value our talent and we believe everyone deserves a second chance. So, the Partners will pardon all of you, but we'll have to enroll you in our performance improvement plan—"

David McCallen, the fifth Grad caught on film and the face in the center of the collage, let out a scoff that only those near him could hear. He flung his badge at the wall and held up a middle finger above his head as he stormed out without looking back. He moved overseas two weeks later; didn't say goodbye to anyone. Jonathan Douglas, son of a hedge fund manager and an art dealer, followed suit. "This is retaliation. I'm gonna sue you fucks." He slammed his badge on the granite floor as the door shut behind him. He did speak to his family lawyer about legal proceedings against the firm, then he found out that his dad had to collaborate with the brother of a Frenell Partner on an ongoing deal, so that was the end of it.

"Is that all?" Colleen asked. No one spoke or moved, so she carried on. "Each of you will receive a warning letter, and a write-up in your RAP, but if you successfully pass the evaluation at the end of the PIP—"

"We didn't start it!" Adam shouted.

A ghostly grin emerged on Colleen's face, but she waited for more.

"Yeah . . . we got carried away . . . we're sorry!" Another made a noise that could be a nervous chuckle or the first note of a sob.

"I had a family emergency last night!" one of the Grads said in a shaky voice. "It wasn't a protest!"

"Guys, we are better than this!" one of them said. While his comment was buried under the pleas of his one-night comrades and the uncomfortable sniffs and coughs from the rest of the Grads, Adam's voice cut through the waves and repeated:

"We didn't start this—"

"I did." Keahi stepped forward, and a hush fell over the crowd. She walked to the front and stopped two steps away from the stage. Four robots scooted over and circled her.

"I'm the one who started this," she said.

"And you are?"

"Keahi Ka'uhane."

"Exactly what was the point that you were trying to make, Keahi Ka'uhane?" Colleen smiled.

"I wasn't making a point. I finished my work, so I went home."

"Do you consider that appropriate when your colleagues were clearly under the gun and needed assistance?"

"It was ten p.m., and I think it's management's responsibility to provide reasonable working conditions and have realistic expectations about workload and turnaround time."

"So you have a point to make after all." Colleen leaned against the podium and stared at Keahi, amused. "In succinct language and small words, tell me exactly what you want changed."

"The Graduate cohort has been working extremely long hours since we started," Keahi said. "The delegation of work also seems disproportionate. We think the complexity of certain work exceeds our level—"

"'We'?"

"It's a common observation."

"Will any of your friends here endorse this 'common observation'?"

"I can't force them."

"Do any of you think your work is too much or too hard?" Colleen asked the crowd and received silence.

"It's a known fact that a lot of Grads have been sleeping in the office," Keahi said. "The communication and management styles of some senior staff are questionable. The level of anxiety is high, and some of us have turned to . . . unhealthy solutions because of the stress."

"You want to say drugs, don't you?" Colleen laughed. "Are you going to tell me which one of your buddies is a secret junkie?"

Keahi held her tongue. She was planning to have another chat with Luc before next week to persuade him to participate in the *Grand Ivory Post* interview anonymously. That reminded her—

she hadn't seen him around today. Maybe he was on a business trip.

"I won't give you names," said Keahi. "This is not a safe environment for people to talk."

"Thank you for reminding me." Colleen nodded. "It is crucial that our people can share their feelings freely, which is why we allow emotional support in confrontational situations. Keahi, you can nominate a friend to join this conversation as your champion."

"I'm fine."

"It's okay—knowing how to ask for help is a sign of mental resilience."

Colleen retrieved Keahi's Timekeeper Profile with her smart ring and zoomed in on her Relationship Map.

"Is So-yeon here?" Colleen asked.

"I don't need any support right now," Keahi repeated. Two robots located So-yeon in the crowd and brought her to the front nevertheless. Keahi tried to make eye contact, but So-yeon never shifted her gaze from the tips of her shoes.

"So-yeon, are you helping Keahi with her little revolution?" Colleen asked. As So-yeon remained silent, Colleen changed her question: "Is there anything you'd like to share with us?"

"No," So-yeon said after a moment of hesitation.

"We encourage our staff to voice their concerns as we believe that's best for morale, so you really shouldn't be afraid to speak up."

"I don't have any concerns." So-yeon sighed. "Everything is—"

"We know you had some silly drama with an Associate on your team and you complained to OATH." Colleen's smile turned into a smirk. "You accused her of bullying, didn't you?"

So-yeon snapped her head up, eyes wide in shock.

"You're only a Grad, aren't you, So-yeon?" Colleen asked. "Do you think it's wise to pick fights before even claiming your Associate badge? Or do you think as soon as you've passed probation, everything is on the table?"

"I specifically asked OATH not to escalate the claim." So-yeon clenched her jaw. "And they specifically promised they wouldn't without my consent."

"That's interesting. Why would you want to keep it secret if you had a legitimate claim?"

"Because I don't trust–"

"So you can take matters into your own hands and stab us in the back?" Colleen sneered. "Let me ask you again, So-yeon, are you participating in Keahi's Great Walkout?"

"This is not her interrogation," Keahi said.

"We haven't forgotten about you, young lady," Colleen said. "Since you were talking about 'unreasonable hours,' let's take a look at your metrics–"

She swiped Keahi's Relationship Map away and opened her Productivity Summary.

"Your self-recorded utilization is over one hundred and fifty percent, but our in-house data scientists have helpfully verified that against your PADU records, including your email and instant message exchange rates, calendar entries, conference call durations, mouse-moving frequency, typing speed, clicking and scrolling patterns, inactive time of your computer, and suspected absence detected by the sensors under your workstation. They've reconciled some discrepancies and reached a very intriguing conclusion–there's an over fifty percent chance that you may have inflated your time sheets–"

"That's not true," said Keahi.

"–an over forty-one percent chance that the seemingly excessive working time was caused by misinterpretation of instructions, lack of planning, and general inefficiency. There's also a twelve percent chance that you've installed an unauthorized mouse jiggler."

"I request a copy of that investigation report and its source data."

"That information is firm property, which we have no obligation to divulge," Colleen said. "But we'll afford you procedural fairness--you have twenty-four hours to submit the evidence supporting your claims. Failing to substantiate any allegations you've made to other Frenell staff or external parties will result in termination of your employment. The firm also reserves its rights to commence defamation proceedings against you."

Without waiting for a response from Keahi, Colleen signaled the robots to take her and So-yeon away. Instead of the front doors next to the stage, four bots wedged the crowd open and paraded the two girls across the floor. Every Grad they marched past turned their head to the side and kept their gaze on the ground. As the back doors closed and muted the footsteps, the room fell quiet like a graveyard.

"As we mentioned earlier, we value constructive feedback, but there's a right way to do it," Colleen said in a tone deprived of amusement. "Undermining the firm brand with petty, specious, even fabricated claims is counterproductive and deplorable. The only effective approach is to have an honest, transparent, and balanced discussion with your team, your Handler, and OATH. We're always here to listen."

She dismissed the crowd and let the leftover patrol bots herd them out. As the Grads shuffled away in silence, Colleen ended the assembly on a joyful note:

"Remember to charge zero point eight hours of 'Non-billable: Personal Development' for this meeting. We suggest you use 'Participate in training on workplace culture enhancement' for narrative. Those who are attending the anniversary party tomorrow, you have by COB today to sign your acknowledgment of firm policies on responsible alcohol consumption at firm events, and acceptable use of mobile devices and social media. There will be clients attending, so the Frenell Business Development Code of Conduct applies. We look forward to seeing you there, and we wish you all a wonderful time."

11

NOLAN TOOK A sip of his fifth vodka tonic and decided that lopsided smirk was Wade's natural feature instead of an acquired quality from his virtualization, so he'd stop worrying about it.

"We are proud of where Frenell stands today, but we must not stay complacent, and we must strive to go above and beyond. For one of the last few great things left in this world, a hundred and fifty years is just a blink."

The speech was supposed to be five minutes. Nolan had cut it to three. The longer Wade's face stayed on the screen, the more likely someone would notice something. He strolled along the walls and gauged people's reactions. There were clusters of whispers, but the sporadic giggles and the casual swaying of their bodies suggested they weren't talking about a dead man. Some had a light pout—the bored kind, not the suspicious kind. Some were more interested in the Scorpius constellation over their heads than Frenell's hopes and dreams—Office Facilities had retracted the dividers between the four meeting rooms on Level 31 to make a grand venue the size of a basketball court, and a virtual background spread across the ceiling to paint an illusion of an arched glass roof under a starry sky. The visuals were breathtaking, indeed. Had Nolan's life turned out as he'd expected two weeks ago, with him cruising through his notice period at this point while getting ready for Chalet & Gravelines, he would've for sure enjoyed it. He settled down in a corner, back against the wall, so no one could read what was on his screen over his shoulder.

Wade already had the inbox of someone who'd died in their apartment pending discovery. Over thirteen thousand emails were "Unread" and there was no evidence of any filing in the last five months. The project-related ones were easy. Nolan would forward them on without adding a word, and the Special Associates on those cases would figure out what to do. The ones calling for Wade's executive decisions were trickier, but he'd gotten a handle after going through the latest messages in Wade's Sent folder, which could be categorized into "Approved," "No," "Details?" and "Do not engage." Limited punctuation. No emoji. Occasional confusion between *there* and *their*. Nolan was a fast learner, and sometimes people didn't give him enough credit for it.

Yesterday, after he'd taken over virtual WPF, he'd found the number of Wade's wife in his personal phone and sent her a text: *Have to go to Europe for urgent business. Could be away for a while. Miss you and the kids.*

She hadn't replied until an hour ago: *I know about that bitch in Milan.*

Well, that was a freebie.

The lights in the ballroom dimmed as a door near the front screen grated open. A spotlight rained down from the ceiling, capturing and following what came in. The gasps of amazement rippled from the front rows to the center of the room and radiated further. Nolan couldn't see a thing from where he stood, but he knew what it was. The panorama screen walls glowed up and brought everybody onto the same page.

The egg looked less flattering in real life than in the demo and could be easily mistaken for a spherical bollard. The maker of the patrol robots wanted a more minimalist aesthetic for this line, so people would pay more attention to the fact that they lived in an age with such slick and futuristic toys and focus less on what these things could do.

The egg pulsed silver as the ribbon of headshot slots below its crown started flashing. Each unit could be associated with up to ten Timekeepers, and the finished product would resemble a communal headstone for ghosts who couldn't afford individual housing. The provisioned egg would faithfully record all activities on each associated account, and wash the mash of data against a vault of preset rules to analyze and rank the Timekeepers by productivity, efficiency, and "value for money." The system would then distill the data from the top performers to train a "Shadow Associate" and fine-tune it by rewarding the qualities Frenell approved and penalizing the attributes that were less than optimal. The accounts ranked below average of the batch would be replaced by new candidates each month, and all the human Associates would be evaluated against their collective Shadow every quarter. Once the Shadow had outperformed the humans for two consecutive quarters, it'd be time for a new batch.

"We retain only the best of the best," said virtual Wade. "So our clients will receive the finest services this profession has to offer."

"Bet you twenty that's a fucking AI talking."

Nolan turned to the voice and saw a woman with a disheveled bun, wrinkled blazer, deep lines under her eyes, and expired deodorant that would mark a female "cattle" from miles away. The guy next to her scoffed in agreement and scanned the room to see if Wade would pop out of a dark corner and start a duet with his virtual self.

"If he pulls that stupid stunt, I'm gonna be so pissed," the guy said.

"Is he trying to say 'I'm not that old,' like those Boomers on TikTok, or is he just rubbing it in?"

"Definitely rubbing it in. Like, hey, I can be replaced too, but guess what, I already own this fucking place."

"I need another drink—"

The female Associate stumbled away with the empty wineglass dangling upside down from between her fingers. She probably shouldn't have had "another drink" two drinks before this one, but she hadn't found anything else that could make her feel better. After she'd bumped into three guests in a row, a patrol robot started tailing her.

As Wade announced that AS28HGC6-F was scheduled for rollout across all Timekeepers below Partner level from Monday, the ribbon of headshots stopped flashing. The slots were filled with faces, and the silver pulsing turned into a still glow. A moment later, the flawless oval shape elongated and undulated with bulges and spikes. Amid the unsettling stretching noises and faint groans of disgust from the audience, the egg morphed into a humanoid and stepped off its display base. Wade's voice turned solemn—perfect for a prophet.

"This is our response to the future. Frenell has always been—and always will be—one of a kind and the leader of the pack."

The room blacked out on Wade's last syllable, then the Shadow opened its eyes under the remaining spotlight.

"Diligent, loyal, available, and now efficient," it said in a natural voice with a natural smile. "All instructions and complaints will be addressed within twenty-four hours. Call the Frenells for impeccable service and utmost satisfaction. Any day, anytime."

As it identified several guests in the front row as "clients" by the color of their wristbands, the Shadow bowed slightly, then it withdrew to a respectful distance and settled by the side of the OATH assistant who'd wheeled it in. Its social cues module decided it was too soon for it to initiate human contact, so it stood with its hands clasped in front of its body, looking professional and tame. The OATH assistant snapped her fingers, and the lights came back on. After a moment of silence, some guests approached the Shadow and squished its limbs like picking an avocado in a supermarket.

The Shadow wore a perfectly symmetrical and ethnically obscure face. As the Associates tried to decipher the vague familiarity, the panorama screens displayed a line of headshots and revealed the ingredients in the first batch–the ten Associates who'd participated in the Spontaneous Walkout, including the two who'd quit at the assembly. Keahi wasn't among them. OATH reckoned she'd poison the well of elixir.

After the open trial of the Spontaneous Eleven, Frenell had dedicated a new channel in Sensible Echoes to collect "anonymous feedback" on any practices that the Associates believed would undermine the firm's "supportive and collegial culture." The landing page looked like it was designed with Microsoft Paint. "Your voice matters," said the banner on top, while the fine print at the bottom reassured that no one mentioned in the feedback would ever know the source of the comment. OATH had announced the launch of this campaign on LinkedIn and promised to release the results to uphold Frenell's commitment to ETA–engagement, transparency, and accountability. The channel would remain open for six weeks. So far, they'd gotten only crickets.

As for the *Grand Ivory Post* interview that was supposed to happen next week, Keahi had called it off, as the "football team" had fallen apart. Without enough firsthand testimonies, the narrative couldn't even make a decent Facebook rant.

Guess it's time to say goodbye :), she texted Nolan. Her twenty-four-hour "grace period" was about to expire.

He typed out a few words in response, then deleted all of them. Staring at the empty input box, he wished a coherent message would appear on its own and accurately convey how he felt. Part of that was shame–like he'd had the chance to stop a murder via time travel, yet he'd sat and watched it happen anyway.

Chilling on Lv 20, she added. *Join me for some fresh air?*

He entered a thumbs-up emoji and chugged the last of his vodka tonic. The alcohol punched his brain, and he felt less hopeless. Before he hit Send, an outburst of laughter distracted him. He looked around and found the same circle of four he and Fischer had used for alibis at the café the other day.

"Cringe!" The Year 3 winced at whatever James was showing them on his screen.

"I know it's only May," James said, "but this is the most pathetic shit of 2028. Change my mind."

Last night, the leftovers of the nine Grads caught on film had made a separate video explaining that the original footage had been taken out of context. It was never meant to be a strike or a protest, but merely to preserve a slice of the "professional" life with no disgruntled undertone, like how people would photograph their brunch just for its documentary value. The group then expressed their gratitude for Frenell's understanding and celebrated the 150th birthday of this prestigious establishment with a collaborative rendition of Lennon's "Imagine" that began with "Imagine life without purpose." After two verses praising the rewarding lifestyle of this job in shifting keys, the clip transitioned into a montage of the Grads saying "Thank you, Frenell" to a swelling Hans Zimmeresque soundtrack.

"Still not the worst version of that song," said Ben. "So what happened to the chick who started all this?"

James dragged his forefinger across his throat and grinned at Ben. "You owe me five hundred."

"What an absolute joke!" Ben rolled his eyes. "I thought she had a million dollars sitting in her bank or at least a trust fund or something, so they could make a whole season of that shit show. Turns out she's fucking nobody! Um, hello?! If you don't have any superpower, don't try to be a superhero, then make an ass of yourself!"

"She'd be a nice con artist," said the Year 3. "Like, one of those motivational grifters who'd tell people 'life is short, so pursue your dreams.'"

"Hold on, we still don't know who's behind that," Suspenders said. "Maybe there's some Partner politics and we'll see a plot twist soon."

"You got something to add?" James noticed Nolan staring and pointed his bottle at him. The rest of the group turned their heads in unison and waited for a response. Their glazed-over eyes projected the boredom of an unimpressed audience, as if all the chaos crossing their paths were merely contrived scenes to fill time. A taste of repulsion rose up within Nolan, reeking of the cheap beer he could smell on them.

"What do you get out of this, exactly?" he asked. "Sometimes I can't tell if you're real people or just the dead skin of this fucking place in human shape."

The group shared a grimace among themselves, then roared with laughter like a chorus of pond frogs.

"Deep!" the Year 3 hollered and raised her glass for a salute, turning several heads and getting a few stares.

"We're dead skin. You're foreskin." Ben nudged James.

"Fuck off." James kept his eyes on Nolan. "What's your problem, Mr. Nice Guy? You bet your house on the idiots and now you're homeless?"

"Fuck you," said Nolan.

"Easy, buddy." Suspenders took his free hand out of his pocket. Nolan ignored him and glared back at James.

"You want to be a pig, be a pig. Stay in your pen and roll in your manure. Nobody cares. But you seem to enjoy shitting on everyone who doesn't want to be a pig. That, I have a problem with."

James scoffed and strolled over, one step at a time, until his nose almost brushed Nolan's cheek.

"We all had to bend over and get fucked like we liked it. What makes that broke bitch so special she can just waltz in like some royal and have what we have without the bullshit? She ain't born into it. And you? You've been rolling in the same manure with me for five years straight. You think you get to call me a pig now 'cause some dumb chick redeemed you?"

He scanned Nolan from head to toe and chuckled.

"How was it? Please tell me you got a piece."

Nolan felt his lips curve up against his will. The sardonic grin on James's face reminded him of Wade right before Goldman had jabbed the dagger inside his skull. He was 90 percent certain he'd seen the corner of Wade's mouth twitch when the blade sank in.

Was that a smile or just a spasm?

WPF WAS DEAD. The world had not exploded.

In fact, the world had yet to notice this tragic loss. As far as Frenell's record went, Wade had been rather active in the past twenty-four hours. He'd delegated client instructions for half a dozen projects to half a dozen Special Associates in his pocket, voted on the menu choice for the next Partners' retreat, attended a virtual seminar hosted by the Bank of Pollyanna on wholesale investment trends, and asked Angela to open a new matter for a certain "Hate Monday Streaming LLC" in relation to their catalog development and the potential cultural risks associated with their programs. The work was entertaining and the client was reasonable—not cost sensitive and always provided the right information. The sole Timekeeper in charge was Associate RM23AGI6-L—Ryuka Murong, of all people.

With a simple email sent from Wade's account, Ryuka's Handler had officially changed from Morse Sachet to Wade Pendleton-Fitzpatrick, and like that, Ryuka was emancipated. The crippling pressure to "exceed expectations" was lifted because the dead complained very little. The constant battle to "manage up" was no longer necessary because she'd gained much better control over the feedback she'd get. Next Monday, she'd have her first briefing for "Project Spectre" with her silent mentor, where she'd rant about the continuous decline of quality in horror movies in recent years and the endless production of flying mutants in tights, and he'd sit through the whole session without interrupting her even once. Afterward, he'd write in her Timekeeper Profile that "Ryuka Murong consistently demonstrates creative problem-solving skills and produces surprising results. She maintains a positive attitude under pressure and delivers timely, high-quality work, adding great value to the team as a proactive and determined member."

Every Frenell Associate would claim they could work autonomously with minimal supervision. Ryuka was the one who delivered in the most truthful sense.

I just wish I could be less invisible.

She read her old message in Perspective and laughed at herself. Now she'd rather be a glitch in the Matrix so she could commit the one true crime this place would never condone: loss of productivity.

It was a delicate sin, and moderation was key. Filling all her time with made-up assignments could tank her collection rate and quickly attract unwanted attention, so Ryuka sourced her limited real work from Michael Clervaux, one of those Teflon Partners who were physically incapable of retaining any memory about an Associate's capabilities or existence. No matter how many years had passed and how much work you'd done for him, he'd still act like he knew too little about you to sustain any "relationship" you assumed you had with him. The Associates had mixed feelings about this, depending on how much they liked Michael on a scale of one to ten. The zero to three called him "impersonal," "cold," or straight-up "arrogant." The eight to ten said he had "good boundaries," "high standards," and a "professional management style." A ten had once called him "surrealistically gorgeous yet surprisingly tame," which was unexpected but informative. If you sat somewhere near five–like most people–you wouldn't think much about Michael Clervaux in general, until he called you on a Saturday because he couldn't turn bullet points into numbering in Word, or until you had to email him from a hospital bed explaining that you were in a car accident, so you wouldn't be able to get that letter to him until eleven in the morning, and he replied with "*11 is fine*," period.

If you rated Michael a five out of ten, you'd simply see him as "Your Average Frenell Partner," or "Not-the-Worst."

Not-the-Worst was running a merger due diligence on a vitamin distributor, and Emma, who was leading the case, had put Ryuka on PPT duty. The slide deck was supplemented by a fifty-page Word table organizing the findings in accordance with their priority and gravity. The latest task Ryuka had received from Emma was to underscore section headings, standardize paragraph indents, and ensure the rows containing medium-risk findings were shaded in apricot with 20 percent opacity.

If you could go through the whole document and fix those, it would make everybody's life so much easier, Emma said in her email.

Sure, happy to help! Ryuka replied.

Clean up formatting at $950 an hour? No problem. Make everybody's life easier? What else would she rather be doing? You're wasting your life on meaningless jobs like this! Aren't we all? It's not "orange." It's fucking apricot.

As for Project Rhapsody, other than the one-liner from Hayden telling her to know her place, she'd never received any further update on the Cheong report, and she didn't care to follow up. That'd be her new approach to the new financial year and beyond: do what she was told and ask no questions. It'd be the same figure on the paycheck anyway.

Before the end of May, she'd like to try time padding. She wanted to see if she could be a Star Biller by billing nothing at all.

It did cross her mind whether she was too heavy-handed, too spiteful, or too cynical. Then she watched the ten headshots on the screen blend into an unrecognizable face on the Shadow and realized she still had so much to learn.

Sauria Street firms had yet to find the magic button to replace their Associates with machines immune to fatigue, resentment, doubt, and disdain, but they'd found the breadcrumbs that would lead them there. Everything is a metric, and data doesn't lie. One could always be more productive, more efficient, more cost effective, more hit-the-ground-running, more get-things-right-the-first-time, more self-sufficient, and more make-everybody's-life-easier. Drop your Associates in an environment where resources are scarce, competition is fierce, security is absent, and anxiety is constant, and the rest will take care of itself.

That is the real industrial revolution AI has promised humanity—automated self-exploitation.

So, without a single ounce of guilt, she calculated her unproductive hours of the day and how much money the firm could've made on her but hadn't. Today alone, she'd cost Frenell roughly four thousand dollars. She could reach sixty grand in two weeks.

Sixty thousand—that was how much more she would've made in the past three years had they made her Special at the end of Year 5 instead of holding her down one year after another. Now Frenell would lose twice as much on her in one month. That filled her heart with joy and put a grin on her face.

"Look who's happy." Morse crept up with a beer. The sick sweetness on his breath suggested this wasn't the first one.

"Hi, Morse." Ryuka kept her smile but let her gaze roam the field behind him. *Don't look at him, maybe he only bites when he's startled*, she thought.

"I just heard about your Handler change." Morse cut to the chase. "That's disappointing—I always thought you had great potential, and I enjoyed being your mentor."

Ryuka squeezed her glass and suppressed the urge to throw it. Why would people only tell you how much they "appreciated" you when you were getting rid of them? It was like they had some universal training material that said, *Try some lip service in case this one hasn't burned out yet. Let's get that last fucking mile.*

"I have to say I find it rude," Morse continued, "that you didn't communicate this to me beforehand so we could have a mature discussion about it."

"Well, it's the firm's decision–"

"I know you asked OATH about changing your Handler behind my back," he sneered. "That's disrespectful, to say the least. Pretty sly of you, Murong. Pretty sly."

Ryuka drew a deep breath and pushed out a smile. This would be the last pointless conversation with Morse that she got caught up in, and the first of many that she could walk straight out of.

"I never *chose* you as my Handler, Morse. I had to deal with you because you were put in my way. You abused your position to undermine my progress, punch me down, and leave me in a dead end. I'm done with you, and I'm delighted."

She turned on her heel to get the hell out, but Morse skipped ahead and planted himself in front of her.

"You know, Wade got the same feedback every year that he'd need to do something about the lack of 'diversity' on his team–guess he's finally sick of the nagging. Good for you. These stupid times work in your favor. But careful, Murong: a duck will never be a swan."

He bounded away before she could say anything. Ryuka watched the back of Morse's skull and clenched her glass. For a second, she wondered how much effort it'd take to virtualize this one. She looked around and met eyes with the OATH manager who had spoken at the assembly after Tim Kwan's funeral. She'd been standing a few steps away from them throughout the conversation. As Ryuka tried to gauge from her reaction if she'd seen or heard the exchange, the OATH manager averted her eyes and walked away.

Ryuka heard a groan behind her and spotted a table of familiar faces. Two of them were in the Mortification Teams chat group–the Year 5 who'd had to tell Morse about their witness's chemotherapy at the Grads' Debut and the Year 4 with the version control drama. Then there was Emma between them.

"Joining," Ryuka announced as she took the last empty spot. After a second of silence, she realized they were staring at her.

"Sorry, is this seat taken?"

The chemo Associate, who was talking before Ryuka sat down, shrugged and raised an eyebrow at the rest of the table. No one else spoke or looked at her, then the group returned to their customized "would you rather" drinking game.

"I'd have to choose Michael for this one," said Emma.

"Of course you would." Version Control pointed at Chemo. "You always give her the easy questions."

"I give everybody the same questions," said Chemo.

"Bullshit." Version Control rolled his eyes. "What, she was gonna choose Gerald? Get a room, you two."

"Will let you know when we do so you can jerk off in the corner. Your turn."

"How am I supposed to choose?" Version Control downed his beer. "Colleen Oakland or Lindsay Frenell. It's fucking impossible."

"I got an easy one for you," said Emma. "Lindsay Frenell or WPF."

Version Control thought about it, then said "WPF" with a serious face. "The guy is capricious, but he's top gun," he added. "I actually have a lot of respect for him."

Ryuka chuckled.

"You wanna play?" Chemo asked Ryuka. "Which Partner would you rather become in twenty years?"

"Make it thirty." Version Control shared a giggle with Emma.

"We already know this one." Emma grinned. "Morse wants Ryuka all to himself."

"Not in the mood, Em." Ryuka shook her head.

"Explain why he's so obsessed with you, then." Emma leaned forward and poked Ryuka's kneecap. "He's like those creepy kidnappers who'd catch them young and raise their own brides. You'll just turn into him with a wig."

She laughed wholeheartedly as her red wine breath hit Ryuka in the face. It was out of character for Emma to be so verbally blunt. *That can't be the first glass*, Ryuka thought. Then Version Control slammed the table and chanted:

"Morse! Morse! Morse! Morse!"

Chemo attempted to grab him, but Version Control had skipped away and hyped the people nearby to join in. The group of five next to them responded with utter confusion, but one of them gave a few claps to save Version Control the embarrassment–force of habit from the Red Sea. Seeing a patrol robot coming toward them, Emma danced away, but not before she made sure Ryuka heard her hum the "Bridal Chorus." Version Control jumped in front of Ryuka and kept chanting while hopping from side to side like a gibbon.

"Here, have some water." Ryuka grabbed a glass from the table and emptied it in his face.

"What the hell!" Someone standing too close backed off to brush the splotches off his jacket, glaring at Ryuka.

The patrol robot sped up and charged forward as Version Control grabbed Ryuka's lapels. A glass shattered in the opposite corner. Through the crowd, Ryuka saw James Taree fall to the ground, while his gang tried to wrestle Nolan off him.

AFTER THE LIGHTS went back on, the guests gathered around the Shadow, loosening the crowd. Colleen stretched her neck, searching for the sight of Wade.

The rollout time for AS28HGC6-F was a whole month earlier than the date confirmed in the previous Partner group email. *The boys are about to close the deal*, she thought, and she'd had to find out about that like the other lowly employees who didn't own a piece of this business. She swallowed her wine with annoyance. This place never seemed to run out of ways to remind you of all the little clubs you couldn't get in.

There was something strange about that speech as well. Not the content, the speaker. Over the past decade, she'd seen different shades of Wade—the parts other Frenells had seen and the parts they didn't get to see. Wade wasn't what you'd call a soft man, and he could pack a hard punch whenever he felt some tough love was warranted, but the person on the screen a minute ago made her feel something she'd never sensed in her years of dealing with him.

A chill to the bone.

She craned her neck in a different direction—couldn't spot Nolan either. The boys thought it'd be a good idea to pack the party like a *Pride and Prejudice* ball so people could see Frenell was still the hottest thing in town, but she wondered how much of this would convert to actual business, and how many of them would pay their bills without bitching or whining for a discount first. "Relationships" are for humans. If they think of you as a dog, the only matter is whether they toss you a bone before they kick you in the belly, or after.

But it was a game of perception, and the show wasn't over yet, so she held her head high and smiled.

"We live in scary times, don't we?" A voice followed her as she threaded through the crowd, giving an equally respectful hello to everyone.

"Not now, Morse."

"Well, well. I guess making Partner does change a person."

"What do you want?"

"I don't have to 'want' anything to hang out with an old friend, do I?" Morse caught up and walked alongside her, raising his glass as he nodded to a passing face. "But if you feel like sharing some queue-jumping tips, I shall welcome that with all grace."

"It's not time based—"

"I know, I know. It's all about 'merit.'" Morse laughed. "And being liked by the right person. Where is he, anyway?"

Colleen stepped out of the current of moving bodies and found a quiet spot against the wall, placing herself on the centerline of the room.

"I know things, Colleen." Morse settled down next to her. "But I have class, and I still value our friendship."

"And you want that friendship extended to Wade."

"I have a strong case; I just need a stronger sponsor this year. He wouldn't have to do anything more than a nod, and I'd be forever indebted to both of you."

"I don't know if that's the problem, Morse. They've told you this three years in a row—Partners have to be good people managers. You can be a bit . . . alienating."

"My team respects me."

Colleen chuckled.

"I've spent more time with the juniors than anyone above Level 26." Morse leaned in and ground his teeth. "I know how to handle Millennials, even Gen Z. Do you know how many of them would line up for my guidance at events like this? I can't even have a quiet drink! If only you could see the fire in their eyes!"

Right then, someone in the back started chanting Morse's name. Colleen frowned, and Morse lifted a hand in that direction. His face sparked with resentment of injustice.

"Listen to that. Listen to what people want. Those kids are more resilient and discerning than you'd assume, and they know what's good for their career in the long run. They're not petty. They want me to be honest. They need me to straighten them out."

He gulped his chardonnay and swallowed hard.

"But it seems I'll never be their leader."

Colleen glanced at Morse's profile and recalled that, a year ago, he'd had the same wounded expression at the party for new Partners right before he'd asked in front of everyone if that child she'd almost had was half-WPF, and now he had the audacity to ask her for a favor like he deserved it. There was something clinically wrong with this guy. In the back of the room, a glass shattered, hushing the chants and igniting a sadistic spark in Colleen's mind.

"Fine." She grinned. "You want a friend on Level 28. You just might have one. Leave it with me, and remember—I don't do this for everybody."

"THIS IS CREEPY," Marcus said as he watched limbs grow out of the egg.

"I'm so glad I don't have to work in a place like this." Diane snorted, then turned to Sai. "So, how are you enjoying it?"

"Don't be a mean girl, Di." Genevieve sighed and gave Sai a look that said "This is just who she is."

Sai flashed a smile and shifted her glass to a less sweaty hand. Suffering through Wade's speech without breaking down in public had exhausted her. She didn't have the bandwidth to care about the tone of someone she'd met five minutes ago. The group that had taken her in occupied a pocket near the west end of the ballroom, a territory that no outsider might intrude on. Sai spotted several clusters of Frenell Partners across the floor. No sight of Wade. Pretending to follow a passing waiter, she moved a few steps to the side and let the clique shield her.

"Should you be drinking that?" Henry asked.

"What do you think *zero* means?" Genevieve tapped the alcohol-free label on the bottle in her hand.

Henry shrugged and turned to the panorama screens showing the Shadow open its eyes. His brows knitted as he looked at the humanoid squarely, drinking his neat whiskey at twice his usual speed. Genevieve's gaze stayed on Henry for a moment before she returned to the discussion with Marcus and Diane about their summer plans. Sai watched the two and bit her lip.

Other than Henry, Genevieve was the only person in the circle that Sai had known anything about. "Know" as in she'd seen her in Henry's Facebook updates, tagging him in photos of events they'd attended with their families. Genevieve had turned up tonight in a dark-gray sheath dress matching Henry's charcoal suit. No decorative items other than a gold coin necklace that looked like an heirloom and a rectangular watch that was clearly an antique. She wore makeup the way makeup should be worn–to polish the face she already had instead of painting a new one she preferred. Her lips would draw an innocent smirk when she said something witty, and her eyes would stare you down when she heard something unpleasant, just like Henry.

They had the same natural presence in any place they felt like being.

Back in college, she'd asked Henry about Genevieve once. "Gene is just Gene," he'd said, without more to offer, like talking about a sibling.

The lights came back on. Sai flinched and pushed her framed glasses higher above the bridge of her nose as she bowed her head. The bruises were easy–she'd covered them with foundation and concealer. There wasn't much she could do about the blood spot in her eye, but the colorful frames did a decent job of distraction. She kept her face down to avoid eye contact with her fellow Frenells. They might recall that video again, they might have learned about her "change in responsibilities," or Pace might have told people what she'd seen.

But Sai wouldn't need to worry about Pace anymore. Pace had been crying that Wednesday because the Whore had blocked her number–after all, she had nothing left to give him. Then she'd made the unwise choice of turning up at the house that he'd brought her to once when things were "light and fun" between them. There had been no announcement or questions about her departure.

"But why do you have to fly all the way to Paris for a concert?" Diane asked.

"He's more experimental over there." Genevieve shrugged. "So he'd do things like those highly conceptual B-sides that didn't do well here. Paris and Dublin, those are where the *real* fans go."

"And also pick up a new Birkin on the way." Marcus grinned. Genevieve wrapped an arm around his waist and slapped him in the chest.

"Get out, you got the matte croc?!" Diane's mouth gaped open. "You. Bitch."

"It's not for me." Genevieve rubbed Diane's back. "Mom's birthday. We'll go back to California this year. Mammoth Mountain, five days plus a bike park pass. You guys coming?"

"I'm a bit sick of that snow, to be honest," Henry chimed in.

"*Nobody* gets sick of the Mammoth snow." Genevieve groaned. "What's the matter with you?"

"Well, you know Henry," Diane said. "Sometimes he'd pick Taco Bell over a steak just so he'd seem less . . . basic."

She gave Sai a closed-mouth smile.

"I can't do July." Marcus shook his head. "Got a family thing in Durham."

"Wait, I thought you were from New Jersey," said Genevieve.

"We moved to Jersey when I started school, but my mom's from Durham, North Carolina, and my grandparents still live there."

"I like North Carolina," Sai said, clutching at any topic she could contribute to that didn't involve six-figure handbags or ski holidays in summer.

All four heads turned to her, which knocked what she had to say out of her mind, so she just stood there, caressing her half-empty glass.

"North Carolina is a peculiar state to like," said Diane. "Did you go to Duke?"

"Oh . . . no," Sai mumbled. "I was just there for a road trip. It was good . . . lots of mountains and waterfalls . . ."

They nodded, then shared a moment of silence.

"I think we might have done the same trip," Marcus said and smiled at Sai. "Blue Ridge, yeah? It's a gorgeous drive. I'd totally do it again."

"This is a disgrace." Henry shook his head as the Shadow had finished entertaining the front rows and paraded deeper into the crowd. "They're literally turning people into drones. It's like they don't even bother hiding anymore."

"Well, if it improves productivity, people can work less," said Genevieve. "Then they'll have more time for their families and what they really want to do with life."

"Trust me, any saved time will immediately be consumed by ads, debt, and a second job," Henry scoffed. "Late capitalism."

"Keep your voice down," Genevieve said and glanced around them. "Your dad is already getting called a socialist for that rehab bill."

"That's actually one of the few things that make me proud of him."

"Aren't you a bit too old for this kind of college-freshman bullshit?" said Diane. "Don't tell me you still got a Che Guevara in your bedroom. That hippie stuff is like chickenpox—you get it young, then you get *over* it."

"Not everything that's against extreme greed is socialism, Diane."

"I'll take you seriously once you've stopped calling proper business management 'extreme greed.'"

"And I'll take your advice once you've discovered human hearts—not as a snack."

"It's not your table, Henry." Diane sighed. "There's no way you could say anything on that side without being a total hypocrite. You think we don't 'get it'? The point is, what are you gonna do? Are you gonna give away what you have personally? If not, just be glad you're born into *this* life and stop being a fucking buzzkill for the rest of us who don't hate ourselves as much. Live a little, jeez . . . actually, when is your concert again?"

She opened the calendar on her phone as she turned to Genevieve.

"Maybe I'll come with you. My mom bought a DeChambord and didn't realize it was bigger than the wall she wanted to hang it on until it was sitting in our front yard. Ugh, that woman . . . so we might ask around and see if a gallery wants it. And"–she poked Henry's shoulder with a forefinger–"we should definitely swing by your brother's vineyard in Tuscany and talk about your pseudo-Marxism over a nice bottle of Carmignano."

Of course, she didn't miss Sai. "I'm sorry, do you know where Tuscany is?"

"Yes, I know where Tuscany is." Sai looked at her squarely. "I went to college."

"Touchy." Diane held her glass-free hand up in surrender.

"Di, you've had enough," Genevieve said.

"I'm angry for *you*, Gene–"

"I can't take you anywhere if you behave like this."

So Diane shrugged and finished her wine, then she swapped the empty glass for the sparkling water that Marcus grabbed from a catering lady for her. Henry sealed his lips and looked in all directions except at the people in front of him. His eyes lit up as the Shadow and its OATH chaperone approached the group.

"I hope you're enjoying the evening." The Shadow smiled.

"We're having a great time." Henry smirked. "Not that many animal-free circuses in town."

"It takes time for people to accept any new inventions that seem powerful and destructive. I understand." The Shadow sustained the professional smile. "But for humanity to break through the evolutionary bottleneck, a certain degree of societal contraction and discomfort is inevitable and also necessary. Besides, I, for one, agree that animal shows for human entertainment should be abolished. It's needlessly cruel and arrogant."

The group was impressed for a second. They'd thought the thing would pop a dry laugh, then find a reason to excuse itself, like a normal person being dissed.

"Are you waterproof?" Henry handed over his glass with one shot of whiskey left. "Let's see if you can do *everything* humans do."

"I'm afraid I do not have a protocol for food and beverage consumption. I'd like to avoid substances in general, as it might interfere with my–"

"Oh, oh! Let me try!" Diane pumped one arm in the air like an excited schoolgirl in a science museum. She leaned in and whispered to the Shadow as if talking to the latest Alexa: "Do you know who his father is?"

The Shadow glanced at the OATH assistant, who seemed to have crashed into a reboot, then it took the glass and poured the contents into the chamber connected to its mouth and left the empty glass on the tray of a waitress nearby without her noticing.

A moment later, the Shadow lost its face.

Its smile was the first thing gone, followed by the head and the shoulders. Like in a reversed sculpting time lapse, its top half melted to a column of waxlike substance.

"Ew!" Diane cringed and pulled Genevieve away from the thing. The others also took a step back, leaving the Shadow in the center of the broken circle, reverting to an egg. The OATH assistant snapped out of her stupor and desperately searched for an answer in the FAQ section of her admin app. The egg spun and skidded and charged toward the group of five, aiming at their thighs and hips. It hit Sai in the back of her knee and brought her down onto the floor. As she tried to get back on her feet, the egg made one last attempt to return to human. In a wave of strange chanting breaking out at the back of the room, a shapeless limb stretched out of the oval body, swirling and whipping in the air, and slapped Sai across the face.

The same pain. The same loss of control. She fell on her hip, and the same darkness she'd tried to forget gripped her ankles and climbed upward, spreading to the wound between her legs.

Then she felt a hand on her arm.

"Don't touch me!" she screeched and smacked the hand away.

"Sorry!" Marcus backed off. "I didn't mean to–"

A glass shattered somewhere in the back, and they heard noises that sounded like a fight. The crowd around them split in half and made a thin path for a line of patrol robots. The OATH assistant couldn't handle the situation, so she'd called for backup. The bots secured the egg, which had returned to a freshly unboxed state with an empty ribbon of accounts. They hoisted Sai off the floor to mop the spill around her, comforted the guests with sincere apologies on their screens and some meditation music, then left the room like nothing had happened.

Sai covered her mouth with one hand and hunched her back, hoping people would forget she was there if she stared at her feet long enough. One peek at Henry and her heart sank–he was studying her with a light frown. Then he blew an inaudible sigh and looked away.

"This sucks." Diane summoned a catering guy to take her glass of water, then dismissed him with a yawn. "Let's go to Lanchester. My tab."

THE PATROL ROBOTS escorted the "disruptors of peace" out of the building and revoked their access to the party by ripping off their wristbands. Edmund printed a warning on its screen, urging them to leave. Nolan fumbled his phone out of his pocket and saw the unsent message ending with a thumbs-up emoji. He tried to reenter the building, but the bot wouldn't let him.

"I'm going to Level 20, okay?!" he reasoned with it, but Edmund stood its ground. Holding a "stop" gesture with one mechanical arm, it retreated inside and settled in front of the turnstiles, keeping watch.

"Nolan, let it go," Ryuka said as she sat down on the steps in front of the revolving door and watched Henry's friends gather near the line of taxis, holding some light chatter while waiting for him to wrap it up with the girl who wouldn't be joining them.

"I just want you to know that I think you're compassionate and sensible," Sai said. "What Diane said was unfair. Don't listen–"

"It's okay." Henry smiled but averted his eyes. "She can have her opinion."

"Do you want to go somewhere, just you and me?"

"Look, I'm really tired . . . you should get some rest too."

"Henry–" Diane raised an arm and tapped on her watch with a finger.

"Sai, maybe you should stay with us?" Ryuka said from behind them.

"I know I acted weird earlier." Sai laughed nervously. "I apologize! I didn't mean to embarrass you–"

"It's not about that–"

Out of the blue, she hooked him by the neck and tried to kiss him. Wide eyed, Henry grabbed her wrist and pulled his face away.

"Oh, wow! Okay . . . um, we both had a bit of a strange night. Now might not be the best time to talk. Let's regroup later when we've both sobered up, how about that? I'll call you."

He mimicked a phone call next to his face and pursed his lips, then he sauntered away and caught up with his friends.

Sai watched them cram into the same taxi and take off. She continued facing that direction for a while after the cab had turned a corner and disappeared. The moment she turned around, both Nolan and Ryuka dodged her eyes.

"Go ahead," Sai said.

Leaning against a handrail over the steps, Nolan hung his head low. Ryuka closed her eyes and let out an exhale of exhaustion into her palms.

"Go ahead," Sai said again.

"With what?" Nolan frowned.

"Say whatever you want and call me whatever you like, but say it *to my face*! Don't talk shit behind my back!"

"We've never—" said Ryuka.

"It must be so easy to pretend you have your shit together when the worst thing that's ever happened to you is what? Your Handler hates you?"

"You really don't know what you're talking about." Ryuka shook her head.

"Or, maybe you get to act so mellow and in control 'cause you're doped out of your fucking mind the whole time. You—stop acting like I don't exist! Look at me!"

"I'm not gonna engage right now. You're clearly upset," Nolan said, keeping his eyes on the ground.

"You think? Did you know people can smell the alcohol on you? No, cologne and chewing gum can't remove the stink of an addict!"

"Leave him alone," said Ryuka.

"I'm sorry, am I breaking your heart?" Sai snorted. "You know he's not into women, don't you?"

"Get a hold of yourself, Saidah." Ryuka frowned. "Not everybody is a frustrated, lovesick little girl, and no one needs advice from a gold digger."

"How long has that been in there?"

"Stop it," Nolan said. "Both of you—"

"She's not entirely wrong, you know." Ryuka turned to Nolan. "What's your deal, exactly? You said you'd quit. We've promised each other!"

"I did! I . . . I'm really unhappy, Ryu."

"But what are you so unhappy about, Nolan? You have *everything* you could ask from this place. Anything you want, people just assume you deserve it–"

"That's not true."

"Sure, tell us how hard *your* life is," Sai said.

"I'm not better off than either of you, okay? This place fucks all of us! They fuck all of us and they pit us against each other! We're friends, for fuck's sake!"

"Are we . . . still?" Ryuka asked.

"Were we ever? Mr. and Mrs. Private School." Sai chuckled.

"What does that have to do with anything?" Nolan closed his eyes and drew a deep breath. "Sai, I see you must be going through a rough patch, but please stop being so bitter. It's really hard to watch. And, Ryu, I know it seems like I've had it easy, but I assure you, you don't want my life! Every morning I wake up . . . why are we even having this stupid fight? We could all be dead this time next year–"

Something fell from the sky and landed on the pavement behind him. It made a thud. For many years that followed, it was the loudest thing in his memory.

Sai was the first one who saw it from where she stood. Her light gasp led to a whimper, then a sob. She turned away and paced back and forth on the side of the road to calm herself, but tears kept rolling down no matter how high she held her head, as if someone had switched on a faucet, and everything in her vision weighed like a mountain. Ryuka had walked down the steps and caught a glimpse of the shadow on the pavement. "Don't look," she said as Nolan swiveled his head, and she looked for him. Her eyes lost focus, but she kept her stare in the same direction, just to avoid facing him.

A group of pedestrians gathered around the spot. Amid their cries and urgent calls for an ambulance, Nolan turned around. The last thing he remembered about that night was a whisper from Ryuka.

"Don't do this to yourself, Nolan. You can't change anything."

12

"WHAT DID YOU take?"

Nolan shielded his eyes with one hand and dodged the light. The person asking the question pulled his hand down and nudged his face back to the front.

"Tell me what you took," the nurse repeated. "The regular stuff or something novel?"

"I . . . I don't know. It came in a–"

"Nasal spray?"

"Yeah."

"Am I a pelican?"

"No . . . ?"

"Do I look like any other animals?"

"Not really."

The nurse spread Nolan's eyelids and examined his lenses. Then she cracked his jaw open and ran both thumbs along the inside of his lips, checking his gums and teeth. She asked several basic questions about him and matched his answers to the registration. After jotting down a few notes on her pad, she moved a finger before his eyes. With the same finger, she showed him the blue line on the floor that'd lead him to the Rapid Assessment Zone, where he'd wait to be inspected by a doctor.

He remembered who he was and where he lived. His body, although sore and frail, was in one piece and able to carry him through the corridors. The night had turned windows into mirrors. The face reflected on the glass was his own, and the dirt and wrinkles on his suit made him realize he must've stayed in this outfit for days. His shirt gave off a fermented stench of old booze, the collar soaked stiff and stained yellow. The screen of his phone said May 26, 2028. Once he'd unlocked it, it greeted him with a chat that'd stopped a week ago, ending on a draft message from him that contained only a thumbs-up emoji.

Ah, that's right, he thought. That was how he'd ended up here.

He was looking for that girl.

As he sat down in the last booth of the waiting area, an overpowering ammonia reek rose up from below his knees. He bent down and sniffed his shoes, then he remembered—the last time he'd gotten someone's piss on his feet was on the wrong side of the Athena River.

The weeping in the booth behind him faded as his brain traded the fluorescent lights for a dying sunset and brought him back to the tent city. A girl with short red hair was closing his hands around the plastic container of a free meal. He handed the food back and told her he didn't live here.

"Are you family?" the redhead asked, gesturing at the shelters behind them.

"No . . . I'm looking for one of your volunteers. Her name is Keahi." He took out his phone, then realized he didn't have a picture to show.

"Okay . . ." The girl eyeballed him a sanity assessment, then retreated to the minivan on top of the embankment, where she exchanged some whispers and glances with her team. She returned seconds later and said: "I'm afraid we don't have anyone by that name."

"That can't be right. I've seen her work here. She wore an Uphill shirt–"

"Our dispatcher manages the roster. It's possible she's with a different squad at a different site."

"Can I see the roster? I need to know where she is."

"No."

"Let me speak to someone who knows." Nolan stepped toward the van. "I'll be quick."

"Look, I'm told we don't have a Keahi." The girl stopped him with one hand on his chest as she flashed the Revilox gun under her windbreaker.

The sight of Revilox gave Nolan a pinch under his left collarbone. He winced and suppressed the pricking pain with his hand. When he reopened his eyes, he was back in the waiting area. The woman in the adjacent booth had stopped weeping, and a man was comforting her in a low voice.

Nolan stretched his collar and examined the triangle between his neck, his left shoulder, and his breast. The injection wound had swollen to a pink mosquito bite, throbbing with his pulse. He assumed the redhead had shot him and Uphill had dropped him at the ER. Then he peeked inside his open jacket and saw the Revilox gun strapped under his arm.

"I really liked some of the stuff he did with the Traveling Wilburys. What do you think?"

Nolan snapped his head up and found himself sitting in the corner booth of the IPC café. Fischer was chewing his meat sauce linguine, waiting for a response.

"How long have I been here?" Nolan asked.

"Since . . . the beginning of lunch?"

He looked down and saw the same dish in front of him, untouched. The stains and smell of alcohol were still on his clothes, but no filth on his shoes. He flipped the phone lying face down next to his plate. It said 2:30 p.m., May 24, 2028.

"If Roy Orbison hadn't gone so soon, it'd be awesome to see what else might've come out of that," Fischer continued. "Then Chateau was like, he sounds too much like the Beatles. No, he doesn't. If you'd only listened to–"

"Wait, Chateau?"

"Yeah?"

"So you two hang out now? When you're *not* trying to get drugs? What are you, friends?"

"Gotta socialize with your team," said Fischer. "They're quite fun people, actually, and helpful."

He took out his staff badge and showed Nolan the button-sized transmitter attached to the back, then proceeded to explain the mechanism of Chateau's latest invention. It came in pairs, and the other half was stuck under Fischer's desk at that moment. It'd hijack the signal of the badge and practically "mute" the real thing. That was why Fischer had the luxury of having a sit-down lunch at 2:30 p.m. on a Wednesday. As far as his firm PADU was concerned, he was still at his workstation. This new device, BodySwap, was in beta testing, and sometimes the transmitters would cross-fire and pair up with multiple receivers, making the trick more detectable as the system would pin you in different locations at the same time. Chateau needed more debugging, but he was getting there.

"We're going on a ski retreat in Mammoth Mountain after the end of the financial year," said Fischer. "Goldman was asking about you."

Nolan stared at his linguine in silence. The chef had left two pieces of arugula on top as ornaments. The setting, the characters, the topic, the mood, none of them seemed right. He was forgetting something, and it wasn't drug gang team building.

"I . . . gotta go, sorry." He stumbled up on buckled knees, grabbing the back of the booth to stop him from falling back into his seat.

"Already? Again?" Fischer sighed. "I know it's twenty-five fifty, but you gotta take it easy once in a while. You look like shit, man."

"I'm late."

"Late for what?"

"Someone is waiting for me at the Frenell café."

"Who?"

"Keahi."

"Do I know him?"

"You met her twice."

Fischer tilted his head and slowed down his chewing to allocate more resources to his memory. Nolan wanted to remind him she was the Uphill girl who'd almost shot him twice, then he remembered Fischer had been high both times he'd met her.

"I think when you were on Rhapsody," said Nolan, "she looked like a wolf?"

That got half a nod out of Fischer. "A wolf. That's cool," he mumbled.

His smartwatch beeped once. Fischer dabbed his mouth with a napkin, found a bottle of Rhapsody in his pocket, and took a hit as if taking his prescription meds. Then he opened an app on his phone and ticked a few boxes—the managed-use solution tracked his consumption and graphed his "performance," as in how consistently he'd complied with the tailored program, how his overdose risk changed, whether he should modify his allowance according to his long-term goals, and his customer loyalty credit. Once High Hopes had completed the internal trial, it'd roll out the application across its end users and gradually reduce the support for its legacy tiered Advocates network till its full retirement in 2030. For now, the users had to manually enter their daily activities, until the launch of the wearable trackers.

"The platform is quite intuitive," said Fischer. "And thorough. We've made something that will help people, and you can let it help you, you know, if you want to be responsible."

"I don't do drugs–"

"When you first start using, that's the most dangerous stage." Fischer took Nolan's plate, stacked it on his empty one, and got on with his second lunch. "You think you got a pristine engine with low mileage, and you're fascinated by what the drug can do for you, so it's easy to go over."

He took the Revilox gun out of his jacket and laid it in front of Nolan where his plate used to be.

"There will be better days. Don't die."

The café dissolved and faded as the fluorescent lights flickered over Nolan's head. He drew out the Revilox and checked its magazine. One antidote and that was all. He put it back under his jacket, then gave himself a frisk search and found a bottle of Rhapsody in his pants–the leftover from Luc with a few drops left. The nurse at the desk between the waiting area and the treatment rooms called out a name, and someone coughing in the distance stepped forward to get the instructions for his blood tests. The partner of the woman in the adjacent booth approached the nurse and was told they'd have to wait a bit more. A doctor walked an old man out and summoned his next patient. He wore a smile and asked about her weekend plans–the best possible spirit for a Friday-night shift. Nolan reckoned he probably wouldn't die in this place, so he twisted off the cap on the spray and sent it into his nose.

It hit harder than the first vodka tonic he'd had after a two-month dry. As soon as he tasted the bitter mist, he knew this wasn't the first time he'd used it. He tilted his chin up and let the juice drip to the back of his throat. The lights weaved a blinding tunnel and transported him to a space with a similar ceiling.

The Courage Room was designed with a TEDx venue in mind. The elevated platform and the sturdy walnut podium had assembled a throne with ostensible credence. There was something dishonest about that presentation–given the kind of speech that usually took place up there, that podium should've been covered in muck like an overbooked guillotine.

"It's easy to criticize in hindsight. Some might give you a generic list of 'early signs.' Some would resort to the platitude that we should be more mindful of our well-being–"

The Frenells knew that shit had gotten real when Katherine Waycross was the one preaching. If it was about harassment, a Partner had been MeToo'd with solid evidence. If somebody had died, they'd died on premises.

"Let's be honest, so many of those unfortunate incidents were avoidable. That makes me angry, and it should frustrate you just the same." She raised her fists to her chest. "We're not here today to cry on each other's shoulders–we're way past that. Now it's time for action. Therefore, we're rolling out a Herd Resilience Plan with immediate effect."

She flicked her wrist, and Christie brought up the slide without a split second of delay.

"One, there has been ample research on social media's detrimental impact on mental health. It has also become a common space where the weak and bitter reaffirm each other's victimhood. We have blocked these counterproductive platforms across firm devices in the interest of morale. Access through personal means during business hours will be considered a workplace policy violation and result in a RAP write-up. Two, our Well-Being Helpdesk remains operative and offers free, strictly confidential counseling sessions. We strongly encourage you to utilize the service or speak to your Handler and your team in order to correctly navigate your feelings. Three, OATH has designated two full-time members to curate a newsletter in Perspective that follows industry development to ensure we stay on top of the game in creating a caring and safe environment. Four, we're opening a new channel in Sensible Echoes for intel on anyone who might be struggling. As mentioned in previous training: if you see something, say something. This time, please understand we're serious. This is a challenging job. If someone is not fit for duty, it's in both parties' interests that we seek alternatives. After all, life should be lived the best way that suits."

Nolan checked his work phone and saw 103 notices of new emails under the time banner that said "11:03 a.m., May 23, 2028." The last email he'd opened came on the Saturday morning after the anniversary party. Its subject line read *The 150th Anniversary*, and its message was succinct: The Partners regretted to inform all staff that a terrible incident had happened the night before. Given the ongoing investigation, fellow Frenells were urged to refrain from speaking to the police or media unless they had been nominated to give information in the presence of an OATH representative.

Although the investigation had not yet concluded, Frenell had released its preliminary findings through a *Grand Ivory Post* interview, which stated that it had not discovered any evidence of misconduct involving any supervisors or colleagues with whom "the employee" had worked. For additional context, it'd highlighted certain relevant details, such as that "the employee" was a recent Grad who'd only been with the firm for a limited time; that she'd had a lot of extracurricular activities, which the firm had been accommodating despite the regular working-hour conflicts; that she'd volunteered in an environment with continuous exposure to drug users; and that the firm would assist the authorities with any inquiries about her social network and relationships. At the end, the article reemphasized Frenell's commitment to mental health advocacy and casually mentioned its nomination for the Employees' Choice of Best Workplace award.

The two dedicated OATH newsletter writers had been working around the clock. Before the Associates left this assembly, they'd receive the first issue, which would provide ten tips for handling stress on a budget, such as a hot bath or a pint of chocolate chip ice cream; an op-ed article advising young people to get their hands dirty and learn more by expecting less;

a news report on the latest accident in a local warehouse causing at least two casualties; then an exclusive scoop that both Miller and Calder had announced they'd turn 30 percent of their staff part time on reduced pay with dynamic scheduling—there were even rumors of layoffs.

"We're in a generational productivity crisis." Katherine gritted her teeth. "Our prosperity is under attack, and each one of us must take responsibility. It's time we ask some tough questions—"

She leaped off the stage and landed in front of the first row. The tail of her long blazer flapped as if she were in a low-budget gangster movie. Lunging forward, she reached her arms behind the nearest head and locked her fingers, tugging the astonished face to her forehead.

"What's your contribution to humanity?"

The Associate stuttered, but it was okay since Katherine wasn't expecting an answer. She let go of him and grabbed the one in the next seat, then the next, and the next. When she'd run out on this side, she reached across the aisle.

"Do people respect you, or do they only pretend they do?"

"How have you fulfilled the purpose of your life? Will your children be proud of you?"

"Has the world changed for the better or for the worse? How much of that are you responsible for?"

"If a war breaks out tomorrow, if a disaster hits us, if this country falls into an endless cycle of crises, exactly what can you do to help?"

"Are you okay? Yes or no?!"

When she was done with the last one, she looked like she had steam coming out of her skull. Christie raised her laser pointer tentatively, querying if they should move on to the next order of business, but Katherine dismissed her with a flick of the hand, as she still had some excess fury to walk off.

"You don't want us to help you, we won't bother. You want to make a point with your self-destruction, be my guest. No one will dignify your tantrum," she raved as she paced back and forth. "We will not submit to the emotional blackmail of the brittle and the entitled. We will not forfeit our century-old glory to the cancer of nihilism that's plaguing our workforce. Not on my watch!"

"Who's she talking about this time?" an Associate behind Nolan asked and followed with a big yawn.

"Da fuck knows," the voice next to her said. "Are we gonna be here all day? I've got a con-call."

Then it dawned on Nolan—he hadn't seen a mention of Keahi anywhere. Not in the firm-wide gag order. Not in the *Grand Ivory Post* article. Not in Katherine's spit-spewing, face-grabbing manifesto.

Keahi Ka'uhane—KK28DIP3-C to Frenell—became inactive on the night of May 19, 2028. Her bus memo was up to date, so all the projects she'd participated in had been successfully restaffed with Associates and Graduates of comparable capabilities—less than thirty minutes of downtime achieved. Products of her work had been converted to KM precedents that belonged to a universal author: "Frenell Library." With her Timekeeper Profile archived, her existence had been reduced to grayed-out cross-references in a handful of Relationship Maps. If you searched her name in Frenell's project management system, the only hit would be an Excel name list created for the 2028 Graduates intake buried at the bottom of the last page. In seven years, once the statutory recordkeeping period had expired and that Excel spreadsheet had been deleted, "Keahi Ka'uhane" would be two words with no discernible meaning in the Sauria universe.

"Say her name," Nolan said, but no one around seemed to have heard him.

"We're not victims of our own minds." Katherine shook her head and turned to those at the front. "Because who are we?"

"We are the Frenells," the front-row Associates responded.

"Say her name." Nolan said it louder.

"I can't hear you!" Katherine yelled.

"We're the Frenells!"

"Say her name!" Nolan shouted.

"Frenells! Frenells! Frenells!"

"Will you say *my* name, Nolan?" someone whispered in the next seat. Nolan turned around and met Luc's face of death. His bloodshot eyes were complemented by a permanent grin, emitting the joy of a long-awaited reunion. Nolan gasped and sprang off his chair. As the metal frame hit the floor, the Courage Room reverted to the RAZ waiting area.

The startled couple stuck their faces out from their booth. A warthog and a meerkat–hmm, maybe they were meant to be. Nolan glanced at his reflection in the window. The creature stared back at him with kaleidoscopic eyes while the color of its skin shifted in a hypnotic rhythm.

As it happened, Fischer couldn't tell a gecko from a chameleon.

None of this was real, and he just had to ride it out, Nolan thought. He gave the couple an embarrassed smile over his shoulder and sat down. As he turned away from the window, Luc's face appeared on the glass next to his own.

"I think I like my new form." Luc chuckled. "Now you can't get rid of me like a bag of rotten potatoes."

"You're not real." Nolan groaned.

"I just wanted to get ahead a little so I could breathe. Do some frontloading. Build up some credit. So when they have to give the short end of the stick to *someone*, they'll think, Luc is a good kid, he works hard, be fair to him. I worked hard, Nolan, but that's not how people remember me. They don't remember me at all–"

"You're not real–"

"–so you'll have to remember me on behalf of everyone else."

Luc's ice-cold fingers clutched Nolan's wrist and pulled it upward. Nolan realized he was still holding the Rhapsody, and Luc was forcing it to his face. It went over his nose and stopped in front of his left eye. His mind went blank for a moment, then his hand squeezed the bottle hard, and the spray hit him in the eyeball. He dropped the bottle and squeezed his eyes shut. Half of his face went numb.

"Don't worry, it will pass," Luc said. "As long as you still feel the roller coaster come down, you're all right."

Nolan covered his eyes and breathed through his nose, keeping the grunt behind his clenched teeth. His disjointed mind scanned for a fragment of memory to escape to. An alternative reality where Luc wouldn't exist.

In his self-inflicted darkness, he heard an incoming Teams call, then someone haphazardly plugged in their headphones and apologized for not picking up on the first ring. He blinked the tears off his lashes and saw the empty Word document in front of him.

"You have not recorded any billable hours today."

A soft female voice flew out of the earpiece he was wearing. It sounded pleasant enough, if you disregarded the content of its speech. Nolan saw the date and time at the bottom of his screen: 09:45 a.m., May 22, 2028. From there, his gaze traveled across the floor and landed on the eggs cruising through the open plan and collecting faces.

"If you have capacity, it's the right time to ask your team if anyone needs assistance."

The smart agent for AS28HGC6-F put up a chart on his screen, ranking the Associates in his batch based on the live feedback of what they'd achieved for the day. Nolan saw that he was in the group with all the top billers on Level 13, like Emma Abilene. That explained the empty slots yet to be filled–most Associates had picked an easy team to pair up with first thing in the morning. The ones who'd missed the ship were in hiding, hoping some poor bastards would fill up the Group of Death, leaving them with the leftovers from lower floors.

Nolan raised a hand to turn off the earpiece, then he noticed the peculiar gear under his shirt.

A slim latex tube was taped to his left forearm, inner elbow, then his shoulder. One end of it extended down into the flask stowed in the inner pocket of his jacket; the other end poked out of his sleeve. Anytime he wanted a sip of fresh bourbon, he just needed to put on his thinking face and cradle his chin.

Now it makes sense. He sucked on the straw as he watched a patrol robot grab a rogue Associate before he could jump into a Meditation Chamber and hold him up for the egg to take his mug shot. This was the reason he still felt calm and hopeful with that happening around him.

The Meditation Chambers on all floors were the size of a train compartment and had a standard off-white interior. Padded with soft panels and devoid of embellishments or distractions. Against the wall stood an IKEA-style fiberboard desk. They called it "the Peace Altar" and gave it a matching stool for extra ritualistic flair. When no one was screwing inside, the Meditation Chamber was the perfect spot for a quiet moment, free from bloody-eyed ghost boys, or silly girls whose faces were becoming obscure. A quiet moment was what Nolan needed.

In the tranquility, the alcohol flow in his veins steadied. He'd even dozed off for a few minutes with the straw in his mouth. Maybe he could live with this. He woke up to that thought. Clock in; clock out. Work for a bot; become the bot. It wasn't all gloom and doom; he'd made it to Level 21, after all. In a way, he'd reached the opposite bank of the river before the bridge burned down. Some people had it worse than him. Way, way worse.

Then he saw the new email to his alter ego.

Ninety-six hours after his death, WPF had become more powerful than ever. The manufacturer of AS28HGC6-F had sent through a training video to the twelve Olympians, bringing them up to speed on the technical basics and their Master User privileges. The rollout had been progressing as planned, with over 70 percent of Frenell accounts synchronized, and the "inventory taking" was on track to be completed by COB today. After that, each Master User would have full access to the repository, where they could see the performance of their portfolio, reproduce well-performing assets, repurpose misfit resources, or decommission the deadweight. It reminded Nolan of a childhood game–Tamagotchi, scaled to farm level.

None of that was a surprise. What tickled his bourbon-soaked brain was a Reply All response from another Level 28 Partner, attaching a slide deck marked "Strictly Confidential" and a multitabbed spreadsheet titled "2028 Financials." The body of the email said, *Updated for Pollyanna.*

He opened the slides and skimmed the executive summary, forgetting about the straw in his mouth for a moment.

The Bank of Pollyanna had been diversifying its investments in recent years to hedge against the consistently underwhelming economic growth and increasingly frequent market collapses. In the old days, it hadn't much cared for professional services–human businesses were messy: the conflicts of interest, the lack of passive income potential, the management of educated laborers with too much mind of their own.

But that was about to change. Once the collective know-how had been virtualized and the workforce had been optimized, selling professional services wouldn't be that different from selling chef-cooked, preportioned, live-assembled poke bowls. A team of five could be streamlined to one Intelligence Architect, someone like Subway's Sandwich Artist.

Frenell was selling the farm.

"Occupied!" Nolan yelled at someone knocking on the door of the Meditation Chamber.

"You have spent over thirty minutes in meditation," his designated egg said. "The staff manual recommends a mindfulness session of no more than fifteen minutes. If you're experiencing an abnormal level of unproductive emotions, speak to your Handler and team for guidance. On a scale of one to ten, how would you rate your peace of mind–"

Nolan flung the door open and towered over the egg. Its social cues module sensed incoming confrontation and decided the best approach to de-escalate was to add a "human touch" to the communication. In front of Nolan's eyes, the egg hatched into a Shadow Associate, stretching its face while adjusting its grin to the appropriate degree of friendliness. Maybe because the egg had assimilated only six Associates instead of ten, Nolan found a shard of himself in that smirk, and that was worse than not seeing himself at all.

He kneed the Shadow in its abdomen and cranked its head backward, attempting to sever the face from the neck. The Shadow's smile froze for a second, then slipped into the uncanny valley before its body melted back into a sphere and skidded in circles. Nolan swung a leg to kick the egg. The mechanical arm of a patrol robot struck him from behind and knocked the wind out of him. He fell forward, and another robot grabbed his lapels, tumbling the flask out of his jacket and tearing the straw off his arm. Neat bourbon splashed over his chest and drenched his collar. The front bot retracted its arms to wipe the liquid off its bald head, while the one in the back secured the egg. Nolan seized the moment and jumped inside the Meditation Chamber. As he darted through the door, the off-white interior transformed into the café on Level 20. All lights were out except the illumination from the vending machines. Someone was sitting at the table in the center of the space. He could only see their back.

"No . . ." he murmured and turned around for the exit.

But there was no exit. What should've been the lobby with the elevators was a pitch-black void, and the café was perching on a cliff. He trudged back to the table and saw the face of the one waiting.

"You shouldn't be here," said Nolan.

"I can be anywhere now." Luc shrugged. "You take me places."

"It's not you . . . I didn't have this with *you*. Where's . . ."

"Where's who?"

Nolan's mouth opened and closed, but his mind drew a blank.

"The girl . . . that girl who started something . . ."

The girl who'd told him something was not right about Frenell. Who'd say naive things like "the world is not supposed to be like that." Things like she was more expensive to buy than thirty-five dollars an hour.

"There's no one like that in this place." Luc chuckled.

"She was the one who walked out–"

Luc tutted and typed something into his phone, then he played Nolan the clip of the Spontaneous Walkout.

"See? She wasn't there," said Luc. "You want to look her up in the system? Bet you won't find anything. You were here with *me* that night. We were Buddies, remember? So we had some coffee and a good time."

"It couldn't have been you."

"Why not?"

"Because you would've been . . ."

"I would've been what, Nolan?"

You would've been dead by then.

Luc gave Nolan a genuine smile, one that pacified his bloody eyes.

"This is your chance, Mr. Nice Guy. If you want to forget her, the whole world will help you. I can carry these memories for you, and you get one ghost off your conscience. You've already got enough of us, haven't you? Or"–he stopped smiling–"should we go through everything you've done and see what you really are?"

Nolan Haut had two options.

He looked the kid in his dead eyes for a moment, then he sat down opposite him and held his gaze.

Behind Luc, the void shrank and the cliff expanded, restoring Level 20 to its true form. As the floor rolled forward, Nolan saw a pair of Chelsea boots, then a slim back, then the raven curls bouncing off the square shoulders. The last glimpse of Keahi was longer than Nolan remembered, long enough for him to recall that he could've helped her with what he knew, but he hadn't, and the last thing he'd said to her was, "What is wrong with you?"

Before she stepped into the elevator, she looked back once. That night, lost in his own thoughts, he'd missed it.

He laughed a little. Now he understood what Fischer had meant when he'd said Rhapsody gave him a comfortable paralysis and led him to places he didn't want to look. Nolan closed his eyes and opened himself up to the warmth spreading from the center of his face. Back inside the waiting area, the flickering lights tapped the bridge of his nose rhythmically, one by one, counting his sins.

If he'd had less to drink at the anniversary party, he might have stayed on track, gotten to Level 20 in time, and had a chance to stop her.

Or, if he'd acted like James Taree since he'd first met her, maybe she wouldn't have gotten the wrong idea about Frenell or dreamed about finding an ally in that place at all.

Rewind further. If he'd refused to entertain Wade's drug-dealing bullshit, maybe Luc Edward would still be alive. Nolan would've been out of a job, maybe even squeezed out of Sauria Street for good, so the fuck what? The kid was only twenty-three.

What else?

What else?

If he hadn't helped Colleen get rid of Aaron Patucchi, Richard wouldn't have been reassigned to Lindsay Frenell.

He buried his face in his hands. As long as no tears came out, a sob was the same as a laugh. He rubbed his cheeks with the heels of his palms, trying to erase the unwanted grin. But his lips curved fuller, his mouth stretched wider, because as he was going through all the deeds that made him hate himself, the back of his mind had been cheering—now he had enough reason for another shot of bourbon.

A hollow pain gripped his heart, and he felt he was plunging down an abyss inside a dream. The first thing that crossed his mind was the desperation in Fischer's eyes when he'd said he didn't want to come down. He picked up the Rhapsody from the floor, and with one deep inhale, he finished every last drop in the bottle. Then he drew out the Revilox gun and pressed the muzzle against his chest.

His heart slowed down for one beat, then he felt a punch from within. It manifested like the first heart attack he'd ever had, but it didn't scare him. It brought him a twisted sense of relief, for paying something worth more than an apology.

As long as you still feel the roller coaster come down, you're all right.

He waited. Gradually, his chest muscles lost their strength, and it cost twice as much effort to breathe. He waited more. His lungs stopped contracting, and his brain fired up a siren as urgent as the screams of a drowning man. *Sit still*, he scolded himself. He waited till the desperation spread to the tip of every limb, then right before the roller coaster flew off the rail, he pulled the trigger.

He still wanted to live.

He dropped the gun and kicked it under the seat as he fell off the banquette onto his knees. The muffled shot and his grunt of pain alerted the couple in the booth behind. The woman came over to check on Nolan, but her partner pulled her behind him and called for the nurse at the desk.

"I'm okay . . ." Nolan sat up on the floor and rested his head against the cushion. "Fuck, that hurt . . . I'm okay . . ."

He kept his eyes shut and his face turned to the side until he could no longer avoid the nurse. As he felt the rush turn into sweat and evaporate from his skin, he opened his eyes and saw her face. An exhausted human face with a frown of concern.

"I'm okay." He smiled at her.

"What happened?"

His gaze slipped to her desk and caught the can of coffee sitting next to her stapler—the same brand sold in the vending machines on Level 20.

"How much is that coffee?" he asked.

"What?" She followed his stare and realized what he was asking, so she said, "Twenty. What happened?"

"Sounds about right." He nodded.

He pulled himself up, refusing anyone's help. With a laugh, he explained he'd had a nightmare. As he wiped the sweat off his forehead and plopped down in the booth, the doctor came out and called the weeping woman in for examination. Nolan sat in silence until he was alone again, until fresh oxygen had numbed the pain in his chest, then he took out his wallet and thumbed out the only banknote inside.

When Keahi had slipped the twenty dollars under her can of coffee, the sweat of chilled metal dripped onto the paper. By the time Nolan had picked it up, the water had dried in the fiber, leaving a crescent scar over Andrew Jackson's face. He rubbed the wrinkled bill between his fingers, feeling the subtle embossment and the friction.

The twenty was real. The water stain was real.

So must be the girl too.

13

"THIS WILL BE a difficult conversation," Christie said over Teams.

"Okay?" Ryuka turned her chair a quarter to avoid direct eye contact with Christie's giant face. At the end of the long table, Morse was sizing her up like a bail judge. So she swiveled back and stared at her own laced fingers.

"The team has expressed concerns about your performance," said Christie. "Our record says that you failed to deliver an important piece of evidence, which resulted in a very disappointing outcome for an important client."

A sense of relief rushed through Ryuka. She thought the virtual WPF operation was busted and these two were going to give her a farewell speech, then let some cops take her away. It turned out they just wanted to throw her under the bus.

The "strictly confidential DSA memo" that Frenell had acquired from Henry Carrollton said the DSA was considering a "low-risk" classification for B9-3T and a staged regulation plan, which would leave Serotane available for prescription, subject to additional safeguards such as score-based evaluations, regular checkups, and robust recordkeeping. The memo also stressed that the DSA should "defer to industry leaders" for interim measures that could help medical professionals transition to the new norms, especially with the marketing of medicines containing the controlled substance. It even cited numerous public surveys and international best practices for reference. Henry had whipped up the whole thing while Sai was in the shower. All it took was some AI writing, the right letterhead, and an e-signature.

Team Rhapsody passed the memo among themselves like a golden ticket discovered inside the wrapper of a chocolate bar. As the outlook of keeping B9-3T off the Schedules grew bleaker by the day, the memo presented the best alternative closest to the status quo. Wushan Yang, the Grad who "never talked back" and did everything for a fraction of a Special Associate's hourly rate, was tasked to draft the advice that outlined the strategy for the DSA hearing and scripted responses for a dozen anticipated questions. Wushan wasn't an expert on addictive prescription drugs, or dealing with physicians and insurers in general. Luckily, he found a case study on the open internet, which he could almost use as a word-for-word playbook. Pharmaceuticals are one of those industries that constantly pump out new stars but never change their stories, like Hollywood—remember the old days when OxyContin was the A-list babe on the market? How time has flown.

Wushan was a top-notch Grad, and 80 percent of his work made it into the final advice. Hayden spent an hour making it more Hayden-ish and fixing some phrasing and typos, then Wade signed it off the same night he gave the memo to Andrej.

The advice went to Osireion tied in a bow, and Michelle and Andrej walked into the hearing thinking they were ready.

So imagine the pleasant surprise they received when none of the prepared talking points came up and the dialogue was clearly steering toward an immediate Schedule I ban, meaning that B9-3T had "a high potential for abuse" and "no currently accepted medical use in treatment," and there was "a lack of accepted safety for its use under medical supervision"—the most stringent category that also included heroin, LSD, and ecstasy, and the literal worst-case scenario in Osireion's board reports.

Twenty-four hours after the DSA published a final order in the Federal Register confirming the ban, Osireion discharged Frenell from all legal representative duties. Osireion waited twenty-four hours to fire Frenell because that was how long it took to find out that Frenell had shared the same DSA memo with its other pharma clients who had been engineering their dupes of Serotane. It was hard to tell which offended Osireion more: that the useless plan of attack from Frenell had screwed everyone, or that its seemingly loyal puppy was eating from more than one bowl.

"If you mean Project Rhapsody," Ryuka said, "I wrote a comprehensive file note explaining—"

"You were asked to deliver a witness statement, and you did not do that, yes or no?" Christie asked.

"The witness disagrees with our proposition—"

"That's a no. The record also says that you willfully ignored the instructions from senior members of the team. I'm obligated to remind you that insubordination is a trigger for termination without notice under your contract."

"I was essentially asked to—there's no other way to put it—blackmail him."

"Let's be careful with the language—"

"Rhapsody was a hopeless case in any event. We were already in a corner when I got involved—"

"We're not here just to discuss Rhapsody." Morse opened his mouth. "And do not cut people off when they're still talking. It's vulgar. This is exactly the kind of attitude issue you need to fix–"

He scrolled on his tablet with a finger and read from it.

"My file says right here: You have been pushing back on work while you clearly have capacity. The quality of your work also falls short. At your level, your work should've required minimal input from your superiors before it goes to the client, which you have *never* achieved. You take longer than average to do your job and can't deliver something that makes sense even after multiple rounds of rework. Some team members have also observed a hostile attitude that made them uncomfortable. On several occasions, you were rude and aggressive, which upset people and exacerbated their work stress."

"Um, who are these 'team members,' and exactly what did they say?"

"We obviously can't disclose that information to you, can we?" Morse tutted. "We owe people who speak up a duty of confidence. Now, tell us how you propose to improve your performance."

"Maybe this is something I should discuss with my Handler?" Ryuka sighed. The meeting was already getting too long.

"Ha! Quit name-dropping. Wade can't help you anymore!"

"What do you mean . . . ?"

"Let's just say, he won't be as relevant in the future." Morse smirked. "It takes ten Partners to undo the damage of one. He'll have a lot to answer for–once they track him down. In any event, I'll likely get the Talent and Resources portfolio once my partnership is confirmed, so you'll be a problem on my plate anyway."

He paused until Ryuka uttered a hesitant "Congratulations."

That morning, Colleen had updated Morse on a quick call that she'd spoken to Wade about "that delicate matter" they'd discussed at the anniversary party. Despite her disclaimer that nothing was set in stone yet, she practically told him that the

Frenell Olympians had thoroughly evaluated his continuous contribution to the firm and believed that his inauguration to Level 26 was overdue. They'd formalize the decision and initiate the process immediately instead of waiting till August when this type of conversation usually took place because, as she quoted, he "should've been up there ages ago."

"Thought you could start Friday with a win," she said, and he could hear the delight in her voice. "Well done, you've earned this."

Goddamn right I have, he thought, but he kept his voice bored and ended the call as if she'd just hit him up to report the weather. Then he had a huge breakfast with six pancakes and his special-occasion manuka honey. He'd thought the big guys would use that unhelpful incident on the night of the anniversary party as an excuse to put off any important discussions, but the universe was finally paying him the credit he'd long been owed. As he relished that rich honey from his memory, he noticed Ryuka was checking her watch.

"You don't seem so excited." He frowned.

"Um–"

"You're thinking, 'Oh, that miserable fuck is finally a Partner. Too bad his friends will always be ahead of him.'"

"That's not what I'm thinking, Morse–"

"Why do you look dead inside all the time?"

"I do not look dead–"

"How are you gonna build any meaningful relationships with that face? What's happened to you? You used to have so much enthusiasm! Don't you have a little fire inside you anymore?"

The little fire inside Ryuka was reignited by the mention of "enthusiasm," which sounded like the name of an exotic bird in a zoo. Its feathers held allure and its beak spoke words of promise, envisaging a land of prosperity that made you pursue it, obey it, worship it, until you realized none of its words meant what they seemed to mean, and the land was a garbage dump that you might not even have a ticket to enter, and that was the day you remembered you were in a zoo and it stank. Even the pronunciation of *enthusiasm* was forced–it wasn't a sound that your tongue and throat would voluntarily make.

"Look at how you responded to my partnership," Morse grumbled. "If a client tells you he just closed a billion-dollar deal, that's how you're gonna respond? It's rude and really makes me question your social skills and your commitment to this job. You wanted to make Special Associate so bad, remember? Reengage that feeling and channel it. Don't you want to be a Partner one day?"

"No."

The word slipped out before it registered in her mind.

"What do you mean, no?! What are you doing here if you don't want to be a Partner?"

"Well, a job is a job."

For a moment, Morse had the expression Ryuka had seen when she'd asked about her Special Associate nomination in the elevator the other day. The expression of utmost disgust.

"That's the most pathetic thing I've ever heard from anyone," he said. "If that's how you see this role, pack up and get lost now. What we do is cutting edge. It's important. It's a privilege and an honor. It changes the world for the disenfranchised–what's so goddamn funny?!"

Ryuka realized she was chuckling.

"You are incredibly arrogant. You know that?" said Morse. "Walk around like you're better than everyone else."

This is unproductive. Ryuka clenched her fists. The low-grade fury that had been brewing in her stomach was rising and might gush out if she didn't leave. She'd take virtual WPF from Nolan and defuse the bomb after this–that'd also give her a reason to talk to him again.

"I appreciate the feedback, and I'll discuss it with Wade. Technically, he's my actual Handler." She stood up from the table.

"Morse, congratulations, again, but I don't want to become who you are. Not everybody enjoys treating people like dogs."

She headed for the door, and Morse said behind her back:

"This is why we should've never taken a chance on you."

She snapped around, and her glare fed his smugness.

"You know how many much more qualified people we could've hired, but we ended up with you because of some stupid quota?"

"That is low–"

"Somebody has to say it."

"Are you just gonna sit there and watch?" Ryuka turned to Christie. "Even at Frenell, surely it's still not okay to say shit like that."

Christie gave zero reaction as if she'd been disconnected. After Ryuka called out her name, her lips moved, and she had the dazed look of someone fresh out of a dream:

"Sorry? My audio is acting weird. Let me see if I can fix it. Don't mind me!"

She turned off her camera and muted her microphone.

"You've never met the Frenell standard since day one." Morse jabbed a finger at Ryuka. "You think I'm the only one who sees right through you? I've heard things about you, and they're across-the-board unflattering. Nobody has any faith in you and nobody trusts you with serious responsibilities."

"That's not fair–"

"Not fair? Explain what happened with Rhapsody. You had one job and you were useless!"

"What I was asked to do was inappropriate–"

"It's not *your* place to decide what's appropriate, Murong," Morse sneered. "It's not up to a *low-level* Associate to tell *anybody* what to do. By the way, are you Year 8 or Year 9 now? Let's see if you break into double digits, shall we? You don't *want* to be a Partner. Right, like you were cut out for that! I didn't want to be brutally honest, but I've had it with you! You know how many people were frustrated with you? How many of them wanted to give you a chance, then they saw what you are and decided not to bother? Because of the ridiculous amount of work needed to get you in shape?"

"I don't know, actually. How come no one ever mentioned any of this?"

"When we raise the issue with you is irrelevant! What, you expect people to say 'You suck' to your face? Ever wonder why you could only get 'cleaner jobs'? If you were even remotely competent, you would've been buried in good work. Look at Hayden! Look at Emma! Read the room, for Christ's sake! God, this is exhausting . . . you have no self-awareness."

Ryuka felt her mind overloading as she tried to make sense of the blizzard of "harsh truths" from Morse. Something felt off, but it was so slippery she couldn't grasp it.

"You still think I'm being 'unfair,' don't you? Look at your pompous face." Morse narrowed his eyes. "Fine. Explain why you can't get decent work! Explain why you can't get promoted! Ah, right, I know—what card are you gonna play now? The race card? The gender card? Go ahead, I dare you. You got a rainbow card too?"

Ryuka went quiet and forgot she could walk away. She didn't want to play any "card." Morse seized the moment and summoned Christie back into the conversation. She jumped on screen instantly—guess the audio issue had gone away.

"Do what you gotta do with this one." Morse flicked his hand in the air as if swatting a fly.

"Um, okay," said Christie. "So . . . we've covered a lot of ground and there's a lot to unpack. Overall, Ryuka, we're looking at some quite alarming patterns that we should address immediately. Have you heard of a performance improvement plan?"

Everybody had. At Frenell, PIP was the equivalent of that red laser dot you'd see on your body right before a sniper put a bullet in you. Theoretically, it was a system to steer an underperforming employee "back on track." Practically, it was a precious window for the firm to construct a watertight paper trail leading to the employee's termination. In the past decade, about 15 to 20 percent Frenell employees were put on PIPs. The number of Associates who had been successfully "rehabilitated" and released back into the Frenell community? Zero.

"During the six weeks of the PIP," said Christie, "you must document your daily activity by the hour in a comprehensive log, including the specific tasks you were asked to do, the time you spent on each task, a brief explanation justifying the amount of time spent, and details about any Idle Time during the day. A template will be emailed to you—"

"I'm still sensing a lot of contempt and hostility in your body language," Morse interjected. "Face people when they speak to you! And what the hell is this when you talk—"

He made an animated imitation of the way Ryuka would sometimes raise and move her hands when she was making a point.

"What the hell is that?! If someone takes you to a client meeting, you're gonna flap like a goose throughout the presentation?"

He signaled Christie to continue after making that side note.

"You must provide two work samples every week to a designated senior staff member for review. At the end of each week, you will prepare a report documenting the feedback you've received and your proposal for improvement. We'll also assess whether you should report to our in-house clinical psychologist, who has over thirty years of experience in workforce optimization, to evaluate your interpersonal capacity and guide you through a series of behavioral exercises that will enhance your fitness for the role. A final opinion will be issued at the end of the PIP, which we will rely on to determine the next step. Do you understand everything I just said, Ryuka? Ryuka?"

Morse scanned Ryuka from head to toe, then he told Christie to end the call and strolled over. He drew a bottle of water out of the ice bucket on his way and twisted the cap off before he slipped it into Ryuka's hand. Something he'd learned from one of those *50 Rules of Power* and *12 Communication Skills of Highly Influential People* books--first grind them into the dirt to show them who's the alpha, then kill them with kindness afterward, and they'll forget you were the one stomping on their faces a minute ago.

"Look, I'm the only one in this entire place who'd be honest with you and take the trouble to guide you," said Morse. "As a Partner, it's in my interest that every Associate reaches their full potential. We have invested a lot of time and resources in you and we want to see you thrive! Help us help you."

Nausea filled Ryuka's stomach as goose bumps crawled down her spine, making her want to jump out of her skin, but all she managed to do was stand there, paralyzed. Morse held her by the shoulders and gazed into her eyes.

"There's only one way to succeed in this profession: quit whining, put in real hard work, and get on the good side of the people above you. Follow the PIP and redeem yourself. After you get back on the right track, you'll tell everybody you'd never consider working anywhere other than Frenell, and you'll thank me later."

She lost that bottle of water somewhere she couldn't recall. She also lost some time on the way back to her workstation. When she recognized her surroundings again, she was staring at a new email from Christie, summarizing the wisdom of the day:

Ryuka,

At today's meeting, we provided you with constructive feedback in relation to your unsatisfactory performance and interpersonal skills. Examples of problematic conduct include inability to deliver work as instructed, which resulted in disappointing results for clients; poor quality of work for a sustained period of time; and behavioral issues such as attempting to leave without permission, using inappropriate language, and calling Morse a dog.

We are particularly concerned about the hostility and resistance observed at the meeting, which raises questions as to your willingness to engage and improve. You have also admitted that you do not see yourself with Frenell in the long term.

You have agreed to participate in the six-week Performance Improvement Plan and report your progress in the form of the activity log attached. We encourage you to utilize the abundant resources we provide to help bridge the expectation gap. Please note that refusal or failure to complete the PIP will result in termination of your employment.

Have a great weekend.

"HELP'S ON THE way, ma'am," the 911 operator reassured Ryuka after taking down her name and address. Ryuka stumbled out of her door and curled up on the concrete steps, gasping like she was down to her last breath.

It was twelve minutes to midnight, and the streets were empty save for a handful of warehouse workers in overalls who seemed too tired, too sad, or too angry to notice anything around them. Normally, she wouldn't be out at this hour, but she needed to be seen by *someone*—someone who could describe how she died.

She'd gone home around eight o'clock that night and put the news on while she assembled an evidence bundle for Rudy on Level 21. It was distracting and slowed her down, but when the room was quiet, a very specific fear would creep in and remind her that someone could call her up the next second and scream about her "incompetence" and "lack of self-awareness." She knew exactly what that caller would sound like. He had a face and a name—he always did. Was it still about your "self-esteem" when your negative voice was a real person?

A bloody phone call scares you? You can't fucking hang up? Grow up!

She wished she had a set of Productivity Shields to insulate her from her own home. The thought of another professional "fuck you" email popping up in her inbox made her jittery, but not checking her email for over an hour made her even more anxious. She stopped her Timekeeper clock and stepped away from her computer, not knowing where to go or how to be. The noise from the news did nothing to quiet her mind. Dinner was premade, microwaved, and half-wasted. Her heart had been pounding after eating, slow but loud, and her skin felt swollen, as if her veins were pumping twice the amount of blood through her body. So she changed into her gym clothes and thought she'd go for a run.

That was when she realized she couldn't breathe.

Can't even do this right, huh? Just suck in the fucking air, it's not that hard!

She panted and heaved. The air must've been diluted or her lungs must've been malfunctioning, as she seemed to be getting only half the oxygen she needed. You'd give someone Heimlich or an EpiPen if their passages were blocked, but what could you do when a greater force was draining the oxygen from the air?

Outside her home, she folded her body and buried her face between her knees, flattening her lungs so maybe she'd need less to breathe. When she counted over a hundred, she heard a short blurt of siren, so she wobbled toward it.

"Why did you call an ambulance?" The paramedic, who had been dispatched for a heart attack, wasn't expecting someone standing up.

"I can't breathe," Ryuka said and stumbled inside the vehicle on her own. They sat in awkward silence for a moment, then she repeated: "I can't breathe."

You know this is not what emergency services are for, don't you? Some poor bastard could be dying right now 'cause you can't manage your stress, you know that? Pathetic!

"You're breathing really fast right now," said the paramedic. "Let's try some deep breaths–deep and slow, there you go. Can you tell me what happened?"

Ryuka synchronized her breathing to his demonstration, drawing deep breaths and inflating her chest to the maximum.

Yet the air still felt thin, and she continued to gasp like a fish on land.

The paramedic wrapped a blood pressure cuff around Ryuka's arm and clipped an oximeter on her finger. "It's all good." He read her vitals with a bored face. "Everything looks good."

"I'm not getting enough oxygen," Ryuka said.

"But you are. Your blood oxygen level is one hundred percent."

"How do you know it's one hundred percent?!"

"See?" The paramedic pointed at the monitor next to him. "This measures your blood oxygen. It says one hundred percent, right there."

"Is that reliable?"

"Yeah . . . I think so."

"But why am I not feeling the oxygen?!" She tried to force her brain to register everything she saw like she had before, but this time, her mind was a carnival with blaring announcements from millions of frequencies. She was in a real ambulance with real medical equipment and two real paramedics. They were having a chat sitting down, and he didn't seem too worried, so maybe she shouldn't be either. She probably wouldn't die in this thing—not immediately—and even if she did, these guys would know what to do with her body without letting it go to waste. Among the swirling musings, somehow the one thought that stood out was that if she dropped dead tonight, the last thing she'd done with her life would be putting hole-punched pages behind numbered tabs while checking if everything was printed single-sided in full color.

She started crying. It wasn't a sadness-induced cry to numb her pain with tears but a compulsive cleansing to keep her alive, like vomiting.

"I think you're having a panic attack," said the paramedic. "And you still have a pretty high level of anxiety right now. Did something trigger it?"

Did something trigger it?

That turn of phrase could open a floodgate, but people asking that question always seemed to expect one or two words, like *peanuts*.

Where should she begin? How about, she'd given *years* of her life she was never getting back to what was, frankly, a pretty fucking disgusting job. She'd done her best, but it wasn't enough, and it seemed nothing ever would be. Those people she wanted to respect, even admire, treated her like she owed them money or her life, and the one piece of career advice they'd given her was "You've always been shit, we just never cared to tell you." She used to consider herself an "ordinary" Associate—maybe not brilliant, but decent. Now she didn't know if that was true anymore. In fact, she didn't know if that had *ever* been true, as she could no longer trust her own thoughts, like she couldn't trust the readings on that hospital-grade BP O_2 monitor right in front of her fucking eyes. Was everything she'd believed about herself completely false? Did she know anything at all? Then a terrifying thought befell her: *What if Morse is right?*

What if she'd really been hopelessly incompetent, and she'd only wormed her way into Frenell as a DEI token? Had people been dropping her enough hints about how they truly felt about her, but she'd missed them all? Had she just been an insufferable, clueless clown this whole time, and people were finally fed up with her? What kind of future could she have if she had no idea what to think or how to behave and she couldn't even tell if she was stupid or not?

Oh, and she'd also had to handle two bodies. Not one. Two.

Did something trigger it? She couldn't possibly make her answer comprehensible to this young paramedic who had never asked for any of this, so she blurted out:

"I work for a dead man."

"What?"

"My boss is dead."

"Oh, um, I'm sorry to hear that . . . was he . . . a good person?"

She laughed.

Then she remembered that was the wrong emotion, so she started her second wave of crying. The tears were real, and she looked only half-insane. It sent the poor guy into a round of random troubleshooting. He pressed the stethoscope against her back and asked her to take a deep breath. "Loud and clear," he said as he proceeded to take her blood sugar, followed by a string of rapid-fire questions as if they were playing a conversational game of catch called *Guess What Will Kill You One Day*. Are you on medication? No. What kind of diet do you have? Normal. Nothing taken out except sugar. Low-carb, not keto. No smoking. No drinking. No drugs. No cutting. No eating disorders. Binge, sometimes, but no vomiting. Depression? Not in recent years.

"Good." He gave her more encouraging nods. "All that is very good."

"Is my heart failing?"

"What?"

"My heart rate dropped below fifty for a second there. That's the 'polar bear' range! Do I have bradycardia?" She grabbed his wrist so he could feel her freezing fingertips.

"Fifty is still within the normal range—human range, and it's possible you have a low resting heart rate."

"I don't think I should be alone tonight."

He stared at her for a moment, then nodded gently.

"We will take you to a hospital, and they can run some further tests to see if there's anything serious, like bradycardia . . . or if it's something mental."

He instructed his partner in the driver's seat to locate the nearest available emergency room. When the dispatcher asked for a "reason for visit," he glanced at Ryuka, who was tapping the top of the monitor as if to see whether the readings would change, then said, "Situational crisis."

ᘓ

"WHAT DID YOU take?" the nurse asked.

"Like . . . drugs?" Ryuka said.

"Yeah."

"I don't do drugs."

"Are you on medication?"

"No."

"Want to?"

"Are they addictive?"

"They can be."

"Then I don't want them."

The nurse jotted down her notes on her pad, then asked Ryuka to follow the blue line on the floor to the waiting area for the Rapid Assessment Zone. She left before Ryuka had a chance to ask which hospital it was and whether it was part of her insurance network, so Ryuka found the information on Google Maps with her location. This visit would cost her.

She pocketed the ID that the paramedic had handed back to her. "They'll take care of you," he'd said after registering her in the system. She felt grateful that he didn't tell her "Everything is gonna be fine" or "You'll be okay." It gave her more confidence in what he'd actually said.

The waiting area looked like a diner without a bar. That impression quickly faded as she walked past the patients inside those colorful booths. One girl seemed to be vomiting her entire pack of organs into a plastic bucket, and the splashy sound was getting concerning as the water level rose. Another had run out of space on her arms for needles and tubes and fallen into, hopefully, a sound sleep. A college-age boy in a wheelchair was asking his dad about the cost of chemo in a tone that was too light even for a fishing-trip discussion. Ryuka caught her reflection in the windows. She looked okay, and that made her embarrassed for not feeling okay.

Go ahead, play the victim in front of these people. I dare you, you lazy, spoiled brat! Life is meant to be hard, and everybody is pulling themselves up by their bootstraps. Get your shit together!

She reached the last booth and met eyes with the waiting patient. He seemed like he hadn't slept in days, but his lethargic eyes gained a little bit more life when he shifted his stare from the twenty-dollar bill in his hand to her face. As she tried to come up with something to say, he scooted over and made some room.

"Hi." She sat down next to him.

"Hi," said Nolan.

"What happened to you?"

"I almost killed myself, I think. You?"

"I thought I was dying."

"Hmm . . . how did we get here?"

"I wanted a promotion."

"I was trying to deal drugs."

"Is it a better job?"

"Depends on the kind of person you are. Not for everyone."

"Hmm."

"You've never told me why you wanted that promotion so bad. It's not about a tree, is it?"

That question started a reel of memories, and Ryuka settled on a fresher piece. About a year ago on Level 12, she'd sat in an obscure corner against a wall. An abstract painting hung above her workstation and would collide with her monitor when she elevated her desk. So she took the painting off and leaned it against the wall to be dealt with later. One of the Olympians for whatever reason was on the floor and happened to walk past at that moment. He reprimanded her loudly in front of everyone that she must speak to their "in-house curator" and have the painting handled with proper care because they were, in fact, quite "valuable." She responded with a smile that she'd do as he said, then he glared at her and walked away while muttering something under his breath. She didn't catch his last words, but she still remembered the look on his face to this day, because it was a look that said, "If murder were legal, I'd murder you right here, right now, by strangulation, so I could feel your neck snap under my thumbs and watch your bulging eyes burst, you bitch."

She googled that artist afterward and found that his global-record sale was three hundred dollars—not three hundred thousand, three hundred. That was how much she was billing in twenty minutes. Nevertheless, she called the curator, who relayed the matter to Office Facilities, and all they did was stack that painting in a Meditation Chamber with a bunch of equally "valuable" pieces from the same artist in a corner, on the floor, against the wall. One of them ended up slashed, and nobody was fired for that.

Throughout her time at Frenell, she'd seen people get away with things from sexual harassment to manslaughter, and she couldn't get away with taking one cheap, useless painting off the wall.

"I wanted to be able to get away with things," she said, then laughed a little. Now she'd gotten away with more than she'd ever imagined. They weren't lying when they said this job would challenge you to your full potential.

"I'm really angry, Nolan. But I don't know if what I feel is justified, or if I'm just entitled and spoiled for thinking this way. I don't know if I'm good at my job, ever, or if I've been a charity case all along. I don't even know if, when I ruminate like this, I'm reconstructing my own memories and stirring myself further away from the truth. All I know is I didn't go *into* that job like this . . . if a job and the people you work for make you give them everything and leave you feeling you deserve nothing, and you end up not even knowing what is 'real,' there has to be something wrong with them . . . right? Or am I crazy for feeling what I feel?"

"You're not crazy, Ryu."

"Are you just saying that because you're a friend?"

"I am your friend, but I didn't say that to comfort you. I told you what I believe, and I think this is one of those occasions where I'm the one you should listen to. I'm not saying put your faith in me. I'm saying don't put your faith in them. That place and those people have a terrifying ability to make you question what is real. They have to. What they tell you will never be the whole fucking truth–never. If you let them get under your skin, you'd lose everything that actually matters to you in a life that's already too short."

She laid her head on his shoulder, and he hugged her with one arm.

"It's been a really strange month," she said.

"I know."

The doctor walked the weeping woman out and collected her ECG results from the printer next to the nurse's desk. He gave her some final instructions before sending her on her way and calling the next name. The father wheeled the chemo boy forward, and the three exchanged some laughter as they strolled down the hall. In the distance, the girl took a break from vomiting and held a casual chat with the wired-up lady, who'd woken up. Every single one of these people sounded like they needed to be here more than Ryuka and Nolan.

"Should we . . . go?" Ryuka asked.

"How are you feeling right now?"

"Better." She sat up. "I still feel hopeless. But it's not the kind that will kill you immediately. More like the 'only eat junk food and never go to the gym' kind."

"Some days are like that." He nodded.

They flagged down a street taxi outside the front door. After Ryuka had given the driver her address, Nolan stuck his face in through the window.

"I think something big is about to happen at Frenell. They're gonna fuck everybody and get away with it like they always do. I don't know what to do yet, but I need your help, Ryu. We're in this together."

She kissed him good night on the cheek and gave him an apologetic smile.

"I don't know, Nolan. I'm kinda exhausted."

The homeless guy hovering outside the ER disapproved of the holdup with a grunt from the bottom of his belly, so Nolan let go and watched the taxi drive away. He crossed the road to wait for one heading the opposite direction. Under a streetlamp, he took out Wade's work phone and checked his latest. On top of his inbox lay a flood of emails pronouncing their significance with either a red exclamation mark or subject lines in all caps, inquiring about the recent development with Osireion and the other pharma clients. Dozens of missed calls and unread Teams messages, likely about the same thing. But what caught Nolan's attention and muted the honks of the taxi that'd stopped in front of him was a simple text from Colleen with two words—

Hello, Nolan.

14

SAI EXAMINED HER family house from across the street. She couldn't recall if it had looked better in the brochure. With the facade sketched in sharp, angular lines and the walls clad in sleek slate-gray paneling, the two-story structure resembled a stack of shipping containers. Being 170 miles away from the heart of the city and part of Clover Hill's industrial and utilitarian aesthetics, it didn't seem like a place for someone to build a tomorrow but a spot for them to forget yesterdays.

She'd never dreamed about home ownership that much, but after countless excruciating rental hunts for a family of six with an autistic son, pooling funds and taking out a monstrous loan for a three-bedroom "turnkey package" in one of the most promoted neighborhoods for "upcoming middle-class" had sounded like a good deal back then, until things began to break around the house months later.

The day they moved in, the family took a photo in the driveway. The labor was brutal. She was drenched in sour sweat, and she couldn't lift her arms above her shoulders for two days straight, but she was smiling in that picture. She'd genuinely thought she was on her way to "making it."

That was one thing no one had taught her in college: you can look at a lie in the flesh, know it's a lie, remember how it cut you with its rough edges, yet still want to believe it.

Ina slammed her drawer shut and guarded it with her hip when Sai walked into their room.

"Oh . . . you actually made it." She scanned Sai while adjusting her smile.

"Well, I said I'd come."

"Yeah . . . just thought you might cancel, again."

Sai was supposed to be home last weekend, as they'd agreed on the phone, but she really hadn't been in the best shape for this, physically or mentally.

"Where are Mom and Farid?" Sai dropped her bag on the floor so she didn't have to touch anything Ina had piled up on her bed.

"Backyard. Idris and Rafi are out for work."

"Lanchester has day hours now?"

"They got a gig at Shelby's. Then they go to Lanchester after."

"That's like a whole day gone."

"They really want to go to that robot camp."

"If their grades tank, no robot camp will help them."

"They're not babies, Saidah."

Sai left it at that. She felt she'd lost the license to lecture her siblings by being chronically absent.

Something hit the wall behind Ina's back. Sounded like a tennis ball. Then Sai heard the cheer her brother would make when he saw a bird.

"What's this new treatment?" she asked.

"Oh, it's pretty complicated," said Ina. "They'll put him through twelve sessions of behavioral therapies in a pressure chamber and take his biomarkers to personalize his medication. It's like designer gene editing."

"Does it work?"

"He's only done it twice."

Farid made more noise behind the wall. This time, Sai heard a question: *What do robins eat?* Most likely, he was echoing that back to someone, buying himself time to recall how he'd answered something similar before—if that memory was still there. *What do robins eat?* he repeated, louder each time. Sai frowned. He'd probably get caught in a loop again, and it'd take mountain-moving effort to calm him down.

That was one of the first symptoms people would notice about Farid, and one of the lasting memories Sai held about her brother. The day Sai left home for college, as she was hugging everyone on the front lawn of the house they lived in back then, a squirrel caught Farid's attention. He followed it to the fence and watched it scamper into the neighbor's backyard. Their neighbor asked Farid if he would like some acorns, and that set him off. He started repeating the question while bobbing his head behind the fence with his eyes fixed on the sweet old lady, whose friendliness soon turned into suspicion, until Mom rushed over and recited the script that she'd repeated thousands of times. Sai was running late, so she shouted her goodbye across the lawn. Mom didn't hear her at all. Nine years later, that part of Farid hadn't changed. He was the only one in the family with a frozen clock, while all of them were getting old for him.

"So how's Mom?" Sai asked.

"Mom's all right. Just tired. The clinic and the chamber are in two places for whatever reason. The commute is a bitch but—"

"No, I mean, is Mom still upset . . . about me?"

Ina mouthed an "ah," then looked down at her shoes.

"We never mentioned it again."

Sai nodded. She wanted to ask Ina about college and, maybe, love interests, but she decided to save that for later so they could even out the awkward silence throughout her stay. To her surprise,

Farid calmed down faster than he normally would. Maybe the new treatment was different this time. Amid Farid's mumbles, Sai heard the soothing yet exhausted second voice. She pointed at the backyard, meaning she'd go check on them, and left the room. Ina waited till she could no longer hear Sai's steps before she reopened her drawer. From underneath her notebooks, she fished out a canvas pouch and counted the nasal sprays in there.

SAI DIDN'T ANNOUNCE her presence when she found her mother and brother near the single crabapple tree in the yard. Mom caught Sai in her peripheral vision, but she didn't look at her. Farid had returned his attention to the tennis ball. He lay on his stomach, dropped the ball in the center of a patch of taller grass, then cupped the ball with his palms as if to bury it under the stalks. This might be his favorite spot, judging from the dent around his body. Sai sat down next to him. Once Farid had gotten into this state, he'd be too engrossed to notice anyone or anything else near him, but she spoke to him anyway.

"What have we got here?" Sai made her voice sweet and chirpy. "Ah, a tennis ball. Should we dig a hole for it? Maybe we'll find some worms–"

"Don't talk to him in that voice. He's not a toddler."

Sai looked up and met her mom's scornful eyes.

"Okay, I just thought–"

"He understands, Saidah. He's an adult, and it upsets him when you talk to him like that."

"Okay, I'm sorry–"

"He can't use words the way you and I do, but he's not stupid. It's about time you get that, don't you think?"

"I get it, Mom–"

"If you'd paid more attention, you wouldn't need me to tell you something so basic–"

"Is this about that video?"

Mom pressed her lips thin and turned her head. Sai took a deep breath.

"Ina has given you everything we have and everything we know. I don't know what else to tell you. It wasn't me. It's not me."

"Worm!" Farid burst out—he'd found the answer to the question earlier.

"You were supposed to be here last week," said Mom.

"Worm! Worm!"

"I'm sorry, okay? I had a lot of . . . work."

"You're never around. Ina, Idris and Rafi, no matter how 'busy' they are, I can count on them, but you're never around. I made dolma last week—"

"Worm!"

"—and you didn't show up."

"Worm! Worm—"

"Will you people cut it out?!"

Harun stormed out of his house and yelled at the Sulaimaniyah family from his porch. He'd finished a graveyard shift at the local hospital that morning, followed by another four hours at the data center on the other side of the town. In total, he'd had two hours of in-and-out sleep since Thursday night. He was finally drifting into an episode sound and deep when the kid went squawking in that weird voice of his. He'd shut all his windows and drawn his curtains, but it didn't help. The builder had definitely cheaped out on the material. The walls were paper thin.

"Feed him some sleeping pills! Or I will!"

Mom was right. Farid understood things, especially strong emotions with a threat underneath. He hushed and froze, then he pushed a flatlining noise through his nose as he pulled his hair with his hands. Mom made a "stop" gesture at Harun, half an apology, half a warning for him to back off. She tried to soothe Farid, who kept dodging and struggling away, while keeping that nonstop nasal noise on maximum volume. Ina had come out of the house with a backpack over her shoulder. She caught up on the situation with a quick glance and dashed over to help Mom. Harun came to the fence and seemed like he was about to have another go, so Sai thrust herself into his path, shielding her family with her body.

"Let us mind our own business, Harun."

Harun's sleep-deprived brain took some time to recognize Sai's face.

"Wow, celebrity in the house." He yawned with his mouth gaping open. Sai took one step back to avoid the smell of overnight tobacco and cheese, or just Harun in general. His entire being reeked of dilapidation.

"Go back inside, please," she said. "We'll take care of Farid."

"You know if you don't sleep, you go crazy? I'm feeling motherfucking crazy right now."

"Look, we're sorry about this. Let me see if we can find you some earplugs, okay?"

"Earplugs . . ." He ran his eyes along her body. "I'd love to plug something in you."

"Leave us alone." Sai shot him a glare and turned to leave.

"Worm!" Farid shouted.

"What did you call me?!"

"That's not what he meant, Harun," Sai said.

"All right, I've had it. Today is the day."

Harun snapped his head around to call Zayn out, then he remembered his son was working this weekend. Grunting and mumbling, he slapped his insect screen out of the way and retreated into his house. Sai heard the faint noise of Harun stomping between rooms and throwing things around.

Then a chilling thought gripped her.

Does this guy have a gun?

"Go inside!" She sprinted toward her family. "Mom, go inside!"

Ina looked up at her sister while Mom knelt next to Farid, who was lying on the ground with his face between elbows, refusing to get up. As Sai tried to usher her family to safety, Harun reemerged with a bucket of brine and marched to the fence, then he emptied the bucket with a heave and coated his neighbor's lawn with vinegary slop. Ina hopped away in time, and Sai also dodged the spill–although it was a close one. Farid was still lying on the grass, and Mom had moved his head to her lap. The liquid mess landed a few steps away from them and splashed over their clothes, like the backwash from a car driving through a puddle on the side of the road.

"You son of a–"

Ina sprang off the ground and charged toward Harun, but Sai grabbed her from behind.

"Ina, you don't need this. You don't need this bullshit. Go check on Mom. He's not worth it. You don't need this."

Harun tossed the bucket to a corner of his yard and strolled back to his house. From his porch, he pointed a finger and yelled at Sai's mom.

"Your great daughters. One is a whore; one is a thug. Mark my words."

He slammed the door shut, and Ina stopped struggling. She brushed Sai's arms off her in silence and picked her backpack up, rounded the house to the front, and grabbed the steel gate.

"Where are you going?" Sai asked.

"I have an appointment."

"What appointment?"

"I have my life."

"When are you coming back? We need to file a police report–"

"Good luck with that!" Ina laughed. "You don't need me anyway. You saw as much of that as I did."

"Is everything okay, Ina?"

When you first met these two, you might not assume they were sisters. Ina looked like a time-travel version of their mother, while Sai took the sable hair and perky nose from her father. They'd both get stares walking down the streets, but far fewer boys had approached Ina because of this exact look she was giving Sai. Sai was glad about that. This coldness might protect her baby sister.

"You're not the only one who wants to be done with this, Saidah."

She took off without looking back. Sai watched her turn the corner. Ina's seaweed-like hair covered her face. Sai couldn't see her expression.

Mom said nothing when Sai returned to the backyard. She got up and checked her clothes for stains, then decided a change was not worthwhile and went into the kitchen. Farid had stopped stimming, but he was still lying on the grass with one arm over his head. Sai called out his name a couple of times, like checking if someone was asleep before making a confession.

"What did I do wrong, Farid? This isn't how I imagined life would turn out."

She lay down next to him and peeked under his elbow. This whole time, he'd been protecting the tennis ball next to his face, and he'd done a great job.

"What do robins eat?" she whispered as she brushed his hair.

After a moment, Farid muttered:

"Worm."

IT WAS A cloudy day, and the sky looked like it was ready to wrap things up at four in the afternoon. For the first time in a while, Sai remembered how dark the house could get, and it reminded her of her city apartment. The floor squeaked even when someone as lightweight as her walked on it, and one of the bathroom doors was slightly misaligned—she had to grab the knob and heave the panel upward to close it. Maybe this was the one Ina had been saying needed fixing.

If she weren't here today, Mom would be in this house alone with Farid.

"Do you want to make dolma? I'll help." Sai found Mom in the kitchen. The dicing paused for a second, then resumed to its steady tempo. Farid was walking along a square path outlined by the fence and the wall and passing the kitchen window every ten seconds. For a moment, it seemed like he was using the chopping sounds for pacing.

"We eat tabbouleh today," Mom said.

"Okay, tabbouleh it is." Sai opened the fridge. "We're running low on green onions. Okay if we put more tomatoes—"

"If you want dolma, you need to tell me early."

"No, no, tabbouleh is totally fine."

"Not because I don't want to make it for you. Dolma is hard work."

"I know, I know."

"Lots of preparation. A lot of things can go wrong. I can show you the recipe, then you'll see."

"It's okay, Mom." Sai chuckled. "Sorry I haven't been around—"

"I don't want you to make the mistakes I made."

Mom dried her hands on the kitchen towel and took another tomato out of the fridge, then she returned to the sink, giving Sai her back.

"We'll have dolma next week," she said.

Sai helped Mom set the table for three. None of her other siblings would come back for dinner. Farid had a very limited diet, so it was rare to get anything other than grilled chicken, tabbouleh, or kleicha on their menu. Idris and Rafi sometimes got leftover bar snacks from Lanchester, and Ina, well, Ina was always able to sort herself out.

She dragged her fingers across the rectangular table that could fit six people and six only. If her memory was correct, the family had picked this one together. The six of them could fill a full table, because they were a full house.

Mom had returned to the backyard to get Farid "ready" for dinner, which involved walking alongside him for as long as he wanted until he felt like coming in. Now, passing the kitchen window wasn't one head, but two. In the somber light under a gloomy sky, Sai saw that Mom was becoming an old woman.

And this could become her life too.

"HEY, YOU. WHAT'S up?"

Henry picked up on the first ring. The upbeat greeting lifted the corners of Sai's mouth. He didn't sound like he was sulking.

"Nothing, just . . . kinda want to see–"

"You know, I was just about to call you, literally. This is wild, ha ha. We must be doing something right."

"Oh, were you–"

"Sorry I haven't been in touch, but I've sorted something out, and I've got big news! Actually, I'm at Oleander. You wanna come?"

When Sai dashed out the kitchen door, Mom and Farid had turned a corner and headed toward her. Mom saw the bag over her shoulder and the phone clutched in her hand, then they locked eyes. Sai wanted to explain that the North Line would finish at five today, so she had to leave now if she wanted to get back to the city, and she *needed* to get back to the city. But her lips were glued tight, and her feet were not moving. Mom marched closer, holding Farid's arm and following his pace. When they were steps away from Sai, Mom broke eye contact and turned onto the next line on Farid's path. Sai stared at their backs for a moment, then she crossed the backyard and left through the front gate.

SITUATED ON OLEANDER Island and perched on the "right side" of the Athena River, le Fleuve du Soleil offered panoramic views of the shimmering water down below. From the second floor, the glass-and-steel structure seemed to be floating in an ethereal realm with a 24/7 interdimensional portal, waiting for its patrons to teleport themselves off as soon as they decided to be done with this world. Sai walked down the aisle that was flanked by empty tables with greasy plates and scattered silverware as she looked out the curved wall of floor-to-ceiling windows. The glittering high-rise condos and corporate towers of Grand Ivory formed a skyline that looked like a crowded motherboard. From this distance, she couldn't catch a hint of the tent city even if she squinted.

Fresh off a cross-city train ride and having run all the way from the station, she wanted to check herself in a mirror, but the flashback of what might be lurking inside a public bathroom deterred her. Having retreated to a corner near the entrance, she looked down at her front, then over her shoulders. Her heart sank when she spotted the stain on the outer thigh of her jeans—Harun had gotten her with that pickle juice after all. She extended the strap of her cross-body bag and swung it to the other side, managing to cover half of the blemish. After getting rid of a piece of streamer stuck to the bottom of her sneaker, she strode down the hall, smoothing her wild hair with one hand while stealing a sniff under her armpit, relieved that her deodorant seemed to be holding up.

"May I help you?" A waiter inserted himself in the middle of the aisle before Sai could move farther. He gave her a head-to-toe scan that he didn't mind if she'd be displeased with.

"I'm with friends," she said as she tried to maneuver around him.

"What name is the reservation under?"

"Carrollton." Sai sighed. "Henry Carrollton? I think."

The waiter stared at her for a second longer before he moved out of her way and gestured at the staircase leading to the rooftop garden. Sai ascended the curved marble steps while the waiter fixed his eyes on her, as if to see if she'd suddenly start running or cast a suspicious furtive glance.

Through the manicured lawn, she reached the west end of the garden, where sculptural agave plants and leather couches carved out a private lounge laced by an ornamental oasis. Her chest tightened when she saw the identical clique she'd collided with at the anniversary party, all in impeccable cocktail attire and gathered under a merry halo. Tugging the strap of her cross-body bag, she flushed. Her feet began to turn, ready to carry her far, far away. That was when Henry disentangled himself from the cluster and bounded over with his arms spread wide, as if to catch her before she fell.

"You made it!" He bear-hugged her, which almost made her burst into tears. The harmonious soapy scent from his hair to the open collar of his shirt soothed her like a cup of warm tea on a snowy morning and made her want to believe that all that had happened in his absence was nothing but a bad dream. What they had was stronger than petty drama and the abyss between Tuscan vineyard and disabled brother who sounded like a broken record. She was desperate to tell him that.

"Listen—"

"Charlene!"

Henry pulled away and waved at a brunette with the enthusiasm of a fair lady bidding farewell from a departing ship in a silent movie.

"Get yourself a drink. There's a tab." He rubbed Sai's shoulder as he walked away. "I'll catch you later."

She tried to grab him but missed, so she shuffled to the bar next to the lounge and ordered something that wouldn't require her to answer any questions from the bartender. Genevieve sat in the center of the main couch, having an intimate debate with Diane that seemed to be conveyed mainly through giggles and hand gestures implying disbelief. They noticed Sai's presence but didn't acknowledge it with more than a glance. Clutching her cider, Sai settled against the balcony railing between the bar and the couches, a safe distance from both, where the waterfront breeze ruffled her hair as the shadows of sunset concealed her chagrin.

"Hey." Marcus smiled at her and took a drag on his vape pen.

"Hi."

"Good to see you again."

"Thanks. Sorry about . . . you know."

"Oh, don't worry about it." He turned his face and blew the smoke into the evening air. "So, you and Henry, you're a thing?"

Someone had asked her that question years ago, right before her graduation. Back then, she'd responded with a shrug followed by a shot of tequila.

She blushed a little and took a sip of her cider, then she nodded: "Yeah . . . yes, we are."

Marcus bit his lip as he studied her face, then he asked, hesitantly:

"Did someone ask you to be here?"

"What does that even mean?" She frowned.

"Look–"

Genevieve let out a squeal and covered her mouth with one hand as she peeked inside the jewelry box she was holding. She rocked Charlene in her embrace and rubbed her cheek against her own, mumbling something that was most likely "I love you." Henry picked up an empty champagne glass from a side table and clinked it to quiet the room. As a hush fell over the periphery beyond the clique, Sai realized half of the people at the bar were here for the same cause.

"Okay, my favorite people, well, most of you." Henry fished a laugh out of the crowd. "Thank you so much for coming tonight. Gene and I truly appreciate all your kind words and blessings. You know me. I'd always thought marriage wasn't for me, but I guess eventually we all find that one person who makes us willing to change what we believe–"

Sai didn't hear the words after that. Nevertheless, her eyes continued to film the events before her. Genevieve snuggled up to Henry and stamped an approving peck on his cheek. Charlene peeled Genevieve off Henry and swept the girl into her own hug while Diane rested her forearm on Henry's shoulder and teased him. The rest of the group cheered and clapped, then lined up for another round at the bar. Henry finally broke out of the circle and headed toward the balcony. Marcus peeked at Sai, turned off his vape, and slipped away.

Henry was saying something to her. She tried to give him a reaction, but she seemed to have lost control over all her facial muscles. There was a reason to cry. But she didn't want to. Not in front of these people.

"Congratulations . . . I guess." She raised her glass and forced a smile. "When is the wedding?"

"July 2030, maybe? Her folks need to work out their tax plans first." He rolled his eyes. "They don't have their act together."

Then he leaned in for a kiss.

"What are you doing?" She dodged his lips, startled.

"I've missed you," he said with an innocuous face.

"But–"

"Oh, don't worry. Nothing will change between us–I've told everyone about you. Gene knows. My parents know. You remember Marcus? He's with Gene. We're open."

Marcus had settled down next to Genevieve on the couch and thrown an arm over her shoulder as she tried on the pearl necklace from Charlene. He was watching Sai and Henry but glanced away when she met his eyes.

"How does this work?" Sai's voice cracked coming out of her dry throat.

"Thought you'd never ask." Henry grinned. "My parents bought me a loft in the city for my birthday last year. Superb location. Literally *everything* within a five-minute walk. I'll get it painted, and we can move in before the end of summer! We'll get a dog and take it to the park on Sundays. We can get brunch, check out some new shows, go to games–anything you've never tried before! Gene has her own place four blocks away, so it's hassle-free if I need to visit. Don't worry, it'll be, like, once a month or something. She prefers I leave her alone. Okay, I've worked *real* hard to get my parents on board–almost had to tell them about my brother's drug problem to give them some perspective. So, remember, I did this for *us*."

Her lips opened and closed several times with no words coming out. Henry thought she needed more convincing.

"Look, my parents were pretty pissed about that DSA memo, so I gotta give them something. They've been nagging me about settling down for ages, so now it's the best time to make the most of it. Gene is two months in and somehow she wants the baby—not mine, obviously, and now she owes me one—a favor, not a baby. Her family's Q2 isn't looking great, so they could use some good publicity as well."

"How is Marcus okay with this?"

"What does Marcus have to do with anything?"

"Isn't he . . . the father?"

"No, I don't think so . . . is he? I don't know, you'll have to ask Gene. The point is, the timing is really opportune. It takes a lot of pressure off things, and we might never get another chance like this. If you think about it, this is the best objective outcome for everyone. Now we can be together and I'll take good care of you!"

"Take good care of me . . . like that dog you want us to get?"

"Don't put it like that." Henry frowned. "You know how I feel about you, but we have to be . . . strategic. Gene and I have known each other since we were born, and our parents went back, like, two more generations. It just . . . it makes sense. It's what *needs* to happen in my life, but it's not what I want. I want *you.* I said this before—you're different. I can be honest with you."

She shook her head and let out a chain of airy, nervous laughs like she was about to cry. The glee on Henry's face faded, and he looked at her with the same expression she'd seen at the anniversary party.

"I thought I was doing what's best for us, but fine." He shrugged. "C'mon, Saidah, be reasonable. You can't possibly expect me to burn the bridges with all my family and friends for someone—"

"For someone like me."

Someone who looked like she wouldn't know where Tuscany was. Someone who had practically been an escort when they'd reunited. Someone who didn't have an estate that could even make the tax benefits for marriage worthwhile. Someone who was damaged and had to be discounted. Maybe Henry was right: nothing had changed between them—the child who shouted out "the emperor is naked" at the night sky had never forgotten where the two of them came from.

"This is unproductive." Henry pulled away and tapped the tip of her nose. "Saidah is being a five-year-old right now, and Henry won't engage with this until she's eighteen again."

He finished his scotch and jiggled the empty glass, meaning he needed another one. "Sleep on it." He made a "call me" gesture before blending into the crowd, leaving her in a sea of festive sentiments that drowned her absurd presence.

"MISS?"

Sai finally noticed the tissue whipping in front of her face like a flag and heard her own sobbing. The taxi driver was an immigrant in his fifties. Thick South Asian accent. Listening to Mahler. Might or might not have a PhD in his home country.

They were at a red light, and the bridge between Grand Ivory and Oleander Island was behind them. She couldn't remember crossing the water, which was a shame, as that was supposed to be the best part of this route. Outside the rear windshield, the jumbled blur and colors veneered the looking glass that she'd fallen out of. She had exited her sparkly realm, and what glittered like gold had returned to mere flecks of teary reflection.

She accepted the tissue and soaked it in seconds. The driver turned down the music and opened the windows, letting in some fresh air with white noise, as well as the smell of the wrong side of the Athena River. Curled up in the back seat, Sai spent the rest of the ride scratching the stain on her jeans, which had become part of the fabric.

After they pulled over next to her apartment complex and she stepped out, the driver rolled down his window and handed her a bottle of soda.

"It's not open! You can see for yourself." He laughed nervously. "I just don't have anything else with me . . . I meant to give this to my daughter when I brought her dinner, but she said she's on a diet. I thought something sweet would cheer her up—she's been working too hard lately."

Sai hesitated. The man's hand was trembling slightly, his smile restrained, yet he extended his arm a little farther until the cap of the bottle brushed her fingers. She took the soda and thanked him.

"What does your daughter do?" she asked. That question illuminated his face.

"She's a consultant. Well . . . I can't explain clearly what she does, but she works in one of the best firms in the city. Her first job! Already with the best . . ."

Sai gave him a faint smile and loathed herself a little when she couldn't help but picture the handful of brown faces she'd come across at Frenell and the Red Sea, wondering if any one of them could've been this man's daughter.

"I should get going." The driver restarted the engine. "You have a good night, miss. Try that, you'll feel better. It's not open."

In the fading taillights, Sai checked the receipt to see if he'd added a tip for all that unsolicited kindness. He hadn't. Her remaining energy was only enough to carry her up the stairs and through the door. She sat on the floor with her lights off, turning the soda in her hands as she read the label under the moonlight coming through her oddly positioned window. The bottle wasn't opened indeed. The tiny ring of plastic around the neck snapped and splintered when she twisted the cap off, and she saw no needle holes when examining it up close. A caramel foam climbed up the neck, oozed over the rim, and dripped onto her carpet, sending the distinctive carbonated sweetness into her nose. Maybe this sugar bomb would make her feel better indeed. She held the bottle an inch from her lips but couldn't convince herself to take a sip. Eventually, she got off the floor, grabbed a glass, and filled it with tap water in her kitchen. She clinked it against the soda bottle and raised the water over her head as she muttered a thank-you to her silent room. Then she finished her tap water and threw the soda into the trash.

The line to Officer Haley was busy as usual. She got through on the fourth try, and he sounded like he had been shaken out of a coma.

"We're still investigating." He yawned. "I told you this last time."

"I was assaulted," she said.

"You got in a fight?"

"No–"

"So you got raped?" He rephrased when he didn't get an answer from her. "Are you reporting a sexual assault or not–"

"Yes."

There was a brief pause on the other end.

"When did this happen?" he asked.

"Last Wednesday."

"And you're calling *now*. Did you do a rape kit?"

"No, I didn't."

"Why not?"

She had no idea how to explain that she had gone to the hospital, then gotten spooked by her own reflection, dreading what people would see when they spread her under the sun like an animal hide stained with blood. Fortunately, Officer Haley understood that this question was meaningless at this point.

"Can you describe how it happened?"

"I was . . . it happened in the office building I work in. . . . I went to the bathroom–it was the women's bathroom, but he was there, behind the door. He grabbed me when I walked in, and threw me across the room. I hit the sinks. It hurt so much. . . . He grabbed me again and tried to kiss me. I pushed him away, then he . . . he hit me. I think he was high. I wasn't drunk."

She took a breath before she got to the part after she'd lost the fight. Her voice dropped lower with each word forward.

There was a sudden rustle of fabric and creaking of furniture, then the line crackled as a heavy exhale gusted through the microphone. She pictured him cradling the receiver between his ear and shoulder as he shifted in his chair to a more comfortable position.

Then she heard something that sounded like the unbuckling of a belt and a zipper sliding open.

"And?"

15

WHEN THE "FIVE minutes left" reminder went off, Ryuka put all her remaining Idle Time in the meter as her final attempt to postpone the inevitable.

"I'm afraid I can't make you a coffee." Calais set down a glass of tap water. "They've already counted the inventory, and the machine is locked."

"Do you feel . . . lost?" Ryuka asked.

"Why would I?"

His gaze glided across the empty café, avoiding the balcony.

The investigation of Keahi's fall remained ongoing, but Frenell needed a PR update. Since it'd been established that the incident could be attributed to neither the work nor the team, they'd picked the next in line. To Frenell's pleasant surprise, Calais had volunteered a way out. They'd reached an amicable agreement on terms kept confidential between the parties. In its subsequent statement, Frenell stressed that the task force was still considering all the evidence available but highlighted certain key facts such as that "the responsibility for property maintenance and on-site safety lay with the tenant of Level 20 and the provider of catering services." However, the firm had adopted a fault-neutral language and omitted Calais's name and face from its press release.

"I thought you had this business forever," said Ryuka.

"It's a job. I have other things in life."

"Like what?"

"'Like what?' You think I have nothing in my life other than an office café? That's hurtful."

"You don't tell people anything! You could be a . . . tofu-making monk and part-time glassblower for all I know."

"Fine, I'll be a tofu-making monk and part-time glassblower to you, then."

"What's the attraction of Valleria anyway?"

Valleria was the biggest city of Alpinelands, a country four thousand miles to the northeast. It had cross-country trains, legends of gods, and long winters. People there spoke different languages, and there was a lot of drinking.

Calais considered the question and smiled. "It's not Grand Ivory."

"I'll miss you," said Ryuka.

"It's actually easier to hang out outside this building, once nobody times your coffee breaks anymore. Excited?"

It was her turn to go silent. June 26, 2028—four weeks from now—Frenell would become something in the past tense.

She felt a familiar disquiet rising. A bizarre sense of powerlessness, like she was a stick figure on the edge of a cliff watching the mountain being erased under her feet. She finished the water and took a pulse oximeter out of her pocket—a handy gadget she'd bought for a hundred bucks—and clipped it on her forefinger. An animated strip of pixels appeared on the screen, pulsing like her heart, and the readings settled after a few seconds. Her SpO_2 level was 99 percent, and her heart rate sat at fifty-five.

She stared at the readings, forcing her eyes to engage and her mind to believe. *This is real*, she told herself. *You're not gonna drop dead for no reason, so pull yourself together and breathe.* Calais refilled her glass and watched her in silence.

"I just can't help but think I'm running away," she said after her breathing steadied. "It feels like giving up, like forfeiting a fight."

"Have you heard of the zombie-ant fungus?" Calais said. "It's a parasitic fungus that hijacks an ant's body and releases chemical signals—essentially hallucinogens—into its brain. This allows the fungus to control the ant physically and mentally, which compels the ant to leave its nest, climb up a plant near the colony, and carry the fungus to a place with the perfect temperature and humidity for its growth. It also forces the ant to lock its mandibles to a leaf so it'd stay in that position forever. At that point, the ant is no more than a container of nutrients. The fungus eats the ant from the inside out and grows a stalk out of the ant's head. From that stalk, more fungal spores rain down on the colony underneath and continue the cycle of zombification."

"Gross, dude." Ryuka winced. "You could've minced your words—"

"This is not normal, Ryuka." He leaned in and tapped on her oximeter. "*This* is not supposed to be normal, and it's exactly what you *should* be running away from. The ant can't run because it's infected, drugged, and dead, but you're not an ant, and you're very much alive. I know after a couple of years in a place like this, it can feel like the world is ending when you leave. But the world is not gonna end. It's right there."

He tilted his head at the balcony, and Ryuka looked outside. From a hundred meters above the ground, any city could look just fine unless it was explicitly on fire. The sky had cleared up after a week of nonstop rain, giving the city the appearance of a tourist attraction postcard, tactically composed and meticulously polished. But there was a whiff of lurking phoniness, as if this grandiose tapestry would crumble into a pile of false promises as soon as she stepped outside, and reveal the manufactured despair that had been the skeleton of this reality all along.

Otherwise, it was a beautiful day.

BEFORE SHE ENTERED the open plan on Level 13, Ryuka ran the script in her head one more time: She'd go straight to her workstation, grab her laptop charger, and gather her personal belongings—only the ones that couldn't be replaced—then get out. The whole process should take less than five minutes, and she'd speak to no one. For the rest of her notice period, she'd work from various spots inside the building and stay mobile—whatever it'd take to avoid running into that one specific fire hose of indignities, not because she couldn't take what might come out of his mouth, but because she might believe him.

She swiped her badge and dashed across the floor diagonally as soon as the glass doors slid apart. Lucky for her, Morse was on the phone with his car dealership about a discount that he believed had been stolen from him.

"What do you mean it's ineligible?" His voice pierced the silence over the heads of the breath-holding Year 5 Associates. "I liked and reposted your ad on both Instagram and Twitter and shared it with three friends. What more do you want from me?!"

Ryuka ducked under her desk and pulled out the drawers of her file cabinet one by one from bottom to top. She stuffed the charger in her backpack, then rummaged through the rest of the contents, searching for what was hers to take.

There was nothing.

She'd never decorated her workstation with photos, trinkets, or motivational stickers. Not even a neglected succulent. The only evidence drawing any personal connection between her and this designated endpoint of production was the colorful Post-it to-do lists stuck to the frame of her monitor, and a mug she'd gotten from last year's Secret Santa that said "The World's

and cabinets, she couldn't find a single item with a blade. Every surface, every nook and cranny, stripped bare, leaving not even the most harmless utensils. Office Facilities had done a remarkable job minimizing the risk of "human error and momentary lapse of judgment." After the Chateau incident, the department had undertaken a firm-wide "rampage and weaponization assessment" and introduced necessary safeguards, including the metal detectors downstairs and entry security checks. Before anyone had a chance to complain, disposable razors had disappeared from the overnight grooming kits in bathrooms, all the scissors at stationery bays replaced by childproof abominations.

Sai slammed shut the last cabinet and pressed her back against it, gnawing at her fingernails as the place taunted her with its sterile emptiness. A faint whistle hooked her and led her to the far end of the kitchen, then into the side room. In the corner stood what looked like an ordinary back bar refrigerator.

She slid the doors open, and a hollow shaft greeted her. The whistle rose from the dark bottom and pitched higher as it ascended, like the distant call of a spectral flute. She pressed the switch and worried for a second that the portal might have been shut down with the kitchen. Despite the groaning cables and the slow, unnerving pace, the car made its way up. Sai stepped inside and closed the doors.

They'd done a surface cleaning of the Red Sea, one that had not removed the stains on the carpet or the tenacious stickiness of spilled liquor. Behind the bar, she scoured for anything usable. She found a crate of empty bottles under the counter. A blunt peeler lay in the sink, unwashed and practical for hardly anything other than making orange twists for Negroni. Corkscrews? All of them had a cap lifter.

As she searched for something that could stab and slice, the facade clock struck eleven, and a ray of morning sun streamed through the glass, illuminating the husk of revelry surrounding her. This was the first time she'd set foot in here while it was still bright outside. She followed the light and came to the windows, casting her stare over the roofs of the business monuments that stitched the sky to a cleft and smothered her every time she walked down these streets. Now, towering over them, she still couldn't breathe with ease.

In a mesmerizing haze, she returned to the bar and went through the last of the compartments. Before she left through the way she had come, she looked over her shoulder and caught the view outside the windows one last time. Then she climbed back inside the dumbwaiter, clutching in her pocket a slender ice pick.

"HE'S IN EUROPE." Angela glanced at Sai without stopping what she was doing. "And you need an appointment."

"When is he coming back?" Sai asked.

"No idea, honey."

Angela stapled a stack of receipts to a reimbursement form, then she saw Sai was still standing outside Wade's office, staring at the throne missing its emperor.

"May I help you?" she asked, elongating every syllable and raising her pitch at the end.

Sai came over to Angela's cubicle and studied her with utter amusement. As someone who had been around since inception, Angela seemed to have marinated her appearance in golden memories about the '70s, yet only the perpetual frustration of a true modern-age office worker could breed that permanent scowl on her face. The woman was within her reach, Sai noticed, and the aisle was open. If she snapped her head to one side and punched a hole in her neck with the ice pick, she should have enough space to hop away without getting any blood on her shirt.

"What's the difference between today and tomorrow, Angela?"

Angela raised an eyebrow and squeezed her stapler hard, but the loud ka-chunk did not drive Sai away or erase the grin from her face.

"Let me guess," Sai said. "This morning, you peeled yourself off the mattress after six hours of sleep; headed into the kitchen, where yesterday's mess was still to be cleaned; assembled a breakfast with processed food to feed your family; drove your kids to school and got stuck in traffic; dropped your kids off and got stuck in more traffic, worried about the hundreds of things on your plate and the hundreds of ways to stretch your budget while cursing clueless drivers and pedestrians behind your windshield. But deep down, you were glad the traffic wasn't moving because you wanted something–anything–to prolong the trek to this soul-draining job you had to keep. Yet you still arrived on time because you were told that was important. You finished everything you were asked to do the way you were asked to do because you thought it'd be appreciated. However, all that time as you worked your way through those receipts, you were thinking that if a comet struck this very building and wiped out the entire Frenell force, you'd be okay with it."

"What the heck is wrong with–"

"Do you have any evidence that you'll be able to repeat all that tomorrow?" Sai asked. "Or do you simply assume that's the case until proven wrong?"

Angela stiffened as Sai's smile widened to an ear-to-ear mask of mania. As Sai squeezed the wooden handle of the ice pick inside her pocket, a familiar voice traveled from the end of the aisle.

"What are you doing here?"

Hayden strolled over and leaned against the partition panels of Angela's cubicle. Nobody noticed he tickled the small of Sai's back and cupped his palm on her hip for a feel before he retrieved his hand to where it belonged–away from another person.

"What's the goss, ladies?" He winked.

"Please leave, both of you." Angela squared her back to shake off the unease and returned to her paperwork. "I have too much work and no information about what Wade is up to."

"Shame, I thought we could use a threesome." Hayden had a good laugh on his own as the Productivity Shields wrapped Angela inside.

"Threesome? Am I not enough for you?" Sai whispered into Hayden's ear, which stunned him for a moment. He pulled away and rubbed his chin as he studied her, but his suspicion disappeared as soon as Sai ran the tip of her tongue along her upper lip.

"Look who's come around," he said under his breath as he pinched Sai's butt. "A bit late, but you know, be a doll, and maybe I can give you a reference."

A GROUP OF first-year Special Associates gathered in the Level 21 kitchen for their snack break. One of them saw Sai and nudged the guy next to him, then the rest caught on, crooning and hooting as the pair walked by. Hayden rolled his shoulders back and widened his grin, snatched a bright-yellow banana from the fruit basket as he strode past the granite countertop, and left the crowd with a wink. Sai didn't pay attention to Hayden's friends and wished they'd reciprocated the indifference.

The Meditation Chamber sat on the other end of the floor. Hayden elbowed the sliding door to one side and skipped in. Sai followed and flicked the latch to red.

"Well, well, well." He scanned the room with bored eyes. "Look where we ended up after all. Was the fight worth it? If you think about it, all this mess was just about a silly banana—"

She grabbed him from behind, muffling his yelp with one hand as she jabbed the ice pick into his neck. A streamlet of blood gushed out and whipped a trail on the wall as she pulled the spike out and drilled it into a second wound. The resistance from Hayden's flesh when she pushed the ice pick in stimulated her—no wonder men enjoyed sticking themselves into places that didn't want them. He grabbed her fingers and pulled her hand off his mouth to scream. She slipped out of his grip, shoulder-charged him to the corner of the chamber, and thrust the ice pick into his chest. Hayden let out a squeal and shoved Sai away. Covered in his blood, the handle was slick as an eel. She lost her grip as she stumbled backward, leaving the ice pick inside him.

Wobbling and whimpering, Hayden reached for the wooden handle as if dabbing a steaming pot. With fresh blood streaming down his neck and drenching his shirt, he didn't know what to do with this sharp object protruding from his chest like an alien's dick—whether he'd be mitigating the damage or pulling out a plug. Glaring at Sai with a "Look what you've done" face, he broke down sobbing.

"Help . . ." he cried, in an airy voice that wouldn't even penetrate a ski mask, let alone these padded walls.

She booted him in the groin. As he knelt down, she grabbed his hair and rammed his head on the edge of the Peace Altar to rhythmic thuds. Hayden no longer made a sound, and his limbs became noodly. A small crimson puddle began to form under him. Sai flipped him over and heaved his torso over the surface, yanked the ice pick out, then punched it back in between his ribs, in his lower belly, under his armpit, several more times in the chest. The vesicles of repugnance that had been festering inside her finally burst and flooded her body, making her hands move on their own, as if each stab would rewind time by an instant, bring her back to a crossroads where she had the choice to go a different way. A salty, metallic aroma permeated the chamber. Amid the squishy noises and her grunting, she heard someone banging on the door.

"Occupied!" she yelled.

"Jesus." The guy chuckled. "Take it down a notch, you two. People are still trying to work."

More laughter followed. A squad had gathered outside, sharing muffled banter and reminding Sai of the existence of a world that she couldn't fit in or leave. She let Hayden slump to the ground, surprised to find that he was still alive. Frail gasping and gurgling came out of his battered face, his eyes half-shut to slits.

"Can you see me?" She spread his eyelids. "Do you know who's killing you?"

There were subtle changes in his gurgling, the closest she'd ever get to an answer. Sai took a step back and watched Hayden suffer. He'd die and she wanted him to, yet the sporadic twitches of his limbs still saddened her.

She let him lie on his back and knelt next to him, marked the spot of his heart, then raised the ice pack over it. With rapid, shallow breaths, she tried to return to the state of frenzy, but her arm froze over her head, refusing to fall.

Right then, the squad outside the chamber started chanting.

"One, two, three, four."

"One, two, three, four."

"Come on, wrap it up already!"

"One, two, three, four!"

Faster, louder, closer, as if they were in there with her. Sai let out a moan, then plunged the ice pick into Hayden's chest.

One clean strike through the heart. She pressed her body on top of the handle until the spasm stopped. Two fingers on his neck, no pulse. Behind the door, the chanting had morphed into guffaws after an imaginary climax.

"You done yet?" asked the guy who'd been banging on the door earlier.

"It's okay, Hayden," said another. "We know stamina isn't your strength."

The laughter died down, followed by indistinct chatter, followed by more banging, then silence. Sai sat down against the wall and took out her phone. She opened a video she'd filmed last night. Her no-makeup face looked sallow and distorted under the glaring lights in her living room. Good, that girl looked like a stranger.

"My name is Saidah Sulaimaniyah. I'm an Associate at Frenell & Co., and I'm about to tell you things you might not believe, or don't care about anyway. But they happened, and I hope they never happen again–"

She swiped to the next clip in the gallery, the one with Pace sitting on the lap of a suited man, keeping her face as far away from his as she could without getting herself in trouble. Then the next, with the hazing boy getting through a line of tequila shots. He had to take a breath after the fifth one, and someone refilled the first four he'd finished as a penalty for the break.

Then the next, of Wade passing a document on to Andrej and whispering with a smirk.

The next, of a cozy conversation between a public company CFO and a fund manager who'd unloaded his holdings just in time before the crash.

The next, and the next.

One by one, she logged on to her dormant social media and posted the videos across platforms. She didn't have a huge following, but people would be watching them. Oh, they would.

The gang regrouped outside the chamber. This time, they had their business voices on.

"Hayden? You all right?"

A moment of dead silence, then they started ramming the door. She pictured them breaking in, horrified by what they saw. Some of them might puke, some would drag her out and beat her to suppress their fear. Or, best-case scenario, they'd run away screaming as they realized any one of them could be next. Strangely enough, the only thing she felt was a gentle hunger.

She scanned the room and noticed the banana under the Peace Altar. Hayden had dropped it on her first strike, then one of them had kicked it out of the way. Thanks to that, it remained intact, save for the smear of blood it had picked up from the streams on the floor. She peeled it and took a bite. It was slightly hard at the core and a little astringent, but the sweet aroma was pleasing. The balance of the universe had been restored, now a banana was just a banana.

The ramming continued. She watched the sliding door tremble and rattle. The lock would surely come loose after a few more strikes. She took another bite, and a faint bitterness coated her palate—part of that might be the blood dripping down her cheeks. The taste gave her a flashback of a forty-dollar whiskey Henry had mixed into the bogus Ravenmore ACE-50. It'd had a grassy undertone, and a raw, tannic note that'd clung to her throat and fought on its way down. She missed the tingle it'd left on her tongue—just the right amount of burn to remind her it hadn't all been a dream. She closed her eyes to visualize the bottle but couldn't recall the brand no matter how hard she tried.

The tip of a crowbar poked through the gap between the sliding door and its frame, making way for the prying and wrenching that followed. A familiar tune resurfaced in her mind. "Everybody Loves Somebody," the song Pace had sung in the Red Sea the first night Sai was there. The song Henry and she had danced to the first night she'd trespassed in his kingdom. She started humming. Maybe the melody would help her remember.

C'mon, it was a tall, green bottle, with ridges at the bottom of the neck. Bold white letters on a black label. One made-up word.

Shit.

What was it called?

"YEAH, FUCK THEM," Nolan said into the phone as he locked his eyes on Colleen.

Colleen laughed a small laugh through her nose and reclined in her chair, watching Nolan finish the chat with she-knew-who.

"That's an unfortunate answer," she said.

After the anniversary party, the disconcertment she'd felt watching Wade's speech had stayed with her. The suspicion had deepened when Wade had suddenly turned on his auto reply and claimed to be on another business trip to Europe. She ran a search for his activities in PADU. What stood out was the location data collected from his staff badge and his Frenell account log-ins. In the week following the anniversary party, "Wade" had appeared in several recurring spots within Grand Ivory. That was when she'd thought to compare his tracking record with those of the Associates. Once again, that really narrowed things down.

"You want his share of the sale." Nolan got the point without her spoon-feeding him all the details. That was why she liked working with him.

She'd replayed Wade's speech a couple of times at home, before bed and over a glass of red. It was a decent job, sufficiently well done, and intrigued her to identify Ryuka Murong, who hung around that warehouse Nolan had visited. But it wasn't perfect. The more she stared at virtual Wade, the more telling flaws she saw. Granted, not everybody knew this face as well as she did and wanted to acid-wash those features off, then carve each line back with a chisel.

Tracing Wade's final hours, she worked out a rough time of death. Those bright young things deserved some credit for getting this far, but they were pushing their luck, and they'd have a hard time keeping up this amateur act. Then she realized she could refine this package with what she had and they didn't–a position of authority; immunity to shame, fear, and anxiety; and all the nonpublic knowledge about this man. His family, his upbringing, preferences and pet peeves, traumas and insecurities, even the quirks in his handwriting when he signed checks.

She had everything one would need to become Wade Pendleton-Fitzpatrick.

That conclusion had pleased her, and she'd laughed till she spilled her wine on her bedspread. This would work so much better than digging up dirt on the mighty WPF, then taking over his book. The universe wanted her to have this one.

"Some people are more valuable alive than dead," she explained to Nolan. "Especially at this crucial point. We can work together and get a slice of the pie–even the tip of that would be more than you'd ever make in twenty years. Win-win.

Or"—she rested her elbows on her desk and clapped once—"you go your own way with a hot potato you simply can't handle, and I let people find out what really happened to Wade. I'll miss out on some big bucks, and not only you but all your little friends who have touched this will be in big trouble. Lose-lose, and that will make me very, very unhappy."

Right then, Nolan's phone rang. Colleen saw Ryuka's name on the screen and signaled Nolan to take it.

Ask her, she mouthed, then she sat back and watched the call end on "Yeah, fuck them."

"You're both making a huge mistake." She shook her head and reached for the key on her laptop that allowed her to summon the patrol robots.

Nolan hopped on top of the desk, tore Colleen's laptop off the dock, and hurled it at the wall. His ankle brushed the tortoise paperweight. This time, he grabbed it and smashed it into her curved monitor.

Right then, Colleen's office door busted open. A young man with rumpled hair and blood smeared all over his shirt barged in. He froze when he saw Nolan and the mess he'd created. Nolan seized the moment and fled, shoving the young man against the doorframe on his way out. The young man seemed confused for a second about his priorities, then he snapped out of it and, with barely coherent words, conveyed the message to Colleen that something horrible had happened on Level 21, and it involved one of her Assets.

16

IN THE LAST week of May 2028, Frenell made its name outside Sauria Street because of two women.

Sai's posts took a while to gain traction. At first, her old contacts assumed she'd healed, and those videos were her comeback announcement and party footage to celebrate her bounce. Some new followers who had joined after the release of her deepfake debut thought she had finally decided to go OnlyFans with her social media, and were rather excited about what was in the production pipeline. By the end of the statement, both groups were convinced that the girl had lost it and gone full-blown delusional. Not until the news about the Frenell office killing broke the next day did they realize maybe they should talk about this thing.

The problem with this type of kamikaze exposé was that you'd hardly ever get corroborative firsthand testimonies from any Associates of the firm in question. There might be sweeping comments from anonymous former employees or hearsay from rival firms about how "toxic" the culture was or how "bitchy" some of the seniors were, but any specificity would inevitably trace back to the individual making the claims, costing their current job or future prospects. The only reliable way to get insights on a Sauria Street firm was through private word of mouth–see how hard people cringed at the mention of the firm, and how many had disappeared from that place without a decent goodbye. The same way you'd find out if that Tinder match with six mutual friends was a serial killer.

Occasionally, local papers like *Grand Ivory Post* may touch on topics like "Do professional services have a culture issue?" or "What bullying really looks like on Sauria Street," but such content suffered from the same lack of depth due to the limited concrete evidence available and often failed to capture the nuances of those incidents that, in isolation, just smelled like an unpleasant odor, but could accumulate and cause lasting health damage through chronic exposure, like the naphthalene in mothballs. As a result, when someone asked "Exactly what happened?" all they got from those articles would just be, "Someone has been passive-aggressive, or active-aggressive in some cases." Then they'd google how much these "poor things" got paid for the job, choose the highest amount they'd like to believe, and decide: *Sure you can get over that, honey.*

That was why outsiders often didn't take those allegations seriously, and that was exactly what OATH counted on.

The day following Sai's posts, Frenell issued a short statement that said the firm was investigating the authenticity of the footage and reminded the public how easy it would be to fabricate so-called evidence in the age of technology. With respect to the clips where the crowd appeared to be chanting Frenell's name, and the hosts who'd been identified on LinkedIn, the statement emphasized that the firm would not interfere with its staff's personal lives, and nothing captured in those videos represented Frenell's official practices. As for that one clip that had caught the facade clock and suggested that the striptease had clearly occurred inside the Frenell building, OATH had ignored it until it couldn't, and its response was standard—Frenell had a robust code of conduct that was provided to every Timekeeper at the time of onboarding. The Associates always had the choice and means to seek guidance on any aspect of their career, including the acceptable ways to network and build relationships. Most importantly, nobody was forced into anything. We tried. We cared. We did nothing wrong.

What happened after that was largely natural laws at play: Sai's failed sexual harassment claim surfaced and raised questions as to whether she had a pattern of making unfounded claims. Some "insiders" stated that she was on the verge of getting fired due to "poor performance," which, despite the firm's endeavors to move her within the organization and help her thrive in a more suitable capacity, fueled her paranoia and prompted her "hell-bent retaliation." Her old-time "acquaintances" from high school and college came out to testify that Saidah Sulaimaniyah had never had the best reputation when it came to boys, and provided evocative details in short essays that all started with "Not to victim-blame, but." One of them got carried away and elaborated on her connections with "political figures and the ultrarich." That thread was deleted before it had the chance to spiral into an Epstein-style conspiracy. And of course, someone reposted that fake porn to jog people's memories about "what she was," if not to entertain the crowd during stoning intervals.

At this point, Frenell could pretty much sit back and watch the cesspool drown the witch with its own force. But as a classy move, OATH followed up with a statement acknowledging that people suffering from mental health issues might perceive certain events through a distorted lens, and the firm was willing to forgive any misleading claims Sai had made about its "toxic culture" for an apology. However, it urged people to focus on the real elephant in the room—in cold blood, the girl had slaughtered a rising star of the community. Someone who had great potential, so much promise, went to great lengths, and cost significant investments from both his family and Frenell to accomplish what he'd achieved before his future was cut short. OATH then directed the readers to the firm's tribute on LinkedIn, titled "Remember Hayden Hins," where they could find chains of heartfelt comments from his fellow Frenells, mourning the loss of a loyal friend and echoing one simple, catchy message: *Violence is never the answer*. Hashtag #saynotoviolence. Hashtag #staycivil. Hashtag #toxicfeminism.

Clumsy attempts like Sai's exposé might look like a bombshell at first glance: loud, unexpected, and capable of making a lot of mess. But ultimately, they were child's play on Sauria Street, and there was nothing novel in their blueprints. "Deny, deflect, destroy." Follow your Frenell bible and cut the right wires, then you'd stay in one piece just fine. The second woman was way more pesky—it was just Frenell's luck that Keahi Ka'uhane hadn't killed herself.

Around lunch hour on May 30, 2028, when the Frenell drama was losing momentum and the audience was yearning for something other than Sai's character and motive, a piece of surveillance footage offered a fresh angle. It was taken on the night of May 19—Frenell's 150th anniversary. Around 9:33 p.m., a line of patrol robots escorted a unit of AS28HGC6-F to Level 20 of the Frenell building, where the egg-shaped Ultimate Scalable Streamliner Replica cruised around the open space, disoriented and tipsy. Once it'd discovered Keahi, who was sitting at a table on the balcony, it refused to leave her alone and kept bumping into her shins and flashing lights in her eyes for a whole minute. The peculiar act caused some confusion at first, then people realized—the face-hungry droid was taking her mug shot. Keahi dodged, blocked, and ignored the droid to no avail. Finally, she picked up a chair and wielded it at the egg.

Four patrol robots charged forward and cornered Keahi. Two of them held her up by her limbs while the third neutralized her with some de-escalator. The last one strolled over after the other three had done their part. Instead of spring-rolling her up according to the standard protocol, it lifted her body by the legs, pivoted her against the balcony railing, and let go. Part of the forensic details were lost in the soundless video, but given the lack of struggle when she flipped over the rail, the de-escalator must've knocked her out before her fall. Most likely, she did not suffer.

Had the girl jumped of her own will—like everyone assumed the moment they'd found her—Frenell would've gotten this contained in a week. The key was to grab the mic early on and characterize the incident as "another one of those," then the rest was nothing but chores. The firm would have to take some initial blows, give the miserable a chance to vent, then wait for them to move on. They always did, because on Sauria Street, every dead body was just a fucking well-being training coupon and nothing more. Shock ran out; people got used to it. Once the family had been financially compensated and the tide of fury had subsided, the firm could then slowly and gradually release the "uncomfortable but honest truths" that would anesthetize the industry in the years to come: This has always been a job where people might kill themselves. It's not for everyone, and it's not meant to be. People have the choice to leave, but they stay for the prestige. At the end of the day, nobody threw them off the building. It is what it is. Hashtag #professionallife. Hashtag #resilience. Hashtag #noregrets.

Except that somebody—something—did throw Keahi off the building, and that something had Frenell's fingerprints all over it.

At first, OATH attempted to steer the conversation with questions like "What was she doing there at that hour anyway?" But it didn't take off as it would with certain other claims that had higher standards for the victim. Mind your own business on company property and get killed by company property to protect company property—now that's something that could happen to *anybody*, even if you're not a whore or a nutjob. Since regular inspections and maintenance of the patrol robots fell under OATH's responsibilities, Katherine Waycross stepped down from her position as Frenell's Chief Culture Officer in response to the uproar. She announced the decision on LinkedIn with grace, and a "close friend" in the comment section blamed the outcome on "a string of bad luck," then pointed out that Frenell had never had a major employment dispute or workplace scandal on her watch.

She could end her watch now. The firm appreciated her contribution.

Unfortunately, one HR casualty couldn't satiate the ravenous mob. The situation got really sticky when the audience got philosophical about the existence of firms like Frenell: *Um, what do these people actually do, and do we really need them?*

That question ruffled more Sauria feathers than any actual deaths had ever been able to. Timekeepers pounced on those threads to defend their honor, liking and reposting every claim about the values they upheld at the front line of making the world a better place, and giving their HR and marketing colleagues the pat on the back they'd long deserved. It was a beautiful moment of allegiance and a belated reminder that, irrespective of their differences, the chickens and the dogs lived on the same farm, and they only had each other when the foxes got an idea.

One active contributor under the username "yolo_eric69"—the same account that had bumped Sai's fake porn back on top of the internet—was particularly vocal:

If firms like Frenell added no value, nobody would be hiring them. Do you even know what a Venn diagram is, bro?

lol, simple minds can't stand gray areas in life coz their tiny brains can only see the world as good and bad. Sad!

Ya'll just mad coz ur losing the game. If you losers ever make it to the top, which you won't, you'll act exactly the same. Every single one of ya.

These responses, which faithfully demonstrated the psyche of a Sauria Street beneficiary—hear you, feel you, fuck you anyway—attracted public attention and collective hatred. Someone noticed the same username in the Facebook hookup group Sauria Street

Adventures and kicked off a round of wild speculation about the user's identity. As some old memories began to surface and morph into a name, the account deleted all previous posts, leaving only one profound remark:

Wow, what a bunch of whiny babies! Wallow in your self-pity, be my guest, but only those who roll with the punches and go the extra mile will thrive and shine. Enjoy ur therapies and I'll see ya'll at interview ;)

Like a brave spectator jumping into the arena to lure the bull away from an injured matador, this faceless warrior made the bystanders forget about Frenell for a moment and join forces to track down "Yolo Eric" and his current employer. At one point, Frenell seemed so close to the end of the sewer it just might come out of it clean.

Then, Lord M happened.

For reasons unbeknownst to anyone even to this day, Lindsay Frenell believed that what the firm needed to put an end to its PR saga was a YouTube live stream. In the hour-long video filmed in the backyard of his Oleander Island mansion, Lord M reprimanded the general public for letting themselves be manipulated and stoking what was clearly a smear campaign orchestrated by Frenell's rival firms. With a stern face and a mournful tone, he lectured his twelve-thousand-plus viewers about the importance of critical thinking.

"Humans have larger brains than other primates so we can reason, deliberate, and engage in independent discourse instead of mindlessly following the herd. This is your moment to be on the right side of history."

Then he addressed "the hopeless generation":

"You're paid to do a job. The job is not done, so you put in extra hours. What's wrong with that? You want something easy, go be a barista.

"It's not like you'd make good use of all that free time anyway. How many of you are watching stupid TikTok videos as I speak right now? When was the last time you kids read a book?

"If you can't do your job properly, you're gonna get shouted at. These days, this is offensive, that is insensitive, and now we have to whisper to each other so we don't scare the babies? You want 'respect.' Have you earned it?

"Young people need to be more humble and patient. Focus on improving yourself instead of money at the early stage of your career. You don't know anything and you're not special! When was the last time any of you called your parents and told them you're grateful for what they did to build this country you live in? Huh? Does anyone still remember what JFK said about 'Ask not what your country can do for you'?"

All great questions. But the streaming took a strange turn when a squirrel dashed across Frenell's lawn and stirred up some strong emotions.

"We were preparing for a family vacation to Australia, and we were all so excited about it!" He fought back tears and shuffled away from the screen, dragging his half-packed suitcase into the frame to show his audience, then spilled its contents all over the grass. "Now we can't go because of this stupid drama. I'm so tired . . . God knows I needed that break so bad, but even if we go, I won't be able to enjoy it now! Is that what you want? Are you people happy? Ruining lives like this?!"

Gracefully, he regained his composure. Then he sat in silence for another twenty minutes, muttering under his breath and shooting sidelong glances at the camera, as if blanking his viewers remotely, until his wife called him in for his meds and stopped the filming.

Grand Ivory Post, which usually published its daily issue on its website before seven o'clock in the morning, took an extra hour the next day to weigh its editorial options. The final issue put Frenell's "I'm as mad as hell and I'm gonna make this your problem" moment in the second lead under the title "That Was Weird." Subtitle: "We Sat Through Grandpa's Breakdown So You Don't Have To." The piece recapped the bizarre performance, then enumerated recent

Frenell Associates' departures by "unnatural causes," which seemed to have become alarmingly frequent over the last two months. From Richard Shaw to Ronan Seymour to Tim Kwan to Dan Barton to Luc Edward to Keahi Ka'uhane to Saidah Sulaimaniyah to Hayden Hins, then a dozen others, totaling two confirmed suicides, three murder casualties, two drug cases, one fatal accident, and a string of ostracizations following unsuccessful complaints. After stating that the firm had declined to comment except to say that Lord M's speech had not been communicated to the firm in advance and could only represent his personal stance, the article ended with, *Time will not solve all problems, but hopefully, it will solve this one.*

All the above coproduced the biggest freak show in the first half of 2028, but a show was all it was. It gave OATH some overtime, and shamed some thin-skinned Frenells, but it was never the kind of blow that could dent the brand. Sauria Street firms don't die for screwing their Associates or losing the popular vote with the part of the internet that can't afford them.

What killed Frenell was something else.

"WHY ARE THEY late?" Colleen stared at the closed door of the Fidelity Room on Level 53 of the Pollyanna Palace. No one at the table answered her. One of the three wrinkly faces who were there to represent all the Olympians picked up the power of attorney that Colleen had dropped on the table the moment she'd stepped in, as if to inspect the authenticity of its contents and Wade's signature. She was used to it. These guys always needed something signed by another man to understand her presence in the same room. This time, they were actually right, so she wasn't taking it personally.

At a quarter to eleven—forty-five minutes after the signing was supposed to happen—the general counsel and two directors of the Bank of Pollyanna barged in and sat down on the other side of the table.

"Apologies," one of the directors said. "But I'm sure you'll understand the delay—"

With a hook of a finger, he instructed the legal counsel to project what was on his laptop to the screen wall. Colleen squinted and realized it was an email from Wade's account, sent last night with the subject line: "So you think you're cashing out?"

"Would anyone be so kind as to walk me through what's going on here?" said the director.

The email attached two Excel spreadsheets. They both contained Frenell's financial details, such as its latest balance sheet and cash flow, and they were likely created by the same author given the consistent style. However, the version labeled "updated for Pollyanna" gave the firm's Grand Ivory headquarters a $150 million boost in revenue. Frenell hadn't pulled that figure out of thin air as simple padding. It reflected how hopeful it was in its recovery of outstanding fees.

As of May 2028, the top twenty clients of the firm had accrued $516 million in service fees for the financial year—one of its worst years in every sense—30 percent of which remained overdue, down from 32 percent at the end of 2027. Frenell hadn't given up on reclaiming its hard-earned revenue, although some clients had stopped responding to the "gentle reminders."

"Here, in your raw data"—the director pointed at the Frenell internal version—"you've recorded a twelve-point-eight-million-dollar receivable from Pollyanna, which you seem to have included in the price. Surely you're not expecting that payment in full?"

He glanced at the legal counsel, who nodded to confirm that their position hadn't changed.

"We sent you a notice six months ago contesting the value of services provided," the director continued. "We've paid what we considered fair, and we haven't received any new evidence or convincing arguments for the remainder, so I'm struggling to see how you could treat that amount as anything other than a write-off. If I may, I'd say you're also being overly optimistic about some of your other collections on this list."

He tilted his chin at the screen, and the counsel highlighted Osireion's name with a double click.

"We're in the process of creating a solution that will best serve the interests of both parties," one of the wrinkly faces said. "We value our relationships with our clients—"

"And we remain readily available to provide any objective evidence supporting our work and its value," said Colleen. "In fact, we think this sale could be a good chance to settle the books and steam out the wrinkles in our relationship, which we believe relies on mutual respect in the long run—"

The Frenell Olympian who had been interrupted coughed once, and the other Pollyanna director chuckled at "mutual respect." Colleen ignored them both.

"Our services have been documented in itemized time sheets with detailed descriptions. If our clients prefer to have an independent cost assessor verify our fees, we're more than happy to make some contacts."

She made a quick mental note to herself. Accounts kept copies of the original invoices issued, and PADU retained all time sheets for up to two years, so if she had to "show their work," she should have the formula and the variables at her fingertips.

Under normal circumstances.

"WHEN THEY PREVIEW or navigate to this attachment with a single click," Ryuka explained, "it invokes the built-in Windows Support Diagnostic Tool and calls out to a web server hosting a script that downloads a virus onto the machine. The virus will then scan the version of PADU on the host and exploit the timekeeping feature. The attachment is macro-less and saved in RTF format instead of Word, so they don't even have to open it. They just need to touch it, then it's done."

"Did you make this yourself?" asked Nolan.

"I don't have to," said Ryuka. "This isn't a complex program, and it's a pretty old attack, so I got a bundle deal for both the doc and the virus on BreakStuff–it's basically Upwork for hackers, and GitHub is their Home Depot."

"Is it a bit . . . extravagant?" Fischer asked. "I mean, email everyone as Wade . . . don't people normally send a phishing email to some easy targets, like someone in Accounts, or, you know, OATH?"

"A couple of things," said Ryuka. "One, it spreads faster. We don't have the time to social engineer from scratch and jump across different subnetworks, and everyone in that place will for sure open something from WPF. Two, let's not pin this on some poor minion who's only there for a paycheck–even if they've ended up in OATH. And most importantly, three, having a few isolated points of compromise at the bottom of the pyramid probably wouldn't fuck up their insurance claims, would it? Which is also why I'm not using a zero-day that doesn't have a patch yet. If you're gonna chop someone's dick off, throw the dick away. What, you want them to stitch it back on?"

Nolan and Fischer stared at her for a second.

"You have a mean streak," said Nolan.

"I've learned from the best."

"It's an old attack, you say?" Fischer asked.

"Yeah, it came out eight . . . nine months ago?"

"What if it's already patched?"

Nolan and Ryuka exchanged a look, then burst out laughing. It was a good laugh–they needed that.

If Jake the poor IT guy couldn't even get those fancy pants to listen to his password policy, imagine the amount of effort and belittling he'd have to go through to make them install a patch that "blocks Office applications from creating child processes and disables the MSDT protocol," then stop their billing clocks for multiple rounds of reboot.

At the group induction of every annual Timekeepers intake, OATH would hand out copies of a two-pager written by some

Partner in the '70s. It contained practical tips for surviving professional services, such as "Be nice to your secretary. She can make your life miserable." These days, those wise words should also include "Be decent to your IT. They have more than enough reason to be sick of your shit."

"Four, this might be the last thing we do together," Ryuka said. "Let's make it count."

So, when the three Olympians and Colleen were in the Pollyanna meeting, Nolan sent an email from Wade's account to the group address including all Grand Ivory Timekeepers and attached an "internal memo" informing them of the imminent change of ownership. Minutes later, the virus swept Level 9 and above as the Frenells downloaded the attachment and forwarded it to their confidants with different degrees of profanity in the message. For those who hadn't updated to the latest version of PADU, which turned out to be the vast majority, their time sheets for the last two years were wiped, then repopulated with one twenty-four-hour entry for "Evaluate the financial ramifications and mortality risks of leaving work at 5 p.m." Every day, all weekends.

They wanted every available second of time to have a dollar sign. They got it.

The bygone days hold only sentimental value. Unless time is literally what you sell, then they hold monetary value. Of the $150 million Frenell attempted to recover, over 80 percent no longer had supporting evidence except the invoices sent to clients at the first demand for payment and the descriptions of work that made a prima facie case for the costs. Frenell had long esteemed itself for the powerful connections it'd developed across industries throughout Grand Ivory. In the months that followed, it had abundant opportunities to put those good relationships to the test—maybe clients would do the right thing.

Turns out, you can help them build an empire by standing on the necks of the voiceless; you can conceal anything and manipulate everyone to help them get away with the unspeakable;

you can be their lapdog, their pimp, their ass-wiper, the most entertaining clown in the room and bend over backward to lick their boots—nothing beats real dollars written off the books.

The peasants below Level 26 were not supposed to learn of the sale until later that day and certainly not in this manner, so Wade's unexpected "memo" prompted some frowning and whispering among the three Olympians. Colleen clenched her jaw as she read the email. Maybe she should've gotten Wade's account disabled the moment she'd identified its ventriloquist. As she pondered ways to contain Nolan, an alert popped up on her phone confirming that Timekeeper WPF97JLG1-C had just scanned his badge at the building entrance.

Wade Pendleton-Fitzpatrick, a.k.a. Nolan Haut, was in the office.

With a smirk curtained by her long hair, she activated her administrator console for the patrol robots and sent a squad to secure Wade's badge and the person holding it. Right then, the Pollyanna director spoke again:

"We're not here today to dwell on the past. Frankly, what we're most interested in is the rollout of AS28HGC6-F. May we have an update on that front?"

"Certainly." Colleen flipped her phone face down on the table. "We have completed the pairing of all Timekeepers, and the provisioned units of AS28HGC6-F have been deposited in a safe place. Once the deal is finalized, they'll be handed over as part of the assets—"

"Let's see some eggs, shall we?" The other director rubbed his palms together in excitement.

"Of course." One of the Olympians connected his laptop to the screen wall and opened his Master User portal. The Dashboard showed an inventory of over one hundred batches, each offering a profile with detailed metrics about the quality of the batch, graded and ranked from AAA to DDD.

"Shadow training takes a lot of resources, and it's more effective in a live working environment," said the Olympian. "So, for now, we keep them dormant. These seeds have encapsulated the Frenell excellence, so if you don't want to carry any staff on board, you don't have to. After the transfer, we can fine-tune the batches with your existing talent and new hires to make it more . . . Pollyanna customized."

The Pollyanna representatives shared a few light nods among themselves and asked the Olympian to open the profile of the top AAA batch. This batch had received a premium grade based on the productivity ratings of its Timekeepers; the revenue they'd generated for the firm; the clients they'd served and the presumed strength of their relationships; their expertise and their estimated recession-proof ability; certain fluid attributes that might affect the value they'd add to the business—like their cultural background and socioeconomic status; and potential risk factors that might adversely impact their commitment—like a human child or terminally ill parents. The application had also predicted the batch's "growth potential" in the next five years and displayed the results in a reassuring up-trending curve.

Then, in front of their eyes, the metrics nosedived. Key productivity parameters plummeted and the overall grade dropped, lagged, then froze due to the constant recalculation. The Olympian closed the batch overview and navigated to the page listing its paired Timekeeper accounts. What was shown there drew a gasp of terror out of the Pollyanna team.

Colleen grabbed her phone and saw two dozen muted alerts on her screen. PADU had detected irregularities in Wade's movement. The tracking showed that he'd gone all over the place after he'd entered the Frenell building—even turned up in multiple spots at the same time. *The user may have installed an enthusiasm defect device. Further investigation recommended*, said the app.

She then searched in the tracking records with Nolan's staff code. The badge of Timekeeper NH23BRT9-C, which should've been sleeping at the bottom of the Athena River as detected last night, was located inside the office.

FISCHER COUNTED THE BodySwap receivers in his palm, then stuck one on top of Edgar's head. The little robot lifted its face and reached out a hand to scratch it, like a puppy with a leaf on its forehead. "No, leave it on. Good boy." Fischer gave it a gentle pat. So Edgar kept the receiver and snaked down the hall and into an elevator, holding the doors open.

"I'll tell Goldman you're coming to Mammoth Mountain," Fischer said as he stepped over the de-escalated security guards and leaped into the elevator without waiting for a response from Nolan. Edgar scanned its key fob and lit up the buttons of all floors.

"Good boy," Fischer said again.

As Fischer and Edgar swept the building from the bottom up, leaving Wade's footprints all over the premises on a bot-fishing mission, Nolan worked the other way from the top down. There'd be over a hundred eggs. If Frenell had gathered them in one place, it'd most likely find that much space above Level 29. Yet, dashing from one empty meeting room to another, he didn't even see a shadow of those bone-colored droids.

His next guess was Mount Olympus. Maybe the owners of this place decided to keep the eggs close, like how some people would keep all their valuables in a safe next to their bed. The moment he set foot on the Partner Floors, an alarm went off in his mind. Not a single soul spotted in those messy offices. The extensive traces of human activity thickened the eeriness of the empty place and layered a postapocalyptic doom over the silence.

Then he tried his luck on Level 13. The Meditation Chamber was empty, and there was no sight of the eggs in any spare space, like the nook with emergency supplies or the stationery bay. Maybe Frenell kept them in the less populated spots, like the data room or the library below Level 8. He tested that idea but received a "Negative" from Fischer.

He glanced across the floor. Most of the Associates had their Productivity Shields on, working or pretending to, not knowing what would happen before the day ended.

Then an ominous revelation dawned on him.

What if they've already shipped the eggs out and abandoned the building?

"I can't find them anywhere." He pressed his lips against the phone and kept his voice low. "They're not in the open plans or the meeting rooms–"

He strode past the bench in the center of the floor, and his eyes caught a shriveled succulent on an otherwise empty desk. It looked limp because Sai hadn't been around lately to take care of it. *And now she'll be away for a long, long time.* That reality had finally gained mass in Nolan's mind. It reminded him why he was doing this. It also reminded him of certain details in Sai's testimony.

"I think . . . there's one more place we can look," Ryuka said over the phone.

"Yeah," said Nolan. "You know how to get up there?"

THE BYGONE DAYS hold only sentimental value. Unless you live in an insidious time loop where nothing changes, then they hold cautionary value.

Nolan crouched down on the bar counter and panned his gaze from one side of the field to the other. He was looking at an end–an unsatisfying one, as he still had so many questions unanswered. But one thing had become clear–

He understood why he drank.

He was not supposed to fear the future, let alone resent it, yet the view of a hundred brain-stealing eggs nesting in a secret cave that'd been over his head for five years made a rather bleak case about hope, and turned him a whole lot more indifferent about tomorrow.

The facade clock struck eleven. He hopped off the bar and maneuvered among the eggs. Their silver pulsing was steady and synchronous. A new species sleeping the same sleep. One of them seemed to have heard the clock. The lens cap over its front camera retracted into its shell, unveiling one gleaming onyx eye.

Nolan held up his phone and let the camera scan what was on his screen. The unit took several moments to locate the profile in the system, and Nolan held his breath until he heard the two faint beeps suggesting a successful pairing. He then logged in to Wade's Master User portal and replicated the new intake across the entire inventory. The process started off slow, given the recalibration of the batches following the changes. As more Timekeeper Profiles were substituted, the homogenization accelerated and flushed the remaining stock in seconds. A thousand accounts, a thousand faces and minds of the entitled and the ungrateful, fed into the furnace and cast a new mask of pride, unified as one man to whom Frenell's legacy belonged, in the literal sense.

Lindsay Frenell's headshot was at least ten years old, taken when there was still substance in his smirk. Once the entire brain reserve had been Frenellized, the field of eggs returned to their hibernation in an absolute hush, as if no one had yet invented sound.

Ashes to ashes, dust to dust, Frenell to Frenell.

"It's done," Nolan reported over the phone.

"Good work. Maybe I should've been there to see," said Ryuka.

"Should I be feeling something stronger? Like sad, happy . . . or lost?"

"All that will pass anyway."

"I hope so."

"You'll visit Sai for both of us, yeah?"

"Yeah . . . what's the attraction of Valleria anyway?"

She thought about it and said:

"It's not Grand Ivory."

ᘓ

WHEN THE FACADE clock struck eleven, Christie marched into the Level 13 open plan with a dozen patrol bots. A firm-wide announcement flew out of the speakers, thundering over the chime of the hour.

Dear Frenells,

Please stop what you are doing and step away from your desks. Listen carefully to the OATH representative designated for your floor and follow the instructions. You'll be given sufficient time to hand over company properties and collect your personal belongings. We encourage you to remain calm and professional in this final stretch of what has been, without a doubt, a life-changing journey.

The firm appreciates your contribution and wishes all of you the best of luck in your future endeavors.

In the morning of May 30, 2028, Frenell's Timekeepers were given an hour to pack up and leave the building, under the supervision of the task force consisting of one OATH human and two lines of bots for each floor. When the firing squad arrived on Level 21, some Special Associates wrestled away and made it to the Partner Floors. They were captured by the bots almost immediately, but they had enough time to see the ghost town and take in the fact that no one was there to answer any questions.

The only Partner who came in that day was Not-the-Worst. He was there to pick up his set of golf clubs he'd kept in the office for spontaneous BD eighteen-holes. He'd gotten the email advising the Partners to work from home and "leave it with OATH," but there was only so much you could do with a driver. Having arrived only after OATH had secured the workspaces because, well, traffic, he went straight to his office on Level 27, grabbed the bag leaning against his shelves, and left. In and out. The Level 13 Associates caught a glimpse of him in the descending elevator as they gathered near the entrance of the open plan. No one thought to dash out and chase him down the lobby for an explanation because that was when Christie got to the part about severance.

The State of Grand Ivory did not mandate severance pay under the law. However, as a gesture of generosity, each Timekeeper's contract—if directly signed with Frenell—allowed for a one-off payment equal to the value of certain billable hours corresponding to the employee's number of years with the firm. So, a Year 5 who had increased their billing rate from $600 an hour to $800 incrementally, met the annual target of 2,550 hours consistently, and billed at least $8,925,000 during their five years at Frenell got to keep $4,000 when the firm no longer needed their services.

Once you've crunched the numbers, it only makes sense that Sauria Street doesn't give a shit about its people. The God of Net Worth wouldn't allow it.

Each Timekeeper also had to sign a separation agreement, which provided further details on how to handle this divorce with grace.

The one-off payment represented the exhaustive remedy they might claim. If they wished to keep their health insurance, the cost would come out of that windfall. If they had sexual harassment or discrimination claims against the firm, they could no longer pursue them. They'd also become ineligible for unemployment benefits if they took the severance pay.

The nonsolicitation clause prohibited them from approaching the firm's key clients for a certain period of time. Whatever they'd built for the establishment stayed with the establishment. The nondisclosure and nondisparagement clauses prohibited them from making statements about their employment and termination, or negative comments about the firm—even if true. Better wipe their drool off the gag if they wanted to keep their four thousand.

Lastly, they got a flag for "Laid Off" on their RAP and a gap on their CV that they'd need to justify at every job interview, if they got one.

A layoff was one of the very few transactions where you got to call both parties "cheap" with a capital C.

Emma Abilene dunked her collection of stress balls into a cardboard box, making deliberate noises as if anyone were there to witness. The email congratulating her for her promotion to Special Associate was still warm, yet now she was cleaning out her desk.

After five years, what she could take with her barely covered the bottom of one medium cardboard box. Two mugs. A tube of lotion. Family photos. Her pills. Two resistance bands. Instant energy drinks. Then every gadget she could find on the market to help her stay calm and reduce stress.

Emma is a good girl.

She'd overheard a Partner make that comment to another one as she'd walked away to freshen up her drink at the last Christmas party. Two months before that comment, she'd turned thirty-four.

She hadn't become a "good girl" until she'd spent three years, two months, and fourteen days with Frenell. That day marked the seventh anniversary of her decision to take out a loan and pursue a law degree, and she started the day by crying in front of her mirror with a toothbrush in her mouth.

She'd landed the best option her investment in herself could've bought her. She was on the "right track." She was the "golden child" her relatives would use as an example of determination and discipline. Successful. Envied. And profoundly miserable.

That was the day she began to think: maybe she shouldn't be "happy."

Maybe she wasn't entitled to happiness or any psychological comfort because a job was never meant to be pleasant, especially not this one. She'd heard all the horror stories beforehand and she had gone in anyway. What alternatives did she have if she wanted her own house and a family, with kids? Go back to retail?

So she changed her perspective and reshaped her expectations, seeing what the firm wanted from her instead of the other way around, questioning what she could do to make life easier for her superiors without even being asked, pondering what the one true secret was to survive this battle royale without getting disfigured.

Then she heard it.

She'd been overthinking. They all had been. What the Masters wished they'd understand had always been one simple message:

The firm must prevail.

The firm must prevail.

The firm must prevail!

That changed her life, and she became a "good girl." Good girls knew their place, got their work done, and kept their heads low. The Frenells noticed her change and praised her "maturity." They began to dump last-minute assignments on her, day or night, 24/7. They sent her on business trips to rural areas with no support or resources. They got comfortable making inappropriate remarks about her Frenell colleagues, and pretended they heard nothing or laughed it off when clients were being sleazy or rude. All of the above became okay because Emma would deliver on short notice. Emma would find the track with only breadcrumbs. Emma would sit and listen and laugh along with them. Emma wasn't petty or woke. Emma was a good girl.

She wasn't happier, but things made better sense. Stop fighting the current, then maybe it'd take her to somewhere safe.

It did. It'd wrapped her into a merciful flow. Although it was still hard to keep her head above water at times, she was no doubt going upstream. She'd secured a few sponsors within the firm—without having to sleep with any of them or indulge their ideas about the chance of that. She continued to get work that had actually made her a better professional. Her brain was wired in such a way that she'd never thought about hurting herself no matter how challenging her days got. Compared to some of her peers, she was indeed one of the lucky few. Be a good girl, then things just might work out on their own. This comfortable numbness had been more reliable than any sense of "security" or "fulfillment" she'd once expected from this place, and it made her think: *I might have a future in this.*

Then the Masters manifested and told her to get out and clean up after herself.

Looking down at the half-empty cardboard box, she saw the real reward for her virtue.

Her rent had tripled in five years. She'd made a habit of buying near-expiry groceries for the discount. She hadn't had a vacation, even a domestic one, in three years because there hadn't been a window when she'd had both time and money on her hands. Another romantic interest had died a premature death earlier this year because of her unpredictable schedule and nonnegotiable priorities. Last week, she'd had an invigorating discussion about a one-bedroom in Clover Hill. Now she'd have to ghost that Realtor.

She wasn't even a cog in the machine; she was just the fuel that burned through it. It seemed the Masters had squeezed out the last useful drop of her, so they were scraping her residue off their pristine pipeline and wheeling her out in a trash can marked "biohazard." All the health issues, the missed family time, the promises she'd broken, and the regrets she'd perpetuated, she could deal with those in her own time, at her own expense, off company premises.

She stood in front of the entrance of the open plan with her box. For some reason, the automatic glass doors didn't sense her presence and remained shut. A metaphor for her life—they'd lived in a house sustained on her flesh and blood and treated her like a maid. Now the house had caught on fire. Not only had they sneaked out without warning anyone, they'd dead bolted the fucking door behind them.

A patrol robot noticed her inaction and cruised down the aisle, playing a prerecorded clip reminding the Associates to stay calm and efficient on their way out. It stopped at her feet and printed out an order on its screen, urging her to leave peacefully without making a scene. She chuckled, then she threw her box to the side and stomped the robot in the face. It skidded backward but stayed on its wheels. After pulling back some distance, it charged forward at full speed as its mechanical arms spread open, one of them holding the tranquilizer. Emma lowered her core and held her hands in front of her body, eyes fixed on the bot. As the tranquilizer nozzle approached her face, she dodged to the side, grabbed the bot by the arm, leveraged its momentum, and threw the metal junk at the sliding doors. The glass shattered, and the robot flew through. It crashed into the elevator frame, then slumped onto the granite, motionless. Emma dusted off her clothes, picked up her belongings, and stepped over the broken glass.

"Bravo! Woo-hoo!"

She snapped her head around and saw James cackle behind her. He was already an odd man without the chaos, and what happened today seemed to have turned him into a proper lunatic. Hovering his phone over the smashed entrance and the demobilized robot, James added some commentary to explain what would no doubt be one of the highlights when the film was released. "Smile for your fans, baby," he said to Emma, catching her back and that manicured middle finger in her final appearance.

James then panned his camera over the open plan and zoomed in on a Year 5 who was trying to pull a "Chateau." He didn't get as far because of the bots. James followed him as he fled to the back of the Meditation Chamber.

"So there was this guy in my cohort–" James provided the helpful context as he moved to the window side of the open plan. Better lighting over there.

When his peers were struggling to reconcile with the news, he'd already taken out his gear and started filming. There was only a fleeting moment to capture that candid despair in the air, and he'd made good use of it. He had to suppress his giggles to keep the camera steady. It wasn't easy–hearing that layoff announcement was the first time he'd felt alive in months.

Years later, when he made Partner at another Sauria Street firm across the road, he'd remember this day as one of those rare life experiences where you'd voluntarily dive into a war zone, then livestream your way out of it. He'd describe it in vivid detail as a joke. When asked if he was disappointed about how Frenell had handled the event, he'd say, "Absolutely, which is why we should remind ourselves to treat our people with respect and decency." Then he'd make a mental note that the Associate asking that question was a deluded snowflake whom he should keep off his A-team list.

Would anyone be "disappointed" when a live volcano swallowed a village at its foot? That was a stupid question.

"Frenell" wasn't one firm, and "Sauria" wasn't one street. They were an idea and a practice much older than Grand Ivory. It might seem like Frenell was dying, but it was only disintegrating. In no time, its shards and shadows would resurface, flaunting their pedigree and rekindling old connections. They'd either be assimilated by their competitors or open up new fronts in the same neighborhood, doing all it took to win back the same clients who'd screwed them over. "Ex-Frenell" rolled off the tongue easily, and it'd preserved some goodwill—a neutered bulldog is still a bulldog. Most of those who had already ascended above Level 26 would go on to have lasting, lucrative careers. Most of the people who'd been escorted out as collateral damage wouldn't.

Even that disintegration was only regional.

Global firms like Frenell who'd aggressively expanded through local mergers and acquisitions would often organize their counterparts across jurisdictions under a "Swiss verein" structure, which was essentially a Subway-style franchise. The member offices shared the same trademark but remained independent in managing their profits and liabilities. What had happened in Grand Ivory had very little impact on the rest of the Frenell clan, except that, maybe, it was time for another rebranding.

Haters and outsiders would like to believe this was the end of Frenell, or the end of "something," but as long as money continued to flow from relationships to relationships, by relationships, and for relationships, Sauria Street would never die, no matter how many individual careers or lives had to rot to fertilize its soil. There'd always be the next Frenell. There'd always be the next superior breed. The next prestigious farm that prided itself on "making a difference in a better world."

Same plot, new settings.

Only people who could discern this truth were worthy of his respect, and he'd always be the best of them all—even though they all knew nothing would change, he was the one who'd exterminated useless complaints from his vocabulary.

"Don't forget to like and subscribe!" he reminded his audience before turning off the camera. Then he made a semi-surrender gesture to the approaching robot and strolled to his workstation. After filling one box and making it halfway to the exit, he sauntered back and grabbed the mini pot two seats down the bench.

He got to keep Sai's succulent after all.

"WHAT DOES HE mean this is the end of Frenell?" Morse caught Colleen outside the Fidelity Room.

Oh, right, there was one more person who was also not pleased with this development.

"How did you find me here?" Colleen sighed, not stopping for the chat.

"I've got eyes," Morse scoffed.

He'd found Colleen here after hurling his monitor off the desk because of that "internal memo," then bombarding Angela with nonstop calls and texts on both her work and personal numbers until she showed him Wade's calendar.

"I think that email is pretty clear," Colleen said as she tried to get around him.

"But what about me?!"

"What about you, Morse?"

"Well, what about my partnership?"

She halted and stared him in the eye.

"You can still be a 'Partner.' Or 'Director.' Or 'Manager.' Actually, 'Principal' is a title that's really catching on. Call yourself a Founding Father if you want, Morse, but nothing you do will ever be our problem from now on. You can be whatever you want, treat people however you like, wherever you go, just not around us. The sooner you get that, the faster you can set up your own shop and go back to shitting on people who must've committed murder in previous lives to deserve crossing paths with you in this one."

She left him with that and marched away, going through her contacts to work out a list for "catch-up" lunches and coffees she'd have to set up. People would tease her once more details about Frenell's fiasco came out. Big deal. It'd get better. She just had to endure the first month or so that'd suck the most.

"Hey! How's it going?" She practiced her greeting in the elevator down as her calls continued to ring out. *It's probably just too soon. No need to overthink.* She gave herself a slap and some deep breaths to get her heart beating and her blood pumping. There was no downtime in this business, and she'd better be ready to go now.

AS NOLAN WANDERED through the ravaged open plan on Level 13, he deciphered the emptiness he'd felt in the hidden floors—they hadn't won anything.

If he had his finger on the scrub bar of this reality, he'd see that, after today, more Associates came out to beat the dead horse—anonymously—while they looked for a new job and dealt with the psychological aftermath of the event that'd permanently scarred some of them. Months later, a handful made it to other firms, hoping to prove that not everywhere was the same, or learning to accept that everywhere was the same. Some left the industry altogether and retrained in other fields, pausing their careers and lives for the transition. Some left the country, and only they'd know if it was for better or for worse. Eventually, life did go on.

But he couldn't see that at this moment, so he continued to traverse the bodiless graveyard, counting headstones, remembering the ghosts.

He caught a faint droning sound and thought someone was weeping. As he approached Morse's office, he realized it was a gleeful tune.

Christie didn't notice him at first. She swiveled in Morse's chair with her back to the door while she savored the chain of missed calls and ignored messages she'd received from one of the Olympians shortly after all hell broke loose.

Stop the layoff

Abort

ABORT

Answer your phone

?????????????????????

She heard the calls and saw the messages—even counted the question marks. But she considered the request and decided that wasn't what she felt like doing. She chuckled a little, then let out a sigh as she cast her pitying gaze over Morse's copy-room-turned-office—no wonder that sorry bastard was going insane in here. She'd definitely ask Eric for something with a window after they moved into the new place for their staffing agency.

It'd be nice to work for themselves, and they'd niche down to hiring for professional services. After five years, she knew these firms and their Associates. She could tell with one glance who was Partner material and who was only good for a temp, and she'd had firsthand experience with all the dirty little tricks the Associates would play to game the system and cheat the firm for their own interests. They'd need her help. No firm would lose any productivity due to underoptimization and regretful human error, not on her watch.

Finally, she turned around and spotted Nolan.

"If you need more boxes, you can find some in the Meditation Chamber." She gestured in that direction and smiled. "Don't leave anything behind."

Nolan looked at her for a second, then he let her be and moved along. As he was about to round the corner at the back, an acrylic painting hanging behind the Meditation Chamber caught his attention. It was a strange placement, facing a narrow corridor hardly anyone would pass. He typed the artist's name into Google and checked the price of the piece. Three hundred valuable dollars.

He examined the painting and tried to understand its existence in this obscure location. It was as if the in-house curator was determined to share her taste with the team, while reluctantly acknowledging the obtuseness of its underlying message. It felt like a practical joke. A convoluted prank from someone who taunted everybody with their tongue in cheek. A promise from someone who knew all the right things to say but had no intention to honor a word of it. In the end, this duality was the one thing by which he remembered Frenell and Sauria Street.

The painting depicted a postapocalyptic Earth and featured a parent-child combo in astronaut suits. The landscape, mostly desert, sprawled ahead under an invisible sun until it reached the idea of a cityscape in the distance. Holding the child by one hand, the parent pointed at the bleak wilderness in front of them as the sun stretched their shadows thin on the desiccated dirt, guiding the viewer's eyes to the single line at the bottom of the canvas—

One day, all this will be yours.

Also by Lavi J. Yves

The Eleventh Hour: Stories

Printed in Great Britain
by Amazon